PRAISE FOR JEAN STONE'S PREVIOUS NOVELS

"Stone is a talented novelist whose elegant prose brings the Martha's Vineyard setting vividly to life. . . . A very good read."
—*Milwaukee Journal Sentinel*

"Stone's graceful prose, vivid imagery, and compassionately drawn characters make this one a standout."—*Publishers Weekly*

"Jean Stone is a truly gifted writer. I wish I could claim her as a long-lost sister—but I can't. I can merely enjoy her wonderful talent." —Nationally best-selling author Katherine Stone

"A wrenching and emotionally complex story. Sometimes, if you are very lucky, you can build a bridge across all obstacles. A very touching read." —*RT Book Reviews*

"A very smart and well-written book." —*Fresh Fiction*

"Stone herself lives on the Island, and we can feel her love for it throughout." —*MV Times*

A VINEYARD SUMMER

JEAN STONE

KENSINGTON BOOKS
www.kensingtonbooks.com

KENSINGTON BOOKS are published by

Kensington Publishing Corp.
119 West 40th Street
New York, NY 10018

All Kensington titles, imprints, and distributed lines are available at special quantity discounts for bulk purchases for sales promotion, premiums, fund-raising, educational, or institutional use.

Special book excerpts or customized printings can also be created to fit specific needs. For details, write or phone the office of the Kensington Sales Manager: Kensington Publishing Corp., 119 West 40th Street, New York, NY 10018. Attn. Sales Department. Phone: 1-800-221-2647.

Kensington and the K logo Reg. U.S. Pat. & TM Off.

ISBN-13: 978-1-4967-1665-1 (ebook)
ISBN-10: 1-4967-1665-5 (ebook)
Kensington Electronic Edition: July 2019

ISBN-13: 978-1-4967-1664-4
ISBN-10: 1-4967-1664-7
First Kensington Trade Paperback Printing: July 2019

10 9 8 7 6 5 4 3 2 1

Printed in the United States of America

For Kathy

Acknowledgments

With my ongoing thanks to my friends at the esteemed Edgartown Library Book Group for putting up with me: Annie (no relation to my main character!), Carol, Cathy, Debbie, Dot (with special thanks to Dot for introducing me to the Indian Burial Ground on Chappaquiddick and to the Chappy "family"), Ellen, Jane, Joyce, Judy, Marcia, Pat, Peg, Sharon, Sue, Sydney, and especially to our fearless leader, Lisa Sherman, who also happens to be the tireless, dynamic Edgartown Library Director. (If I've omitted anyone, please forgive me!) Thanks, too, to the wonderful author Susan Wilson for our delightful lunchtime writers' group.

Also, thanks to Detective Michael Snowden at the Edgartown Police Department for his knowledge and research that pointed me in the right law-enforcement direction for this book.

And to so many of my neighbors whose names I've yet to learn, thanks for being here, and for keeping the island filled with peace and love.

Chapter 1

"You have to leave."

Annie Sutton stood in the doorway of the cottage on Chappaquiddick. Her jaw went slack; her thoughts tumbled into one another.

Her landlord, Roger Flanagan, pressed his thin lips together as if attempting an apologetic smile. "I'm sorry, Annie. You've been a wonderful tenant. But my grandson, Jonas, is moving to the Vineyard." He averted his eyes and stared off toward a cluster of scrub oaks in the side yard. "He recently completed the master's program at the Art Institute of Chicago; he's an exceptional artist—his medium is acrylics—so it makes sense for him to live here, what with the growth in tourism and an uptick in disposable income among the seasonal residents who are also discerning collectors. . . ."

Blah, blah, blah.

She barely heard a word he said after his opening line. It was already July first—the day that the entire island of Martha's Vineyard launched into high season, which meant it would be nearly impossible for Annie to find a year-round rental. She'd heard that the feat was tough enough off season even on

Chappy, which depended on a tiny ferry to connect with civilization or at least with the Vineyard—the stores, the gas stations, the medical facilities. Chappy was the nickname for Chappaquiddick Island, which technically wasn't an island at all except on the occasion when the surf broke through a narrow strip of land on the South side. Chappy also was technically (and legally) part of Edgartown, the easternmost town of the six that were scattered around the Vineyard. Annie had learned that, when it came to geography and a few other things, the Vineyard sometimes made up its own rules.

Drawing in a slow breath, she asked, "When do I have to go?" Her voice quaked. If he'd already mentioned a move-out date, her brain hadn't processed it yet.

Roger's smile morphed into a sheepish look. For a seventy-plus-year-old man that *Forbes* magazine had proclaimed a hedge-fund piranha, he looked oddly embarrassed. "As you know, your lease was a winter rental. It expired June first. After that, we'd agreed you'd be here month to month, with a thirty-day notice required by either party. So shall we say mid-August? That will give you a couple of extra weeks to find something else. Jonas can live in the main house until then."

A couple of weeks of "extra time" would hardly make a difference. As much as Annie wanted to say, "No! This is my home!" Roger Flanagan was right: She had no choice. She'd known from the beginning that renting the cottage might not be long-term. She had not, however, chosen to believe it.

"Thank you," she said, without meaning it. "The extra time will help." Before she could add something polite about wishing Jonas success, Roger folded his arms.

"Big wedding here on the Fourth. Hope we won't disturb you."

She leaned against the doorjamb. With the Flanagans in New York most of the year, she'd lived alone on the property for such a long time—nearly ten months and counting—that she'd almost forgotten the place wasn't hers. "Weddings are nice."

"It's for our daughter, Dana. She's all we have. Dana and, of course, Jonas."

Of course, Annie's mind echoed with a twinge of disdain. Then she realized that Roger's remark must mean that Jonas was Dana's son. Annie had seen the woman flit by the cottage once or twice, but was surprised she was old enough to have a child out of college. *The master's program at the Art Institute of Chicago,* she corrected herself. "Well, don't worry about disturbing me. I grew up in Boston. I'm accustomed to living with noise." Besides, she expected that any sign of protest would be pointless.

He tipped his Tilley hat and shuffled away in his Tevas.

Closing the door, she slumped against it and said, "Damn." She loved the little cottage. She loved Chappy, where she'd landed when she'd traded city life for the peaceful island. She'd made friends, connections with people she now cared about and who cared about her. She did not want to be forced to leave.

"Damn," she said again.

At age fifty-one (a fact she found startling), Annie had lived long enough to know not to envy anyone who had a life of privilege. As a writer, she knew that every individual, every family, had a story (often a dark one, an *underbelly,* her old college pal and best friend, Murphy, used to call it), and that having *beaucoup bucks* (Murphy again) was no guarantee of happiness.

"But money helps when you need a place to live," she said out loud now. Then she did what she did best in times of stress: She put on the kettle for tea.

While waiting for the water to boil, she plunked down on the rocking chair and stared at the wall. Or rather, she stared at the bookcases that stood against the wall, the ones she'd bought when she'd moved in, then packed with her favorite volumes. Along with the corner desk, the bookcases fit perfectly into the snug space and created an inspiring nook where she'd finally been able to settle in and conquer her writer's block.

Where would her things fit now?

She was almost finished with her latest novel—*Renaissance Heist: A Museum Girls Mystery*—but with less than a month until her publisher's deadline, she needed time to focus. How the heck could she do that if she had to hunt for a place to live and then actually move? Should she simply shove everything but her laptop, her thesaurus, and a suitcase of clothes into storage? She'd blow her budget if she could find a quiet, single room (shared bath, kitchen privileges) at an exorbitant summer rental rate, but at least she'd be able to get the book done. Then, come September, she could begin a realistic housing search.

It was a lousy plan, but it was the only one she could come up with at the moment. Her priority, after all, had to be *Renaissance Heist,* as her editor, Trish, often reminded her. Aside from the deadline that was designated in indelible ink in her contract, Annie had been counting on book sales to replenish her savings now that she'd finally paid off the huge debt her former husband had bequeathed her when he'd disappeared. But how could she be creative with this new crisis dismantling her thoughts?

"Damn," she said for the third, self-pitying time. She hated that at her age she needed to worry about how and where she would live. Mostly, she hated that her idyllic dream-come-true world was about to come crashing down.

She gazed out the window. The view from the cottage was of the scrub oaks, not the water. Ocean views were reserved for the Flanagans of the world, the "haves" in a world of "have-nots" like Annie. Unless she got really lucky. Really fast.

The kettle whistled.

★ ★ ★

"You can move in with me," John Lyons said over dinner that evening, a simple meal she'd created from fresh bass and carrots and last-of-the-season asparagus from Slip Away Farm. John was handsome—*tall, dark-haired, and well muscled,* Murphy would have noted—with soft gray eyes and one of those magnetic smiles that made people instantly think he was on their side, though Annie wasn't certain if anyone he arrested would agree. Even better than his good looks, John was kind. Caring. Sensitive. And Annie adored him. They'd been dating since New Year's Eve: Things between them were still wonderful, sexy, fun. Yet she'd wanted to linger a while longer in the lovely beginning of their relationship—that magical time when all things were new and exciting—before she made any kind of commitment. And she certainly didn't want to feel forced into one because of the island housing crisis.

She toyed with a carrot slice. "I think it's too soon for that, don't you?"

He cocked his head and grinned the half grin that made Annie feel like a fifteen-year-old girl with a crush on the best-looking boy in the school. "Maybe. But I can't pretend I haven't thought about it."

Neither could she. But before she spoke the words, he added, "Of course, you might not want to be too picky if you're going to wind up being homeless."

Annie knew he was joking, but his remark stung. "Right," she said. "It will be tough to finish my book if I have nowhere to charge my laptop."

"You can always camp out on the sofa in my father's study. You know you'd be welcome there."

"I do know that. And it's a good feeling. But your parents have a busy household now that's complete with a beautiful, but sometimes fussy, baby. Which isn't conducive to writing, either."

He set down his fork, reached across the table, and took her hand. His expression turned serious. "Look, Annie, whatever you decide, I'll do what I can to help. The last thing I want is for you to have to leave the island."

It was the last thing Annie wanted, too. But she'd had enough ups and downs in her life to know that just because she wanted to stay there didn't mean it would work out.

Just then, John's cell phone rang.

Annie forked a piece of fish while he checked the call. Born and raised on the Vineyard, John was a police officer in Edgartown and did not turn his phone off. Ever. He looked back to her and mouthed, "Sorry," then stood, walked toward the front door, and stepped out onto the porch.

"Hi, honey," she heard him say. She deduced it was one of his teenage daughters, who lived off island with their mother. They were only up in Plymouth, but John once said that having a wide berth of water between his ex and him had been essential after the divorce. Annie had not been surprised. She imagined it would feel disturbingly claustrophobic to live on an island where a former spouse remained, too, where they would no doubt run into each other at the market or the post office or even at the movies. As wonderful as life was on the Vineyard, there were simply few places to hide.

"What does your mother say?" John said into his phone.

She hated feeling as if she was eavesdropping, but her one-bedroom cottage was not built for privacy, and he had not shut the door behind him. She took another bite of the fish.

"That's not acceptable, Lucy. You know that."

Oh dear, Annie thought. Lucy was the younger girl—thirteen going on thirty, according to John.

"Put your mother on the phone." His voice was stern but not threatening; Annie would bet he was a soft touch when it came to his girls.

"When will she be home?" He paused; he sighed. "Never mind. I'll call her myself." He did not say goodbye.

The screen door opened. He walked back to the table and sat down. He stared at his dinner plate.

"Everything okay?" Annie asked, though, clearly, it was not.

Picking up his fork, he poised it over his dinner. "Consider yourself lucky that you never had kids." Then he closed his eyes and shook his head. "Oh, God. I am so sorry."

Annie smiled. He, of course, had momentarily forgotten how close she'd been to becoming a mother, that the abortion had been one of two life choices she wished she'd handled differently. The other bad choice had been to marry her ex-husband in the first place.

John dug into his dinner, just as his cell rang again. He glanced at it and muttered, "Crap." He let it ring twice, then said to Annie, "I hate to do this, but I gotta go. It's Jenn."

"I understand," she said, but her words dissolved before she knew if he'd heard them: He was too busy standing up, pulling his truck keys from his pocket, and going back out the door while asking, "What the hell's going on?" to the woman he had once married. Then he disappeared into the night.

Annie tried to finish her meal but could not. She set the leftovers aside for the compost bin and reminded herself she was on her own now. She tried to have faith that she'd find somewhere to live, and that it would be fine, because she was resilient and had learned how to land on her proverbial feet.

If only she could shake off the feeling that this time there was much more at stake. Maybe she'd feel more hopeful after a good night's sleep.

Donna.

The thought of her birth mother's name jolted Annie from the edge of fretful dreaming.

Of course! She bolted upright in bed, her heart softly pounding. Families help one another out. Or, at least, her adoptive parents had helped each other. Blood relations would, too. Wouldn't they?

She switched on the nightstand lamp and wondered if she dared to believe it. She'd met Donna only a few months earlier. The woman was open and ebullient and seemed truly happy to finally meet Annie. But she'd recently sold her antiques shop on the north shore of Boston, happily retired, and was now on a long-awaited, four-month world cruise with Duncan, her current gentleman friend. "We're almost seventy," she'd lamented with a grin. "Please don't call him my boyfriend."

But Donna wasn't due back until mid-August: far too late for Annie to make a decision.

She wanted to stay on the island, wanted to live and breathe and keep writing there. She also wanted, very badly, to continue her relationship with John, wherever it led. And she wanted to perfect the craft of soap-making that she'd learned from her friend Winnie Lathrop, who was part of the up-island Wampanoag tribe.

But she didn't suppose she could live in Aquinnah with Winnie and her family, because Annie's roots were Scottish, not Native American.

She wished she could ask Donna for advice. She also wished she could talk to her adoptive parents, the Suttons, who had known her in a way Donna never could. Annie still found it disturbing to think that a mother did not really know her child.

"It will take time," Donna had said the day she'd arrived on Chappy after Annie had finally responded to the woman's letter that began with the powerful words: *I am your birth mother.* . . .

Donna had stayed with Annie nearly a week, sleeping on an air bed on the living room floor. They'd talked and talked about important things and about nothing special. They'd walked for hours, exploring the dirt roads of the island, getting used to each other's presence amid the sounds of the waves and the occasional cry of a gull. It had been in January, when most folks had the good sense not to be there. But for Annie, the togetherness had been like a warm quilt.

Annie looked like her, or at least how Annie had looked before she'd traded her designer clothes for jeans and flannel shirts and had stopped having manicures that weren't conducive to harvesting herbs, plucking wildflowers, and making soap. They had the same dark, almost black, hair that was now streaked with silver, though Donna admitted to having more streaks than her stylist allowed her to show. They had the same long-legged, lean body, the same careful stride, the same happy laugh. The same hazel, not green, eyes.

Mother and daughter. The tree and the apple.

Donna had promised to return after the cruise; they'd agreed that the Vineyard would be a wonderful place to cement their new bond. Which was one more reason it was imperative that Annie found a damn place to live.

There was always Kevin, she supposed. But Annie was still getting used to the idea that her birth mother was in her life, let alone that Annie had a half brother who was nine years younger than she was. She'd met Kevin only once—over lunch, in Boston—when he'd joined her birthday celebration with Donna. She'd told Annie that he'd recently sold his construction business and, like her, he was single again.

"I spent all of an hour with him," Annie now said to herself with a small laugh. "It might be a bit presumptuous to ask if I could move in for a while."

Still, she had his phone number.

She could always send a friendly text.

If she knew what to say.

Or how she thought he could help.

She punched her pillow to rearrange the fluff, then snapped off the light again. *Tomorrow,* she thought. *I'll think about it tomorrow.*

Or the day after.

Then she closed her eyes again and prayed that sleep would come quickly.

Chapter 2

The following afternoon, Annie stood on the sandy path that led from North Water Street down to the Edgartown lighthouse—officially, the Edgartown Harbor Light. Along the dune grass and rock jetty, beach roses were in full, scenic bloom, a pink-and-white symphony with summer-green leaves against a backdrop of sapphire water and aquamarine sky.

She looked back toward Chappaquiddick, across the channel and the harbor that was sprinkled with the confetti of white-masted sailboats gently bobbing at their moorings. From where she stood, she could see her landlord's big waterfront house that would soon be filled with God only knew how many wedding guests. Jonas, the budding artist, would no doubt be among them.

She hadn't heard from John that morning, which wasn't surprising. He was on the night shift now, twelve hours on, twelve off, to keep the summer as peaceful as the Chamber of Commerce brochures promised. Besides, John knew that Annie needed to write every day in order to meet her deadline. And now she'd have to shorten her work hours to allow time to walk around Edgartown, talk one-on-one with rental agents, and hope they'd put the word out that Annie Sutton needed somewhere to live.

In the evenings, her new plan was to get back to work and edit what she'd written earlier—as if she'd be able to concentrate while her housing issues swirled in her mind the way the winds had swirled outside in winter. She'd hardly have time to see John. She hoped he wouldn't think she'd lost interest in him, that it was the real reason she'd turned down his offer.

Pulling her gaze off Chappy and the waterfront property that wasn't hers, she took her cell phone from her purse.

"I know you're sleeping," she said when John's voice mail kicked in. "But I wanted to say I hope things with your daughter have worked out all right. Life can be unpredictable, can't it? Anyway, I'm thinking of you." With her last words, a soft ache rose in her heart. "I'm in Edgartown, off to see rental agents. Hope to see you soon." She quickly pushed the red "End" button, swallowed her emotions, and headed up the path toward the stanchions of historic, white, sea captains' homes that weren't hers, either.

The first real estate office was only a block away; a tiny bell jingled over the door as Annie stepped inside.

"Year-round rental?" the young woman at the reception desk asked. She wore a sea-glass necklace and too much eyeliner that was smudged from the warm day. According to the nameplate, she was Hannah Smith.

"I know," Annie said. "I might as well ask for the moon, right?"

"Or Jupiter. Or Mars."

Annie dropped onto a chair that no doubt had been strategically placed to combat client exhaustion.

"We had one last week. A one-bedroom right here in the village. Thirty-five hundred a month. We got the listing in the morning, and it was rented by noon."

Great, Annie thought, knowing that she might have been able to afford it if she hadn't spent all her money paying off her ex-husband's debts.

"Are you checking social media?"

"I will. Later today."

"Put a listing in both newspapers?"

"Not yet."

"Asked as many people as you know?"

"I'm working on that. I only found out yesterday that I have to leave. What about weekly rentals? Do you have any-thing from, say, mid-August until I can find a winter rental? Something in a realistic price range?" As much as she didn't want another temporary fix, one could at least buy her the time to finish her book.

"Depends on what you mean by 'realistic.' Even then, most of our properties have been booked solid for months. I can let you know if we have any last-minute cancellations. But we mostly handle four- and five-bedroom homes. Family homes, you know?"

Yes, Annie knew.

"We might get a few year-round ones after Labor Day," the girl said as Annie stood up and went to the door. "So if you don't hear from me, stop back then."

Annie gave her contact information to Hannah. Then she thanked her and went out the door, the little bell tinkling more loudly that time as if to say, "Good luck, you're going to need it."

She walked. She pondered. She tried not to panic, a mind-set that was becoming more challenging with each hour that passed, with each stop she made at rental offices—five in all—where she was given the same advice:

"Leave your contact information."

"Check back after Labor Day."

And the most disheartening: "Don't give up," which was delivered with a sympathetic smile.

By the time Annie had threaded her way through throngs of sunglassed, flip-flopped men, women, and kids who strolled willy-nilly along Dock Street, her usual optimism that the right attitude and a happy smile could overcome obstacles had vanished like the tourists after Columbus Day weekend.

When she reached the ferry, the *On Time II*—which, along with the *On Time III*, provided Chappaquiddick's only public means of conveyance—she squeezed between two day-trippers who were equipped with water bottles, backpacks, and hiking shoes, and sat on one of the small metal benches that hugged the wooden railing on either side. Within moments, the boat chugged away on its 527-foot, ninety-second journey. She didn't need to see the red, white, and blue buntings that draped Memorial Wharf to be reminded that the Fourth of July was a mere three days away; she only had to look at the three SUVs aboard the *On Time* that sagged from their cargo of suitcases, coolers, and, no doubt, lots of bug spray, and from the colorful kayaks strapped to the roofs; she only had to gaze at the herd of bicycles on one end of the boat or at the animated faces of the passengers. She wished she could capture even a glimmer of the enthusiasm they were exhibiting.

The *On Time* inched closer to the tentlike tops of the red-white-and-blue–striped beach club cabanas that garnished Chappy's shoreline like children's pinwheels ready to spin into action.

Annie tried to remember what it had felt like the first time she'd come to the Vineyard at ten or eleven, when her parents, Bob and Ellen Sutton, had rented a small cottage for two magical weeks that turned into an annual pilgrimage. The island had been different then, softer, quieter. Annie had loved flying kites, building sandcastles, and riding bikes with her dad up island, past miles of rolling hills, ancient stone walls that framed breezy pastures, and expanses of shoreline that offered postcard kinds of views.

Back then there were few inns and fewer restaurants. Once, when her mom forgot to get corn for dinner, Annie and her dad went to a nearby farm. He'd forgotten his wallet, so they stole six ears right off the stalks; the next day, they went back and paid for what they'd filched. The cottage they'd rented had indoor plumbing but no electricity; at night they ate strawberry shortcake and played Parcheesi and Sorry! by the light of kerosene lanterns. Her dad loved the island. After he was cremated, she and her mother sprinkled his ashes off South Beach as he'd requested.

As much as Annie cherished those vacations with her parents, her favorite Vineyard memory was the year she was fifteen, when she gathered the courage to wear a two-piece bikini and sat on the beach savoring John Irving's *The Hotel New Hampshire,* while peering over the arc of her sunglass lenses at the cute boy, a few blankets away.

Years later, the cute boy became her first husband. Most people said it wouldn't work: Brian's family, after all, spent all season on the island; they were among the haves. The marriage was filled with love and joy but hadn't lasted—not for the reasons some had predicted, but because Brian was killed in a car accident when he was twenty-nine.

But, yes, if Annie thought hard enough now, she could remember what it had been like to feel happy.

The *On Time* bumped the piling on the Chappy side of the pier. She waited for the flip-flops to scurry off, then, as she sauntered down the ramp, she spotted Earl Lyons—John's father—leaning against the tiny gray-shingled information booth.

"Coffee?" he asked when Annie joined him.

"How'd you know I'd be here?"

In April, Earl had hung up his red-and-black-checked wool shirt for what he called his "seasonal wardrobe," which that day included a brown T-shirt with the colorful logo of Offshore Ale. Earl wasn't much of a drinker, but he often said that advertising local establishments was good for the economy. Between the T-shirt, his trademark jeans, and well-worn sneakers, it was hard to believe that, despite a crop of white hair and thick, spiky eyebrows, he was nearly seventy-five.

"I'd like to say my timing is due to my supernatural powers, but it isn't. I came down to pick up cedar shingles for one of my customers. The lumberyard delivered the boxes to the Edgartown side and shipped them over on the ferry. While I loaded them onto my truck, I saw your car in the lot. Then I stopped to say hello to a neighbor, Charlie Beebe—do you know Charlie?"

Annie shook her head.

"Great guy. Lost his wife a few years back. Anyway, he got off the same boat that the shingles did. By the time he left and I was done loading, along came the next ferry and here you are." As usual, Earl's explanation involved a long story, though he always had a way of putting Annie in a good mood: In many ways, he reminded her of her dad.

"Follow me," she said. "It's too late in the day for cinnamon rolls, but I might be able to unearth a cookie or two." When the season had officially started, they'd had to curtail the morning coffee-and-pastry routine that they'd fallen into last fall. Earl said that most things changed in summer because folks didn't have enough time to breathe. She was beginning to understand what he'd meant.

"I'll be a few minutes behind you," he said. "Might as well drop the shingles off on the way."

Annie waved, went to her car, and drove the short distance to the cottage. Off season, if the weather was decent, she walked, but that day it was too hot and there were too many people and vehicles to enjoy a peaceful stroll.

As a reminder that quiet time had grown rare, when she pulled into her driveway, she saw three delivery trucks parked by the main house, and a crew of ten or twelve men hoisting a white tent on the lawn that led down to the water.

"Big wedding this week," she said once Earl arrived and took his usual place at her table. "Roger's daughter."

"Dana."

"So I heard."

"She was a nice kid. Not phony like her father or too sweet like her mother."

"You never said you weren't fond of the Flanagans." The percolator on the woodstove had done its job; she set it on a cool burner so the grounds could settle.

"Roger could be worse, but it's always been hard to tell what he's thinking. His grandparents bought this property before I was born. When Roger inherited it, he renovated the place. I think he likes it here: He supports a few island causes, like the hospital and community services and the garden club that Claire's in, though I've often wondered if he only does it so he can tell folks he does. You know what I mean?"

Annie nodded.

"And then there's his wife, Nicole. When she sees you she acts like you're her long-lost best friend. But she's real good at ignoring you if one of her spa-going lady friends is around, like she doesn't want to be seen mingling with the locals. She's been known to grouse—in a real syrupy way—about the fact that there's no restaurant on Chappy; that there are too many seagulls on their beach; and what a shame it is that there aren't more tennis courts at the community center. She says all of it with her lips kind of pursed as if she's not complaining, but

I've always figured she'd secretly rather be on Nantucket." His monologue included a few cartoonish gestures and one or two well-practiced eye rolls.

"Then why do they stay?"

"My guess is Roger feels like a big cheese here. With all his money, he's certainly one of them."

Money. Annie had never understood why some people embraced it to the point of letting it define their lives. Then again, if she had, she might have never signed the prenup that Brian's uppity sister had insisted on. Because Annie and Brian had been married only six years when he was killed, Annie had received nothing. There had been no protection against him dying—Brian had been so young, his family had longevity on both sides, and tragedy only happened to other people, didn't it? After the accident, Annie kept teaching third grade. But on her income alone, she had to move into a smaller apartment, a one-bedroom, no bigger than where she was now.

"Well," she said, "I won't need to think about the Flanagans much longer. Have you talked to John?"

"Yup." Earl plucked a peanut butter cookie from the plate Annie had set out. He took a considered bite, chewed, then swallowed. "What are you going to do?"

She didn't mind that John had told his father about her housing crisis, though she wondered when he'd found the time to call Earl, since she'd assumed he'd been sleeping all day. Not that John had to answer to her.

"I saw some real estate agents today. No luck, though. It's a terrible time of year to find a year-round rental."

Earl looked over her shoulder. "That coffee ready yet?"

She filled two mugs and waited for him to say whatever else he wanted to say. She'd known him long enough to tell when he had something on his mind.

"John says you won't move in with him?"

Annie didn't know what she'd expected but that was not it.

Though Earl probably knew she and John often had dinner together, she'd never let on that it had become real dating, the kind that involved spending time together that often included overnights. Apparently, however, John had.

She set the coffee on the table and sat down. "John is an amazing guy," she said with a smile. "But I'm still getting my feet on the ground here. Still shaking off the soot from too many years in the city. Do you understand?"

"Nope." Earl always seemed to have a comeback for which she wasn't prepared.

"Okay. Then how about this? It's too soon for me. Moving in with him feels too much like a commitment. I don't want to make one unless I'm absolutely certain it's the right thing for me. And that he is absolutely certain it's right for him, too. In other words, I don't want to rush into anything just because I've been kicked out of my house."

"Fair enough." He took a long gulp of coffee.

"Besides," Annie continued, "I've only met his daughters once. And that was for a quick breakfast at Among the Flowers." She decided not to say she'd felt awkward then, that John had introduced her as an author and that, because his older daughter, Abigail, was a reader, he'd thought the girls would like to meet her. He'd never implied that they were a couple or anything more than mere acquaintances. "Anyway," Annie added, "I don't think it would be fair to suddenly move into their father's house, do you? The girls don't seem to want to come here as it is. If I was there, it might make things harder for him."

"Have you talked to him today?"

"No." She took a cookie, and broke off a small piece. "His ex-wife called last night while we were having dinner. He left before he barely touched his food." She tapped the cookie on the edge of the plate as if it was a sheet of paper and she was Rachel Maddow. "I could tell he was upset." She resisted adding that she also wasn't crazy about the idea of living with someone who had to step away from her when his ex called, as if he had secrets he did not want to share. Annie's ex-husband, Mark—her post-Brian "mistake"—had done that too often; the sting was still fresh.

"They have a small problem with Lucy."

"I gathered that, but he chose not to explain. And he doesn't have to if he doesn't want to." Annie wasn't, after all, married to John, though she had been to her secretive ex. *Semantics,* some people might say; to Annie, it was about trust.

"I think he's trying to protect you from his troubles. He knows you have your own problems right now, and he doesn't want you to feel like you have to take his on, too."

She smiled again. "Well, I guess true love never runs smoothly, right?"

Earl guffawed. "No kidding. Claire and I have been married going on fifty years, and I'm still not sure how it works." He folded a napkin around another cookie and stood. "Speaking of Claire, with all you've got going on, do you still think you can help her with the garden club tour? It's only two weeks away."

The tour was the annual crowning joy of Edgartown horticulturists who showed off their floral blossoms and beds in the good name of charity. As always, Claire was the chairperson for the event. Annie wanted to say she couldn't help after all, that she needed to finish her manuscript and find a place to live. But Earl and Claire had done a lot for her when they could have turned their backs. So she stood up and said, "Of course I'll help. I'm looking forward to it."

"She'll appreciate it." He sighed. "As much as she loves Francine and Bella, some days I worry she's taken on way too much."

"Whatever you need, Earl. Please. Just ask."

He nodded. "Thanks for the java and the snack. You going to the big shindig at your landlord's Thursday?"

Annie laughed. "The wedding? I wasn't invited. You?"

"Nope. Wouldn't go if I had been. From what I hear, the men are all wearing white tuxedoes." He pocketed the wrapped cookie and moved toward the door.

"I'll hide in the scrub oaks and take pictures for you."

"Well, then, I guess my life will be complete."

Annie followed him onto the porch just as an amplifier blasted some sort of music, followed by a voice that boomed, "Testing, testing," so loudly it surely had been heard up island at the Gay Head Cliffs.

Earl shook his head. "Yup. Looks like you're in for a real treat."

She laughed as he trotted toward his truck. Then he stopped and turned around.

"If you don't hear from my son, give him a call, okay? Tell him I said that you two need to talk." Then he waved and climbed into his pickup, covering his ears as if to shield them from the music that shrieked from the amplifiers again . . . not unlike how John was apparently trying to shield her from his problems.

Annie wondered if that was true and if—or when—she'd feel safe enough to truly believe in a man again.

Chapter 3

John finally called later that evening. He told her that things were already revved for the long holiday weekend. "God help us, they started the *Jaws* marathon tonight. At the town hall, some kids have covered 'Edgartown' with a sign that reads 'Amity'—that happens every summer. And they added it to the banner that advertises the parade and hangs across Main Street. Maybe we should leave it that way year-round."

"It would give people something to talk about. And it would probably go viral."

He groaned. "It already has. Yesterday, three kids asked me if I was Chief Brody."

Annie laughed. "I don't envy you your job."

"Me, neither." He fell silent for a moment, creating a somber pause. "How's the book coming?"

"Okay. Fine."

"And the house hunt?"

"Lousy. How's Lucy?"

The silence fell again. "The same. Listen, I'll do my best to see you over the next few days, but no promises, okay?"

She wished she could shake the uneasy feeling she'd had

since Earl told her that she and John needed to talk. Was John angry that she'd turned down his offer to move in? Or was he one of those men who had a hard time communicating? "John," she asked, "is everything all right? With us, I mean."

He hesitated again. "It's fine, Annie. But I have extra duty right now. Tourism is already at an all-time high, which is great, but with more people come more problems. Okay?" End of story. End of discussion.

Resigned, Annie simply said, "I understand. Call when you can. Or come over. In the meantime, stay safe." She tried to sound lighthearted. After all, his hesitation really could be about work, or might be due to whatever was going on with his daughter. Maybe it had nothing to do with Annie. Or with their relationship. Whatever the problem, she decided she had neither the mental energy nor the time to dwell on it.

They said goodbye, and Annie went back to work until loud voices and laughter erupted from the grounds of the main house and made it impossible for her to think. She wondered if the wedding celebration was going to go on all week.

In the morning, coffee in hand, Annie decided to take advantage of the quiet. She sat down at her small corner desk and prepared to dive into her manuscript when a soft knock came on the screen door. She glanced out the window and saw Francine—the one person Annie would never ask to go away. Or maybe Earl. Or John. Or Claire. Or Winnie, her up-island friend.

Annie laughed. She loved that so many wonderful people had come into her life. "Francine! Come in!"

Francine pressed her face to the screen. "Are you sure? You look hard at work."

Annie stood up. "I'm never too busy to see you. The door's open. You want coffee?"

"No thanks, I can't stay long," Francine said as she stepped from the porch and into the cottage. "Looks like they're ramping up for a party at the main house."

Sometimes Annie forgot that Francine had spent a few unfortunate days in the neighborhood.

"Wedding tomorrow," Annie replied. "Their daughter."

"Oh, cool! They'll get to see the fireworks over the lighthouse." She seemed sincere, not envious of the bride-to-be, who, unlike how Francine once had been, would no doubt never need to wonder where she would live or who would pay the bills. Annie hoped Francine was content on the island now, to be with a real family, to have made real friends, to get up each morning and dress in the sleek black skirt, crisp white shirt, and black bow tie that she now wore, the uniform for her job as a concierge at one of Edgartown's popular inns. She looked healthy and well fed, no longer waiflike and malnourished, as she had when Annie first met her. At twenty, Francine was a pretty girl, with big dark eyes, long black hair, and a shy smile. A girl who seemed happy, at last. "I just wondered if you can go to the parade with Bella and me tomorrow. It will be her first Fourth of July parade—and mine, too. I have the morning off, but I have to be at work by noon. I thought if you could . . ."

"Absolutely. And, before you ask, yes. I can bring Bella home when the parade is over so you can go straight to work."

Averting her eyes, Francine added, "If it's too much trouble, don't worry. Earl and Claire are going. But I thought if you went, too, they'd get a break from babysitting."

"I'd love to help. And I'd love to go to the parade. It will be my first one here in Amity, too."

The girl's expression turned puzzled. "Amity?"

"From *Jaws*." Then it occurred to Annie that Francine hadn't been born when the film had caused such a sensation in the mid-1970s. "Did you ever see the movie?"

"Sure. It's a classic."

"Well, the town they called 'Amity' in the movie was really Edgartown."

"Holy cow," she said, "I never knew that. I didn't know much about the island until . . ."

Annie smiled. "Until last Christmas. One of my happiest holidays. Now, please, have some coffee? I have a fresh pot."

But she shook her head. "Can't. Thanks. I'm on my way to the little ferry. I have to work today."

It was cute that Francine called the *On Time* the "little ferry" to differentiate it from the big boat she'd arrived on last December, when she'd brought only a few clothes, a basket, and a whole lot of problems. Then Annie realized what Francine had just said. "You walked all the way from Earl's?"

"I hitched a ride. But I can walk from here. The little ferry's not far."

"I'll drive you."

She shook her head again. "I'm fine. I like to walk. And you need to get to work, too. But there is something else I wanted to ask."

"Ask away."

"Well . . . I guess I really only wanted to be sure you're okay."

Annie frowned. "Right. I guess you've heard that I have to move." By now she supposed that everyone on Chappy, if not the whole island, knew of her dilemma. "Thanks, but I'm fine. I'll find a place." Francine didn't need to worry about Annie. She had enough of her own responsibilities now and seemed to be handling them well, thanks in great part to Earl and Claire, and in no part to the other side of baby Bella's family.

"I know you'll find a place. But I was wondering if you're okay about John."

"John? What about him?" The question popped out quickly. Maybe too quickly.

"Well, I know you two are close." The girl fidgeted with her bow tie. "So I thought, you know, that you might be upset that he'll be gone for a while."

Annie stared at her. Then blinked. "Gone? Gone where?"

Francine's hand covered her mouth. Her large eyes grew larger, wider. "Oh. You didn't know. I assumed . . ."

Gathering her wits, Annie saw that the girl was confused. And embarrassed. She put her arm around Francine's tiny waist and guided her to the rocking chair. "Sit," she said. "And please tell me what's going on."

"I can't. Well, it isn't my place. . . ." She sat. And rocked. And chewed on a thumbnail.

"We have no secrets, Francine. You and I. So please. Tell me." A small pool of acid had risen in Annie's throat but didn't deter her from wanting an answer.

Extracting her thumb, Francine drew in a breath. "I guess one of his girls is having problems."

"I know. It's his daughter Lucy."

"So he's going to Plymouth."

Annie sat on the small sofa next to the rocking chair and tried not to let her overactive writer's imagination leap to hurtful speculation. "Well, that's good news, don't you think? That John wants to see her? If he can spend a little time with her, if he talks to her in person, maybe he can help with whatever's been troubling her." And Plymouth, Annie reasoned, was only an hour away. Not counting the ferry. The big boat.

Francine's eyes flicked to Annie, then away. She focused on the woodstove. "But it's more than a little time, Annie. He'll be gone for two weeks. Or three."

Okay, Annie quickly thought. *Two weeks. Or three. Not forever.* Still, it seemed strange that Francine was the one who had told her. Had John really been too busy to call? "When does he leave?"

"Sometime next week."

Of course he would stay through the jam-packed holiday weekend. With his job, it would be essential.

"I hope it's okay that I told you."

Annie smiled. "It's fine. His girls have to come first. They're young. They need him." She stood up and went into the kitchen, holding back the pressure of tears forming behind her eyes. "I know you have to go. But I'll give you something to munch on for your long journey across the channel." Hoping her feelings would settle while she kept her back toward Francine, Annie slipped three cookies into a sandwich bag. "Should I meet you at the dock tomorrow morning at eight? That should give us time to cross and to find a perfect parade-watching spot."

"Great. Bella and I will ride with Earl and Claire and meet you there. Thanks, Annie."

After drawing in a slow, balancing breath, Annie turned around. Francine was already at the door; Annie put the small bag into her purse, then gave her a hug. "No, thank you. For caring enough to worry about me. I'll be fine. And so will John." She kissed Francine's cheek and opened the screen door. "And since you insist on walking, you'd better scoot. You don't want to be late."

Annie would not, could not, think about John. She had too much to do to get caught in the dark web of "thinkies," as her dad used to call it when she wasted time worrying about things over which she had no control. Her dad never allowed himself to succumb to thinkies, which she'd always suspected was why he'd smiled so often.

Knowing it would be pointless to try and find a place to live until after the weekend, she returned to her desk and forced herself to boot up her laptop, open the file for her manuscript, and figure out where she'd left off. Then she got down to business, writing and rewriting, cutting and pasting, double-checking her research on Renaissance art and museum thefts. She didn't think about John, well, maybe she did once or twice, but she overrode the thinkies and plowed through one word, one scene, one chapter at a time until long after the sun had gone down and she'd worn herself out. Then she went straight to bed. But between the pre-wedding hoopla out on the sloping lawn, growing worries about becoming homeless, and nagging doubts about John darting in and out of her thoughts, Annie did not close her eyes until the first light crept over the sky.

When the alarm sounded two hours later, Annie somehow managed to pull herself together, meet Francine and the others, and make it to Edgartown in time to find a prime spot on Main Street. Despite her exhaustion, Annie volunteered to push Bella's stroller, hoping that by having a responsible task, she'd stay awake.

Many of the marching contingents were similar to those from the Christmas parade, although instead of Santa tossing out candy canes, a papier-mâché great white shark flung packs of Goldfish crackers and bumper stickers that read: I SURVIVED JULY 4TH ON AMITY ISLAND into the cheering crowd. Annie promised to take Francine to see *Jaws* before the summer ended so she could see the Vineyard locations where it had been filmed. Not only would they have fun, but it would also provide Francine with a trove of trivia she could share with hotel guests while impressing her boss.

Between the gaiety of the marchers and the gleeful crowd highlighted by kids on bikes that were decorated with patriotic crepe paper, Annie was reminded of when she'd been young and the days had seemed simple. Not every day, of course. True, it had been a different, slower era, but life still got complicated, bad things still happened, and people still hurt one another. She tried to remember that now as she struggled to keep the knot in her stomach at bay, and tried not to worry that, once again, it felt as if all that she'd grown to love was quietly sliding away.

When the parade ended, Francine went to work, and Annie politely declined Earl's invitation to the cookout at the Chappy Community Center, saying she needed to get back to her manuscript. She was relieved when Claire offered to take Bella with them; despite what Francine had feared, they apparently did not need a break.

"I don't expect you'll get much writing done, though, with the wedding going on," Claire added.

Ugh. The Flanagans' wedding. Annie had conveniently forgotten about it. Still, she needed to go home if only to sulk. Not that her father—or Murphy—would have approved.

Ugh, she thought again.

But having learned long ago that the best way for her to battle the blues was through writing, as soon as Annie arrived home, she retrieved an old pair of earplugs and got to work. Thanks to the earplugs, the commotion from the main house was dulled to a bearable level. For a short time, there nearly was silence; perhaps that was when the ceremony was taking place.

Annie worked in relative comfort for a few hours, until, as dusk set in, the band grew louder, seeping through the earplugs and teasing her with distraction. Still, she kept typing. But when familiar strains leaked into the cottage, she realized the band was playing the song she and Brian had danced to at their wedding—"When a Man Loves a Woman," the Michael Bolton remake of the old Percy Sledge tune. Brian's sister had snarled that it was juvenile for them to select a Top 40 tune; Brian snarled back that it was obvious she'd never been in love.

They would have celebrated their thirtieth anniversary this year.

"Okay!" Annie shouted and flicked off her computer. "You

win! I will stop working but you are NOT going to make me cry!" She might have been talking to Brian—after all, since Murphy had died, Annie had taken to conversing with dead people.

In an effort to regain her senses and drown out the sounds, she yanked out the earplugs and decided to take a shower. Standing under the pelting hot water for a long time helped. A little. Then she put on a white cotton robe, wrapped a towel around her hair, and decided to make tea. But as she walked toward the kitchen sink, wondering if it was too early to go to bed, a glint of bright colors flashed outside the window: The fireworks had begun.

Annie couldn't remember when she'd last watched fireworks. If she stepped out on the lawn she might be able to see the lighthouse, the harbor, and the night sky illuminated . . . Maybe she should take a few photos.

"Great idea," she said, finally feeling more cheerful.

Slipping her phone into her pocket, she tightened the belt on her robe, went out to the porch, then stepped down onto the lawn in her bare feet. Cool grass licked her toes; she almost giggled. The band had stopped playing; the air was now filled with cracking, popping, and startling booms as rockets shot upward and exploded into sparkling clusters. From where Annie stood, she could hear the wedding guests hoot and holler with delight.

She then sensed a woodsy scent of warm embers drifting up toward the cottage; her gaze moved down toward the beach, where a fire pit glowed. Hoping for a better view, she raised her chin back toward the sky and carefully tiptoed around toward the corner. That's when she tripped. Over something large. And unmoving.

Having lived in the cottage as long as she had, Annie knew there were no rocks on the lawn—only snowdrifts in winter and verdant green grass in summer. This wasn't winter. And whatever she'd tripped over wasn't grass. It was something . . . solid.

Grabbing her phone, she hit the flashlight app and beamed it at the ground.

That's when she saw a body at her feet. A woman. Dressed in a strapless lavender gown. And clutching a bouquet of lavender and white hydrangea blossoms.

Annie sucked in a breath. *A bridesmaid,* she thought. *Dear God.*

Chapter 4

Though it felt like it took several minutes, Annie composed herself faster than that. She shined the phone onto a youthful face. The skin was pale, the eyes were closed, and something that looked like water trickled from the nose and the mouth. She moved a strand of pearls and touched the slender throat. There was a faint pulse—the bridesmaid was alive.

Annie knew that a pulse—even a slight one—meant she shouldn't do CPR.

After all, given the festivities going on, the girl might only be drunk. But the weak pulse, combined with the discharge from her nose and mouth, were . . . weird. The bridesmaid might be in real trouble.

With trembling fingers, Annie searched the phone for her "Contacts." She remembered that the Chappy emergency number would bring faster results than if she called 911.

"I think there's a pulse," Annie cried to the voice that picked up. "But you'd better hurry." Not knowing if the system could ping her location, she quickly spewed out her address. Then she rang off and stared at the bridesmaid—she hadn't moved; the water from her nose had dribbled down to her chin.

Cover her, a distant voice—Murphy's voice—whispered in Annie's ear. Though Murphy had died nearly a year ago, she still found a way to offer sound advice on occasion.

Annie plucked the bouquet from the bridesmaid's clutches, then propped the phone up against it. With light shining on the lavender dress, she was assured that the EMTs would see the girl, and no one else would trip over her. Then Annie raced into the cottage and scooped up the nearest blanket—her mother's quilt.

Back outside, she draped the quilt over the bridesmaid. Next, she needed to tell someone at the wedding reception. "Someone," of course, should be Roger Flanagan. Father of the bride. Annie's short-lived landlord.

Without thinking or caring that she was barefoot and clad only in a robe, she dashed down the lawn toward the tent and the laughter, her footsteps accompanied by a round of red, white, and blue sparks splayed out overhead. When she reached a corner where the tent was anchored into the ground, she stopped, hoping someone would notice her, a statue in white, with hair that must look as if, like the sky, she, too, had been electrified. But no one was strolling among the linen-covered tables that were adorned with blue and lavender hydrangea centerpieces; no one sat on the chairs that were clothed in matching table linens; no one was removing the empty champagne flutes or the fine bone china plates that sported cake crumbles. Even the bandstand had been evacuated except for a drum set, a saxophone, a piano, and two electric guitars—all blissfully idle. The laughter and chatter now rose from the opposite side of the tent, where the guests had congregated, no doubt for a better view of the fireworks.

Annie wanted to scream.

Instead, she squinted, trying to pick out Roger in the crowd. It didn't seem right to disrupt the whole group, including the bride and groom, especially since help was on the way.

Even in the dim light, from Annie's vantage point she could see the tops of a number of fashionable hairdos: ladies' milk-maid braids and waterfall twists; undercuts and Mohawk fades on the young men. If Roger had worn his Tilley hat, he would be easy to spot, though it hardly would have suited a white tuxedo.

Suddenly, a figure stepped from the shadows right next to her. "May I help you?" The tone was cool and testy.

Annie turned and looked into light-colored eyes whose far corners tipped up toward the temples. She did not know the woman, did not recognize the impeccably tinted blond hair, or the cheekbones that seemed too high and too chiseled for someone whose décolletage revealed tiny ripples of aging.

"Roger," Annie said. "I need Roger Flanagan. Fast."

A single finely arched eyebrow raised. "I am sorry, but this is a private party." Despite the gorgeous blue satin sheath the woman had on, she reminded Annie of a character she'd once created—a bitchy one.

"I'm well aware of that. But I still need to speak to Roger. It's an emergency."

The woman pursed her full lips that might also have been "done." "I am Roger's wife, Nicole Flanagan. I don't believe that we've met?"

So. This was Nicole. She did not seem drunk, merely rude. Not even falsely sweet, as Earl had described her. And had she not heard the word *emergency*?

"I'm Annie Sutton. I rent the cottage. Roger needs to know that what looks to be one of your daughter's brides-maids is unconscious on my lawn. I've notified the EMTs." Without waiting for a response, she tightened her robe belt again, turned on a bare heel, and walked briskly back toward the unresponsive, drooling girl.

★   ★   ★

Because it would be hard to hear the wail of a siren over the pops and pow-pows of the fireworks, Annie kept her ears perked. She waited next to the bridesmaid, who remained motionless, a mannequin bathed in a circle of high-tech, cell-phone light. Though the night remained warm, Annie shivered. Other than in the case of her adoptive parents, she'd never seen a dead body, or even one that was still alive but unresponsive. Brian's brother-in-law had identified Brian after the accident; he'd assured Annie that she should remember Brian the way he had looked, his bright smile, his gentle eyes. Brian had wanted to be cremated, so she'd never even seen him dressed up in death.

"Annie?"

The sharp voice pierced the darkness like an angry bat. Her body jerked.

Then a man stepped into the light. His hair was white, his shirt was white, his pants and shoes were white. Despite the brusque voice, he could have been an angel who'd come to collect the girl in the lavender silk and organza. But it was Roger, minus his Tilley and Tevas.

"What's this?" he demanded. Not "who's this," but "what." He stared down at the bridesmaid.

"My guess is she's one of yours," Annie replied. She was appalled that she, too, could sound haughty when it seemed necessary.

He crouched the way Annie had moments earlier. He pressed two fingers against the girl's throat. Then he reached for her wrist as if he had witnessed Annie's earlier actions and now mimicked them. "She's still alive," he said.

"Yes."

"Well, then, we can't do CPR."

"Right." Annie had known that, thanks to the training she'd had when she'd been a teacher. She looked back toward the street. "I called the ambulance."

Roger leaped up. "You did what?"

"I called the ambulance," she repeated. "The EMTs."

He raked a hand across the arch of his forehead, then through his thinning hair. "But it will be on the scanners. Broadcast all over the island. Oh. This is unfortunate."

Annie didn't know what to say. She'd forgotten that some people in the world actually cared what "the neighbors" thought; people who prized perception over compassion, people like Brian's sister, who, years earlier, hadn't allowed the public to be told that Brian was killed by a drunk driver, as if it would somehow stain the family name.

Roger sighed. "I should alert Colin."

"Colin?" Annie asked, her eyes dropping back to the bridesmaid so she could avoid looking at him.

"Colin Littlefield. This girl is Fiona. Colin's younger sister."

Annie knew that the waterfront property next to the Flanagans' belonged to the Littlefield family. But the original owners had died a few years ago, and the place had since fallen into disrepair. Earl had told her that the heirs were arguing about what to do with it; meanwhile, the place was wasting away like a seagull with a broken wing. Fiona must be one of the heirs; Colin, another.

She was about to tell Roger that alerting Colin was a good idea when she realized it didn't matter because Roger had disappeared into the darkness as quickly as he had emerged. She also realized that the music was blaring again; the fireworks had ceased.

As Annie stood, trying to decide if there was enough time to hurry into the cottage and throw on some real clothes, headlights bobbed down the clamshell driveway; a pickup truck slammed to a stop by Annie's front porch. A cab door flew open; the driver jumped out, a black bag in hand, long auburn hair spilling down her back. It was Taylor, Chappy's nosy neighbor, Annie's near nemesis, and, apparently, one of the island's emergency personnel.

Great, Annie thought with an edge of sarcasm. She and Taylor had not gotten off to a terrific start when Annie had first moved to the Vineyard. She'd done her best to keep her distance since then.

"The ambulance is coming from a hospital run, so it might take a few minutes," Taylor said as she brushed past Annie and dropped to her knees by Fiona. "Fill me in."

Annie wondered if Taylor was one of "the neighbors" that Roger had feared would find out.

Then, craning her neck up to Annie, Taylor said, "FYI, I'm one of three EMTs on Chappy. The ambulance comes from Edgartown, so one of us shows up 'til they get here. You wanna tell me what happened?"

Annie cleared her throat. "I have no idea. I'd just taken a shower. I started to make tea when I saw the fireworks. I stepped outside for a better view, and I found her."

"Fiona Littlefield."

Of course Taylor would know who the bridesmaid was. Few people crossed the channel onto Chappaquiddick that she didn't know, or at least know where they were headed and why.

"Well, she's still breathing." Taylor opened the black bag and took out what looked like a blood pressure cuff. It was impossible to tell if she was pleased or annoyed at having been rousted from God only knew what for someone who did not need CPR or who wasn't dead.

Then Taylor yanked a phone from her denim shirt pocket and hastily relayed Fiona's vital statistics to someone on the other end—perhaps someone in the ambulance or at the hospital.

"Roger Flanagan has gone to find Colin," Annie said.

Taylor shook her head and turned away from the cell. "He

won't find him. Colin's Porsche rolled off the *On Time* leaving Chappy when I was on my way back from the movies."

It was hard for Annie to believe that she hadn't heard Colin's car when he'd left the party: She was all too familiar with the low rumble of the Porsche engine. Husband number two, her ex, Mark, had had one. Like so many of his toys, she'd wound up paying for it, though the car had vanished when he had. But Annie wasn't shocked that Taylor knew the kind of car Colin Littlefield drove; what was surprising was that she had gone to the movies. It seemed like such a normal thing to do, and Taylor was anything but that.

"I know what you're thinking," Taylor said, setting the phone down but, Annie noticed, keeping the line open. "But the best time to go is when folks are whooping it up at their own Fourth of July parties. Nobody bothers with the movies then, so it's quiet. I like watching *Jaws* on the big screen. It brings back memories."

Many islanders had been used as extras when the movie was filmed, but Annie doubted that Taylor had been old enough to make her debut. She made a mental note to ask her at some other time, like when there wasn't an unconscious bridesmaid on the lawn.

Then Taylor sighed and glanced at her watch. "They'll be here any second. The *On Time* is on alert, waiting. All other traffic and passengers have to wait. They're our number-one cutter."

Probably because Annie looked baffled, Taylor added, "We call them cutters because they get to cut into the ferry line. Like the mail truck, FedEx—you know. The vehicles that have first dibs. Cops and ambulance are at the top of the list."

Annie said, "Right now, Edgartown seems far away."

"It's only five hundred and twenty-seven feet. You'll be stunned at how fast they get here. Way faster than in a city. Emergencies always happen in slow motion, though; it's been less than three minutes since you called." She gestured toward her phone. "And we're in constant touch."

Less than three minutes? Was that possible? Then, as Annie was about to ask if it would be okay for her to duck inside and change out of her robe, the distinct sound of a siren wobbled through the air. And Fiona Littlefield went into a convulsion.

Chapter 5

The Edgartown Police SUV pulled in first and parked behind Taylor's pickup. John Lyons jumped out; the ambulance came next. John swept the beam of his flashlight across the lawn, directing the vehicle onto the grass. Then two men thundered out and raced toward the women: One carried a large LED lantern; the other, a black case. With practiced precision, they squatted on either side of Fiona. One man tore open the case while firing razor-sharp medical terms at the other, who repeated them into a phone.

"Water was dribbling from her nose and her mouth," Annie reported. "But it looks like it's gone now."

The EMTs examined Fiona's mouth. While they worked, John motioned for Annie to join him by the porch.

"What happened?" he barked. He held a small notebook; a pen was poised above it.

Annie stared at the page. As if their relationship wasn't tenuous enough, now he was going to interrogate her. She clenched one hand; her fingernails scored the flesh on her palm. Then she told him the story, starting with when she'd stumbled over the bridesmaid and ending when Taylor arrived. "I didn't know she was an EMT," she added.

"Did you hear anything or anyone?" he asked, ignoring her comment about Taylor.

"No. Only the fireworks."

"Did you see anyone?"

"No. But I wasn't looking. Before I went outside, I was in the shower. I have no idea how long Fiona was lying here."

When he was done writing, John closed his notebook. "I tried to call you. When the call came in. I heard the address; I thought something had happened to you."

Under other circumstances, she might have found his comment endearing. Right then, she wasn't sure. "There are two hundred people at the main house. Chances are, it would not have been me."

"The dispatcher said 'the guest cottage.' "

"Oh," she said. Then she remembered he had no way of knowing that she was upset. After all, he didn't yet know that she knew he was heading off island to Plymouth. He didn't yet know that she knew he'd be seeing his ex, or that Annie had no idea how to handle that, what questions would be okay for her to ask, and which ones might be off-limits. Even at her age, she did not know the boundaries, only that life had changed since she and Brian dated in the eighties, and since she and Mark had, in the nineties. Morals, values, expectations—the rules had all changed. If any, in fact, still existed.

She resisted the urge to check her phone to see if John had really called. "You must have called when I'd gone to find Roger."

Looking into her eyes, John cocked his sweet half smile, the one that made her feel like a schoolgirl. "You went to the Flanagans' dressed like that?"

She laughed. "I did."

He chuckled as if in approval, then capped his pen and moved back to the others. Annie followed.

"Any other Littlefields around?" he asked Taylor. "Like maybe Colin?"

Then the EMT with the lantern and the phone looked at his partner and said, "We need to transport."

Not waiting for an answer, John sprinted toward the ambulance with Taylor on his heels. Apparently, they, too, had done this more than once.

"He isn't here."

The voice startled Annie. It was Roger, who somehow had sneaked back to the scene and now stood beside her. She wondered how—or if—he'd explained the "unfortunate" commotion to the wedding guests, none of whom had accompanied him. "Colin," Roger added. "He's gone and so is his car." He stared down at Fiona, whose convulsion had abated though she remained unconscious.

"I know," Annie said. "Taylor saw him drive off the *On Time* into Edgartown." She scolded herself for her smug satisfaction in knowing something that Roger didn't.

"Well, I can't tell Sheila," Roger added, "because she didn't show up for the wedding."

Annie reached down and plucked her phone from the ground.

Then John and Taylor jogged back from the ambulance toting a stretcher. They set it down next to Fiona; Taylor removed the quilt and handed it to Annie. "Good idea that you covered her up," she said.

Annie gave her a wry smile.

The Edgartown EMTs lifted the patient and carefully laid her on the stretcher, the organza dragging on the grass. In an amazingly caring gesture, Taylor picked up the fabric and spread it neatly, modestly, across the bridesmaid's legs. Then the EMTs strapped down Fiona's feet and drew another strap under her arms and over her chest. Annie noticed they had tossed the bouquet of hydrangeas aside.

"Who's Sheila?" she asked Roger as the EMTs worked.

"The sister. The eldest Littlefield kid. She's an oddball."

"Did you expect her?" Annie didn't know why she'd asked. The instinct of a mystery writer, she supposed. Always scouting for details to help fill in the blanks.

"No. Etiquette was never her strong suit."

"Is she one of the heirs who wants to sell the house?"

Roger hesitated. "I try to stay out of their business. I only know that Sheila's not been fond of my daughter since Dana and Colin split up."

Dana? The bride? "Colin Littlefield dated your daughter?"

"When they were teenagers. Children, really."

The EMTs hoisted the stretcher and headed for the ambulance. Taylor carried the black case for them; John followed, carrying the lantern and his flashlight. The procession disappeared around the back of the vehicle. Their voices faded.

"But Colin came to Dana's wedding," Annie continued, "so he must not have hard feelings."

Roger let out a laugh. "Colin Littlefield is too proud to have anyone think that losing my daughter had been her choice, not his."

Annie might have pried more, but she was suddenly uncomfortable, standing in her bathrobe, staring at an ambulance, while making small talk with the man who was booting her out of her house. Then she heard a clang of metal that sounded like doors being shut. And the night grew still, silent again except for the incongruous party music in the background, the only light glimmering from the ambulance interior.

Then Annie heard John say, "Thanks for the help, Taylor," and Taylor responded, "No problem, Skippy." Annie knew that "Skippy" had been John's childhood nickname, a reminder that the two of them had known each other all of their lives.

They walked back toward the cottage while the ambulance remained in place, the EMTs apparently doing whatever was necessary, maybe hooking up oxygen or setting up an IV. Taylor went to where Fiona had been lying and stood next to Roger, though Annie wished she'd go home. Whatever might be in store for Fiona Littlefield, the Edgartown EMTs were in charge now.

John veered toward Annie's front porch, where he reached inside and snapped on the exterior floodlight.

Annie wondered why she hadn't thought to turn on the outside light earlier. Shock, she supposed. After all, she'd first thought the poor girl was dead.

Then John walked over and addressed Roger and Taylor.

"Do either of you know how to get in touch with either Colin or Sheila?"

Taylor shook her head.

Roger loosened the white bow tie of his tuxedo. "Dana might have Colin's number. They dated a long time."

No one asked why the bride would have her ex-boyfriend's phone number.

"Can you find out?"

Roger blinked. "You mean, like, now?"

"Yes."

He turned his head toward the party tent. "For God's sake, John, this is Dana's wedding. . . ."

"I'd appreciate it, Roger." John's voice was neighborly, yet no-nonsense.

The older man glared at him, then looked back toward the party. "I'll see what I can do."

"Thanks." John handed him his card. "I've got to go back with the ambulance. Give me a call when you know. The last boat left Vineyard Haven half an hour ago. We'll check to see if Colin was on it. If not, he can't get off island 'til morning. Unless he leaves his car here and goes by private boat. Or by plane."

Roger gave a mock salute and tucked John's card into his

short-tailed jacket. "Knowing Colin, he probably slipped away with one of the other bridesmaids." He winked, which, under the circumstances, seemed inappropriate. Then he waddled off down the lawn, oblivious to the fact that his white shoes were no doubt getting covered in grass stains.

Then the lights of the ambulance suddenly flashed; John told Annie he'd be in touch, then he trotted to the cruiser, jumped in, and backed over the clamshells out to North Neck Road. The ambulance departed behind him, emitting no siren that time.

"You going to finish making that tea?" Taylor asked. "Looks like we're all that's left here, and I could sure use a cup."

As far as Annie knew, Taylor hadn't been inside the cottage since Annie had lived there. But she seemed more interested in talking than in commenting on the décor. "The story goes that Colin Littlefield needs to sell the property," she yammered, "because he's in debt up to his eyeballs. Sheila wants to donate the place to the Trustees of Reservations with the stipulation that they'll turn it into a bird sanctuary. Fiona wants to keep it in the family, though 'the family' is only the three of them now. Three squabbling heirs. I wish it was the first time I heard a story like this one on the island."

Annie took another sip of tea. *Tell Taylor, tell the island,* Earl had warned her more than once. Then again, Taylor could be a good source if ever Annie needed to learn something. And writers always needed to learn things, didn't they? It certainly wouldn't hurt anything to at least be nice. "In the meantime," Annie interjected, "the Littlefields' house sits there rotting?"

"Precisely. Word is that Colin even fired the landscaper now, which hardly matters, because in the last year they only paid him to keep the lawn mowed."

"What a shame. It looks like it was once a beautiful place."

"It was. When I was a kid, I hung out with Sheila in the

summers. She was different from the others. Not snobby, you know?" Taylor laughed. "Actually, she was different from most people. But she liked to hike around the island and check out the wildlife. One year, when we were around ten or eleven, we made a scrapbook of all the different animal shit we could find. Excuse me, the *droppings*, as Sheila called them. Did you know that mouse shit and rat shit are shaped differently? That mouse shit has rounded ends, but rat shit ones are pointed? Anyway, her mother was mortified, which I thought was hilarious. I don't know what Sheila thinks the Trustees can do with the property, though. It's boxed in by the Flanagans on one side and by the Astleys on the other. The Littlefields' is a three-acre property, but that's hardly enough for a preserve." She stared into her tea as if she were searching for the answer.

"You've lived here your whole life, right?" Annie asked.

"Yup. Except for fifteen years."

That wasn't the answer that Annie expected. Taylor seemed so entrenched on Chappaquiddick, it was hard to picture her not living there, not being part of the daily, ongoing fabric. "Where were you then, if you don't mind my asking?"

"Boston. I was a city girl. Went to college and everything. What about you? You're a writer. You must have gone to college."

"Boston as well. I grew up there and went to BU. Before I was a writer, I taught third grade for nearly twenty years."

Taylor nodded as if she already knew that, which she probably did.

Small island, Annie thought. *Few secrets.* "Do you ever use your college degree here?"

Taylor snorted. "I'm a caretaker, which was hardly offered as a major. Besides, I don't need a college education to tell a glacial stone from a rock, which is important because it helps the excavators who come over to Chappy to build, to dredge, or to try and stave off erosion. They come to me with questions. Which is fine. I like taking care of other people's properties. It gives me the freedom to be me. And to do my part to try and keep Chappy out of danger. Safe from unwanted species, both animal and human." She laughed. "Speaking of properties, how's your house hunt coming along?"

Of course Taylor would know about that, too; her reputation was well earned. "Not great. If you hear of anything, please keep me in mind."

Taylor stood up. "Will do. But sometimes it's best not to mix business with pleasure. And now, I have to get home. Time for Mother's pills."

Annie thought her reference to mixing business with pleasure must be some kind of joke. She and Taylor were barely friends, let alone "pleasurable" ones. Annie stood up, too. "Well, thanks for your help tonight."

"Part of my job. As a volunteer. By the way, I'm sorry to hear about John's problems. I know you two are, well, close." So she also knew that John would be going to Plymouth. Had he told everyone on the island except Annie?

Setting her jaw, she remembered that Earl had once said that Taylor once had—maybe still had—a "thing," as he had called it, for John. Maybe she was trying to get under Annie's skin. And maybe it was why Annie shouldn't expect her to help in Annie's house search: The woman might be happier if Annie was long gone.

"Well," Annie said with a smile, "family first."

"Ergo, Mother's pills," Taylor replied, as she pulled out her keys and swept from the cottage, her auburn mane leaving a slight breeze in its wake.

Annie watched the pickup drive away while wondering if she, too, might be happier if she were long gone from the Vineyard. Then her text alert dinged. It was John.

I'm off at 8:00 am. Meet me at the diner for bkfst? 8:30?

Though Annie dreaded the conversation they needed to

have, both Earl and Francine had insisted that they had to talk. She hesitated a few seconds, then typed: **Sure. I'll try to be in my clothes by then.**

If he grasped her attempt at a humorous reference to the bathrobe she'd been wearing at "the scene" of Fiona's mishap, he didn't acknowledge it.

Chapter 6

The morning was sultry and hazy, a red sun already smoldering on the horizon. After her shower, Annie slipped into a pale-pink sundress and flip-flops and coaxed her hair into a short ponytail. She carefully applied a light layer of makeup and mascara, then drove to the *On Time*. She knew that by the time she had finished having breakfast with John, it would be even hotter, too uncomfortable to walk back to the cottage. With enough "city girl" spirit still lingering inside her, Annie thought an air-conditioned car was preferable to needless perspiring. Still, she parked in the lot on the Chappy side to avoid having to hunt for a parking space in Edgartown.

Though she was early, the diner was open, its black-and-white checkerboard floor gleaming, its red vinyl chairs and turquoise vinyl booths scrubbed clean, its retro chrome-and-white, Formica-topped tables polished to a mirrorlike shine. The place was packed; despite it being the day after the holiday, few people seemed to be sleeping in. It was summer, after all.

The waitress, whose name was Esther, also worked nights at The Newes, a favorite year-round pub that Annie frequented with John. Esther gave Annie a hug and escorted her to the booth in the back. "Your handsome man called and reserved it," she said with a wink. "Coffee?"

"Please," Annie said as she sat and picked up the laminated menu. She tried to look pleasant and happy, though inside, her stomach churned. The last thing she wanted was food. Gazing out the window at a gaggle of tourists with island maps in one hand, coffee-to-go in the other, Annie decided to distract herself by reviewing her duties for the garden tour. She took a spiral pad from her purse. Her list was short because, in spite of her venture into natural soap-making, Annie still had trouble telling a wildflower from a weed. But she could take direction fairly well, and Claire had issued specific tasks:

- Make sure refreshments are at every house.
- Remind greeters at each venue to limit viewers to six at a time. No one wants their gardens trampled.
- Double-check that judges know the criteria and have enough ballots.

That was all. Annie decided to also try and have fun. It certainly could be a pleasant diversion from house hunting and writing. And dwelling on John. And stumbling over a body in her yard.

She was so engrossed in her efforts at distraction, she didn't see John until he set a porcelain mug in front of her.

"Special delivery from Esther," he said.

Annie blinked. "Oh," she said. "Good morning."

He set another mug across from her and slid onto the vinyl cushion. "Or 'good evening,' if you pulled the night shift."

"Right," she replied, managing a small smile. "Tough night?"

"No different from any other Fourth of July. I'm sure you can fill in the blanks." He looked tired.

"How's Ms. Littlefield?" Annie asked.

He shrugged. "That little incident seems like a lifetime ago.

After I saw you we had four DUIs, one overdose, three fender benders, one serious accident, two bar fights, and seven loud parties to break up. No. Make that eight. And two domestic disturbances, to put it politely. In other words, we had about the same amount of activity in one night as we do in total all winter. As for Fiona, I didn't hear anything more. But she was breathing on her own, wasn't she?"

"Yes, but she was still unconscious."

John mumbled, "Hmmph," or something like that. Then Esther appeared and asked what they'd like to eat. And Annie was reminded of the real reason they were there.

John ordered bacon and eggs; Annie, a plain English muffin, which she hoped she'd digest if, instead of butter, she used a thin layer of jam.

She looked across the table at John. *Let's stop the small talk,* she suddenly wanted to shout. *Are you going to tell me you're going to Plymouth?* But she sat, and she smiled, trying to look unruffled.

"You look like a girl this morning," he said. He reached over and took her hand.

"I am a girl."

"You know what I mean. You look young. Like in your twenties or something."

"Flatterer."

"Yeah," he said, withdrawing his hand, "pretty big talk for a guy as exhausted as I am."

She half listened as he told her more about the night's activities; she guessed he wasn't ready to share his news. Waiting until their breakfast arrived, Annie could no longer keep silent.

Lowering her eyes, she spread strawberry jam on the muffin. "I heard you're going to Plymouth." Despite the chill from the air conditioning, she grew warm. And flushed. She picked up her napkin, dabbed her brow, then glanced at John again.

His forkful of scrambled eggs had paused halfway between

his plate and his mouth as if indecisive about which direction
to take. After a few seconds, he set the fork back on his plate,
the eggs not eaten. "Yeah. I've been meaning to tell you about
that."

So Francine hadn't misunderstood. And Taylor's bucket of
gossip was, as usual, right.

Annie reached for her coffee.

"It's Lucy," he said quietly, as if Annie didn't already know
the girl was having problems. "Jenn caught her smoking a
joint." It took a couple of seconds for Annie to remember that
Jenn—or Jenny, as John sometimes called her—was his ex-
wife, mother of his two children. Not that Annie needed to remind herself of that.

"Oh," she said, her feelings mashing together like ice
crushing in a blender. "Well. I'm sorry, John." And she was.
She'd seen it in the schools, back when she'd been teaching,
back when drugs had begun creeping into the lower grades
long before anyone believed that pot would ever become legal.

"It's the worst possible time for the department, but I have
to go. She's my kid, you know? She just finished seventh grade,
for chrissake. *Seventh.*" His lovely gray eyes grew wet.

Annie felt selfish and cross with herself for angsting about
them when he was in such pain. She reached over and took his
hand. "You'll figure this out, John. I know you will. It's so good
that . . ." She didn't know if she should refer to his ex-wife as
Jenn or as Lucy's mother, so she simply said, "Well, it's good
that Lucy got caught now. While she is so young."

"Too young," he said, his chin dropping to his chest.

"When will you go?"

"After the weekend. Monday. Or Tuesday. For a couple of
weeks or so. It might cost me my job. But I don't have a
choice."

"No, you don't." She was not being condescending; she
was being realistic.

They sat in silence a few more moments, clutching their mugs, neither one eating. Finally, John paid the check and they went outside, where he kissed her goodbye and said he'd stay in touch. She walked in one direction, and he in another, and Annie realized she hadn't asked where he'd be staying, though that part probably wasn't her business. It was in that gray area again.

Annie had grown up watching *Little House on the Prairie* and later *Happy Days* and *Family Ties*. On those shows, people always had problems but resolved them together because deep down they loved one another. It had been the same in her house, relatively speaking, so she'd never questioned why anyone had a family or even wanted one. Still, between what Francine had gone through, what John was going through, and now with the drama between the Littlefield offspring, it gave one pause, as her dad would have said.

She boarded the *On Time* and squeezed onto a bench between a family of six and a young couple who wrestled with a stroller and twins. Not that Annie needed a reminder that she had no children, no husband, and apparently no boyfriend anymore. She was alone, which, she decided, was different from being lonely. Solitude, after all, was needed for her job, but was unhealthy for the other hours in her life.

Then she looked up at the hot, hazy sky, pushed a loose strand of hair back from her damp forehead, and smiled as a happy thought crept into her mind: *But I'm no longer alone!* Good grief, she had a family now, didn't she? A birth mother who had embraced Annie wholeheartedly, even though it had taken Annie years to reach out to her. And a brother! Annie had a brother, well, a half brother, which was almost as good. Wasn't it?

She'd met Kevin that one time in Boston, and they'd texted a few times. She'd sent him an eCard on his birthday, and he'd sent a photo of their mother, Donna, in New York Harbor when she'd embarked on her four-month-long world cruise. It wasn't that Annie never thought about Kevin, she just hadn't known what to say.

But now, crushed between perspiring passengers, her knees nearly touching the wheel well of a Cadillac Escalade, she reached into her purse, took out her phone, and looked up his number. Before changing her mind, she typed a quick text:

Hope your 4th was fun. It's dreadful here. Hot, humid, too many people. Last night I tripped over the body of a bridesmaid on my front lawn, but I guess she survived. Ahh, summer on the Vineyard.

She added a silly emoji that had gritting teeth. She touched "Send," dropped the phone back into her purse, and felt better immediately. Connections were essential, especially, she knew, when one's heart was feeling a little bruised.

After arriving on the Chappy side of the harbor, Annie decided to drive over to see Claire under the guise of reviewing her garden tour duties again: Socializing would be smarter than going back to the cottage and watching the wedding remnants being dismantled and listening to the post-party fun from a solitary distance.

"I can't believe you found one of the Littlefield girls on your lawn! Unconscious!" Claire wasted no time launching into what must have been the gossip of the day. Or, more than likely, of the season to date. Her wild white hair looked more like a dandelion puff ball than usual, no doubt due to her excitement. "The Littlefields have been such an enigma. The parents seemed nice, but the kids never took part in any activities at the community center, not even when they were young. There was always something a little 'off' about them. Do you know what I mean? That oldest one, the girl, what's her name? Sheila? I think she turned out to be a lesbian, not that it matters, but she was always hiking and doing boy things before, well, you know, before girls really did that. And that boy insisted on driving fancy sports cars not built for Chappy roads. He was always bumping up and down on our ruts and laughing like he was a trust fund baby and owned the whole island, though I think their assets were a lot smaller than anyone might have guessed. And the one you found? Fiona? Oh," Claire sighed, "she was a timid little thing. Always hiding behind her big sister. Or her parents. And now this. My goodness."

Annie listened politely without interrupting, sipping from a delicate china teacup.

"What happened, anyway? Was she drunk?"

"I don't know," Annie replied. "But I didn't smell any alcohol." There was no reason to bring up the seizure, though Taylor might already have told Claire. Annie didn't know whether or not confidentiality was required between patient and EMT. "But I'm sure she'll be fine," she added, though of course she had no way of knowing if that were true. "What I'd really like to talk about is the garden tour. I've gone over my checklist—is there anything else I can do? Have tickets started to sell?"

"Online, yes. And a few at the library. Other than posting the notice in the *Gazette,* if you have any ideas how to boost sales, we could use them. We get stuck in the same old rut, and this year we're raising funds for elementary school programs, so I want to do better."

"Do you have a Facebook page?"

"Yes! I almost forgot. Francine talked me into it and she set up the whole thing."

"That's terrific, Claire." Annie didn't know if the target audience enjoyed social media, but she was sure Claire was pleased that Francine was now involved, too. "And I'll do whatever else you need. I hope you know that."

"Can you join me Monday morning? I have to go into town and look at the gardens, see what kind of shape they're in, maybe offer suggestions. And take pictures! You can take pictures for the program. And for Facebook. Francine said we should have lots for that. But she'll be working, so we'll have to bring Bella. . . ."

"I'll be glad to take pictures, Claire." Another morning off from working. She was so close to finishing the book, would one more day really matter? She hoped that her editor, Trish, could not read her mind from a distance.

"Are you sure you have time? I know you're looking for a new place to live and trying to get your work done. And now . . . what with John leaving . . ."

It occurred to Annie that she now had her own kind of family right there on Chappy. She laughed, because if she started to cry, she might never stop. She had a feeling she'd be laughing a lot in the next couple of weeks. "I'm fine, Claire, really I am." Then she heard her text alert ding in her purse, and a happy wave rippled through her. It might be her brother, her actual brother. Her blood family. Sort of.

Annie stood up. "It's really important that John helps out with Lucy. That's what matters most, Claire. She's his daughter."

Claire nodded but stared at the floor.

Then Earl appeared in the dining room; Annie hadn't heard him pull into the driveway. "Don't worry about John, Claire," he ordered, then turned to Annie and said, "He'll be back."

That's when Annie understood the real reason she'd been worried about John leaving: She was afraid she'd never see him again.

Pushing down that thought, she told Claire she'd pick her up Monday morning at nine thirty. She thanked her for the tea, said goodbye to Earl, and went out to her car. On the way, her text alert dinged again.

Hey, Sis, it read. **Yeah, the Vineyard sounds interesting. Up here in Boston it's only hot and humid. Like, you can't**

breathe. No ocean breeze, but no dead bridesmaids, either, so that's good, I suppose.

Annie laughed. She wanted to get to know him better, but knew it would take time. Still, four months had passed since they'd met; saying that time passed too quickly had become such a cliché for life.

"September," she said, as she climbed into her car, her head and heart feeling lighter than when she'd arrived. Once the bulk of the tourists had left, once she was resituated with a new place to live, once her birth mother was back home in Boston after the cruise, Annie would invite them to come to the island.

But as she backed out of Earl's driveway, she remembered she could only invite them if she was still there.

Chapter 7

"I have a place for you to look at."

The call from Hannah Smith, the Realtor, came Sunday afternoon. Annie had spent most of the weekend sheltered in place at her desk, reveling in the fact that, in spite of her imagination occasionally trying to drag her into depression, she'd made great progress on the book and was feeling like she might meet her deadline. Just in time for Trish to go on vacation. But at least Annie would be done.

When her phone rang, she'd hoped it was John. The long weekend was nearly over; maybe he'd have time to see her before he left for Plymouth.

But the rental agent might have good news, too, so she relaxed and waited for details.

"It's a year-round rental in the village. And I have a few winter rentals now that should be available in September if you want to look at photos."

"How big is the one in the village?"

"A one-bedroom garage apartment. Sweet little place. About six hundred square feet. Give or take. And it has a two-car garage—one of the bays is yours. Inside the apartment, it's all been redone. Cozy, tasteful. Fully furnished. Vineyard Decorators did it."

Annie wasn't sure, but she thought where she lived now was about that size. "How much is the rent?"

"Four thousand. All-inclusive."

Commanding herself not to use one of those words that years ago resulted in kids getting their mouths washed out with soap, she quickly remembered that to stay on the island, she'd have to pay the price. And that, once she finished her manuscript, she'd get the next half of her advance, so her checkbook would be flush again.

If only she could get the book done.

"Okay," she said. "Let's take a look."

"Tomorrow morning?" Hannah asked. "This one will go fast." It wasn't a sales pitch: Everything on the island that was tagged "year-round" was scooped up faster than Mad Martha's ice cream in July.

"Can we make it early afternoon? Say, one o'clock? I have a commitment in the morning." No matter how important finding the right place would be, she wouldn't go back on her promise to Claire.

Hannah sighed. "I guess I can hold off listing it until then. Only because my bet is you'll want it."

"Thanks. I'll be at your office before one."

They rang off, and Annie was too excited to work any longer that day. But four thousand dollars . . . a month? Even though more income was on the horizon, she'd depleted her savings by paying off the debt that Mark left. Now that she was free of that burden, shouldn't she take a financial break? Take some time to replenish the coffers, as her dad had taught her?

Maybe she'd been too quick to turn John down. Not that moving in with him was an option now.

Never, ever depend on a man, her mantra had become after Mark had done what he'd done.

"He just walked away?" John had asked after Annie had told him about her sleazeball ex-husband.

"He didn't exactly walk," she'd explained. "He went to work one day and didn't come home that night. Or ever again. To his credit, he called that afternoon and said he'd be tied up and would be late." She'd laughed. "He was late, all right."

"Did you file a Missing Persons Report?"

"Yes. But not for almost two weeks. I kept thinking he'd be back. Smart, huh? And to think I was a teacher."

At that point, John had put his arm around her and pulled her close. It had been an unusually warm day in January; they were sitting on a blanket on South Beach, savoring the beauty around them: the tall dune grass that arced a gentle dance in the breeze; the mounds of sand that, so far, had survived winter's blast; the deep winter-blue of the ocean. Before stopping to rest, they'd walked, holding hands. They'd filled their pockets with purple wampum and silver oyster shells that looked like tiny footprints sculpted by the tides.

John had leaned over and kissed her on the forehead. "Would you like me to track the bastard down? You could press charges, maybe ask the court to get you some recompense."

She thought about his offer for all of five seconds, then shook her head. "Thanks, but no. I've always known I was as stupid as Mark was sleazy. I never asked where his money came from. I knew he was in commercial real estate; he convinced me it was lucrative. It's taken a long time, but I can finally sleep at night."

"And him?"

"As much as I'd like to think otherwise, I'm sure he can sleep just fine. It's one of the inequities of life we sometimes have to accept. Or choose to drive ourselves crazy."

"No," John said, "I mean what about him? Do you still . . ."

She faced John, their eyes, their lips nearly touching, the wind threading their hair into each other's. "Do I still love him? Good grief, not at all. I'm not sure I ever did. I'd been so traumatized when Brian died . . . I was so young, and I was crushed. Mark was magnetic. He loved having fun—big, expensive fun. He was nothing more than a panacea for me. Not that I'm proud to admit it."

John kissed her again, that time on the lips. She loved how he kissed her. Loved it more and more.

She looked out the window now, past the front porch, out toward the patch of lawn where Fiona Littlefield had, for some reason, dropped to the ground. And Annie wondered why life—even on the Vineyard—often became so damn complicated.

Later that night, Annie awoke to what sounded like snapping and crackling of more fireworks. She quickly realized it was thunder, not fireworks, that Mother Nature was having the last word on the holiday weekend. Then another sound jarred her: a loud banging on her front door.

Rolling onto her side, she checked the time: one forty-five. In the morning.

The banging came again.

Easing herself from under the top sheet—the only covering she'd needed on the hot, humid night—she grabbed her robe and threw it on top of her sleeveless cotton nightgown. Then she padded from the bedroom into the living room. When she was halfway to the front door, another flash of lightning lit up the porch; through the window she saw John peeking in.

At least it wasn't a leftover wedding reveler.

Annie opened the door. He stood on the porch, his dark

hair wet against his head, his thin cotton T-shirt clinging to his broad chest, an impish smile making him look like one of her former third-graders who'd been misbehaving.

"Hi," he said.

"Hi, yourself." She clawed her hand through her hair.

"Mind if I come in?"

She didn't mind. Rubbing her eyes, she only hoped she wasn't dreaming.

"I was in the neighborhood. . . ." he said, as he stepped inside and took her into his arms.

She didn't know how he'd managed to get to Chappy. It was well past the final *On Time* crossing for the night. "But . . ." she began, until he shushed her with his lips.

The sun rose in the morning as if nothing dramatic had happened in the night: none of nature's electrifying displays; no dispensing of the godawful humidity; no handsome, albeit drenched, man appearing at her door. Except that the same handsome man was walking into the bedroom now, dressed in a T-shirt and khaki shorts as dry as he was, and carrying two mugs of steaming coffee.

"So," Annie said, "how did you do it? How did you get here from Edgartown last night?"

He handed her a mug and sat on the edge of the bed. "Boat."

"The *On Time* was done for the night. Please tell me you didn't request an emergency transport."

"I didn't say I came over on the *On Time*. I said I got here by boat."

She smiled. "Kayak?" It was a joke. She knew he loved to kayak, and always complained that he no longer had time to enjoy it.

"Yes."

Annie laughed. "No."

"Yes."

"In a *thunderstorm?*"

"It wasn't thundering and lightning when I left. And I really wanted to see you." He didn't add, "Before I leave."

Staring into her mug, she tried not to think about that part. "Where did you park it?"

He laughed. "You're such a city girl. Did you mean where did I dock it?"

"Park. Dock. Yes. Whatever."

"Outside."

"Outside . . . here?"

"I pulled in on the edge of the Littlefields' beach. I knew no one was there. Then I hauled it out and came here."

"You carried the kayak here?"

"Like this." He stretched his arms toward the ceiling. "Hey, it was raining. I needed to cover my head."

"And then you put it down here."

"Yes. I docked it on your front steps. So no one would bother us during the night."

She laughed again. "My God, you are incorrigible."

"I was hoping you'd think that."

She took a long drink of coffee, impressed as always with John's brewing skills. No doubt he'd learned how from Earl. "I have to leave soon to get your mother and Bella."

"I know. I believe you and my mother are going to Edgartown to check out the quality of this year's garden entries?"

How did he know that? Once again, she tried not to feel left out that he'd spoken with his mother but hadn't called her. "Something like that," she replied.

"It's all part of my plan. If you wouldn't mind helping me strap the kayak to your car roof, I'll go with you to my mom and dad's, then drop off the kayak there. Then I'll go back to Edgartown with all of you."

"You're bringing the boat to their place?"

"Yup."

"You're leaving it there?" Their roles seemed to have switched, as if she'd become the interrogator.

He drank his coffee, set the mug on the floor, and retrieved his sneakers from the foot of Annie's bed. "Yeah. They're going to keep it while I'm gone."

So there it was. The real reason for the romantic gesture of arriving by kayak in the middle of a storm had merely been a convenient way to transport his damn boat so it would be safe while he was away. In Plymouth. At his ex-wife's. For two weeks. Or three, according to Francine.

Swinging her legs off the bed, Annie said, "I'd better get into the shower. I have a busy morning ahead." She was too annoyed to tell him that, in addition to helping his mother, she was going to meet the rental agent about the apartment. She was growing tired of trying to figure out what this relationship was or might ever, or never, become.

An hour later, with the kayak safely delivered and stored in the Lyonses' barn, and with Bella strapped into the car seat that John switched from Earl's truck to Annie's Lexus, the three adults and the ten-month-old baby made their way to the *On Time*.

En route, the only one who talked was Claire, which was fine with Annie. When they reached the parking area on the Chappy side, Claire turned to John and said, "What time are you leaving, dear?"

His eyes flicked to Annie, then back to his mother. "I'm on the two thirty."

Annie knew that islanders referred to the car ferry schedules by the departure time: "The two thirty" meant John would be on the boat that left the Vineyard at two thirty that afternoon, bound for Cape Cod. "America," some islanders called it. "Abroad," others said.

They got out of the car by the *On Time* slip, where John

took Bella out of the car seat and secured her into the stroller. If the gesture had been meant to show Annie how much he cared, it did not work: She had to resist the urge to shout, "Just GO! You're not needed here!" But she knew she'd regret that, and that shouting would make her eyes and her heart sting even more than they already did.

Somehow, she avoided erupting. They boarded the "little ferry," as Francine called it. By the time they reached Edgartown, her anger had melted into a puddle of unspoken distress.

John hugged his mother first. "Give Gramma's love to the girls," Claire said. "I know you'll make everything right." Grasping the handles of the stroller, she tottered toward Dock Street. Then she stopped and looked back. "Ms. Bella and I will head up the hill to number twelve North Water Street." She obviously wanted to give them privacy.

"So," John said once Claire was out of earshot, "this is goodbye again."

Annie looked off toward the wharf. The *Pied Piper* shuttle had arrived from Falmouth: A few dozen vacationers were disembarking, toting children and backpacks, and wearing eager smiles.

"So," Annie echoed, "I'll see you in a couple of weeks?"

He nodded.

She turned to him, hoping for a hint about their future. But when she looked in his eyes, she only saw her reflection. "I guess we'll see how things are between us when you come home."

He frowned. "Huh?"

The *On Time* was loading again; she scooted to the Old Sculpin Gallery, out of the way. Earl once told her that *sculpin* was the name of a fish species found in fast-moving waters like the channel in Edgartown Harbor.

"John," she said, slowly forming her words, not wanting their last conversation to be hostile, "I wish I didn't feel a little bit angry. I wish I didn't feel as if the only reason you came by last night was because you were bringing your kayak to Chappy, and I happened to be on the way."

He put his hand on her arm. "Annie. That's not true. I wanted to see you. . . ."

In spite of her resolve, tears welled in her eyes. "And you expected I'd be there. I mean, you didn't call. It wasn't like, 'Hey, Annie, I have an idea. I really want to see you. Maybe I can bring the boat over at the same time.'" Her thoughts sounded scrambled, the same way her stomach was feeling. "I feel like I was an afterthought. Or worse, like a booty call."

"Jesus," he said. He pressed his hands against his eyes and held them there for a moment. When he pulled them away, she saw that he, too, was crying. "I didn't want to tell you. I didn't want you to feel like you had to get involved. I figured this is my problem. And, yes, it's Jenn's problem, too." He let out a whoosh of pent-up air. "But, God, Annie. The last thing I want you to think is that last night was a booty call. Maybe I'm not thinking too straight right now. But I should be straight with you. This thing with Lucy isn't about a thirteen-year-old girl with a petty behavioral problem."

Annie wanted to say she didn't think that a thirteen-year-old caught smoking marijuana was worthy of high histrionics today. She supposed she might feel differently if she were a parent, if Lucy were her daughter. She supposed she could try to reassure him by suggesting that the school must have a counselor who was well versed in dealing with this situation, but school was out until September, so Annie had no idea what to say. Besides, he was right. This was his problem, not hers.

Then he took her hands in his, looked down at them, then raised his head and gazed off toward the *Pied Piper,* the way she had done. Her eyes followed his: Like the *On Time,* the boat was loading passengers—continuing the comings and goings of summer.

"Annie," John said into the air. "Lucy's pregnant."

She thought she must have heard wrong. "What?"

He looked back at her, tears now spilling down his tanned cheeks, his pearl-gray eyes glassy and pained. His shoulders started to quiver.

With her emotions bouncing into new territory, Annie guided him toward the Whale Tail iron sculpture; they sat on the short wall in front. She touched John's back, the same well-muscled back she'd clung to during the night when they'd made love, when she'd wanted him badly, and he'd wanted her.

And now, he stared at the ground. "That's the first time I've said it out loud."

"Your . . . your parents don't know?"

He shook his head. "My mother would go off the rails. Lucy's still a baby to them." He heaved a huge sigh, then wiped his eyes. "God. She's still a baby to me. I'm taking her to have an abortion." His voice cracked. "She's only thirteen," he said in a whisper, as if to himself. Then he exhaled a long, somber breath. "She doesn't want Jenn there. It's just as well. They've never gotten along, Not like Abigail and Jenn. Lucy's too much like me. Pigheaded, according to Jenn."

Looping her arm through his, Annie quietly asked, "What do your parents think is going on?"

With a halfhearted shrug, he said, "I told them the same lie I told you. That she was caught smoking a joint."

Under other circumstances, Annie would have been upset that he'd lied. But these circumstances were more than forgivable.

"What about you? Will you be okay?"

He slipped his arm around her. "It helps knowing that you're here. That you'll be here when I come back."

Resting her head on his shoulder, Annie said, "I'll be here, John."

"Even though you don't want to live with me."

"Even though I don't want to live with you *yet*."

They sat for a few more minutes, when John finally said he needed to leave. He kissed her, squeezed her hand, and visibly staving off more tears, he walked up toward Main Street, and she went toward North Water, knowing she'd been gripped by the deep kind of hurt that comes when you love someone you cannot help.

Chapter 8

"Roses and delphiniums create such a delicate garden," Claire chirped, as Annie walked past the gate of a white picket fence that framed one of the town's fabulous colonial sea captain's houses. "Hydrangeas are hearty and vibrant, and God knows they should be our official flower. But this garden captures the island's light and fragrance."

Claire seemed to be in her element. She wore a mid-calf, powder-blue cotton dress, "sensible" orthopedic walking shoes, and a wide-brimmed straw hat that did little to control her perpetually flyaway hair. Her pearl-gray eyes—mirror images of John's—bubbled with enchantment as she leaned down and inhaled the scent of a healthy cluster of tiny pink roses. Then she smiled, straightened up, and pushed the stroller to a grouping of tall, colorful stalks resplendent with lavender blossoms. "Canterbury bells," she told Annie. "Beautiful, aren't they?"

Sometimes, like then, Claire almost seemed innocent. But Annie had witnessed another side of the woman, a controlling, angry side that flared if she felt she or her family were being challenged or betrayed. Annie knew that John had been right not to tell his mother the truth about Lucy; there was no telling how Claire would react.

"We'll want photos of all of these gardens," Claire instructed. "Then we'll select the most vibrant to put in the brochure and post on Facebook."

"Let's not forget Instagram," Annie said. "Francine should know how to do that, too." She mused that she sounded like Trish, who was not only Annie's editor but also her champion of online promotion. "The more people who see it, the more people will buy it," she frequently said. Adhering to that directive, Annie took out her phone now and started shooting pictures. "I have so much to learn about flowers," she said. "In Boston, the only ones that stick in my mind are the magnolia blossoms on Newbury Street."

"Those are trees, dear. Flowering trees, not plants, not like these."

"Like I said, I have a lot to learn."

"Not to worry. We'll have you knowing a foxglove from a hollyhock in no time."

Not wanting to admit the attempt might be futile, Annie didn't say it had taken every drop of her patience to learn which roses carried the best fragrance for blending into her soaps, and that sometimes the strongest scents were not as pleasing as the softer ones. As with hydrangeas—with variations from large pom-pom blossoms to lacy, fragile ones— she'd never known there were so many varieties.

Ambling through the winding garden paths, she took close-ups and wide shots that showed off a striking spectrum of color that accented the freshly painted white clapboard house and its velvet green lawn. Annie began to realize it was fun to shift her creative spirit from words into pictures.

Claire meandered nearby, making a few notes, nodding this way and that. "Next stop, number twenty-three," she announced once she apparently felt they'd given number twelve its due.

Annie fell into step behind her as they went through the front gate and up the sidewalk that was choked with tourists, most of whom were walking toward them. Claire, however, used Bella's stroller almost as a plow, commanding control of the ribbon of redbrick while maintaining a stiff smile on her face. When they reached number twenty-three, she halted abruptly and turned back to Annie.

"He's lying, you know," Claire said.

Annie stopped. Blinked. "Excuse me?"

"My son. He's lying to all of us. He doesn't think I can tell when he is, but I am his mother. I know these things." She leveled her eyes on Annie, who curbed a reaction.

"I'm not sure what you mean, Claire."

"I think you do. I saw the way you looked at him. Or, should I say, the way you didn't look at him in the car. You know that he's lying, too."

Bending her head, Annie pretended to study the camera, the settings, the framing options.

"You don't know Lucy, Annie, but, I'm telling you right now, John is lying. There is no way that girl is smoking pot. She is too smart for that. And too close to her father. She'd know he'd have her hide if she ever did that." She shook her head and started walking again. "No," she said, "he's lying about something. My guess is that his ex-wife is up to no good. I only hope it's as simple as trying to get more child support. He can fight that; he already gives her more than the court ordered."

Annie was relieved for John, grateful that, while Claire knew he was lying, she hadn't guessed the real reason. He'd been right: The truth would crush her. Send her off the rails.

Claire veered off the sidewalk onto a path that led to the garden at number twenty-three. It was a bounty of shades of blue, as if every blossom had been plucked from the sky or the sea. Annie began to shoot again, but her mind strayed elsewhere. Earl had once said he thought his wife was clairvoyant. "*Clair*voyant," he'd said. "So she was aptly named Claire." *Please,*

God, Annie prayed now, *don't let me look or act in any way or say anything that will give away John's secret.*

Clicking her way from one garden to another, she was glad there was no more talk of Lucy or John, only intermittent praising of the gardenscapes and their artful displays and Claire's occasional comments:

"Sallie Franks has agreed to offer her tiny shortbread cookies to our guests again this year. They go so well with lemonade."

"The Allsops have done such lovely work this year."

"The softer shades of impatiens are more agreeable, don't you think?"

After a couple of hours, it was time for Annie to meet the rental agent. Claire had wandered off; Annie found her in a backyard garden, showing Bella how to cup her palms to catch the fragrance of pink roses that were woven through a tunnel of white arbors.

"Claire?" she interrupted. "I have to leave to see that rental place now."

Lifting Bella's hand, Claire helped her wave bye-bye. Then the woman said, "I hope what I said about John didn't alarm you. But I do know my son—"

"It's fine," Annie interrupted. "If he wants to hold back anything, that's his prerogative. Lucy is his daughter, after all." But as she watched Claire with Bella, Annie couldn't help but wonder how happy the woman would be to have a great-granddaughter to fuss over. Unless the mother was thirteen.

"I was only trying to warn you," Claire continued. "I suspect that this isn't about Lucy. If Jenn wants more money, John will take care of it. I only hope that she isn't trying to win him back. And that she's going to use the girls as leverage."

A knot of pain formed in Annie's throat, then wormed its way down to her stomach, as if she'd been given an endoscopy without anesthesia. She put her hand on her chest, then tried to pretend she'd only had an itch. "You said Lucy is a smart girl," she told Claire. "Well, don't forget that her father is a smart man. I'm sure John will do whatever he feels is best for his family." Then she went back down the path, out onto North Water, and wondered how long it would be before she could breathe again.

If Donna MacNeish had had the access and the opportunity to have an abortion, would she have gone through with it? She'd been seventeen when she'd become pregnant, eighteen when Annie was born. "Those were different times," Donna had told her when they'd finally met. "Either you married the boy who was the father, or you gave the baby up for adoption. The standard threat was: 'Your baby should be raised in a good home. Without suffering the stigma of having an unwed mother.'"

As savvy as Annie grew to be, she'd never understood that reasoning. But she did know that when she'd been born in 1968, *Roe v. Wade*—the federal law that permitted abortion—hadn't yet been argued by the US Supreme Court. A year earlier, Colorado had become the first state to legalize abortion, but only in the event of rape, incest, or potential disability to the mother; it was not until 1970 that a state—Hawaii—legalized abortion if a woman simply wanted one, no strings attached.

Annie had known from a young age that she'd been adopted; Bob and Ellen Sutton had assured her that she was their special gift. But around the time she was told the "facts of life," Annie began to question how her birth mother could have given her up. She was about thirteen then. Lucy's age today. It was when she'd researched the facts about abortion.

As Annie threaded her way through the narrow streets of Edgartown now, she remembered she'd felt numb when she learned that she was alive not because her birth mother had so desperately wanted her to be born, but because she virtually had not had a choice. Even later when Annie learned there had been other options—back alley doctors and illegal procedures (by then she'd seen the film *Dirty Dancing*), and other countries where Donna could have gone—the lingering sorrow at knowing the truth had never completely gone away.

"Your birth father and I did want you to have a good home," Donna had explained. "We planned to get married someday and adopt a baby whom we would love, the same way we'd hoped your adoptive parents would love you."

It was the stuff young dreams were made of.

But Donna hadn't wound up with Annie's birth father— and he'd died by the time Annie finally met her. Annie hadn't pried for more information because it seemed too painful for Donna, and it no longer seemed to matter.

And now, so many decades after Annie was born, a young girl in this new world was going to end what could have been a life, what could have been a child raised by loving adoptive parents, the way Annie had been. And though life had certainly changed, and Lucy might even be "allowed" to keep her baby, Annie knew that society did not always jibe with the laws, and that Lucy and her baby would not be totally safe from judgment.

With a small sigh for the sorrow that the creation of life could still cause so many people such pain, Annie tucked a few strands of hair behind her ears and tried not to worry how Lucy would feel not only now but also later. After all, Annie knew from experience that choices of the head—the sensible, practical choices—were not always those of the heart. And that the ones of the heart were those that tended to linger.

Before she could wallow in sadness any longer, Annie reached the real estate agent's office, where her new life might—or might not—await.

★ ★ ★

Too small. Too pricy. No washer/dryer. No parking. And that was only the first listing.

Annie flipped through two more equally unacceptable "winter rental" listings in Hannah Smith's three-ring binder.

"Are you reconsidering a house share?" Hannah asked. "Some clients find that can be an affordable compromise."

Annie had been staring at a page that showed two house-share listings, wondering what it would be like to live with someone—anyone—again after having been alone more than a decade. "Oh, no. Sorry," she said. She turned the page to a large house: four bedrooms, three baths. She didn't bother looking for the price.

"A house share can be good while you're waiting for something else to come up," Hannah continued. "Something more conducive to a permanent home."

Annie nodded, turned another page, which brought her to the "For Sale" section. "That's it?"

"Afraid so. Except for the year-round one we're going to look at. Which is really charming." She grabbed her keys and directed Annie to the door.

They walked three blocks closer to the water. Annie knew that the location played a significant role in the four-thousand-a-month price tag. She tried to look on the bright side: It would be easier to get around if she lived in town and not on Chappy; and it wasn't far from John's duplex, the "affordable" property he'd won in the island lottery, which didn't mean he was given the place for free, only that he paid a much lower cost than the pricy island market value.

She wondered if Lucy might come back with him for the rest of the summer.

"Here we are," Hannah said.

Annie sighed and forced her thoughts back to her current mission. They stood in front of a large white house with black shutters and with window boxes filled with red geraniums and some kind of white flower she should know the name of by now but did not. The driveway was redbrick and had, as promised, a two-car garage. Two sets of arched wood doors featured polished wrought-iron fixtures; window boxes on either side matched those on the house. They went to the right, where Hannah unlocked an exterior door.

"This is your private entrance," she said.

Annie never liked it when real estate agents referred to anything on a property as "your"—your kitchen, your bedroom, your bath—as if a training facilitator had told them it was a subliminal way to make clients feel they were already home, and that they were too naïve to know it was part of the sales pitch. She followed Hannah up the full flight of gleaming wood stairs and through another door at the top.

The apartment was charming, as Hannah had said. It was decorated nicely in the latest pewter and ivory with "pops" of cerulean and chartreuse here and there. The kitchen area had white cabinets, marble countertops, and stainless steel appliances—but there was no room for a table. The living area had a full-sized sofa and chair, a chest, an end table, and a small buffet. But there was no kitchen table and no place to put one. Unless the bedroom was enormous, Annie did not believe it was six hundred square feet.

"And over here is your bedroom," Hannah said, leading Annie to a room that, no, was not enormous. It had a double bed (Annie's queen bed would be a tight fit) and a single nightstand. There was a generous closet, however, though half of it was taken by the stackable washer and dryer. Right next to the bedroom was a bathroom that was nice and newly done, but had a narrow shower stall and no tub.

"I think the owners might have the square footage wrong," Annie said.

"Hmm. Yes, well, you might be right. It does seem a wee bit smaller than advertised."

A wee bit, indeed.

They went back to the living room and Annie looked around. On the plus side, it had lovely plantation blinds at all the windows and a cozy propane heater that looked like a fireplace but would mean Annie would not have to haul wood inside.

"The rent includes cable, Wi-Fi, and all your utilities," Hannah added. "And did I mention it has central air?"

Which, Annie thought, *given the elfin size, might account for a whopping total of four hundred dollars a month, max.*

"And the furnishings are beautiful, aren't they? Everything is brand-new. And it has the upscale look that suits someone of your status."

There were times when Annie wondered if she'd be treated the same way if she were still a third-grade teacher.

Still, she knew she could talk herself into renting it if she weren't careful. Then she realized something critical was missing: a place for her to work. There was no desk or table where she could put her laptop, no room for her bookcases, and certainly nowhere to make soap, which had begun as an enjoyable pastime but now generated a second, though meager, income. But while she supposed she could find another location for that, or, if need be, give up soap-making altogether, Annie could not live without writing. Not financially and, more important, not psychologically. Writing was the fuel that kept her going.

"Like I said," Hannah continued, as if noting Annie's hesitation, "this place won't last long. As soon as I list it"—she snapped her fingers—"poof."

Annie walked around again. She eyed the gleaming hardwood floors, the thickly padded area rugs. "A one-year lease?"

"Two."

That was the decisive moment. While most year-round tenants would jump at the chance to be locked into a lovely island home for two years, Annie knew if she signed the lease she might as well tell John she'd never move in with him. And she'd have to work very hard, and very consistently, to keep up with the exorbitant payments. *Oh,* she groaned inwardly, *why has my life become so complicated?*

Then she thought about John. And Lucy. Annie knew that her housing situation was nothing compared to what they were dealing with. She also knew that no matter where she landed, things would work out, and that settling for something—no matter the reason—often turned into a mistake.

"I'm sorry," she said quickly, before she changed her mind. "But it really is too small. There's no place for me to work. Not even a corner where I could set up my laptop. I need space for books, too. No"—she shook her head—"it's too small." *And way too expensive,* she did not add.

Hannah gave her eyes an unprofessional half roll. "Okay, then, I'll keep trying."

But Annie suspected she would not.

Chapter 9

The afternoon air was still hot but did not feel as humid—"sticky" Annie's dad liked to call it when the warm moisture in the air made his white shirt stick to the back of his wooden desk chair at work.

After leaving what might have been her only chance at a decent apartment, Annie strolled along Main Street. As she approached the ice cream shop, she decided to treat herself to a cone. Maybe she'd feel better after a good dose of fudge swirl, which had been her dad's favorite flavor. But as she put one foot on the doorstep, she was jarred by a loud shout.

"Annie! Annie Sutton!"

With one hand on the door handle, she almost did not turn around. Annie hated being recognized by a fan of her books—she'd never thought that being a writer entitled her to celebrity.

"Annie! For God's sake!"

That got her attention—that, and the fact that the voice was familiar.

Two vehicles honked. One driver shouted an obscenity, either at Annie or at the person who was shouting for her: Taylor.

Taylor was behind the wheel of her pickup truck and had

stopped in the middle of Main Street, holding up summer traffic. She was leaning across the seat, trying to get Annie's attention through the passenger window.

Good grief, Annie thought and bolted to the truck. "You're stopping traffic!"

Another horn blasted.

"I don't care. Get in!"

"Get in?"

"Yes! And hurry up." Taylor's auburn hair was pulled into a ponytail, setting off her amber eyes that looked ready to pop. "Get in!" she seethed again.

Annie sighed, opened the door, and climbed onto the seat. "Okay, now drive. Before a war breaks out."

Taylor made a guttural sound and stepped on the gas.

"So," Annie said. "Are you going to tell me where we're going?"

"To the hospital," the woman replied, making a sharp right onto South Water Street.

Annie swallowed. Hard. "What?" Her question came out in a quiver.

"Claire's had a stroke."

Claire? "Claire Lyons, Earl's wife?" She knew her question was ludicrous. At least she didn't add, "John's mother?"

"Claire Lyons. Yes." Taylor gritted her teeth.

"But . . . I just left her. Not long ago. She was on North Water . . ."

"That's where she was found. In Mildred Atwater's garden. With the baby. What's her name again?"

"Bella?"

"Yeah. I can never remember that name."

Because you are an ass, Annie thought. "Where's Bella? Who has her?"

Taylor shrugged. "She's at the hospital, too. They decided

not to leave her there to poke at the peonies." She seemed to enjoy employing sarcasm as an art form.

"But how's Claire? Is she . . . ?"

"Is she going to make it? It's too soon to tell. She's conscious and everything, and it looks like they got to her fast. It helped that she was in Edgartown and not over on Chappy. The big concern now is that she'll have another. A bigger one. That sometimes happens with strokes."

Annie stared out the window. Poor Claire. Poor Earl! She couldn't believe this had happened. Claire had seemed so chipper that morning. So bright, so . . .

Oh, no! Annie thought. *What about John?* She looked at her watch. It was nearly three o'clock. "Oh, God. John's on the ferry."

"We know," Taylor said, as if she were part of a major investigative branch of law enforcement and not just a caretaker on Chappy who volunteered as an EMT.

Then Annie scolded herself for being irked with the woman who'd obviously been searching for her.

"Earl wants you to get the baby," Taylor said. "Maybe bring her to your house. If that's okay with you."

"He's there? At the hospital?"

"He just arrived when I left."

"Oh, God. Is he okay?"

"Not really."

Claire and Earl had definitely become Annie's island family. She'd grown to feel closer to them than she did to her birth mother, mostly because she'd spent nearly a year with Claire and Earl, and less than two weeks with Donna MacNeish. Drumming her fingers on the dashboard, Annie warned herself not to be thinking about her birth mother when she should be worrying about Claire. And Earl. And . . . John.

★ ★ ★

Earl looked as pale and shaken as Claire did. He sat in a chair, close to the bed, folding and unfolding the brim of the Red Sox cap that rested on his lap.

"She had a stroke," he said when he saw Annie enter the room.

Annie nodded, then looked at Claire. "Gosh, Claire, that was a surprise, wasn't it? How do you feel now?"

Claire gestured that she wasn't sure.

"She had a stroke," Earl repeated, his voice hollow and distant. He went back to folding the hat brim.

Pulling a chair next to Earl's, Annie tried not to stare at the tube that snaked from Claire's hand up to an IV, at another that encircled her head and was clamped in her nose, or at the wires that led to various monitors that blipped and bleeped.

Claire tried to speak, but her words were sloppy and unintelligible.

"It's okay," Annie said, "you don't have to talk."

"She can't," Earl said. "She had a stroke."

"Are they still doing tests?" Annie asked, her eyes jumping between the two people. She didn't want to exclude Claire from the conversation, but understood that the answer would be up to Earl.

"I suppose."

A doctor and a nurse came in. "Excuse us," the doctor said. "We need to examine Claire."

Annie stood up, grateful that the doctor hadn't addressed Claire as "the patient," or simply as "her." Physician education had clearly come a long way since Annie's father had a heart attack more than two decades ago, when a medical person had plainly announced, "I'm sorry. He's dead."

She offered a hand to Earl. "Come to the waiting room. You can tell me what happened."

He stood up in an awkward, sluggish motion, then let Annie

guide him down the hall. Once he was resettled, she quietly said, "Start at the beginning."

"All I know is I was down by Caleb Pond, working on the Andersons' shed. A tree snapped in half during last night's storm and broke through a window." With eyes that looked dazed, he looked around the small, square room that was painted pale green and, like much of the hospital, was decorated with attractive, original artwork of seascapes and landscapes and people, Vineyard people, Annie suspected. He pulled a handkerchief from his pocket and blew his nose. "Pete Denton called me from the scene." Annie knew the name, but not the man; he was one of John's fellow police officers. Earl looked at Annie. "I'm so glad you made me learn how important it is to carry my phone."

She reached over, patted his hand.

"We don't know how bad she is," he continued, "yet."

"She seems alert, which seems like a good sign." Annie had no way of knowing if that was true, but it sounded plausible and hopefully eased Earl's thoughts.

"John's on his way back. He was halfway to Woods Hole. Once they got there, he jumped on the freight boat. The steamship guys are taking care of his truck. He should be here soon."

Annie nodded as if she already knew that.

Then Earl let out a long sigh. "She just . . . collapsed," he said.

She rubbed his hand. "It must have been scary."

"It could have been worse. She landed in the Atwaters' hollyhocks. Pete said if she'd landed on the sidewalk, she'd have been banged up on top of the stroke. She'll be upset about the flowers, though."

Annie let him rest in silence for a moment, then she said, "Earl? Where's Bella?"

His dazed eyes scowled. He quickly stood up. "Jesus. I don't know. I think one of the nurses took her. . . ."

"It's fine. I'll find her. Don't worry."

"Okay. You go find the baby and I'll go back to Claire. God, what a day, huh?"

Bella was safely ensconced in maternity, exactly as Annie had expected. Her friend Winnie's sister-in-law wasn't on duty, but Annie remembered the nurse at the desk. Months ago, she had helped Annie settle Bella's endless crying when Annie had no idea what to do.

"Too bad about Mrs. Lyons," the young woman said now. "Will she be okay?"

"I sure hope so. Among other things, Claire has been a godsend for this baby." She thanked her for helping, then gave Bella a big hug before wheeling her off in the stroller.

Because Taylor had dropped Annie off at the hospital, then had to get back to work, Annie decided to take the bus back to Edgartown. Then, on the way to the main door, as she was passing the reception desk, she had a thought. She knew it probably was none of her business, but . . .

She went to the desk. "Excuse me," she said. "Can you tell me what room Fiona Littlefield is in—if she's still here? I'm Annie Sutton, the one who found her."

After Annie got off the elevator, Fiona's room was not hard to find.

Angling the stroller inside the door, she tried to enter quietly. Once inside, she saw that Fiona was sitting up, staring out the window toward Vineyard Haven Harbor. Unlike in many of the Boston hospitals, the inpatient rooms on the island were all private.

Annie introduced herself, then added with a smile, "I found you on my lawn."

"You're the lady who lives in the cottage?" Fiona's long

highlighted hair was tangled and seemed in need of a good washing. Her skin was wan; her body looked shriveled, which might have been due, in part, to the thin cotton hospital gown she wore. And though she was hooked up to a couple of monitors and an IV, she didn't seem to be in pain.

"Yes." Annie saw no point in adding, "But not for long."

"Thanks, then. For saving my life. The doctor said if I'd been there much longer . . ." She turned her gaze back to the window.

"It was lucky on my part. I happened to step outside for a view of the fireworks and there you were. How are you feeling?"

The girl nodded. "Better, thanks." Her voice seemed as small as her body. "I wasn't drunk, you know."

Annie didn't know how to respond.

"I mean, people probably think because I was at the wedding and it was hot out, I must have had too much to drink and passed out. But I only had one sip from a glass of champagne with the toast. I hate alcohol."

"I didn't care about any of that," Annie replied. "I only knew you needed help."

Fiona gave her a weak smile. "Please. Have a seat. Is that your baby?"

Annie laughed and wheeled the stroller so Bella faced Fiona. Then she sat down. "No, but she's part of my Vineyard family. Her name is Bella."

"Hello, Bella. You're a very pretty little girl."

For once, Bella did not make a sound; she just gaped at Fiona with her big dark eyes.

Then Fiona quickly looked back at Annie. "I was poisoned, you know."

She said it so matter-of-factly, Annie was startled. "What?"

"The toxicology report said I had andromedotoxin in my blood. That's a poison. Someone poisoned me."

The news was bizarre. Not to mention unsettling. "But . . .

who on earth would poison you? Are you sure? Maybe it was an accident . . . ?"

"Believe me, it was no accident. The doctor said they sent the report to the police, who are supposed to contact me, but I have not heard a word."

Annie felt as if she'd walked into a conversation she'd rather not have heard. "The police are awfully busy right now. . . ."

"They'd be a lot busier if I had died." She waved a hand in the air as if swatting a fly.

"But, Fiona, who . . . ?" She sensed she was now treading water in a pool where she didn't belong. She wished she had stood up, said she was sorry, but that she really could not get involved. Instead, Annie found herself . . . curious. Again.

Fiona made a sound that was like a child spitting out an olive. "It's not hard to figure out who tried to kill me. My brother and sister both hate me because I don't want to sell the house on Chappy. Neither one of them has any sentiment. No pride in our family. Nothing. They only want money. Well, Colin wants the money. Sheila wants it to become a bird sanctuary. As if the island doesn't already have enough places for birds. I mean, they're everywhere, aren't they? Why the heck would they need a sanctuary?"

It seemed like a logical question.

But what had begun as a simple check on a girl whose life Annie had apparently saved now felt like a soap opera that she'd tuned into halfway through the first season. "Well," she said, trying to sound agreeable, "the Vineyard does have lots of green space." Why couldn't she wish the girl well and escape from the room? Maybe if Bella would start screaming . . . but, no, for once the baby seemed content.

"It must have been my brother. Sheila never bothered to show up for the wedding."

Though Annie was hardly well versed in family dynamics,

she doubted it was common for siblings to poison one another. Even over a house. "You think your brother poisoned you?"

"Well, someone did, and he's the only one who had motive and opportunity. I've watched enough crime shows to know those things matter."

"If you really believe that, you should call the police. Don't wait for them to get back to you."

"I will. As soon as I get out of here. They told me I'll be here a few more days. Until they're sure the poison has left my system. Speaking of which, would you do me a favor?"

Annie stumbled and stuttered over her words, but after a couple of seconds muttered, "Yes, of course."

"I don't have any clothes, except my bridesmaid dress. You live right next door to my house, right? Would you mind going over? My things are in the upstairs bedroom that faces the water, the first one on the left at the top of the stairs. Would you please bring me a few essentials? I don't have anyone else. . . ." Her voice cracked a little, leaving Annie feeling unneighborly. And, worse, selfish.

"Of course," she replied. "Would you like to make a list of what you want?"

Fiona shook her head. "It doesn't matter. Whatever you bring will be fine. If no one's around—and I guess Colin is long gone—go around to the back. The door to the sunroom probably isn't locked. . . ." She continued giving instructions about how Annie could get inside. Annie, however, only half listened because she already knew how. She'd been in that house on another occasion. A couple of times, as a matter of fact.

Standing at the bus stop outside the hospital, Annie wondered if she should have waited for John. She decided, however, it would be better for everyone if he could be alone with his parents. So she called Francine, gave her a quick rundown, and told her that Bella was with her.

"Claire will be okay," Annie said.

"But it's our fault, mine and Bella's. She worries about us. . . ."

"Stop! It's no one's fault, least of all yours. You and Bella have done more for Claire than you can imagine. She'd grown so lonely after John's girls left the island; you've brought the joy of being needed back into her life." Annie had no idea where her words had come from, but she didn't doubt they were true. "So please, no more talking like that, okay?"

After a short pause, Francine softly said, "Okay."

Then Annie felt her heart flutter. If Claire didn't survive, what would happen to Francine and Bella? *Stop it.* Murphy's voice suddenly broke into Annie's thoughts. *Don't be an idiot. Be strong. You know how to do that.*

God bless Murphy. Annie's guardian angel.

Francine said she'd pick up Bella at the cottage on her way home from work. They rang off, and Annie watched for the bus while she moved the stroller back and forth. She hoped Murphy was right, that she'd find the strength to help everyone she cared about get through whatever would happen next. Then she decided to do what she did best in times of stress: She made a mental list of everything on her mind. Long ago, she'd learned it helped her feel less overwhelmed by providing a false sense that she could regain some control.

That day, the list was short but potent:

- Her deadline loomed.
- She'd soon be homeless.
- Her boyfriend's thirteen-year-old daughter needed an abortion, and there was no way Annie could help.
- He'd gone to be with his daughter, and was sleeping with his ex for all Annie knew. (Until then, she hadn't

realized that possibility had been in the back of her mind.)

- His mother had had a stroke, so Annie would need to help her out. And help Earl. And Francine and Bella. And John from a distance.
- The girl she'd found unconscious on her lawn now claimed she'd been poisoned, most likely by her brother. Which was definitely NOT any of Annie's business.

When the bus arrived, she didn't feel less overwhelmed; she reverted, instead, to feeling numb. She lifted Bella, then jostled the stroller up the stairs behind them. A young man offered his seat; Annie thanked him and squeezed between other passengers. But, for once, rather than being put off by the crowd, she was glad for the company, glad to have Bella sit on her lap and wave at the other passengers, glad that some waved back. It helped stave off a strong urge to cry, not because of her issues, but because of Claire. Annie did not want her to die. It was, she knew, that simple. And it made her feel that sad.

Chapter 10

By the time Annie returned to the cottage and had situated Bella on the floor atop her favorite quilt with a sippy cup of apple juice that Annie had diluted (as per Francine's research on the Internet), she knew there was at least one thing she could quickly cross off her list: She could go to the Littlefield house, gather a few things for Fiona, deposit them back at the hospital tomorrow, and be done with the matter. Fiona could go to the police and handle her own quandary as to whether or not she'd intentionally been poisoned. Annie had no idea whether or not the girl was capable of doing that, but she refused to worry about it.

Then she looked over at Bella in time to see that she'd pulled herself up from the floor and was standing, hands clinging to the cushion of the love seat, laughing.

"Look at you!" Annie cried. "What a big girl!" She clapped her hands.

Bella smiled and giggled and then thumped down, her fall cushioned by her thick diaper.

Annie bent down and scooped her up before any crying could begin. "You stood up all by yourself! We need to celebrate. Let's go on an adventure! We'll take a walk next door to the Littlefield house. You remember that house, don't you?"

In less than five minutes, they were out the door, Bella riding on Annie's right hip while grasping her sippy cup. A large shopping bag dangled from Annie's left hand, and her phone was tucked into her pocket, not that she'd need it. But Earl's comment about always having his with him had resonated, and Annie wanted to be prepared in case Colin Littlefield returned. Not that he'd have malice on his mind, but Annie knew that stranger things could happen than a brother trying to poison his sister—even on the celebrated island of Martha's Vineyard. She reminded herself that the word *celebrated* needed to be spoken with one's tongue firmly fixed in one's cheek.

She went the long way—up the driveway and out to the road—to avoid cutting through the cluster of scrub oaks and taking the path that bisected the Flanagans' lawn. No sense running into leftover wedding guests or Roger himself. Otherwise, Annie might be tempted to ask Roger how well he knew Colin, and if he thought the Littlefield son might have tried to poison his sister. Then she told herself—again—that just because she'd found Fiona on her lawn did not mean she had to save her.

In less than a couple of minutes, she ducked into the sunroom of the cavernous house, scooted through the kitchen, and made her way to the massive butterfly staircase in the front foyer. Standing at the foot of the stairs, she called out, "Hello?" Not surprisingly, there was no answer. She hadn't seen any cars in the driveway, and there were no visible signs of life on the main floor—not a set of keys, a few pieces of junk mail, or a lone cardigan tossed over the sofa in the gathering room. It was easy to tell that the house had once been beautiful, lovingly built, tastefully appointed. Now, however, it had been stripped of elegance, of its family and harmony, if there had ever been any. The house, like Fiona, seemed neglected.

Annie shook off her gloom and dashed up to the second floor.

The room Fiona had indicated was the same one where Francine and Bella had once stayed. Where they'd once squatted, to be precise.

"Here we are again," Annie said to the baby. "Remember this place?" She stood in the center of the large space and took a slow breath. Christmas seemed so long ago; so much had changed since then. "In many wonderful ways, thanks to you!" she said and kissed Bella's cheek, then set her down on the thick carpeting.

Fiona's clothing was in the closet; Annie pulled a sundress from the rack and tossed it, along with a nice pair of sandals, into the bag. She took clean underthings from an open suitcase, then went into the bathroom and selected a few toiletries.

When she was finished, she gathered Bella and headed out the door. On the way, she spotted a paperback novel on the nightstand; she grabbed it, dropped it into the bag, and did not take it personally that the book was not one of hers.

The mission complete, they were halfway down the staircase when Annie's phone rang.

"Damn," she said, instinctively clenching her jaw as if she'd been caught in the house where she did not belong. Reminding herself that this time she was there at an owner's request, she rearranged her bundles (Bella included), reached into her pocket, pulled out the phone, and answered.

Wonder of wonders, it was Kevin, her brother.

"Any more dead bridesmaids lurking around?"

Annie laughed and continued down the stairs. "She wasn't dead! Though now she believes her brother tried to poison her." She flicked her eyes around quickly, in case Colin was lurking under the stairs or around the corner. He was not.

"Hmm," Kevin said. "I'm afraid I haven't known you long enough to want to poison you."

"Good thing." They spoke with ease, almost as if they'd known each other a long time. Annie retraced her steps through the kitchen and the sunroom, out the door, and onto the lawn. "How are you? What are you up to?"

"I'm okay. Not much going on in Boston, though. I was thinking that it might be a good time to visit the Vineyard. And you."

"Me?" she asked. "Here?" Well, of course he meant her and of course he meant there. What was Annie thinking? She was thinking of the million things she had to do in such little time. "Well, September might be best," she said. "Like after Labor Day. I think you'd enjoy it more once most of the tourists have gone." She briefly wondered if she'd still live on the island by then.

Kevin's laugh was warm and friendly. "The truth is, I decided I needed a dose of energy, the kind that comes from large crowds and plenty of sunshine. It's kind of lonely in Boston right now, but don't tell anyone I said that. People might think it's weird that a forty-two-year-old man misses his mother. But the truth is, she's been gone too damn long!"

So Kevin was lonely. Annie certainly knew what an empty, disconnected feeling that was. She walked to the driveway, then back up to the road. It would be nice to see him again, to get to know her half brother better. "When are you thinking of coming down?"

He laughed again. "Actually, I've done more than think about it. I'm in Vineyard Haven. I just got off the ferry."

She stopped, pitching Bella forward, causing her to let out a scream. Annie bounced her and smoothed her hair, trying to ease the noise. "Oh," she said. "Well. Welcome."

"Is that a kid I hear?"

"Don't worry, she's not mine, I'm babysitting. Bella belongs to all of Chappaquiddick. There's never a dull moment here."

"Well, you won't have to babysit me. For one thing, I brought my pickup. For another, I made a reservation at a place called the Kelley House. I was lucky to get a room; they said they'd had a cancellation. Is it far from you?"

Bless him, Annie thought. Kevin was considerate. And he definitely was lucky to get a room at the last minute in July. "The Kelley House isn't far at all," she said. "It's right over the channel from Chappy. Are you headed there now?"

"I don't know where I'm headed. I've never been here."

"You lived in Boston your whole life and never made it to the island?"

"Nope."

Annie tried to think fast. "Okay, first, park your vehicle right there in the ferry lot. Then go into the terminal and grab one of the green maps on the rack by the door. You probably have GPS, but, trust me, that map is invaluable. It gives a clear picture of the whole island, so you'll always know where you are."

"Great. Someone just pulled out of a parking space, so I'm pulling in."

"You must have been born under a lucky star," she said with a snicker. "Once you have the map, go to Edgartown and get checked in at the inn. I have a few things to take care of here, but I can meet you for dinner. You'll see a restaurant, the Newes, on the ground floor of the Kelley House. It's a pub. Nothing like the kind of hotel restaurants you might be used to. But I think you'll like it."

"Sounds great, Annie. Thanks."

"No problem. I can't wait to see you. I'll meet you there by seven, okay?" They said goodbye and Annie stared at Bella.

"Doesn't anyone realize I've become accustomed to peace and quiet? Why are they trying to screw up my schedule?"

Bella didn't answer; she simply threw down her sippy cup and wriggled on Annie's hip as if she wanted to get down. Annie lowered her to the ground; Bella grabbed hold of Annie's leg, pulled herself up on her two chubby, rubbery legs, and took a step—a real step!—then plopped onto the lawn.

It was six thirty before Annie was able to start dressing for dinner. Francine had stopped by to pick up the baby: They'd had a long talk about Claire. They speculated about her prognosis, and about how they might need to rearrange their lives in order to help her once they knew the kinds of help she'd need. And though Annie tried to show Francine that Bella—at only ten months old!—could now take a single step, the baby would not cooperate. She merely sat down on the floor and laughed. At least Bella was nearing her first birthday by laughing almost in equal measure to crying.

Finally alone, Annie dressed in a pink linen dress and white sandals and unpacked a white linen sweater she'd nearly forgotten she owned. For a place that was accustomed to dressing "down" nine months of the year, the streets of Edgartown had become a runway of summer fashion.

She brushed her hair: It was long now, below her shoulders, longer than she was used to. So far, the strands of silver that skated through it seemed to be fairly well under control. Which was good, as she had neither time nor extra cash to invest in having it colored. *Maybe someday,* she thought, as she put on a pair of wampum earrings—pale-lavender and deep-purple shells that John had given her for her birthday.

She had pulled her hair into a ponytail and was tying it with a pink ribbon when there was a knock on her door. Rushing from the bedroom, she hoped it wasn't bad news about Claire.

Her heart quickened and then, through the screen, she saw John.

"Hi," she said, opening the door, eyes wide, anxious.

He smiled; she relaxed. "My mom's going to be okay," he said. "At least for now. All her vitals are under control. She has slight paralysis on her right side, and she's having trouble speaking, but her prognosis is really good. The doc says she was lucky the EMTs got to her as soon as they did." He closed his eyes. A lone tear sneaked from each corner.

Annie stepped forward and threaded her arms through his, enveloping him in a long, deep hug. "I'm so glad. I feel terrible that it happened right after I left her." She rubbed his back, then said, "Please, come in off the porch."

"We have tourists to thank," he said, moving past her into the living room. "A couple of women were walking by, admiring the gardens. They saw her collapse; they called nine-one-one right away."

"Did anyone get their names?"

He shook his head. "Not that I heard."

She made a mental note to post something online and in the newspaper to let the tourists know they really were appreciated, despite the unending lines in Stop & Shop and the traffic snarls at the Triangle that they caused.

"She'll be in the hospital a few more days," John continued. "Then, if all goes well, she'll go to rehab."

"You know I'll do anything to help."

"As if you don't have enough on your plate? Like finishing your book and finding a place to live?"

"It's fine, John. I'll get it all done." She grinned. "And I have a visitor, too. Though I don't know for how long or to what extent I'll be expected to play hostess."

His brow furrowed. Then he looked at her dress. "Oh. You're going out. Which must be why you haven't asked me to sit down." As if, after six months of dating, he needed an invitation. "Well, you do look really nice."

"Why, John Lyons, are you jealous?"

"Not if you tell me your old maid aunt is in town."

"I don't have an old maid aunt. In fact, I don't have any aunt that I know of. But you're close. My brother has come to the Vineyard."

"Your brother?"

"Half brother, Kevin. I told you about him."

He nodded. "Right. Sorry, I'm kind of in a fog. The guy's in construction, isn't he?"

"He was. He sold his business when his wife left him."

John nodded again. "I keep forgetting you have a family now."

"Sometimes, I do, too. Speaking of families"—she checked her watch—"oh, damn, I do have to go. But I'd love to tell you about Fiona Littlefield. I saw her after I left your mother's room."

"How is she?"

Annie bit her lip. "I have an idea. Can you join us? Kevin is staying at the Kelley House, so I'm meeting him at the Newes. I can tell you about Fiona then. And he might like to hear her story."

John checked his watch, too. "I'll tell you what. Why don't you go? I'll run out to the house and pick up a few things for Mom. Then I'll join you there. That way you can have some alone time with him first." He kissed her. Nicely.

"But what about Lucy? Shouldn't you head back to Plymouth?"

"They can wait until tomorrow. I want to be sure Mom is settled."

Annie nodded, embarrassed to feel relieved that he was there.

★   ★   ★

Kevin was exactly as she remembered, though he now sported a summer tan. "Golf," he explained when Annie commented on it as he stood up to greet her. "Too much time on my hands."

They hugged; they sat.

"So," she said after they ordered wine and perused the menu, "what do you think of our little island so far?"

He smiled. His hazel—not green—eyes were exactly like hers. His hair was a shade lighter and his shoulders much broader, but their long-legged gaits were nearly identical. Annie was still getting used to the fact that she strongly resembled her birth mother; now, in the dim light of the restaurant, she could see she resembled Kevin, too. Or he resembled her. However that went.

"It took me a while to navigate the traffic from the boat, but I suppose it's a trade-off. There has to be some downside to living in paradise, right?"

"It's not like this off season. Sometimes it can feel like a ghost town. I have a friend who says the only people here then are the sane ones." The friend was Earl. She thought about him, and about Claire, and hoped they were both going to be okay. "The truth is, he's more than a friend. He's the caretaker of the property where I've been staying, and I've been dating his son, John."

"Nice!" Kevin said. "You have someone in your life."

She nodded. "I went a long time without anyone." She didn't know anything about Kevin's marriage or his ex-wife; nor did she know how much Donna had told him about her two marriages. But though Annie didn't intend to hold anything back from her brother, she wanted this evening to be about him. About them. "I have to warn you," she said, "now that you're here, I'm going to want to know it all—like how it was to have been raised by our mother. I want to know what she was like when she was young. She was still young when she had you, wasn't she? You're nine years younger than I am. . . ."

The wine was delivered; they put in their orders. They both chose the flounder, which made Annie laugh.

"Like minds," Kevin said. Then, after the waiter left, he answered her question. "Mom was great. But I feel funny telling you that. I mean, I don't want you to be sad. To make you feel like you missed out."

"Please, Kevin, I want to know. And I want you to know I had great parents and a good childhood. Not perfect, but most things aren't."

He smiled again. "True. Like, don't forget Mom and my dad split up when I was only four."

"Right. That must have been hard."

"I don't remember. I never saw him again."

They spent the next two hours talking about everything from Kevin's fourth-grade science fair (Donna helped him "build" a volcano that erupted all over the gymnasium floor) to his first semiformal dance in eighth grade (after he'd shamefully stalked her, Louise Bridges, the hottest girl in the class, finally agreed to go with him; she wound up being allergic to the corsage Donna picked out, and Kevin was so humiliated he did not go to another formal until his senior year).

The conversation was even more delicious to Annie than their dinner. They decided to share an apple crisp, and as they fought over the last morsels of brown-sugar-and-vanilla-ice-cream crumbles, John walked into the restaurant, adding another layer to Annie's growing sense of happiness and contentment that she hadn't felt in many, many years.

Chapter 11

Annie introduced the men. "My brother, Kevin," she said to John, then, "My, um, friend, John Lyons." She hated that she'd stumbled over how to refer to John. Should she have called him her boyfriend? It felt silly to call him her gentleman friend, the way that Donna referred to Duncan.

The men had shaken hands and were both sitting down when Annie realized she'd been daydreaming. She quickly sat and smoothed her skirt.

"How was the apple crisp?" John asked.

"John's a police officer," she told Kevin. "A sergeant, actually. Investigating everything is second nature to him."

"The large glass bowl with visible traces of cinnamon and ice cream hardly called for the A-team," John said. "That, plus the fact that the Newes only has a few choice desserts."

"He's been here once or twice," Annie explained with a half smile. John was good at breaking the ice with people he'd just met. It was one of many—probably hundreds—of qualities that Annie liked about him.

"So," he said, looking squarely at Kevin, "Annie tells me you were in the construction business. Hands-on or the paperwork?"

Kevin laughed. "Definitely hands-on. I have an MBA from BU, but I'd rather get my hands dirty. Unfortunately, when you have your own business, most of your time is spent parked behind a desk staring at a computer screen. Doing today's kind of paperwork."

Annie wanted to comment that she'd gone to BU, too, though several years before he had. It was another happy coincidence.

"But your MBA must have pleased your parents," John said.

"My mother, actually. Dad left when I was four. But she— my mom, Annie's, too—always told me to be myself. She said that would guarantee me a happier life."

A dark-haired waitress named Lolleen appeared and set a mug of coffee in front of John. She asked if Annie and Kevin wanted more, but they said they were all set.

Then John turned back to Kevin. "You planning to stay on the island awhile?"

The question seemed to come from out of nowhere. Annie looked for Kevin's reaction.

"In all honesty, I haven't thought about it. I only know I was getting cabin fever, which sounds absurd, seeing as how I live in the city. But it seemed like a good time to get to know my sister better."

Sipping his coffee, John seemed to be thinking. Annie had known him long enough to know when he was doing more than making idle talk. "Can I interest you in a little short-term work?"

Well, Annie realized, she'd been right that he was pondering, though she hadn't anticipated his question. She wondered what on earth he was talking about.

Kevin sat up straight. "Don't know. Like what?"

With a slow sigh, John said, "I don't know if Annie's told

you, but my mother had a stroke this morning. She's going to be okay, but it's going to take a little time."

Where was he going with this?

"My dad used to be in construction," John continued. "He was a carpenter. He's been retired for years, but he takes care of properties on Chappaquiddick. He maintains that if he didn't do something to get out of the house, my mother would drive him nuts."

And then the pieces fell together. And Annie wasn't sure how she felt about it.

Resting his arms on the table, John leaned toward Kevin. "Right now, though, I'm more worried about him than I am about her. I have to leave for a couple of weeks, or I'd be here to help. Would you consider sticking around, maybe taking care of the properties for him? We can't pay you much, but if you wanted to stay at my place that would cover you having to rent something."

Picking up his spoon again, Kevin ran it around the remains of the apple crisp. "Wow. I don't know. How long would you need me?"

"If you could stay for the whole two weeks I'm gone, it would be great. But, believe me, I'll take whatever help I can get. I only know that I need to line up some help for Dad as well as for Mom."

Annie felt a small tug at her heart. John was a good man. And though she'd been concerned about both his parents, she hadn't considered Earl's responsibilities. Still, it seemed odd that he'd ask Kevin before he'd run the idea past her. *Nerves,* she thought. *From no longer knowing which end is up.*

She reached across the table and put her hand on John's. "Don't forget I told you I'd help however I can."

"With my mom, sure. And Bella. But I can't exactly see you patching shingles on roofs if we have a storm." His sad smile tugged at her heart.

"When would you need to know?" Kevin asked.

Draining his coffee, John got up and shook his head. "On second thought," he said, "I'm really sorry. I didn't mean to put you on the spot. You and Annie should just enjoy your time together. My brain's a little screwy right now, so please forget it. I shouldn't have asked."

Kevin stood and shook John's hand. "No problem, man. Let me talk it over with myself, and see what I come up with by the morning. Would that work?"

Annie smiled at Kevin's laid-back humor that eased what could have been an awkward situation.

"Sure," John told him. "But, please, no pressure. I'm on the eight fifteen tomorrow. If you decide to stay, I can call my dad and alert him. Annie can show you where my place is. There's a key under the mat."

Kevin laughed. "You leave a key under the mat? And you're a cop?"

"This is the Vineyard," John said, his smile widening. "Trust is part of life here."

After they left the restaurant, Annie said goodbye to John—again—who said he wanted to check in with Claire one last time. As he left, she realized she'd forgotten to tell him about Fiona. Then again, it wasn't important compared with what he had going on.

To help lift her spirits, she suggested to Kevin that they go for a walk. She led him toward South Water Street, away from the eateries and the drinkeries, as John liked to call the pubs. She pointed out various homes and gardens and the pagoda tree that the sea captain Thomas Milton had brought back from China and planted in 1837. With gnarly limbs that stretched like octopus arms in every direction, it had grown into what was thought to be the largest of its kind in North America. It was amazing that, in nearly two hundred years, it

had withstood ferocious hurricanes and relentless nor'easters
with hardly a quiver.

"You're an excellent tour guide for a city girl," Kevin said.

Annie liked walking beside him. Only an inch or so taller
than she was, he fell into step with her. It felt comfortable, familiar, as if they'd grown up together, had been raised in the
same house.

Then he asked, "So, what's the deal with you and John? Do
I need to play the role of a protective brother?"

She thought about Fiona and Colin; she wondered if Colin
had ever played the role of a big brother with her before he'd
tried to kill her. If, in fact, he had done that. "Sorry to disappoint you," she said, "but I think I stopped needing to be pro-
tected when I started to get gray hair."

He eyed her head. "Hmm. Yes. In that case, it appears I'm
far too late."

She gave him a playful swat. "Even if I were young, you'd
hardly have to worry about John. He's the best. Really, he is."

"So you two are a deal?"

"We have been, yes. But it's complicated right now." She
filled him in on John's ex-wife and his two daughters. She
didn't tell him that Lucy was pregnant, only that John would
be in Plymouth with them. "And his parents are good people.
I was lucky they befriended me when I moved here."

They strolled in silence until they reached Cooke Street,
where Annie took a right. "I'll take you past his place, in case
you decide to consider his offer."

Kevin made no comment.

Passing one lovely home after another, each close to the
narrow road and framed by white picket fences woven with
roses, Annie noticed that indoor lights were on, draperies were
open, and no shades were pulled. Unlike in winter, when the
homes looked cold and deserted with their owners safely re-
siding in Boca Raton, San Diego, or other "wimpy places" (as

she'd heard islanders refer to anywhere that didn't require a snow shovel or a fleece jacket), the interiors cast welcoming glows that revealed classic summer hues, a plethora of original seascapes, and plenty of rich, dark wood accents befitting the nineteenth century, in which many had been built. Even the houses that had been torn down and rebuilt to suit a sophisticated market (*Open floor plans; guest suites; wide, welcoming verandas,* Annie thought with an uncharacteristic, envious sigh) had recreated much of the original décor.

She stopped in front of John's well-kept, gray-shingled, white-trimmed duplex.

Kevin's eyes widened. "Nice place. Don't know what I was expecting, but it's nice."

"It is. It's fairly new and very spacious for a town house. It has three full baths, two up, one down, and three bedrooms upstairs. It can get a little noisy in the summer with the traffic and the people walking by. That's when he closes the windows and turns on the air-conditioning."

"He lives here alone?"

"He does now. He got this when he was still married." She did not mention that she'd been invited to move in.

Kevin didn't ask for details, so Annie didn't have to explain the way the housing lottery worked. She suspected that he wouldn't be there long enough to need to know, anyway.

She opened the gate and they stepped inside for a closer look. A small garden flanked the front steps; Claire always made sure it was filled with colorful flowers. John let his mother enjoy the task, though he'd told Annie he drew the line at window boxes.

"He keeps a few cherry tomato plants on the deck out back," Annie said. "He claims they're the best snack on the planet. Red ones, yellow ones. He eats them like candy. They should come into season any day now." Then she checked her watch. "Oh, Kevin, I hate to do this, but it's getting late. I really need to get back to Chappy. Would you like to do something in the morning? Go sightseeing? Sailing? Gallery hunting?"

"You sail?"

She shook her head. "No. But there are charters."

"The truth is, I get seasick. I almost lost my lunch on the ferry. But what about you? Don't you have to work?"

She smiled. Sort of. "Well, yes. But as a writer, I'm flexible."

"Mom told me you have a deadline."

Mom. The word still rang strangely in Annie's mind. *Mom,* as in Donna MacNeish, not Ellen Sutton, the woman who had raised Annie and who'd been dead so many years now it was tough to remember what it had been like to have a mother. "Well, yes, I do have a deadline." She didn't add that she also wanted to check up on Claire the next day and deliver the things she'd collected for Fiona. But Kevin was important, too. More important, in many ways.

"Okay. How about if I stop by your cottage in the morning? I think I can find my way to Chappaquiddick."

She smiled. "For future reference, we call it 'Chappy.'"

"I think I can find my way there, too."

"I'll have coffee ready. And you'll get to see the place before I'm booted out. That's a long story; I'll tell you later."

"Great. We can have coffee, then you can point me to John's parents' house. I might as well meet his father. The sooner I get started on learning his caretaking duties, the better for all concerned."

Annie blinked. "Seriously?"

"Yeah," he said, draping an arm on her shoulder. "Got to take care of my big sister, you know? Besides, it sounds like it might be fun."

On her way back to Chappy, Annie decided it felt odd to have a protective brother, but the concept was growing on her.

Which brought her to think about Fiona again. Was it really possible that Colin had tried to kill her? What kind of a person must he be that Fiona would even consider that? And what about the other sibling, Sheila? Did she really want the family property converted into a bird sanctuary? And could she have somehow been involved?

Then, Annie had an idea.

The short trip home across the channel seemed to take forever. She was accustomed now to parking on the other side, and once she disembarked, it was only a short drive to the cottage. And though it was late, and she was tired, she could not quiet her mind. So she kicked off her shoes and went straight to her laptop. She might not have the training or the resources of a police detective, but as a writer, she knew how to do basic research.

Colin Littlefield, she Googled. Maybe she'd learn something about him from his social media pages. Then up came a link to his Wikipedia page.

Wikipedia? How many ordinary people had Wikipedia pages?

Colin J. Littlefield.

The photo showed a young man with blond surfer-boy-looking hair. He was good-looking enough, though not in the league of leading-man actor, or even of John, not that Annie was biased. She scanned the data below the image.

Born: October 17, 1979 (age 40)
    White Plains, New York
Residence: New York, NY
Parents: Donald J. and Marina L. Littlefield
Siblings: Sheila B. Littlefield
    Fiona M. Littlefield
Occupation: Filmmaker

Annie blinked. Colin was a filmmaker?

She quickly scanned the biography: *Son of the late real estate entrepreneur Donald J. Littlefield; graduated from Andover 1999, Hofstra 2003, received a master's from Columbia for which no date was given; no spouse, no children; US Marine veteran, Iraq 2003–06.*

He had seemed like a regular, preppy rich kid, until she came to the part about him having been in the Marine Corps, a veteran who had served in Iraq. Annie had conditioned herself to pick up on quirks and incongruous traits; she wondered if this might be a big one.

She scrolled down to a list of film credits:

Dust in Their Boots 2011
Trial by Fire 2013
Airlifted 2014

Only the three titles were listed: It was noted that they were war-related films, perhaps they'd been a catharsis for what he had experienced. Beyond that, Wiki didn't disclose what Colin had been doing in the past five years, and there was no indication that he had any public entanglements (arrests, lawsuits, bitter divorces, etc.). Annie wondered what he did for a living now, and if he might be·broke, in need of funds that selling the house on Chappaquiddick would provide—if only his younger sister would agree.

She returned to the Google list: There were no other significant mentions of him; only the typical list of where she could find his age, address, and phone number if she paid a subscription fee. His name also appeared in obituaries of both of the Littlefield parents. But there were no links to websites, news articles, or any other mentions of him.

Next, she put Fiona's name into the search engine. Though Fiona seemed to have no Facebook presence, no Twitter or Instagram accounts, and not even a LinkedIn job record, a curious entry referenced an article about a small ballet troupe. Aside from the *Nutcracker,* to which Annie and Murphy had taken Murphy's twins when they'd been around five or six, Annie knew nothing about ballet. (The outing had been a disaster: "What was I thinking?" Murphy had howled because the twins had danced in their seats more vigorously than the performers on the stage. "God help me, they're boys!" They left the theater during intermission.)

The article was not about Fiona, though her name was mentioned as having appeared in a lesser work by Tchaikovsky. It was dated four years earlier; there was no photo.

She moved on to Sheila, the eldest Littlefield sibling. Not expecting to find much, Annie was stunned to see link after link, all to good works, all of which involved birds and "critters," as John called them. The woman was a director of a number of foundations and was listed as treasurer of three. There was no Wiki page, but a photo appeared on the website of one of the foundations. Sheila looked happy and engaged, not like the scowling, angry sister that Annie had envisioned. And not like a murderer, either.

As Annie sat, transfixed by the Google screen, she wondered if she should Google her own brother in case he might lead a life of suspicion.

Then she chided herself and shouted, "No!" Kevin was her brother, her blood relation, and she was not going to spy on him. Besides, it was long past her bedtime; she quickly shut down the laptop and got ready for bed. Tomorrow, after Kevin came and went, then after she saw Claire, Annie would drop off Fiona's things. Maybe the girl had come to her senses and decided that her brother—her blood relation—had not tried to kill her after all.

As for Annie and her penchant for research, well, she knew that her curiosity and her unstoppable imagination were terrific assets for her career, but that they could also take her into shadowy corners where she, quite frankly, did not really want to go and did not belong.

Chapter 12

Kevin arrived promptly at seven o'clock the next morning. Annie had woken up early: The heat and returning humidity had permeated the cottage, making her briefly reconsider the four-thousand-dollar-a-month apartment with central air. Then logic helped to abandon the idea, so she showered, dressed, and was more or less ready to greet her sibling.

"Sorry I'm so early," he said. "I wasn't sure how long the ferry ride was."

"Did you time it?"

He lifted his T-shirt and dabbed the sweat from his face. "Less than two minutes. Less than five, if you include getting on and getting off. Waiting in line took longer."

They agreed that, thanks to the temperature, iced coffee made more sense than hot. Kevin also accepted one of Annie's cinnamon rolls that were Earl's favorites.

"I decided to wait to tell John I'm going to accept his offer until after I've met Earl. I want to make sure he's okay with this. That he's okay with me."

"Good idea. Though I can't imagine why he wouldn't be okay with you." Annie didn't know much about Earl's customers or his daily routine, only that typically, like most islanders, he was terribly busy in summer. But she filled Kevin in on a few tidbits, like how she knew that he mowed a couple of places with a hand mower and used an old-fashioned rake to keep shrubbery beds tidy because the owners were from New York City and the drone of mowers and leaf blowers grated on them like the sounds of traffic they'd come to escape. She also knew that Earl usually had a few carpentry projects going, which interested Kevin the most.

Without wasting time, he gulped the last of his coffee. "I'm ready when you are."

Before leaving the cottage, Annie wrapped up a pastry for Earl. Maybe a touch of cinnamon would help ease his troubles. "Follow me," she said. "And because you'll need to know, the speed limit all over Chappy is only twenty-five."

"So much for life in the fast lane," Kevin said.

On the way outside, Annie grabbed the bag of Fiona's things, then tossed it into her back seat. She realized she got a kick out of her half brother. Without the presence of their mutual mother, he seemed to feel free to be himself, unencumbered by the woman who, though delightful, would always have the role as his parent whether he was in his forties or a hundred and forties, and no matter if he were married, single, or the father of twenty kids of his own. He had, after all, been raised as an only child, the same way Annie had been raised by the Suttons.

Francine opened the door when they arrived at the house. "Man, am I glad to see you," she said. "Earl's turned into a freak. All he does is sit in his study, staring out the window. I think he sat there all night. He hasn't eaten or anything."

Annie introduced her to Kevin, then moved into the doorway of the study. She did not announce herself, but Earl must have sensed she was there.

"The doc won't let Claire have visitors until after lunch," he said without turning toward her. "He said she'll have a full morning of physical therapy." His skin tone was ashen, his jowls were sagging, his hair seemed to have thinned. He resembled an old actor without stage makeup. Annie thought of the old cliché about someone having "aged overnight," and knew she was seeing a perfect example.

She motioned to Kevin to stay in the hallway, and she stepped into the room.

"The first few days are the toughest," she said, sitting on the sofa across from him in the room he now called his "man cave" instead of his study. He was surrounded by history books that he loved, paintings of whalers in stormy waters, and framed photos of huge fish, many of which had been caught during the annual island-wide derby in autumn. "But the best news is it looks like Claire will be fine. You believe that, don't you?"

He shifted his gaze from Annie back toward the window. "I'm getting old. Claire's getting old. It's time we started to accept it."

"Well, it's true that you're getting older, Earl. We all are. But the Earl Lyons I know is not old, not in the sense you're talking about. The Earl Lyons I know would get out of that chair and plan his next step. Come up with a way to right the ship, if that's how you say it."

He sighed.

"And I've come to help." She reached into her pocket, pulled out the napkin-wrapped cinnamon roll, and handed it to him. "First, sustenance. Second, someone has come with me who you need to meet." She signaled Kevin to come in.

Earl accepted the pastry, though he held off taking a bite. He did, however, stand up and shake hands with Kevin. He even said it was nice to meet him, and that he and Claire thought a lot about his sister. But when Annie explained that John had commissioned Kevin to take over Earl's duties for a few days so he could focus on Claire, Earl sat down again. And stared at the cinnamon roll he'd placed on his desk.

"Thanks for the offer, young man," he said, looking at the roll and not at Kevin. "John already alerted me to this cocka-mamie scheme. But I'm perfectly capable of taking care of myself. And what's more, my son ought to know that by now." With a swift motion, he grabbed the roll and pitched it into his wastebasket. Then he turned his back to them and looked out the window again, dismissing them without another word.

Under other circumstances, Annie might have been angry. But after her father had died, she'd quickly learned that a spouse without a spouse often becomes scared. And why wouldn't that happen? She'd been scared after Brian had been killed. So scared she'd done a very stupid thing and married the next guy who'd come along, one of the biggest jerks on the planet. As difficult as it had been with Brian gone, they'd only been mar-ried a handful of years. She could not imagine what it would be like to be married nearly five decades and abruptly have your life flipped upside down. It had happened to her mother; Annie had always believed it might have been why her mother had died so soon after her dad. And now, Annie knew it would be best if she and Kevin simply stepped away, let things happen as they would, organically, as some would de-scribe it. Earl should not have to feel that his work and his purpose would be taken from him the way his wife might have been, might still be.

They found Francine in the kitchen, leaning against the counter, biting her nails. "It's my day off," she said, "so I can at least take care of Bella. Maybe later I should bring her to the hospital to visit Claire?"

Annie marveled at how, though only twenty years old, Francine was more responsible than some adults she had known. "I think Claire would like that," she said. "In the meantime, do you have any idea where her notes are for the garden tour? I know she kept them in a folder." Though, unlike Earl, as soon as a temporary cell tower had been raised on Chappy, Claire had welcomed the convenience—and importance—of having a cell phone, she still liked to do "her business" by using paper and ink.

"It's the pink folder, right?" Francine asked, pulling one from a kitchen drawer. "She had it with her when the ambulance picked her up. Earl brought it home from the hospital last night."

"That's it," Annie said, taking the folder and scanning the contents: the previous year's program guide with updated comments marked in red, a few pages of additional handwritten notes, and several forms for the judges that were neatly clipped together. "We might not be able to get Earl to accept help, but at least I can put the brochure together for Claire. And get it to the printer. I'll text you a few photos of the gardens so you can add them to the website and put them on Facebook and Instagram, if you want. And I'll take over anything else that Claire has to do for the tour."

"Yes, send me the pics," Francine said. "I'll post them today." She rubbed her thin arms. "Everything's changed so fast, hasn't it, Annie? Claire getting sick. Earl acting weird. John gone. Geez."

"Geez is right," Annie agreed. "But we'll get through this together. And you, of all people, know we will." She smiled and gave Francine what she hoped was a reassuring hug, then followed Kevin outside.

Kevin opted to stay on Chappy. He said he'd like to explore the land and the trails; he'd picked up a more detailed map at the hotel. He also said he'd call John and explain Earl's reaction. Annie hesitated at first, then decided to stay out of the way. The transaction, after all, needed to be between John and Kevin—her boyfriend and her brother, both labels which still sounded bizarre in her brain. She gave Kevin John's cell number, promised she'd be in touch, and drove off to the ferry, knowing what she had to do first: finish taking photos for the garden tour. She also thought that spending some time among beautiful, fragrant flowers might help put the past few days into better perspective.

The only downside to her plan was that she'd have to bring her car across and take a chance on finding a parking space in the village. But she knew that having her car would make it easier to get to the hospital later; maybe she'd be lucky and all the tourists would already have gone to the beaches on such a sultry, "sticky" morning.

Ten minutes later, she was in Edgartown, and, much to her astonishment, found a place to park. Murphy must have still been watching out for her from her station up in the white, cottony clouds.

Inside the pink folder was a note Claire had made that earmarked the Collins garden as the place for an important photograph; she'd jotted a comment that said the place had been in the same family for seven generations and was renowned for its showcase of roses.

The address was easy to find: Winter Street was directly off North Water, and the property was punctuated by a procession of deep-red, velvety blooms lining the white picket fencing that hugged a path leading straight through the backyard. It was breathtaking. Annie began snapping from one end to the other, determined to capture the radiant display that would not only attract visitors but please the Collins family as well.

"Hellooo!" The voice belonged to a woman who pronounced the *o* at the end of *hello* as if it were spelled *oooh*.

Annie stopped shooting and shielded her eyes from the sun's hazy glare with one hand. A figure in a scarlet dotted Swiss dress with a full skirt and crinoline that swished with each step was approaching at a determined clip.

"Are you helping Claire?"

"Yes," Annie said. "I'm Annie Sutton."

"And I am Irene Landry Collins, seventh-generation owner of this grand home and garden."

Though Annie would hardly call the house itself "grand"—without doing the math, she deduced that it must have been built in the mid-nineteenth century and that the single-car garage had been added later—it was pretty and quaint, a mere "cottage" compared with others in the village, though several of Annie's current place would no doubt fit comfortably inside it. True to historic directives, it was painted white with black shutters and had a white picket fence in the front.

"You must be the girl who is helping Claire this year."

Annie tried not to smile at being called a girl, especially since Irene Landry Collins looked only a decade or so older than she was. Perhaps it made the woman feel important to think of Annie as the hired help. "It's nice to meet you, Mrs. Collins."

With a delicate hand, the woman reached to her throat and toyed with her triple strand of pearls. "How is Claire doing? I heard what happened. Such a shock. And in Mildred's garden, of all places."

Knowing that Claire would want Annie to defend her honor, or at least cover her embarrassment, Annie said, "She's actually doing quite well. It turned out to be a minor mishap, but thank you for asking. I'm sure Mrs. Atwater's hollyhocks will bounce back soon."

The woman nodded stiffly as if she were unsure. Perhaps she thought the year-round islanders were on a secret mission to divest the island of seasonal people—even those whose families had been there since Thomas Mayhew washed ashore in 1642.

"That's lovely news about Claire," she continued, as if the

flowers had not been mentioned. "She does such a wonderful job with the tour. We enjoy taking part every year."

"It's a terrific event for a really great cause. Any help that benefits the Vineyard children is important, don't you think?"

Mrs. Collins twiddled her pearls again. "Yes. Which is why we try to do our part. Really, we do." She looked almost apologetic about the fact that she and her neighbors had more than the rest of the world. Or than many islanders, anyway.

Annie hoped she hadn't offended her. "Well, I can't speak for everyone, but I do know that most of us who are crazy enough to live here year-round appreciate your support." She added a smile. "I was an elementary school teacher in Boston for many years, and I admit that I'm in awe of the education system here."

"Yes. Of course. Education is important. I graduated from Bryn Mawr back in the day." Then Mrs. Collins's cheeks turned a light shade of pink, as if she knew one had nothing to do with the other. "Well," she added nervously, "if there's anything I can do to help out during Claire's recuperation, please let me know."

Annie would have liked to ask if the space over her garage was an apartment, and if she'd ever thought about renting it out. Or if any of her cronies on the tour had any available quarters. But she knew from the rental agents she'd met that most garage suites and backyard cottages in town were reserved for use by the owners' extended family and friends. And that the rest of the time they, like the main houses, sat vacant. "Thank you, I will."

Then she had an idea that might help imply that she really did appreciate Mrs. Collins's offer to help. "Now that you mention it, I'm going to try my best to put the brochure together. As a Bryn Mawr alum, you probably have top-notch grammar skills. Would you be able to proofread the brochure for me? Make sure I have everyone's names right? Claire would be mortified if I spelled a name incorrectly or if I left anyone out." Over the years, Annie had learned that a little schmoozing could go a long way. Besides, the woman seemed genuinely nice, in spite of her elevated station in life.

A broad smile broke through Mrs. Collins's tight lips. "Why, yes, I'd be happy to do that. I've always enjoyed dabbling in writing."

Annie said she hadn't known and wasn't that wonderful. Apparently, the woman had no idea she was speaking to someone who earned a living doing more than "dabbling" in the craft. "I'll drop it off before I take it to the printer. I'm afraid it might be at the last minute, though. We're a little bit behind because of Claire's . . . accident."

"That's fine. All I pretty much do these days is tend to the flowers, sip iced tea, and play an occasional game of bridge. It's been too hot for much of anything else. In the meantime, please do give Claire my best."

Annie nodded, then strolled back through the arbors, pleased that John's mother had clearly established a nice reputation among the seasonal island elite. *Good for her,* Annie thought and reinforced her plan to do her proud.

Chapter 13

With swift efficiency, Annie made her way through the rest of the gardens on the list, snapping what she hoped were enticing photos—the head-sized hydrangea blossoms at the Tuttles', the spectrum of wildflowers at the Elliotts', the bright collage of daylilies at the Coopers'. She had too much to do to waste any time, and was pleased when she finished just after noon. Heading back toward her car, she encountered few tourists on the sidewalks, for which she praised the humidity despite the fact that it glued her cotton tank and loose walking shorts to her skin.

It's all good, she told herself. She had plenty of time to visit Claire, maybe share some of the photos, then get back to Chappy, shift creative gears, and complete the revision of the last chapter—the last chapter!—of her second draft. She would call Trish, alert her to the progress, and bask in a brief celebration before moving on to the final version. Trish would be elated but would, in her grim, teacher-like voice, remind Annie that the *final-final* deadline was nonetheless looming.

Maybe Annie could break for a quick dinner with Kevin—if he hadn't been scared off the island—then work on the brochure. If she could set up and maintain a schedule, she should be able to juggle Claire's duties while keeping a steady pace with the rest of her book. The tour was nine days away; the manuscript deadline in three weeks. Before then, maybe a place to live would drop into her lap.

Right, she thought as she spotted her car and noticed something white waving at her from under the windshield wiper. But it was neither a friendly note nor a pizza delivery menu: It was a parking citation. She looked around. A NO PARKING sign was partly hidden by someone's shrubbery. Yanking at the ticket, she muttered, jumped into the car, and tossed the paper on the passenger seat. She tried to rationalize that twenty-five dollars was worth the price for the space and that parting with the cash would not change her life or affect her ability to come up with a first-last-and-security deposit.

But when Annie reached the hospital, her annoyance was heightened by the fact that she couldn't find a parking space in the lot. Perhaps there had been an uptick in surfing accidents or man-of-war stings, or maybe Jaws had revisited State Beach. She drove around the front and back three times and was ready to give up when someone got into an SUV. Annie waited, her engine impatiently humming, as if this were a week before Christmas and she was at Chestnut Hill Mall.

Finally, brake lights appeared, and a vehicle backed out. Annie signaled a big thank-you, pulled into the space, rested her forehead on the steering wheel, and let out a sigh. She hadn't remembered that the island had been this crazy in summers when she'd been a kid; then again, her dad had always been the driver.

Upstairs, Claire looked better than she had the day before. A tray table rested over the bed; she held half a sandwich in her left hand. It appeared that she'd already eaten the other half.

Her eyes brightened when she saw Annie, though her smile was one-sided and limp. Annie bent down and hugged her.

"How's lunch?" she asked, gesturing to the sandwich.

Claire stuck out her tongue and shrugged.

"Oh, look, you have a fruit cup."

Claire set down her sandwich, placed her hands as if in thankful prayer, and looked up to the ceiling.

Annie smiled and pulled up a chair. "How was physical therapy this morning?"

Picking up a pad, Claire took a pencil in her left hand and slowly, methodically, wrote: *sucked.* Then she laughed, emitting a sound similar to that of a seagull begging for crumbs from a tourist who walked by the water munching a cookie from the Black Dog.

"I'm glad you have a pad and can write! I can't imagine not being able to convey what I'm thinking."

Me, either, Claire wrote. Then, *John brought before he left.*

"Last night?" Annie asked.

He snuck in late. She let out another laugh.

Annie was pleased to see her in such good spirits. She took her phone from her purse. "I have a few things to show you. But first, I don't want you to worry about the garden tour. Everything is under control. I finished taking the pictures this morning. Francine will post some online; I'll write the brochure copy tonight and design it tomorrow."

Claire frowned. She pointed at Annie, then put her hands together again and opened them, palms up, like a book. Then, with her left hand, she pretended to scribble words on her right palm.

"Don't worry about my book," Annie said. "That's under control, too." *Sort of,* she didn't add.

Picking up the pencil again, Claire drew a box. She added a triangle on top, and two small boxes inside the main box. Then she drew what looked like a door. And a small tree in front. She printed: *You find one?*

Annie shook her head. "No. The one I saw yesterday was

about the size of this room. Not that this room isn't lovely, but . . ."

Claire laughed again.

Annie picked up the fruit cup and peeled off the lid. "Finish your sandwich like a good girl, and I'll let you have dessert."

"Oh, boy," Claire muttered, and Annie understood. It was encouraging that the woman's voice seemed to be returning.

Claire went back to her lunch. Annie wasn't interested in eating; she was more preoccupied with silently checking the time.

The food tray wasn't cleared until two o'clock. "Okay," Annie said, "time for pictures. Tell me which ones you like. Especially the ones that should be featured." Turning her phone toward Claire, she scrolled through the shots. When she reached Irene Collins's red, velvety roses, Claire pointed and nodded. "That one," she grunted.

It was almost artistic, a long shot of the stunning blossoms. Sunlight kissed the petals, casting a magical shadow.

"Front cover?" Annie asked.

Claire nodded. "Big . . ." She could not seem to form her next word. She picked up the pencil and drew: *$$$*.

Annie was confused. "People will pay lots of money to see this?"

Shaking her head, Claire tore another page from the pad. *Donor. Collins.*

"Oh! You mean, Mrs. Collins is a donor to the club."

Wrinkling her face, Claire said, "More."

"She'll give more if you feature her roses?"

"All," Claire responded, then huffed in frustration.

"Write it down, okay?" Annie asked.

The writing seemed to take Claire forever. When she was finally finished, Annie took the pad and read: *They are all big donors. Collins. Atwater. Tuttle. They pay for the honor of showing their gardens on tour.*

It was a couple of seconds before Annie understood. Then she said, "Wait. Are you saying that the donation the club makes to the schools isn't only from ticket sales? That it's also from the people who own the gardens?"

"Big," Claire said again. That time, with her left hand, she rubbed her thumb against the inside of her fingers, signifying that the word *big* referred to dollars.

"Every year?" Annie knew she shouldn't have been surprised. Though Earl had told her Roger Flanagan supported island causes, she hadn't considered that the "support" of seasonal people was more than a token donation. She'd assumed they considered their property taxes and money spent at restaurants and in shops as their contribution.

Claire nodded. "Big money," she repeated. "Thousands. Very nice."

"Yes," Annie agreed, "very nice, indeed."

After a short while, Claire fell asleep. Annie gathered her things and dashed away, heading down the hall toward Fiona's room. There wouldn't be much time to chat, which was just as well, because Annie really did not want to get involved with combative siblings, especially when attempted murder might be involved. It was out of her league and none of her business. None at all.

Outside the room, Annie stopped for a moment and drew in a breath. Then she put on what she hoped was a warm, friendly smile, rounded the corner, and went in.

Fiona was sitting up in bed, arms folded, a bit more color in her cheeks than the previous day. One of her IVs was gone, though both monitors were still connected. Her attention seemed focused on someone else in the room; perhaps it was only the television. But when Annie followed the girl's gaze, she saw Roger Flanagan sitting in a chair at the foot of the bed. They noticed her at the same time.

"Hello," Annie said. "I hope I'm not interrupting." *That was a stupid comment,* she thought. What could she possibly be "interrupting" between a seventy-something-year-old curmudgeon and a thirty-something-year-old trust fund baby? Then she remembered she was no longer the third-grade teacher who had worn rose-colored glasses for far too long.

Roger stood. "No problem. I was just leaving."

"I hope not on my account. I only stopped by to drop off a few things." She turned to the patient. "Would you like me to put these in the closet?"

Fiona nodded. "I'll be out of here tomorrow, I think. So thank you." She turned her head back to Roger. "Please remember what I said, Mr. Flanagan. If you see Colin, ask him to wait. Tell him I need to speak with him."

"I'll do my best. But no guarantees. Your brother has always had a mind of his own." He walked to the side of the bed and patted Fiona's shoulder. Then he nodded at Annie and hurried from the room. It would have been nice if he'd asked how she was coming along with her search for a place to live.

"He doesn't agree with me, either," Fiona said. "That Colin poisoned me. Even though he said I was the only guest who got sick. Out of all those people, I was the only one? That tells me it must have been Colin. Who else would do such a thing to me? Anyway, Mr. Flanagan offered to let me stay at his house. I don't dare go home if my brother tried to poison me."

So there had been nothing odd going on between them after all. Still, Annie wouldn't have pegged Roger as someone who visited a patient in the hospital for no reason. Reminding herself this wasn't her problem, Annie wanted to change the subject. "Where is that, Fiona? Where's home?" Google had said that her home was New York, but Annie felt no need to let the girl know she'd done a quick search.

"Manhattan," Fiona said. "I'm a dancer. Ballet."

That matched the search engine results, though it had been a while since Fiona's most recent mention. "Oh, how lovely. When does the season begin?"

"Mid-September. But auditions start next month. Then rehearsals."

Annie knew nothing about ballet except she'd once been told she was "too big" to wear a tutu: too tall, her shoulders too broad. "You'll be busy then. It's good to be busy."

"What?" the girl asked, her light-brown eyes narrowing, making her small oval face look scrunched and older than Annie assumed she was. "Do you think if I'm busy it will help me forget that my brother wanted me dead?"

Setting the bag in the small closet, Annie turned back to her, smiling again. She'd already decided not to take a seat— aside from the clock ticking way too quickly, she really, really did not want to get involved.

She stood next to the bed and called up her teacher instincts to soothe a young student who was overreacting to a bad grade, forgotten homework, or the fact that a classmate had picked a fight on the playground. "Fiona," she said, "I know you've been through a lot. Ingesting poison must have been terrifying. But the most important thing you can do now is get your health back up to snuff. Mr. Flanagan has generously offered for you to stay with them until you're able to go back to New York. Maybe you should consider that. A little time spent in an Adirondack chair in the sunshine, looking out at the water, can work wonders. Will you consider that?"

"Colin is my brother. What he did was a crime."

"Well," Annie said, readjusting the strap of her purse on her shoulder, "if you feel strongly about that, then you must talk with the police. Don't try to handle this on your own."

The girl didn't respond.

"And I'm sorry, but I really must go. I have work to do. A deadline." She smiled again. "As a dancer, you must know what that's like. There's never enough time until the curtain goes up!" It was a silly parallel, and Annie knew it. But she didn't think it was hurtful or mocking, and it helped her exit the room with a little philosophical grace.

Chapter 14

"My son has informed me that I'm an insensitive jerk."

On her way through the lobby, heading toward the door, Annie ran smack into Earl. "Well," she said, "hello to you, too."

He raked his fingers through his hair the same way John often did. "I'm sorry, Annie. For the way I treated your brother. I didn't know he was in tough shape. I had no idea what he's been going through."

Annie had no clue what Earl was talking about, though it was odd that, while referencing Kevin, he'd uttered words that were similar to those she'd just used with Fiona. She opened her mouth, about to say that, when she realized that Earl had said he'd spoken with John. "What did John tell you?"

Taking her by the elbow, he guided her to two chairs by the window that were under a colorful, well-done acrylic of what looked like Old Mill Pond in West Tisbury. They sat, facing each other.

"That Kevin lost his wife. If I'd known that, I hope to God I wouldn't have behaved that way. Especially since I almost lost mine yesterday. Anyway, I'm real sorry, Annie."

She remained a little confused, but let Earl continue.

"And I do appreciate his offer to help me out with my

work. If it will help him get past his grief, I'm more than glad to help out. To be honest, it would be a load off my mind, too, not to have to worry about getting the work done for my customers."

Well, that explained it. John must have turned the situation around. Knowing that his father wouldn't want to admit he needed help, and knowing that one of the many things Earl was famous for was helping others, John must have decided to reposition the situation so it seemed that Kevin—not Earl—was the one who needed the help. And, of course, Earl would not say no to Kevin because he was Annie's brother. *John Lyons,* she thought, *is indeed a good man.*

"I think Kevin misses working," she said. "If he feels someone needs him, it might help him get back in the swing of things. Back into his work and into life."

Earl chewed on that for a minute. "He'll stay at John's?"

"John has offered."

"Well, then that'll be good, too. No sense leaving a place empty at this time of year. We don't have much crime, but every so often, usually in summer, we get a doozy or two. House breaks and vandalism aren't unheard of." He'd used the word *doozy* months ago when he'd told Annie a blizzard was on the way. That particular doozy had changed Annie's life in many wonderful ways. A house break and vandalism, however, would not be what John needed right now.

"I'll call your brother when I leave Claire. Do you have his number?" He pulled out his phone.

She gave him the number, which he promptly entered into his contact information. Annie refrained from mentioning again how happy she was that he'd caught up with the communications age. Instead, she said, "And for the record, I don't think you're an insensitive jerk."

"You haven't known me as long as my son has," he said with a snort. "But speaking of Claire, how's she doing today?"

"I think she's doing great. I'm no doctor, but I think she's amazing. And her voice seems to be coming back."

He beamed. "I knew she'd get better. She's too ornery not to." Then, with a sweet chuckle, the kind that reminded Annie so much of her dad's, he stood, said goodbye, and marched down the corridor to visit his wife of almost fifty years.

Once out in the parking lot, Annie called Kevin. He said he was sitting on what he'd been told was East Beach, having a ham sandwich and drinking lemonade, both of which he'd picked up at the small Chappy Store, only open in summer. His words mingled with the background sounds of the surf and the breeze and the clamor of children playing.

"I'm glad you're still here," Annie said. "Earl changed his mind. He'll call you in a while, so don't say I told you." She explained the angle John had used to convince his father that he would be helping Kevin—that he'd said Kevin had "lost" his wife, apparently, not unintentionally—leaving Earl to think the woman had died and not left him. Then she giggled to herself at the thought that this was what brothers and sisters probably did—kept secrets from the adults. "Do you want to have dinner tonight? I can cook. After today, I'm going to have to dig in my heels and do the final revision on my manuscript—another round of polishing it from page one."

"A job and a free dinner. What more could a man ask for?"

Annie laughed. "Don't forget the free housing at John's. In the heart of the village. Do you have any idea how much a place like that would cost to rent?"

"Not a clue. But what about you? What are you going to do about finding a place?"

"Don't remind me."

"We'll talk later. At dinner."

"My house. Seven o'clock?"

"You got it, Sis."

"Good. Now hang up and finish your lunch. I can barely hear you through the noise of happy tourists."

They rang off. She turned on the ignition and backed out of the parking space, marveling at how often she caught herself smiling these days despite the chaos whirling around her.

Though time pressed on, Annie took the beach road to avoid heavy traffic that would be heading into the Edgartown Triangle. It hadn't occurred to her that a line of vehicles would also be creeping alongside the beaches, their drivers praying for a coveted parking space. Still, it was fun to watch the conglomeration of straw hats and beach blankets; the high-riding windsurfers; and the perpetual conga line of kids who waited their turn to leap off the jumping bridge. It was definitely summer, very different from winter, but still feeling very much like her home.

She wished she could call John. She wished she could tell him about Fiona's situation, and how determined the girl seemed to be about confronting Colin. But Annie didn't think John needed further distraction.

Besides, he would tell her not to get involved.

Slowing at a crosswalk, she spotted two preteen girls who waited to cross. Annie stopped the car, and the pair with not-quite womanly bodies, their tiny bikinis, and their long hair flowing behind them pranced toward the sand, savoring what they surely didn't realize might be their last innocent summer. Or maybe they were no longer as innocent as they appeared.

Annie shuddered. The world was so different now, a thought that her parents, and their parents before them, must have felt, too, in dramatic ways. After the summer Annie had met Brian, after she'd gone home to South Boston and he to Brookline, they lived close enough to still see each other. Annie's mother had taken her to have a gynecological exam; on the way home they'd stopped at the pharmacy and filled a prescription for birth-control pills. It hadn't mattered that

Annie tried to assure her that she and Brian weren't having sex. "Better safe than sorry," was Ellen Sutton's terse reply.

Neither of them mentioned that Annie's birth mother might have been around the same age when she'd become pregnant.

As it turned out, however, the pills had been a good idea, because by Christmas that year, Annie and Brian had "done it."

The girls finished crossing now, followed by an older couple, weighted with beach chairs and blankets, then three boys and someone who might be their father. Finally, Annie was able to resume driving.

She stopped at the market, and, amazingly, found a legal parking space. "Shop early in the morning, late at night, or on a sunny day," Earl had advised when the season was on the horizon. "Otherwise, you'll be picking berries down at Wasque or fishing out at Pogue, to avoid going into Edgartown for food."

Nearly an hour and a half later (twenty minutes in the store, ten to the dock, forty-five in the queue for the *On Time,* five to the cottage—all of which would have taken fifteen minutes total in winter), Annie was safely in the cottage and ready to shuck a few ears of corn.

After that, she'd go back to revising her manuscript.

After that, she would cook.

After that, she'd break bread with Kevin.

After that, she'd work on the program for the garden tour.

She dropped onto the rocker. Something would have to go, or she'd wind up in the hospital in the room next to Claire. Or worse, next to Fiona.

Dinner was delightful. She'd tossed a couple of steaks on the grill that would no longer be "hers" once she found a new place to live, if that ever happened. She made a big green salad and she and her brother ravaged the corn. For dessert, she served brownies she'd made a few weeks earlier and stuck in the freezer, along with a heaping scoop of ice cream for Kevin.

"This will help me keep up my strength for my new job," he said with ardent justification.

He told her he'd spoken with John again, and that they agreed he'd move into John's place the following day. Annie desperately wanted to ask if John had mentioned how his daughter was doing, but she knew he wouldn't have confided in Kevin. She would have felt better if she at least knew when the surgery would be.

But, as with Fiona's situation, Annie knew that Lucy's abortion was none of her business.

After dinner, Annie pulled out old photo albums so Kevin could see what she had looked like when she was a kid. He oohed and ahhed in the right places, commenting on how much they looked alike in grammar school pictures.

"It must have been hard for Mom to see these," he said.

Annie turned another page in the album. "I haven't showed her. I wasn't sure if it would upset her—or upset me. Anyway, I figured it was too soon. Maybe someday."

He put his hand on her shoulder. "Don't sell her short, kid."

She laughed. "Don't call me 'kid'! For one thing, I'm nearly a decade older than you are."

"I'm taller."

"I'm smarter."

"Not really."

"I'm prettier."

Pause.

"Okay, you got me there."

It was ten o'clock before he stepped off the front porch to head back to Edgartown. "One more night at the Kelley House, then I'll move into John's place. Jesus," he added, looking up at the sky, "it sure gets dark out here."

"Black as the night," she replied with a laugh. "And no streetlights. Not one."

They hugged goodbye. After Kevin left, she went back inside and cleaned up the dishes before she collapsed on her bed, totally done for the day. *Done in,* her dad would have called it. She fell asleep without changing into her nightgown.

At some point during the night, Annie stirred from what might have been a dream. But as the blurred edges of awakening became clearer, she could have sworn she'd heard a too-familiar sound: the distinct, low rumble of the engine of a Porsche.

Colin Littlefield, she thought. It had to be him.

Unless . . .

Despite the summer heat, her body turned to ice. She pulled the sheet up closely to her chin.

It's only Colin, she tried to convince herself. There was no way it could be Mark. Her ex-husband would have no way of finding her, would he?

The sound had ceased, as quickly as it had woken her up.

But with her eyes open now, her heart racing to the beat of her imagination, Annie knew what she needed to do. She had to get out of bed. She had to put on her robe and slippers. She had to get her flashlight, cut through the path that led over to the Littlefields', and reassure herself that it had been Colin . . . who had returned to the scene of the alleged poisoning. It was, however, unnerving to realize that coming face-to-face with an attempted murderer would be less frightening than to find her ex standing outside her door.

She stayed still a moment longer, but heard no further sounds. Then she got up, pulled her things together, and ventured out into the darkness.

There was no Porsche in her driveway. Still, she knew she would not sleep again until she was certain the sound had come from Colin's car and not Mark's.

Her mission would have been easier if any lights still burned inside the Flanagans' house, if any leftover wedding revelers had lingered on the premises. But though several cars were scattered around the property, the house was dark, as if people with any sense were in bed at the late-night hour. Everyone except Annie, whose every step felt more treacherous than the one before.

She found the path and tramped through the overgrowth and scrub oaks, tiny branches scratching, clawing at her calves. There would be blood, she knew. But Annie was determined. A little crazed, perhaps, but determined.

Just as she came out the other side, a small critter flashed across her way. A skunk? A raccoon? A water . . . rat? She shivered, grateful that whatever it had been had moved too quickly for identification.

Clutching her robe as if it were a life preserver, she knew by the squeak of clamshells beneath her feet that she'd reached the Littlefields' driveway. She held up her light: nothing. No Porsche. No cars. No vehicles of any kind. Just a long strip of shells that reached out to North Neck Road.

She flipped her light over the grounds and down toward the water. But if a Porsche had been there, it had only been in her dreams.

Standing still, no longer cold, Annie was stunned to think that because Colin Littlefield merely drove the same model of car that Mark had, her subconscious had split wide open, exposing her pain—again. *The Mark pain,* Murphy had called it. The wound must have been deeper than Annie had known.

No longer caring about critters in the night or scratches on her legs, Annie plodded back to the cottage feeling like a fool.

Chapter 15

Having Kevin on board was a huge help to everyone. When Francine went to work, he tackled Earl's morning jobs while Earl stayed home with Bella. At one o'clock Earl dropped Bella off at Annie's and joined Kevin, so they accomplished twice the work in an afternoon. Annie was able to work on her book most of the day because afternoons were Bella's naptime. By the time the baby woke up, they went for a walk. Or rather, Annie went for a walk with Bella tucked into the stroller.

By Friday, she still hadn't heard from John, and she'd resisted calling him. Somehow able to keep her angst at bay, she was making progress on her last draft of *Renaissance Heist,* the *final-final*. It was the part that Annie loved best: closely reviewing word choices, reading the text out loud, checking to be sure she had captured the perfect rhythm for the story. She saw the process as the proverbial light at the end of the tunnel, a sign that she was almost done, that the book would soon be birthed. *The End.*

To clear her head of her world of fiction, she took Bella to the toddler playgroup at the community center.

At first, the children sat in a circle on the floor, their moms or their summer au pairs sitting behind them. The children tossed a beach ball back and forth across the circle, accompanied by lots of shrieks and giggles and the unhappy cries of one young boy who clearly did not want to be there. The sounds reverberated off the beams of the cathedral ceiling and the big stone fireplace. Then the children were given cardboard boxes filled with sensory toys for them to transfer into smaller boxes while the leaders sang nursery rhymes.

After half an hour, Annie had a headache, which must have been apparent.

One of the leaders, who looked to be Francine's age, squatted next to Annie and whispered: "We're going to do the musical segment next. If you'd like to step outside and stretch your legs, I'd be happy to help Bella." Annie hesitated until she spotted another young woman pull several small drums, four miniature cymbals, and a bag of metal triangles from a toy chest. She said, "Thank you," then stood up and stepped out onto the deck.

Which was where she ran into Taylor, who was brushing a new coat of stain across the wood.

"It never ceases to amaze me how people keep volunteering to lead the playgroup," Taylor said. "All that racket would drive me nuts." Her hair was pulled back into a ponytail and fastened with a length of twine; her hands, surprisingly small for all the rugged work that she did, were encased in what looked like the thin type of gloves worn to dye hair. Maybe that was how her hair kept its vibrant auburn color.

"I used to be an elementary school teacher," Annie said, "but apparently I've forgotten how much noise kids can make." The last part wasn't the truth, but Annie really did try and be on good terms with Taylor. She did not need to be her best friend, but being cheerful might make life more pleasant.

"I heard your brother is working for Earl now."

How Taylor learned so much island gossip in record time remained a mystery. "He's helping out until Claire is back on her feet."

"She goes to rehab Monday, doesn't she?"

That was news to Annie, though she did not want to admit it. "I guess that's the plan. She's doing well. Thanks again for tracking me down so I could get to the hospital and rescue Bella." *Rescue* was probably one of those word choices she would change to something less dramatic if this were a *final-final* and not a conversation. But something about being around Taylor made Annie nervous.

"Speaking of rescue," Taylor said, "have you heard any more about the Littlefield girl?"

"No." Not wanting to encourage conversation about Fiona, Annie turned back toward the door. "I'd better get inside."

"Wait," Taylor said, setting down her brush. "You find a place to live yet?"

Annie had no idea whether Taylor had heard about a potential rental on Chappy or if she was simply being nosy. Maybe that was how she knew so much; maybe she was a pro at pestering people with personal questions. Annie shook her head. "I've been too busy to realize how desperate I'm about to become."

"You can always rent my place."

Annie froze, her hand on the door. Her place? What the heck did that mean?

"I have a garage apartment," Taylor continued. "Finished it as one of those in-law things. Mother wanted me to have the house to myself, though God knows why. But she's too old now to do the stairs, so I convinced her to move back in with me. I can keep an eye on her better. Make sure she eats and showers, you know what I mean."

Nodding seemed like a cheerful thing to do.

"The apartment is sitting there gathering mice. It's small, but, hell, it's a roof. Be glad to show it to you if you think you might want it."

If Taylor saw Annie blink, she didn't react. "Really?" She knew the pause that followed was too long and might be too revealing, but Annie could not pull any words together. "Wow," was what finally came out. She tucked her hair behind her ears and willed her brain to engage. "How much are you asking?"

"I haven't thought about it yet. But you could take a look. I'm sure we could work something out."

This was real. Her chance to stay on the island. And it had dropped into her lap from a most unlikely source. "May I come by tomorrow?" The question rolled out before she'd thought it through.

"Four o'clock? I mow lawns on Saturday, but I'm usually home by then." Taylor told Annie how to get there. "Look for the wide-mouth-bass mailbox. My dad was a fisherman."

Annie nodded slowly. "Okay. Well. Okay, then. And thanks, Taylor. Thanks." She ducked back inside, where the music had ended and the children were quietly sitting, tossing the beach ball back and forth. Bella seemed to be well-watched by the young leader, so Annie meandered over by the kitchen, sank into a comfortable chair, and wondered what on earth she'd just agreed to. After all, desperate or not, having Taylor for a landlord might be the most ridiculous thing Annie had ever considered. But if the place was adequate and the price was right, was she in any position to say no?

"You want me to go with you?" Kevin asked after Annie had arrived at Earl and Claire's to drop off Bella. He was at the kitchen table with Earl; they were drinking iced tea while Bella crawled around on the kitchen floor. By the look of the sweat-stained T-shirts and ragged hair on the men, Annie presumed they'd had a long bout of work in the sun. However, it appeared that they'd grown companionable, for which she was grateful.

"Don't you have to work tomorrow?"

"We'll be done before four," Earl replied. "Shouldn't be a problem for Kevin. Besides, bringing a bodyguard to Taylor's might not be a bad idea."

"Oh, no," Annie cried. "What am I getting myself into?"

"I'm kidding." He winked at Kevin. "But bear in mind that the two of you are very different ladies."

"I'm doing my best. And I am pretty desperate. But do you think it's a bad idea?"

"Not if there's a decent roof over your head and the rent's right."

"Have you seen the place?"

"Not the apartment. But before her father died, I was in the house once or twice. Nice enough, for a fisherman. I suppose it's got more of a female look now that Taylor's there, though. You want some iced tea?"

As curious as she now was about Taylor, Annie needed to get home, grab something for dinner, and get to work on designing the program for the garden tour. Having taken the afternoon off, she felt slightly guilty. But the house was so comfortable and Earl so welcoming, she said, "Thanks. Iced tea would be great. But don't move, I'll get it."

"Who's Taylor?" Kevin asked while Annie half filled a small glass. "I've heard the name; I first thought she was a man."

"She's nicer than most people think," Earl said. "Especially when they first meet her. She was a curious kid. Smart, too. Went to Berklee College up in Boston. The music one. She played the cello."

"Taylor?" Annie asked, not hiding her shock.

"Yup. You wouldn't have guessed that, would you? After college she played with the symphony for years until her dad got sick. Cancer. She came home to help her mother nurse him. By the time he died, her mother needed nursing, so here she is. A shame, really."

Annie was stunned. "Wow. From a cellist to a caretaker. That's quite a switch. Did she ever marry?" She took a drink and marveled at how little people often knew about others.

"She's always been single, as far as anyone around here knows. Or is telling. I don't think she has many friends, though. She changed after she moved back. Became a gossip, then. Like everyone else's business was more interesting than her own. But you already know that, Annie. Anyway, I always figured you can't really blame her. Her life kind of went out the window. She became a real island character."

Kevin drained his glass. "That settles it. I'll go with you tomorrow, Annie. If I'm going to be here a couple of weeks, I might as well meet as many 'island characters' as possible. Present company excepted, of course."

Earl chuckled, but Annie was too fixated on what she'd learned about Taylor to join in. "I feel terrible," she said. "I'm afraid I haven't given her much of a chance to befriend me."

"Well," Earl continued, "you two didn't exactly get off on the best foot. And just because she has a sad past doesn't mean her place will be a good fit for you. Her mother's not well, and is a little bit nuts. And, like I said, Taylor changed. But the way I see it, lots of folks have a sad past and still find a way to adapt to the world."

Annie fell silent; Kevin did, too. Those with "sad pasts" were, after all, in the majority at the table.

"Well," she said, finishing her tea and clearing her throat. "I'll take that as my cue to leave. If I want a future that's happier than my past, I need to get back to work. Tonight I'm going to finish the brochure for the garden tour. Speaking of which, Taylor told me Claire goes to rehab on Monday?"

"As long as she behaves."

"That's good news, Earl. Really good news."

"It sure is. My own cooking stinks." He said it as if Claire were the "little woman," and Earl the master of the house.

"I won't tell her you said that," Annie replied with a smile. "But Francine cooks, too, doesn't she?"

He cocked the same endearing smile as John's. "Sure. Well, kind of." Then his smile faded and he let out a big sigh. "Between us kids, Claire's stroke scared the crap out of me. I'm not ready to let go of her yet."

Annie gave him a quick hug. "And you won't have to. Hopefully, not for a very long time. Don't forget, when Francine is here and has a free minute, the three of us need to work out a schedule. When Claire gets home, she'll need one of us with her. At least for a week or two."

Earl looked over at Bella, who must have decided that the basket of clean laundry in the corner was a perfect place for her nap. "First Bella, now Claire. I guess at some time or another, we all need one another."

"That we do," Annie replied. Then she turned back to her brother, still amazed that she'd come to know him so easily. In fact, she still had a hard time grasping that she had a brother at all. "Are things okay for you at John's?"

He nodded. "Yup. Like a good houseguest, I even put the key back under the mat." He laughed. "I still don't believe he does that."

"He's just an island boy at heart," Earl said.

And Annie was learning that she was an island girl. If only the twain should ever meet, she and John might actually live happily ever after. If there was such a thing.

After saying goodbye to Kevin and Earl, Annie started her short drive home. Though Bella didn't require much effort, it was tiring to look after a little one. She knew it would be more convenient for the people she cared about if she rented Taylor's apartment and stayed right there on Chappy. It would be better for Claire, Earl, Francine, and even Bella. And it would be easier for her than to have to schlepp back and forth from Edgartown. It had been such a long time since she'd been part of a family, she remembered now that along with the closeness came occasional compromise. But as she recalled, the bottom line had always been worth it. And now that she knew more about Taylor's backstory, maybe Annie could adjust her attitude.

She was pondering how she could go about that when she pulled into her driveway. Immersed in her thoughts, it took a few seconds before she realized a girl was sitting on her front porch steps, her head bent, her long blond hair draping down both sides of her face. But as Annie stopped and turned off the ignition, the girl lifted her head: It was Fiona Littlefield, who looked more like a girl than a woman, her tiny frame contradicting visible crow's feet at the corners of her eyes. *A ballerina's body,* Annie thought, now that she knew her neighbor's passion.

Annie got out of her car and walked toward her. "You're out of the hospital. That's great." She noticed she was dressed in the short cotton dress and the flip-flops that Annie had packed for her.

"He did it," she said. "My brother. He really did it."

Lots of folks have a sad past, Earl had said. In Fiona's case, she seemed to be having a sad present.

"Has something else happened?" As Annie started to sit down, she saw streaks of tears on Fiona's pale cheeks. "Would you like to come in? Maybe have a cold drink?" *Don't get involved,* her inner voice—or Murphy—warned her. *Fiona's problem is none of your business.*

Fiona stood and nodded weakly. And when she wrapped her arms around her slight middle as if she were shivering, Annie knew she could not turn her away. Fiona had no one that Annie could see whom she could count on, and she needed help. So

Annie led her into the cottage and gestured to the table. "Tea? Hot? Iced?"

"Hot, please. If you don't mind." Her voice was a whisper.

While Annie busied herself making the tea, Fiona sat, silent. Neither of them spoke until Annie set two steaming mugs on the table. With the heat and humidity of the day enveloping the room, she badly wanted to turn on the fan, but it was clear that Fiona was still cold. Fear, Annie knew, often did that. She'd been reminded of that when she'd stood outside the Littlefields' in the pitch dark, scared that because Colin's Porsche wasn't there, it meant that her ex-husband had found her instead.

"Fiona," she said quietly, trying to ease into a conversation, "what happened? Did Colin . . ." She searched her mind for a question. "Did your brother do something else?"

Gently shaking her head, Fiona picked up the mug and cupped it with both hands. "I ate the honey cake. I'm the only one who did. It must be how he poisoned me. But the box is gone now. Colin came back and destroyed the evidence."

Annie was baffled. Could it have been Colin after all? Could the Porsche engine sound have been real and not in Annie's dream? Maybe he had gone back to destroy the evidence . . . and when she'd heard the engine, maybe he had been leaving, not arriving.

But . . . Annie wondered, what the heck was honey cake? And what did it have to do with Fiona being poisoned?

"I don't understand," Annie said. "Can you start at the beginning?" The only thing for certain was that something had caused the young woman to wind up facedown on the lawn, passed out, and then have a seizure. And with the police shorthanded, maybe Annie should help. After all, she did have a history of solving mysteries, factual as well as fictitious.

"The day of the wedding, I didn't eat," Fiona began. "I was nervous about fitting into my dress." By the diminutive look of the girl, Annie couldn't imagine that any dress, short of a doll's, would be too small for Fiona. "Earlier in the day, after the ceremony, but before the reception, I ran home to use the loo. I saw the cake in a box next to our kitchen sink. The label said it was honey cake. I love honey cake, not that it mattered. By then I was so hungry I would have eaten anything."

She was chattering now. Some color had returned to her cheeks; Annie decided not to interrupt.

"I grabbed a huge piece and ate every bit. It tasted strange. Bitter, you know?" She lowered her eyes. "But like I said, the box is gone now. Colin must have thrown it out. So I can't prove anything." The girl seemed frightened and sincere.

"What makes you think the cake was poisoned?"

"It had to be from that. I didn't have anything else to eat or drink all day. And Colin knows how much I love honey cakes. When we were kids, he and Dana made them out of local honey every summer."

Annie deduced it must be some kind of white cake or pound cake, sweetened with an ample amount of honey. Something a child might especially love. She wanted to ask how, if it had already been in a box, had Colin—or anyone—bought it knowing it was poisonous—if, in fact, it was. But not wanting to upset Fiona further by presenting logistics, Annie asked, "And your brother has left the island?"

"I guess. They finally let me out of the hospital this morning. Mr. Flanagan brought me home. I decided to be brave and check Colin's room. Everything's gone. Except his stupid mattress that's still on the floor like we're homeless or something."

"But he isn't there?"

"No. And the Porsche is nowhere around."

The Porsche. The fewer times Annie heard the name of the car mentioned, the happier her subconscious—and her conscious—would be. "Fiona? Why did you come to my cottage that night?"

"Your light was on. Everyone at the party was watching the fireworks. And drunk. But I felt really weird. I knew I needed help."

Annie nodded. "Well, it was good that you came here, then." She wanted to reach over and place a reassuring hand on top of Fiona's, but a voice in her ear warned her to be cautious: *You don't know this girl,* Murphy (she knew it was Murphy) said. So Annie took a sip of the tea that she hadn't really wanted and asked, "Have you talked to the police?"

"Mr. Flanagan indulged me and stopped there. We waited in the lobby a long time, but they were really busy. I could tell he was getting annoyed at waiting, so I told him I'd go back later."

"Are you going to stay at your house?"

"I can't. I'm afraid Colin will come back and try to finish me off. And Mr. Flanagan's grandson is at his house. That artist kid who's going to move into your cottage. I don't really know him, and I'm not comfortable being around strangers."

Annie wondered if by "strangers," Fiona meant men. But for once she was grateful the cottage was so small, or she might have offered Fiona a room. Neither John nor Murphy would have been pleased. "What will you do? Go back to Manhattan?"

"I might as well." She stared down at her mug. "I guess it's the only home I have left. Too bad I'm almost thirty-four." Thirty-four was certainly older than she appeared. With the exception of the crow's feet.

"If you can stay on the island a few more days," Annie said, "I can ask around." She wasn't sure if she should, but she did want to help. Whether or not Fiona's brother had tried to kill her, something had definitely happened to Fiona. And it was anyone's guess what effect it might have on Chappy if the Little-fields' once-lovely house fell to total ruin . . . or into unsavory hands. Besides, how long would it take to solve such a simple mystery?

"Okay," Fiona replied. "I can probably stay at the Kelley House. It's a big place; they might have a room."

Annie didn't say there was a good chance they did because Kevin had just checked out. She gave Fiona her phone number. "Let me know where you are. And please, don't go searching for your brother until we've talked with the police." She realized she'd said the word *we* as if they were in this together. Apparently, she'd become a sucker for girls who showed up on her doorstep. And who had a family at stake.

Chapter 16

With less than a week left until the garden tour, Annie had planned to finish the brochure that night. The next day was Saturday—she could bring a hard copy to Mrs. Collins to proofread. Thankfully, the printer was open on Sunday, so Annie could pick it up from Mrs. Collins that morning, then bring it to Vineyard Haven and cross the brochure off her to-do list. Then she could get back to work on her manuscript and meet her deadline the way she'd met Claire's.

All of which was, of course, if everything went according to plan, if no one else had a stroke or no more relatives showed up.

After Fiona had left, Annie threw together a small salad, then tossed a veggie burger in the microwave and called it dinner. While she ate, she sat quietly in the rocking chair and let her mind wander into Fiona's life: poor little rich girl, not-quite-prima ballerina, certainly about to age out of her profession—if she hadn't already. Not to mention that she was so thin; given the way she'd admitted to not eating or drinking anything the day of the wedding, then wolfing down a huge piece of cake, perhaps she was bulimic. Annie supposed that eating disorders weren't uncommon among performers in the ballet. On top of all this, there did not seem to be any romance in her life, someone to help take the edge off her troubles. No wonder she did not want to give up the house on Chappy. Having lost both her parents at a rather young age, combined with a dicey relationship with her older siblings, the house might represent happier times that she wasn't yet able to let go of. Who could blame her?

Annie had been younger than Fiona when she'd lost both her parents: twenty-five when her dad died, not quite twenty-six when her mom passed. But she'd still had Brian, the love of her young life. He'd helped her get through her grief until he died, too.

Even now, his favorite poem remained fresh in her mind. He recited it often, as if sensing that his early death was preordained.

Closing her eyes now, Annie quietly recited the words:

> When I am dead
> Cry for me a little
> Think of me sometimes
> But not too much.
>
> Think of me now and again
> As I was in life
> At some moments it's pleasant to recall
> But not for long.
>
> Leave me in peace
> And I shall leave you in peace
> And while you live
> Let your thoughts be with the living.

When she was finished, she paused. Then she tried to redirect her thoughts to Fiona, to "let her thoughts be with the living." But Annie's eyes remained closed and, in a short time, she drifted into peaceful sleep.

* * *

In the morning, she half remembered awakening at some point during the night, shuffling into her bedroom, crawling under the covers. She hadn't changed out of her clothes, which were as wrinkled as she, too, felt. It didn't help that her phone showed it was nine o'clock; it also indicated a text: **At the Kelley House. FL**

Good. At least she knew where Fiona was and now had the girl's phone number. But with everything else Annie had to do, she'd have to wait to start hunting for what had really happened.

In the meantime, coffee could not come soon enough. It helped that the skies were gray and pouring; Annie had always loved working on a rainy day. Best of all, once the sun returned, the humidity level should have dropped.

In less than thirty minutes, she was coffee'd, showered, dressed, and at her laptop, designing the brochure, or rather, trying to. When she'd been a teacher she'd used graphics software—too many years ago, she realized now—in order to share assignments with students in a visual, clever way. But though the latest technology was supposed to make things easier, the going was slow: She felt like an old dog trying to learn one of those new tricks. If she'd been nine or ten, it would probably have been a snap.

But Annie persisted, because she always had. It had not always proved the right way to live, but it was her modus operandi, Murphy had once called it, then she'd further declared it had nothing to do with opera, which was good, because Annie had not been blessed with a passable singing voice. *Yup,* as Earl would have said, Annie sure missed her best friend.

But with thoughts of Murphy lifting her spirits, by noon she felt comfortable with the steps of the technology: pick a template, copy, paste, pat herself on the back. She checked the essential information: time, date, proper addresses of each garden on display, names of the home owners, judges, and, most important, donors. Those alone took up a full page. Roger and Nicole Flanagan's names were among them, though the amount they'd donated had not been provided.

"I wonder what they get out of it," Annie muttered to herself.

Three hours later, as she was finishing, Kevin arrived. He was drenched, like a muskrat newly emerged from a pond.

"Too much rain to work today," he said, shaking the water off his hat and onto her porch. "Are you ready to check out your new digs?"

Wow. It was already quarter to four. Annie sighed. "It depends on the place. That and the fact I'm not sure I want Taylor for a landlord. I know she's had a hard life, but she is kind of quirky, you know?"

He laughed. Annie was growing to love the sound of her brother's laugh. It had felt so familiar, from day one. She supposed that was the anomaly of nature, the blood bond that could not be explained.

"Aren't we all quirky? In our own way?"

"I suppose." She shut down her laptop, grabbed an umbrella, and followed him to his truck. Once inside, she reached over and put her hand over the ignition. "Wait a second. I wanted to tell you that yesterday, when I got home from Earl's, I had a visitor waiting. Fiona Littlefield."

His eyebrows elevated. "Ah, yes. The dead bridesmaid."

"You really must stop calling her that! But, yes, that was her. She's convinced that her brother tried to kill her. Using a poisoned honey cake."

"Seriously? A cake?"

She nodded, then filled him in on the details. "And I Googled the brother. He was a documentary filmmaker who produced a few war films. But he hasn't done one in a while. He was, however, a marine. In Iraq. I figure that's what his movies were based on."

"It seems that if an ex-marine wanted to do away with his sister—or anyone—he'd know of a more effective method than poisoning her with a cake."

Annie agreed. "But I did tell her I'd ask around. I've met a couple of the guys John works with. I thought I'd stop by the station after I drop off the brochure to be proofread. I could have sent Mrs. Collins the digital file, but it might be easier for her if I printed it out. I think it's been a while since she's been at a computer."

Kevin said, "I have no idea what—or who—you're talking about. But I'm sure you're right."

She swatted his arm again. "Anyway," she added, dismissing his humor, "the police have the toxicology report, but Fiona hasn't heard from them. I'll see if I can stir up any action."

"Sounds like a long shot."

"I know, but there's something about Fiona that seems so . . . forlorn. And you and I are old enough to know that people are more complicated than they seem."

Kevin nodded, then started the truck. "True. But for now, we need to stop worrying about other people and find you a place to live."

Annie knew he was right.

Taylor was standing on her front porch, arms crossed over a faded Black Dog T-shirt. The garage wasn't visible; the Cape-style house, however, was bedraggled, in need of new cedar shingles and a fresh coat of paint on the trim. But a colorful border of wildflowers rimmed the front steps as if to say, "We know the place has seen better days, but the folks inside are nice enough." Maybe Taylor's mother was the gardener.

By the time Kevin parked and they got out, the rain had nearly stopped. Annie hoped it was a good omen.

"You could have come earlier," Taylor said as she walked toward them. "I didn't mow today on account of the rain." She looked at Kevin. "You must be the brother." The woman was definitely quirky.

Kevin wore a big smile. He stepped forward and shook Taylor's hand, his eyes fixed on her hair.

"Kevin MacNeish," he said. "And yes, I'm the brother."

Taylor didn't introduce herself. Annie wondered if she would ever learn the woman's last name.

"You're working for Earl?"

He nodded. "Just helping out until his wife's back on her feet."

Taylor, of course, already knew that. Annie had told her. And no doubt several others had, too.

She flipped back her auburn tresses and pointed toward the back of the house. "Garage is this way."

They followed in single file, as if they were kindergarteners on a field trip.

"Some of Mother's things are still in here, but you can move them if you want. I'd just as soon sell the stuff, but not many people want to trek to Chappy for a chest of drawers that's been around since Methuselah."

They reached the garage, a tall structure built for two vehicles as high as box trucks. It, too, needed new shingles and a paint job. Not to mention some clippers, as a thick tangle of underbrush blocked the side door. Taylor kicked the rubble aside. "Haven't been out here in a while," she said.

The door was unlocked. She pushed it open and they went up a hardwood staircase—seven steps, a landing, a turn, three steps more, another landing, a turn, up five.

"We had the stairs built this way so they'd be easier to navigate than going straight up." They reached another landing and a door at the top, then stepped into a small room.

Annie bit down on her lip to mask her first reaction: creepy. The place was decorated like a child's dollhouse—it had beige-flocked wallpaper that once might have been white, heavy brocade draperies at two tiny windows, and stiff Victorian-era furniture, including a tufted burgundy settee and a pair of Queen Anne chairs. A tea table set with china cups was between the chairs. Three large wall hangings might have been paintings or mirrors but were now draped with bedsheets. The air was stale and gray: Dust motes were everywhere, which added to the aura of film noir. *Whatever Happened to Baby Jane?*, Annie thought. The single saving grace was a cozy propane stove in one corner of the room; Annie knew it would give off a toasty glow in winter.

"Well," she said.

Taylor planted her hands on her hips and gazed around. "Like I said, you can move anything you don't want."

Annie followed her through a narrow doorway that led into a small kitchen. Kevin stayed behind, which was smart. Otherwise, the three of them would have bumped into one another.

In spite of its size, the kitchen was less offensive. The appliances were outdated, but at least they appeared to have been manufactured in the twentieth century, and they were relatively clean. A small drop-leaf table had been shoved against a back door; there was barely room for two chairs. But above a deep farmhouse sink, a window overlooked an orchard and offered a lovely view.

"Apples?" Annie asked.

"Peaches," Taylor replied. "They're just beginning to ripen. You can help yourself whenever you want. Mother doesn't do much baking anymore, and I don't have time."

That's when Annie realized whenever Taylor referred to

"Mother" it made her think of Norman Bates in the film *Psycho*—the terrifying movie that had, in its time, pushed the envelope beyond noir. She squinted out the window and saw the round, golden fruit. "Very nice," she said.

Then, from the other room, Kevin called, "Great bedroom!"

Annie smiled at Taylor, ducked from the kitchen, and went down a short hall. Kevin was right. The bedroom was surprisingly great. It was bigger than the living room, with plenty of room for her bed, her corner desk, and her bookcases. She could even use the chest of drawers that, indeed, looked as if it had been around since Methuselah. Maybe she could apply a rich, dark stain so it would match her bookcases.

Best of all, the bedroom had sliding glass doors that opened to a balcony. As disjointed as it felt that the balcony was off the bedroom instead of the kitchen or living room, having a private outdoor space was a bonus, and almost made the rest of the apartment seem like a good idea. Then Annie realized she hadn't seen a washer or dryer.

"Taylor?" she asked, then turned and nearly crashed into the woman. She took a step back. "Is there a washer and dryer?"

"No. Sorry. Not in here. You'd have to use the ones in the house, so we'd need to work out a schedule. And the bathroom's downstairs."

"Downstairs . . . in the garage?"

"Not quite. We can see it on the way out. We ran out of space up here."

Though this was far from Annie's dream home, she'd actually considered taking it until then. "Well," she said, "let's have a look."

They headed back down the stairs. On the second landing, Taylor opened a short door that Annie hadn't noticed on the way up. They went down three steps into a small bathroom that had been painted an attractive pale green. It had a shower, but no tub, a tiny sink, and a toilet that seemed child-sized if there was such a thing. The low ceiling suggested the room had been an afterthought.

"Okay," Annie said, "I'll have to think about it for a day or so. And maybe come up with a fair price."

"I figured one out already," Taylor announced. "Twenty-two fifty a month. Year-round. Including utilities. As they say in the shops, 'Take it or leave it.' "

Then Kevin stepped forward. "I didn't see a TV."

"No TV. No cable."

"And no Wi-Fi?" Kevin asked.

"If you mean Internet, no. We don't have that, either. Some folks have it out here now, but not us. This is Chappaquiddick. Not midtown Manhattan."

"I can't take it," Annie said, when they were back in Kevin's truck. "I need the Internet for work." She wasn't sure if she was upset or relieved. Though the apartment was, like its owner, more than a little eccentric, living at the behest of Taylor whatever-her-last-name-was somehow felt awkward to Annie.

"The Internet?" Kevin said. "That was your only problem with it? How about the living room that looked straight out of *The Addams Family* or the bathroom that was made for the Seven Dwarfs? And you'd need to schedule when to do your laundry? Who does that?"

Annie laughed. "You're right! I was afraid I was being too picky. I almost told myself that though the lack of the Internet would be inconvenient, I could always go to the community center. They have Wi-Fi twenty-four-seven."

"Maybe they'd let you sleep there for less than twenty-two fifty a month."

"It is a bargain, though."

"You're kidding, right?"

"I wish."

When they got back to the cottage, Annie knew that it was too late to get over to Edgartown and bring the brochure to Mrs. Collins. If she didn't get it to her until Sunday, then to the printer on Monday, would that leave them enough time?

"Dinner?" Kevin asked when he turned off the ignition. "I'll take you to Edgartown if you're in the mood to slay the crowds. I'll even treat. I got paid today."

Annie sighed. Despite the rain, the humidity hadn't abated; the sky had become a murky yellow, an ideal color to depict how she'd felt since stepping out of Taylor's apartment.

"Rain check?" she asked, forcing her best smile.

"You look wrung out. The same way Mom looks when, as she says, she's 'off her game.'"

The thought that Annie's trait was similar to her birth mother's was somehow comforting. But not comforting enough to want to dress up and enter the realm of happy people drinking wine, cracking lobster tails, and socializing. Loudly.

"Can I do anything to help?" Kevin asked. "Finish writing your book? Build you an apartment?"

"I thought you'd never ask. But actually"—her brain cells began to kick in—"would you mind dropping off a copy of the brochure to a woman on Winter Street? It's on your way to John's."

"Hmm," he said, tapping one finger against his temple as if he'd lapsed into deep concentration. "Hmm. Well, okay. I believe I could work that into my schedule."

Leaning across the seat, she gave him a quick hug. "I'm so glad I have a brother who's a lifesaver instead of a murderer. And I'll tell you what. Tomorrow I will pick up the brochure from Mrs. Collins, then bring it to the printer in Vineyard Haven. I'd email the pdf, but the tour is Thursday, so it will be a rush. I'd rather go over any changes Mrs. Collins makes with the printer in person. If you want to come with me, we can have Sunday brunch at the Black Dog Tavern. And I'll drive so you can look around."

"You had me at 'brunch.' Pancakes and sausage are a perfect way to blow off a Sunday."

She got out of the truck. "Great. I'll pick you up at nine. And thanks, Kevin. I really mean it." She waved and trotted into the cottage, trying not to think about how strange it would feel to pick up her brother at John's. Especially since she hadn't heard a word from her boyfriend, or whatever he was, not since he'd left, come back to see Claire, then left again. Maybe, like her, he was feeling overwhelmed.

Chapter 17

As long as Annie had the Internet, she decided to go online and look for rentals. It would, she supposed, be fruitless and might leave her depressed, but to try and concentrate on her manuscript would be a struggle, and she couldn't be bothered to watch television. She half considered going to the Edgartown Police Department after all to talk to John's coworkers about Fiona's conclusion that her brother had poisoned her. But it was Saturday night, and she knew they'd be extra busy maintaining law and order throughout Amity. And if she ran into Kevin when she was coming or going, how would she explain she'd needed some alone time? He was such a gem; she never, ever, wanted to hurt his feelings.

She put some leftover coleslaw, a tomato, and a hard-boiled egg onto a plate. Then she brought her laptop to the table, Googled *MV year-round rentals,* and clicked and scrolled while she ate her dinner.

Nothing.

Nothing.

Nothing.

House share.

Nothing.

Nothing.

Short of screaming, Annie began to shut down the computer when she had another thought. She went back to Google and typed: *poisoned honey.*

At first she was inundated with scientific names, locations, and details about toxicity. Then she found a list of poisonous plants in the northeast:

Azalea
Mountain Laurel
Oleander
Rhododendron

The list included other shrubs whose names she didn't recognize, but the website reported that, in addition to the leaves, stems, and twigs, the nectar of the flowers could sometimes be poisonous.

She drew in a long breath. "And along come the honeybees," she said, then continued reading until she found an entry that explained if bees made honey from poison nectar, the honey would be bitter, but the unpleasant taste could be somewhat masked if baked into something edible . . . such as a honey cake.

"Holy cow," she said. "Holy, holy cow." She compelled herself not to jump up from her chair. Instead, she focused on the rest of the entry that went on to explain the aftereffects: "Several hours after ingesting the poison, the patient can present with a watery mouth, slow heartbeat, convulsions, coma. Without proper medical attention, death can occur within twelve hours."

All of which was exactly what had happened to Fiona. Except, thankfully, the death.

Annie, however, had no idea if any poisonous plants grew on the Vineyard, and if so, whether or not they were in season.

Because, as a mystery writer, she knew the importance of playing the devil's advocate, she supposed it was also possible that Fiona had read the identical entry and, maybe in need of attention, had faked the rest.

Except, of course, the hospital knew she'd been poisoned. And they'd provided the report to the police. Who would tend to it when they had time.

If John were there, he'd get to the bottom of it. In the meantime, if he would only call, Annie could ask what he thought, and if he knew what she could do to help. Then again, if John would only call, she might not be on a ledge of depression, trying to figure out someone else's life because she could not figure out her own.

Then, as if Murphy had laced Annie's tea with inspiration, she came up with another plan. It might not point a finger at Colin Littlefield, but it was a great place to start.

Picking up her phone, Annie texted Fiona: **I think I have a lead. I'll be in touch tomorrow.**

After a fitful night made worse by the lingering humidity that dampened the bedsheets, her nightgown, her skin, and everything in its wake, Annie finally fell asleep. When she woke up at eight, sunlight blew into her bedroom thanks to a blessed morning breeze that had magically brushed the dampness away with a heavenly, broad summer broom.

She bounded from bed, energized. Then, while in the shower, she had another brilliant idea. Before going to see Mrs. Collins, she could look up one of the garden tour judges. A master gardener. Someone who'd be certain to know something about poisonous flora on the Vineyard. There were three judges: Annie had cut and pasted their names onto the template of the brochure.

It wasn't long before she was out the door, over to Edgartown, and up to Fuller Street, which ran parallel to North

Water. Finding Henri LeChance's home was even easier: A picture-perfect hedgerow framed the property and featured a white garden gate leading onto a brick walkway that meandered through a floral wonderland. It was a definite fit in the neighborhood.

Monsieur LeChance (as, according to the program, he preferred to be addressed) was in his screened gazebo, eyes closed, playing a violin, its mellifluous sounds pirouetting in the morning air. For some reason, Annie had pictured the *monsieur* as a small, doddering man much like Hercule Poirot; instead he was tall and reedy, his arms and knees jutting at sharp angles from the straight chair on which he sat. A blanket of gray hair atop his head was so dense it might have been a toupee, but, on closer inspection, it matched his eyebrows perfectly, so she supposed it was not.

Annie did not speak; she did not want to disrupt his small concert. Yet, as if he'd sensed her footsteps, he opened his eyes and looked directly at her. He set down his bow and instrument and pushed a few stray hairs back from his brow.

"*Bonjour,*" he said.

"*Oui,*" Annie replied, "*bonjour.*" She felt somewhat ridiculous speaking French in an historic New England village. "*Parlez-vous anglais?*"

He laughed, revealing large white teeth, too large, in fact, for his gaunt face. He stepped from the gazebo and greeted her with a firm handshake. "Of course. And you are?"

She smiled, embarrassed. "Annie Sutton. I've been helping Claire Lyons with the garden tour."

"Yes, that's coming up this week, isn't it? I heard Claire had a misfortune. Is she doing better?"

Annie related the good news. Then she said, "And yes, the tour will be Thursday. But that's not the only reason I'm here. I'm a writer; I'm doing research for a new book." In the same way that a honey cake could "somewhat mask" the bitter taste of poison, she'd decided to use her profession to hide the truth of her mission. She asked him about poisonous flowers or plants currently on the island that might lead to tainted honey.

Monsieur LeChance shook his head. "That would be a dreadful thing for tourism, *non*?" His voice was heartier than the subtle tones of his violin.

She smiled. "I write fiction, monsieur. Make-believe."

"*Mais non.* We wouldn't want your readers to think a place as *affiné* as Martha's Vineyard would allow such things to grow?"

It didn't matter that Annie had no idea what the word *affiné* meant. She got the point. "Perhaps something that isn't instantly deadly? Something that could simply make the victim ill at first, then, with quick treatment, avoid death?"

He shook his head again. "*Non, non.* Nothing that would be *appropriés.*"

She ran the names and locations of the other judges through her mind while Monsieur LeChance shook his head again.

"Oh, for God's sake, Henri," a female voice with a British accent shouted from what looked like a kitchen window of the house. "Tell her about the mountain laurel. It's not as if it's a bloody state secret."

He rolled his umber eyes and offered a small sigh. "Mountain laurel," he conceded, "*mais oui.* There is that. Not that you—or anyone—should taste it, mind you!"

"And you're in luck," the voice called from the window once again, "because it's in bloom right now. All over the island."

Having been rewarded with a perfect answer, albeit circuitously, Annie said, "Thank you," toward the window, then added "*Merci,*" to Monsieur LeChance. "I will see you Thursday?"

"*Mais oui,*" he said again. "Unless *le poison* gets me first." He waved and tootled back into the gazebo, where he picked up the violin again, closed his eyes, and resumed creating the soothing sounds.

Annie listened for a minute, then made her way through the picturesque wonderland back to the front gate to where she'd parked her car. She was grateful that she now knew what she needed to do next. And whom she could enlist to help.

After retrieving the brochure from Mrs. Collins (she'd found only three typos and two misspellings, but Annie assured her that her work had been well worth the effort), Annie drove to John's. Kevin was sitting outside on the front steps, for which she silently thanked him. She didn't need any more reminders that John wasn't there.

On the way to Vineyard Haven and the printer, Kevin told her that Earl had called the night before and asked if they could stop at the lumberyard and pick up fencing for the Alvords' chicken coop and some roofing shingles for someone else's barn. Apparently, in the "hubbub," as Earl had called the aftermath of Claire's stroke, he'd forgotten them a week ago.

"Mrs. Alvord has an ongoing problem with her chickens escaping," Annie told her brother. "The fencing is probably fine. The real problem could be she forgets to close the gate." She quickly wondered what her ex would think if he knew she was talking about chicken coops and fencing instead of things she wanted to add to her designer wardrobe. *Those were definitely the bad old days,* she thought. And though another stop would interfere with her plans, she supposed that as long as they were on the west side of the island, they might as well check out the lumberyard.

"I guess Taylor used to take care of the property," Kevin

continued. "That was until Mrs. Alvord had a falling-out with Taylor's mother."

Annie laughed. "The two women have probably been friends for sixty years. Life here can be intriguing."

"Well, I hope I'm not stepping on Taylor's toes with this."

"You won't be."

"But she must need the money more than I do. Or more than Earl does."

Casting a quick glance toward the passenger seat, Annie asked, "Why are you worried what she thinks? I told you her place won't work for me."

"But have you told her yet?"

"No. I'll call tonight."

"Okay, well, it's nice that she offered, anyway."

Annie wondered if Kevin had developed a tiny crush on the hearty woman with the auburn mane. She would have asked, but her mind was already too crowded, and thoughts of Taylor and her brother would be way too complex to consider.

After several trips around the block to park in Vineyard Haven, Annie finally succeeded. Kevin waited in the car while she dashed inside. In less than five minutes, she'd explained the corrections, selected the paper stock, and showed the man at the counter where she wanted spot varnish on the photos so the brochure would look as *affiné* as possible.

Because her business took less time than anticipated, Annie decided to give Kevin a mini tour of West Chop.

Back behind the wheel, she drove all the way up Main Street, past magnificent old summer homes, their dark, weathered shingles a noticeable contrast to Edgartown's heraldry of white. They drove alongside the shoreline that skirted Vineyard Sound, and when they reached the West Chop lighthouse, she stopped the car. They got out and walked to the lookout, where Cape Cod was visible across the calm cerulean water. A flotilla of sailboats, their sails like thumbprints across a canvas of blue sky, was interrupted only by the big, gleaming ferry as it inched toward the island.

"Nice place you have here," Kevin commented.

When they'd finished gaping, Annie drove past more historic homes, circled around tennis courts and a clubhouse, then headed east on Franklin Street, back out to State Road.

The lumberyard was closed, for which she was secretly pleased because it meant she could begin executing her plan.

"I've been thinking," she told Kevin, "that as long as we're out this way, we might as well check out a few things for, as you call her, the dead bridesmaid." She brought him up-to-date on what she'd learned the night before and from Monsieur LeChance.

Kevin whistled. "I can't believe you kept this from me for over an hour. So what's the plan?"

"The cake was in a box so it probably came from a bakery. That's where we'll start." She made a U-turn and drove across the street, straight into the parking lot of the Black Dog Café. "It won't exactly be pancakes and bacon like they have at the tavern," she said, "but they're a bakery, so maybe they sell honey cake. If not, we can at least grab a couple of muffins and be on our way. I know I promised you brunch, but trust me, you won't be disappointed."

She parked the car. They went inside and stood in the Sunday line of people that stretched the full length of the glass case and went almost out the door. When their turn at last arrived, Annie made the inquiry.

But, no, they did not make honey cake. "Sorry," the clerk said.

Annie chose a blueberry muffin, Kevin a cranberry-orange one.

Next stop was the Scottish Bakehouse, whose menu offered succulent treats that were more Brazilian than Scottish. But, no, they did not make honey cake, either. The baker hinted that because they used fresh, local ingredients whenever possible, the cost of local honey would make a cake too pricy.

After a third and then a fourth stop, Annie refused to get discouraged. Then she came up with another idea. "Forget this," she said. "We're taking a side trip up island to Aquinnah."

"Because . . . ?"

"Because I have a friend named Winnie, a wonderful Wampanoag lady, who showed me how to handcraft natural soaps. One of her brothers has a few beehives. He might know someone who makes honey cakes." She didn't know why she hadn't thought of him earlier.

Winnie wasn't home, but her sister-in-law, Barbara, was. Barbara was the nurse who worked in the hospital maternity department; she was married to Orrin, Winnie's beekeeping brother.

"He's not here, either," Barbara replied when Annie asked for Orrin. "Ever since he decided to keep bees and do less fishing for a living, I swear he's fishing more. Even with his godawful arthritis. But he should be back soon. Once the sun starts heading over the yardarm—which, to him, means anytime after noon—he's pretty much done with the fish." She laughed. "He always says that 'yardarm' thing even though he has a trawler, not a sailboat. He likes the way that it sounds." She snickered in a loving way.

They stood in the sprawling, unkempt yard. In addition to the main house, there was a small stone house where root vegetables were sheltered after the harvest; next to that was Winnie's studio, then a separate, round brick kiln that had a stovepipe rising through the top. Leaning against the main house, a stack of framed mesh screens looked like they could be part of Orrin's beekeeping venture. The hives, however, were out of sight, safely tucked away on the expansive land. Annie felt that, even more than on Chappy, up island show-cased the Vineyard at its most genuine; she was glad to be able to share it with her brother.

Then a van rumbled into the driveway.

"Oh!" Barbara exclaimed. "Looks like the yardarm got shorter today!"

Orrin climbed out of the vehicle, gave the group a wave, then went to the back and pulled out a couple of plastic cool-ers. "Stripers for dinner!" he called. He had the off-balance waddle of a fisherman, as if one foot were on land and the other at sea.

"Did they come from Squibnocket?" Kevin asked, then gave Annie a wink. She had no idea he knew anything about Vineyard fishing, or any fishing for that matter. Especially since he'd said that being on a boat made him seasick.

"Yup. Wasque's still closed."

"Nesting birds. I heard about that."

Annie was so surprised by her brother's comment that for a second she forgot why they were there. Apparently, Kevin had really been enjoying his time on the island, talking to lots of people while doing Earl's rounds.

"You staying for dinner?" Orrin asked. "Got four big ones here."

"I'm sorry, but thanks." Annie jumped into the conversa-tion before Kevin accepted. "We'll take a rain check, though. By the way, this is my brother, Kevin." The men shook hands and Annie cleared her mind. "We stopped to ask you about your beekeeping. Well, about the honey, anyway. I just learned it can be tainted if bees get the nectar from something poi-sonous, like mountain laurel. Is that true?"

"True enough. Usually the bad nectar winds up being mixed with so much from other sources that the effects are minor. But once in a great while it can stay fairly concentrated."

"How would a beekeeper know it's tainted? And if you sold your honey to a bakery and they put some in cakes or cookies, how would anyone know they were poisonous before they got sick?"

Though he lacked a couple of front teeth, Orrin's smile was broad. He held up an index finger. "First of all, it's rare that people get sick from it. Animals, yes. People, not so much. But to be on the safe side, we always do taste tests. Every batch of raw honey that goes out of here gets a foolproof test. I spoon out a sample, dip my finger in, take a taste, then, as they say, voilà! It's not exactly rocket science: If the honey's bitter then it's bad—you can tell right away."

It was interesting that he'd used the same word to describe it that both Fiona and the Google entry had: *bitter*.

"Does that answer your question?" Orrin asked.

"It does. Thanks. Have you heard that any on the island was tainted lately?"

"I sure have. Rodney, over at Sweet Everything Farm in Chilmark, on the west side of town. He lost the whole batch he was putting up for the Ag Fair."

Annie knew that, for over a century and a half, the Ag Fair ran for a few days in August. It was famous for its carnival rides and contests, its sheep shearing and skillet tossing, and for the tons of items that were judged, from apple pie to watercolors, and apparently, to honey. She'd been asked to enter her natural herb-and-flower soaps but had declined because she'd had a feeling her summer would be busy. *An understatement,* she thought now.

Returning to the problem at hand, Annie asked if Orrin knew whether or not Rodney had sold any of the honey to a local bakery.

He shrugged. "About all I can do is tell you how to get to his place."

"Fair enough," Kevin said. "And one of these nights, we'll be back for striper."

Annie smiled at the thought that her brother apparently intended to stick around.

Chapter 18

Sweet Everything Farm had a hand-painted shingle that hung on the tree belt where the long driveway began. Cornfields seemed to rise up from the fertile earth in every direction, as if it were the most natural thing to do. They found Rodney in one of several barns, slicing into a bale of hay. He was short and stocky and, over a T-shirt, he wore denim overalls that made him resemble Elmer Fudd.

Annie introduced herself and Kevin and said they'd come by way of Orrin Lathrop. "I'm doing research for a book," she said with a smile. "Orrin said you had a bad batch of honey recently. I'm trying to incorporate that into a plot."

He pursed his lips as if he were about to kiss someone. "You write murder mysteries?"

"I do," she said with a light laugh. "And I'm intrigued by the thought that a food source as pure as honey can be poisonous. I might have a character who wants to try and kill someone with it."

Rodney scratched his chin, then said, "It would be tough for anyone to know how much honey it would take to be fatal. One or two bad batches pop up on the island every couple of years. Maybe there are more, but they're destroyed as soon as the beekeeper discovers it tastes bitter."

There was that word again.

"Anyway," Rodney continued, "lucky for me, my bad batch didn't get far."

Kevin stuck his hands in the pockets of his jeans. "What happened? Did your taste test tell you it was poisonous?"

Rodney broke the hay apart with his foot, then tossed a bundle over the wall of an empty stall. Annie supposed the small herd—there were eight stalls in the barn—was grazing outside in the summer sun. "My allergies were bad one day. So my taster was off." He wiped his palms on his jeans, raised one of his fingers, and tapped his tongue, much the way Orrin had done.

"We only sell raw, organic honey," he continued. "Straight from the hive, unfiltered, not pasteurized. As much as I hated losing the whole batch, my guardian angel must have been watching out for me that day, because only Myrna got sick. From now on, she'll be double-checking me."

"Who's Myrna?" Annie asked.

"My wife. I potted a few jars of the honey the day before Myrna left for her sister's on the Cape. She measured two heaping cups and made two cakes. She does it every July so her sister has them for the big picnic she throws on the Fourth. Myrna wanted to take the early boat, so I drove her down to Vineyard Haven. On the way she mentioned she'd skipped breakfast. I told her to get something at the snack bar on the boat. But Myrna hates to spend a dime. Anyway, while she waited to get on, she opened one of the boxes and broke off a hunk of cake. She knew while she was chewing it that it tasted bad, but the passengers started boarding, so she swallowed fast and climbed up the ramp."

"She got sick on the boat?" Kevin asked.

"Not real sick—it takes longer than the forty-five-minute

trip to Woods Hole for that, and a lot more than she ate. But as soon as her stomach got queasy, she knew why."

"Because the cake tasted bitter," Annie interrupted.

"Right. You wanna talk to her? I gotta head out to check the corn. But she's up at the house making strawberry jam before they're done growing for the year."

"I'd love to talk to her. Kevin, you want to come with me?"

Kevin decided he'd rather follow Rodney around. "Unless you mind," he said to him.

"Can't be any worse than the damn goats," Rodney said. "Try not to eat any fence posts along the way." He snorted, obviously amused at the line he might have said to tourists more than once. Then he grabbed a wheelbarrow and led them from the barn, pointing the way for Annie to get to the house.

As red as the barns and with clean white trim, the house featured a long porch where a row of Adirondack chairs sat, as if poised for visitors. Annie knocked on the screen door while wondering if she should tell Myrna the truth. Because the woman knew the types of reactions someone might have from ingesting tainted honey, maybe she'd be able to judge whether or not Fiona's tale was plausible. But wary of getting anyone—like Colin Littlefield—into trouble if he did not deserve it, she decided to keep the details to herself.

Myrna wiped her hands on her apron and opened the door. She stepped outside and Annie explained why she was there, or at least a watered-down version.

"So you didn't make any other cakes from the bad batch?" Annie asked.

"No. I make more at Rosh Hashanah. And Easter and Christmas. Mostly we sell the raw honey to the natural food stores on the island."

"But you didn't sell any of it to them, either?"

"No," Myrna replied. "No cakes. No jars."

"What did you do when you realized it was bad?" Rodney, of course, had already explained it, but Annie supposed a real detective would want a statement straight from the "witness's" mouth.

"I chewed the first bite and knew right away what I was tasting. But passengers were boarding, and I was already in line, so I swallowed fast. I knew I hadn't eaten enough to kill me. I went into the ladies' room and tried to throw it up, but I've never been good at doing that on demand. Anyway, by the time we pulled away from the pier my stomach felt upset. It might have been all in my head, but I needed to get home to tell Rodney so he could burn the rest of the batch. I knew he'd be out in the fields and he doesn't carry his cell phone out there. We fight about that sometimes, but . . ." She shook her head in silent annoyance. "Anyway, I stayed on the boat and made the return trip."

"What happened to the cakes?" Annie asked.

"I trashed them on the boat. No. Wait. I stayed put in the ladies' room on the way back in case I wound up getting sick, you know? A woman in there asked me if I was okay. I was leaning against the sink; I might have looked a little green. She probably thought I was seasick or something. Then my stomach rolled. I pointed to the counter where I'd put the boxes. I said, 'Those cakes are poisonous,' then I bolted back into a stall. She asked me if I wanted her to get rid of them. I said sure. It never occurred to me I should bring them home for Rodney to examine. I just wanted them out of my sight."

"Do you remember what the woman looked like?"

After a thoughtful few seconds, Myrna said, "No. But I guess she was about medium height." Coming from a woman who was nearly the same short stature as her husband, Annie didn't think that was terribly specific. "She had light-colored hair. Blond, maybe." She pressed her lips together as if in concentration. "I do remember that right when we were about to pull into Vineyard Haven, I came out of the ladies' room, and I saw her standing by the staircase, talking with a man. I thought they were together. But later, when I walked down the ramp, I saw the same guy drive his car off the boat. The woman wasn't with him."

"You're sure?"

"Yes. I didn't have my car, and I felt better by the time we got off. Because I couldn't get ahold of Rodney, I decided to take the bus home. I didn't see the woman again, but when I walked toward the bus stop, I saw the man drive off the boat—and, yes, he was definitely by himself. He was easy to spot because he was in a Porsche."

On the way back to Edgartown, Annie couldn't stop talking. If her ex-husband, not Kevin, had been sitting in the passenger seat, there was little doubt he would have told her to shut up.

"So I guess this means we believe the dead bridesmaid after all?" Kevin asked when she finally stopped to take a breath.

"It's hard not to, isn't it? Which leaves the big questions: Who was the blonde on the boat who took the cakes? What did she have to do with Colin Littlefield? And why did Colin disappear if he wasn't guilty? Not to mention, where the heck is he now?"

If only she could call John, Annie knew she would feel better. But he'd be gone at least another week, and she didn't want to interrupt . . . whatever. She had always been cautious not to overstep boundaries with anyone, and when it came to John, she still had no idea what those boundaries were. It would have been nice, however, if he would call.

Then she realized her thoughts were becoming redundant. Trish would go through an entire blue pencil deleting them.

"I think it's time for you to talk to the bridesmaid again,"

Kevin said, cutting short her moment of self-pity. "Besides, I'd like to meet her."

Annie turned at Beetlebung Corner in the direction of West Tisbury. "I hate to say this, my wonderful brother, but I think it would be better if I went alone."

He clutched his heart, feigning hurt. "You're kidding, right?"

She tried her best to look apologetic. "No. Something tells me Fiona isn't a big fan of men. She might be more honest with me if it's just the two of us. At least this time. Okay?"

"No. I want all the dirt."

She laughed. "I'll come and get you when I'm finished."

"Cross your heart?"

She did.

"When you're done, will you meet me at the Newes? You gypped me out of brunch, but I'll buy you a late lunch."

Annie glanced at her watch. She couldn't believe it was already after three o'clock. "It might be too crowded to get a seat. People tend to linger on weekends."

"Then I'll sit on the stone wall and wait outside."

"You win, brother. The Newes it is."

Then the traffic ahead suddenly clogged, though none was coming from the other direction.

"What's going on?" Kevin asked, as if Annie might know.

But she did know, or rather, she guessed, based on things she had heard. In less than a minute, her guess was validated as one, two, three large silver SUVs with darkened windows came from the direction of the airport.

"The president," Annie said. "Or rather, the former president."

"Which one?"

"Don't know, but I was told to be on the lookout in the summer."

"Right," Kevin replied. "I almost forgot we're on the Vineyard."

They waited a few more minutes before the line was allowed to move. "I heard the traffic was much worse," Annie added, "when either of them was actually in office. It's a good thing no one here except me is ever in a hurry."

When they arrived at the Kelley House, Annie didn't bother to look for a place to park. She dropped Kevin off at the pier (thus saving the *On Time*'s four-dollar passenger fare), then swung around and got in line for the ferry. By some miracle, only five cars were waiting, so the round trip wouldn't take long. Once she made it to the Chappy side, she'd return as a passenger. Annie had finally figured out that living on Chappy often required improvising.

Kevin had dutifully waited; they walked past the Old Sculpin Gallery and the Anchors, the Edgartown Council on Aging, past the Whale Tail, then around the corner to the Kelley House. Annie was impressed with how quickly her brother had learned to navigate his way around.

At the front door of the hotel, she ducked into the lobby, while Kevin progressed up the short hill toward the pub. Before messaging Fiona, Annie decided to text John. Since the trip to Sweet Everything Farm, she'd felt a strong, no, an urgent need to connect with him. The whole situation had begun to feel criminal.

She sat on a soft leather chair that faced the fireplace and admired the striking gallery of photographs adorning the walls. As much as she would have liked to inspect them more closely, she knew she would be procrastinating. The sooner she messaged John, the sooner this could be resolved.

With a resigned sigh, Annie typed: **Hope all is going okay.** She couldn't say, "Hope all is going well," because how could having brought his thirteen-year-old daughter to have an abortion be anything close to "well"? **If you have a chance, I'd love to talk. Your mom is good. But . . .**

She stopped. The story about Fiona and the honey was too complicated to relay in a text. Would it really be wrong if she called him?

Turning to avoid the front desk clerk, she stared at her screen. Her pulse started to race; she felt as if she were a girl again and that it was her first time calling a boy. She remembered that her "first time" had been when she'd called Brian. She'd prayed his parents wouldn't answer, or that he hadn't forgotten who she was, though he'd called her three times since the summer. She'd wanted to ask if he'd go to the harvest dance at the public high school with her even though he went to Milton Academy. She remembered the cold, damp sensation in her hands—*clammy hands,* she'd read somewhere. She'd dialed the number at Brian's house, twice. She'd hung up both times. On the third try she took a deep breath and dialed again.

To this day, Annie couldn't recall who had answered or what her conversation with Brian had been like. But she did know he had taken her to the harvest dance. And after the dance he'd kissed her. A lot. And he'd told her he might be in love with her.

The sharp sound of the phone at the reception desk startled her now. She realized she was being foolish. She was a grown woman, at best middle-aged. And a young woman's life might be at stake. It was absolutely appropriate for her to call John and not send a cryptic text. She deleted the text, tapped his number, and touched "Call."

The phone rang. Annie drummed her fingers on the arm of the chair. She'd start by asking how Lucy was doing. And how he was doing. She would not ask about his ex-wife.

The phone rang again.

And again.

Finally, it clicked on. A woman's voice said, "Hello?"

Annie knew she hadn't called the wrong number. Just as she knew that the voice didn't belong to one of his daughters. It was too mature and too prickly.

"Is John available?" she asked before her hesitation could reveal there was a hole in her stomach from having been sucker-punched.

"No."

The curt reply irritated Annie. "This is Annie Sutton." Then, like the wimpy teenager she'd once been, she added, "I'm a friend of John's parents." She would have rather asked why the woman had answered John's phone.

"I know who you are."

She gripped the chair as if she'd lost her balance. "Earl and Claire are fine. But I need to speak with John."

"Sorry. He's in the shower."

The *shower*? She glanced at her watch. It was after four o'clock. On a Sunday afternoon. She doubted that John was cleaning up to go to church. As far as she knew, the only time he set foot in a house of worship was for the community suppers in winter months. Perhaps he'd undergone some sort of conversion. Or, more likely, he'd just rolled out of bed. In which case it was apparent he was staying in the same house as his girls and . . . her.

Annie's insides fluttered. She closed her eyes and tried to relax. But all that happened was she pictured John in his ex-wife's bed. The bed, perhaps, where they'd conceived Abigail and Lucy.

"Would you please give him a message?"

No answer. His ex must really be enjoying this.

"Tell him I need to speak with him about the young

woman who was poisoned. There have been new developments in the case, and we need his input." She hung up before she felt another dagger pierce through the satellite connection.

Then, on shaky legs, she went to the desk and asked the receptionist to please ring Fiona Littlefield's room and tell her Annie was there. Though she could easily have texted or phoned, the only way Annie knew for her heart to climb back into her chest was if she made some type of human contact. With a real person. Even if it was only someone who would smile at her and say, "Yes. Of course. I'd be glad to notify Ms. Littlefield."

Chapter 19

"It was my horrid sister," Fiona said. "She had to be the woman Colin was talking to on the boat. The lady must have given Sheila the cakes and told her they were poisonous."

"But she didn't come to the wedding," Annie said.

They were sitting in Fiona's room—number two seventeen, not one of the haunted ones, as far as anyone knew. Fiona was cross-legged, her small body barely covering half the cushion of the navy-blue upholstered chair. She stared at the hardwood floor. It was the first time Annie had been inside the Kelley House, which offered a rich blend of colonial décor with both classic and contemporary accents: a writing desk and two small occasional tables were finished in highly polished chestnut; two beds were covered by meticulous white duvets and chunky pillows in intriguing shades of blue; the walls displayed framed photographs similar to the stunning ones in the lobby.

Annie sat on an ottoman that matched the chair.

Fiona raised her head and directed her gaze toward Annie. "I thought Colin was going to pick her up at the airport in Providence. When he showed up alone, I asked him where she was. All he said was, 'You know Sheila. She's a pain in the ass.'

He didn't say anything else, and I didn't ask him what he meant, because he was right—she is. Can you imagine? She wants to turn our house into a bird sanctuary!"

"Do you think she became part of a plan to poison you?" Annie avoided the word *conspiracy* because she thought it sounded ridiculous. This was not, after all, the Kennedy assassination or a case of election meddling.

"More than likely."

"But Colin was seen getting off the ferry alone."

"Maybe Sheila gave him the idea but she chickened out and went home. In spite of the fact Sheila is worth millions, she's a tree-hugger at heart. I never even saw her kill a fly. And she's a lesbian."

Annie was unsure what being a lesbian had to do with being a tree-hugger or not killing flies, but she decided to let the comment go. "Where does she live?"

Fiona's narrow shoulders rose a little, her small bones barely touching the pink fabric ties that secured her flowered sundress. "Somewhere outside Seattle. I've never been there. She does something with computers. And invented some kind of program that keeps paying her royalties. Or at least that's what Colin told me. But according to him, even with all her money, she refuses to help him out with his film business. He makes documentaries about the war. But Sheila says they're too violent, and she won't support violence. Not that it matters. He has a trust fund. Like Sheila and me."

Not wanting to mention that she already knew about Colin's documentaries thanks to her Google search, Annie said, "Well, Seattle is a long way away for your sister to have come here, then gone back simply because she 'chickened out' of trying to kill you."

Picking at her pedicure, Fiona said, "Like Colin says, 'she's a pain in the ass.'"

For the first time, Annie wondered if she'd been on the wrong track, if maybe Sheila, not Colin, had indeed poisoned their sister. But, if that were true, why hadn't Colin resurfaced? Or was it possible that the Steamship Authority had missed the listing of his car as it left the island? She didn't know how that could happen: The SSA had high levels of security. Could Colin have left his car at the airport and flown somewhere, anywhere, out of there? But why would he have done that?

Instead of producing answers, Annie's questions were making things more complicated.

"In any event," Annie said, "I think you and I should go to the police station tomorrow. They need to take over your case. Otherwise, we might screw something up. Or scare off the real culprit."

"Okay," Fiona whispered, as if she were tired of talking about it. "After that I'll go back to New York. There's no reason not to."

"What about the house on Chappy?"

She made a small whimpering sound. "I might as well let them sell it. I really don't even want to go in it again. It's too full of memories. The old ones were okay, but, well, it isn't easy to accept the fact that your siblings want you dead."

Annie bit her lip. She reached over and touched Fiona's arm. "We don't know that for certain. In the meantime, please don't do anything, okay? Not until we've straightened this out. I'll come get you at nine o'clock tomorrow, if that's not too early. We can walk to the station from here. Okay?"

Fiona hesitated, then nodded.

"Have you eaten?" Annie added. "Would you like to join my brother and me downstairs at the Newes?"

"No. Thanks. I'll stay here and read. I'll have something sent up later."

Annie doubted that she would.

★ ★ ★

After leaving the Kelley House and heading toward the pub, Annie heard her phone ping, or rather, her text alert: incoming message.

She stopped, unsure if she wanted to look. It could be from John, offering a fabricated story as to why he'd been taking a shower at four o'clock. She held her hand to her throat and took in a breath. It was the first time she'd thought that way about him, as if she could not depend on him, as if he were going to hurt her, as if he were . . . Mark.

Trying to shake the feeling, she reasoned that the text might actually be from Kevin. Perhaps the Newes was mobbed and he wanted to rearrange their plans. Or maybe it was Earl with an update on Claire. *Dear God,* Annie thought, *what if Claire has had another stroke?* She thought about all the times she'd nagged Earl to always have his phone with him, in case of an emergency, in case, in case, in case. How could she ignore hers now after all the fuss she had made?

She reached into her bag and checked the small screen. The message was from John: **All OK here. Text if you need me.**

Her stomach cramped. That was it? Text if you need me? Hadn't his ex given him the message that the young woman had been poisoned and that Annie needed his input? Why wouldn't his ex have told him? Because she knew that Annie was his lover? Or . . . that Annie *had been* John's lover? After all, it now seemed clear that John was sleeping in his ex's house.

But where?

On a pullout sofa in the living room?

An air bed in the garage?

Closing her eyes, she hated that the awful feelings of distrust that she'd had with Mark still festered in her memory. She thought she'd expunged them long ago.

She wanted to tip her head back, look up into the sky, and rant obscenities.

Then a little boy bumped her side as he struggled to maneuver up the crowded sidewalk, one hand holding tightly to a young woman's hand. Annie stumbled off the curbing, twisting her ankle.

"I'm sorry," the boy said in a soft, sweet voice.

Quickly checking an initial instinct to gripe that the kid hadn't been paying attention, she righted herself as he shrank close to his mom, looking a bit scared. Annie leaned down to him. "That's okay, honey. Sometimes there are too many people here, aren't there?"

He nodded bashfully and put his thumb into his mouth.

"Are you all right?" the young woman asked.

Annie smiled. "No harm done. It's a busy day." She waited until the two of them had melded into the crowd before limping away, grateful for the reminder that most people did the best they could. Even John. And that sometimes everyone, including her, needed to be cut some understanding slack.

With a tender ankle but a fresh outlook, she reached the Newes and threaded around the patio tables that were crammed with people, none of whom was Kevin. She angled her way inside, looked left, then right, and spotted him at the bar. But as she headed toward him, Annie noticed that he was talking with a woman. A woman with long auburn hair. Exactly who Annie least wanted to see.

She went to her brother and put a hand on his shoulder. "Hey, brother," she said, then acknowledged his companion. "Taylor, nice to see you."

"Kevin told me you don't think my place will work on account of we don't have the Internet," Taylor spewed. "You could always go to the community center to get connected."

Annie did her best to look pleasant, while Kevin looked as shamefaced as the bashful boy had. "I know," she replied. "I considered that. But when I'm writing, I'm constantly online.

I'm afraid the center might be too hectic right now for me to concentrate."

Taylor snorted. "Writers have been writing for centuries without the Internet."

"That's true. But they didn't have an editor like mine, who demands I do a book or more a year." She hoped Trish would forgive her for using her as an excuse. "So thanks, Taylor, but, yes, I'll have to decline. I meant to call you earlier today, but I got sidetracked. Claire's garden tour is in a few days and . . ."

Waving away Annie's words, Taylor had apparently heard enough. "Not to worry. I'll find someone. Or not. It's not like we need the income. In the meantime, Kevin has invited me to have lunch with you two, though it's getting late enough to call it supper. In any case, I call his offer a valid consolation prize." She winked at Kevin, and Annie slid her hand from his shoulder.

"Wine before burgers?" he asked.

"Actually," Annie said, "I'm afraid I'll have to leave you two to split my share." She was not about to reveal anything about her visit with Fiona in front of Taylor. Hopefully, Kevin hadn't spilled any information, though the half-full stein in front of him might not have been his first beer, and Annie had no idea how loose his tongue might have become. "Kevin, can I borrow your truck? The printer is having issues with the program, and I need to go back to Vineyard Haven."

"On a Sunday?" Kevin asked. Clearly, he hadn't realized her story was fake.

Taylor took another slug from the draft in front of her.

"Folks here work twenty-four-seven in the summer," Annie said. "I can walk up to John's and get the truck. I wouldn't ask, but it's an emergency."

"No problem," Kevin said and handed her the keys.

"I'd bring you myself if I didn't have a date with a burger," Taylor said, in an obvious but lame effort to be humorous.

Annie took the keys and smiled. "I shouldn't be long." She left the Newes, curious as to whether or not her brother had become attracted to Taylor, but knowing she had far too many other things on her mind to start worrying about that, too.

Annie had no idea how she could find Sheila Littlefield, but figured if she tracked down Colin it would be a start. And the easiest—and maybe the only—way to do that would be to determine if he, or both of them, had left the island in a plane. She'd only been out to the airport twice: once to pick up John, who'd made a quick trip to Boston to testify in an immigration case; the second time when she'd been on her way home from Winnie's and had needed to use the ladies' room. Too much tea, she'd told a woman at the car rental desk as she'd raced past.

In spite of the snail-like Sunday traffic on West Tisbury Road, she finally arrived and headed straight for the parking lot.

As in the wait line at the *On Time* on a sunny day, vehicles sat silent in tight, narrow rows, as if hoping someone would resuscitate them soon. Annie began by cruising the first row, wishing she'd asked Fiona the color of Colin's Porsche, or if she knew the license plate number. Pricy cars, after all, were fairly common on the island in July and August.

The first row harbored models of various high-end SUVs and an occasional Subaru. She looped around to the second row: Range Rover, Jaguar, Audi. Then the next: Mercedes, Tesla . . . *Good Lord,* Annie thought, *this place could be a photo spread in* GQ. She supposed most of the vehicles belonged to seasonal people who dashed to one city or another, doing business as efficiently as possible, then speeding back to their island lair.

She was musing on this as she coasted through the lot, when suddenly there it was: a Porsche. Silver. With a license plate from . . . Nebraska? She doubted that Colin Littlefield had at some point moved from New York to Nebraska. Besides, the vehicle was one of those large four-door ones, and from what Annie had gleaned, Colin traveled solo.

She continued to canvass the area; another Porsche was in the back. But it was a red one. With a Massachusetts vanity plate that read: PGIRL. *Porsche Girl?* Annie wondered. Definitely not Colin.

Leaving the main lot, she was about to give up when she spotted what looked like an older model parked off to one side, nearly out of sight. It had New York plates, which was a good sign; it was black, with a T-bar roof. *A classic,* Annie thought, though cars were hardly her forte. She was, after all, still driving a now eight-year-old Lexus that she'd planned to trade in for a sensible, less costly SUV before winter. If only she could find the time.

She stopped Kevin's pickup in the middle of the lot, got out, and tiptoed toward the Porsche as if she intended to steal it. Crouching down, she cupped her hands on the driver's window and peered in. A map of the island was haphazardly tossed onto the passenger seat; beside it was an empty, crumpled wrapper from what looked like a protein bar. There was also a small white card that at first Annie thought had been part of the protein bar packaging. Then she realized it was a reservation card from the Steamship Authority, the same size as the boarding passes that were issued—both of which were given when a vehicle went into the SSA lot before getting in line. Upon boarding, the pass was given to the ticket taker; the reservation card typically stayed with the vehicle to present for the return trip.

If this really was Colin's car, the card would have been printed with the date he'd arrived and the date he'd planned to leave.

Evidence, she thought, though she wasn't sure how it could help launch a case against him. Unless it could prove he'd been on the same boat as Myrna and her poisonous cakes.

But Colin was gone now, not by boat, but apparently by air. Where had he gone? Had he left right after he was sure Fiona had ingested the poison? Had he wanted to escape in a hurry but couldn't change his ferry reservation because the boats were booked? It had been, after all, the Fourth of July weekend.

Maybe he had abandoned his car and taken off so that by the time the police began to look for him, he would have been long gone. If he'd taken Cape Air, JetBlue, or another commercial carrier, he would have had to show his identification. Now that she'd found his car, it might save the police valuable time. She'd be sure to tell them about it in the morning.

While Annie was still crouched, peering and pondering, she felt a sudden firm tap on her shoulder.

She jumped, whacking her hand on the sideview mirror. "Ouch," she said, followed by, "Oh. Crap," when she saw that the tap had come from a man in a gray-and-black uniform, wearing a hat with a wide, shiny brim and an unwelcoming look on his face: a Massachusetts State Police officer.

"Is this vehicle yours?" he asked, pointing to the Porsche.

"No," she replied, gesturing toward Kevin's truck. "That one is. I was just checking to see if this belongs to a friend. He was on the island last week, but he left . . ." She knew she was rambling; she only hoped she sounded a little believable.

"License and registration, please."

His request was ordinary, with no cause for alarm. Until she quickly remembered she'd not only left Kevin's pickup running, but she had no idea where the registration was.

"Well," she said weakly, walking back to the truck, "I have my license, but the truck belongs to my brother."

The officer didn't comment; she now felt totally intimidated. Should she mention John's name? How well did the state police and the local ones know each other? More than likely, very well. But would it help? Or could she get arrested for trying to influence a cop?

She opened the passenger door of the cab, hoping that the registration was in the glove box. She tried to pull it open, but it was locked. She smiled at the officer, reached across the seat, turned off the ignition, and removed the keys, which jangled as she fumbled, probing for a small one that might fit the lock. She wondered why a man who had sold his company and did not have a viable job would need to have so many keys.

She found a silver one. By then her hand was trembling, though she had no idea why. She hadn't done anything wrong. Not really.

With a half turn of the key, the lid flopped down. But her relief was quickly thwarted as she, and the officer, looked into the compartment. There, sitting alone and looking less than innocent, was a gun, as shiny as the wide brim on the state police hat.

"You have a permit for that?" the officer asked.

Annie's stomach cramped again, the way it had when she'd read John's dismissive text. But now she pressed her hand against it, leaned to one side, and promptly threw up.

Chapter 20

"How was I supposed to know you had a gun?"

"It's a pistol, Annie. I never thought I had to tell you. It's not a big deal."

"It feels like a big deal. It felt like a big deal when I threw up on the statie's shoes. It felt like a big deal when he snapped the handcuffs around my wrists and 'escorted' me into the back of his police car. It felt like a big deal when Officer Williams—that's his name, in case you'd like to know—paraded me through the police station in front of several people—some of whom probably know John and might have recognized me as his . . . whatever."

"I told you, I'm sorry. When you asked to borrow the truck, I was talking to Taylor . . . I'd had a beer . . . I wasn't thinking . . ."

"Mr. MacNeish?" Officer Williams came back to the area where he'd told Annie to sit on a wooden bench and wait. Taylor had given Kevin a ride to the Oak Bluffs barracks. At least the woman had the sense to wait outside. Or maybe Kevin had told her to.

Kevin stood up.

"Okay," the officer said, "you're all set. Sorry for the confusion."

"No, officer," Kevin said, "I'm the one who's sorry. Annie needed a vehicle, and it never occurred to me . . ."

"Not a problem. The glove box was locked, so that was good. And the handgun wasn't loaded. I know you're licensed to conceal, but you might want to make sure it stays locked up while you're on the island. There's really no need for it here."

"Yes, sir," Kevin said, though the officer was at least ten years his junior. Annie wondered if he was going to salute him.

"One more thing. Ms. Sutton?"

She stood next to Kevin. "Yes?"

"Your friend. The one who owns a Porsche? What was his name again?"

Once he'd seen the gun, he seemed to have forgotten that she'd been scoping out the Porsche. "Colin," she said now. "Colin Littlefield. He has a house next door to me on Chappy. I live at the Flanagan place."

"Year-round?"

"Yes. Well, I thought it was. It's a long story, but I'm working on it." She didn't think he'd care to hear about her housing woes. He might, after all, have some of his own.

"Well, I don't know Mr. Littlefield, but I do know that isn't his car. The registration is not in his name."

More than being surprised, Annie was baffled. She wanted to ask whose name was on the registration but didn't want to push what little luck she might have left. Besides, she figured he wouldn't tell her, anyway, thanks to privacy issues and all that.

"Thank you," she said. "I'm sorry for all your trouble."

The officer nodded once and said, "Have a nice evening," as if they'd just met at a cocktail party.

Kevin nodded back, took Annie by the elbow, and guided

her to the front door. Once outside, she said, "I can't believe you have a gun. Care to tell me why?"

"No special reason, other than I live in the city. And I used to own a business. Sometimes I had cash on me. I got a permit for protection. If it's any comfort to you, this is the first time anyone—other than me and the guy who sold it to me—has seen the damn thing. But what's the deal with you? I can't believe you went to the airport looking for Littlefield. For God's sake, Annie, he could be a murderer."

She shook off his hand. "As far as any of us know, he hasn't killed anyone. Yet. And I would have asked you to come with me, but you were too wrapped up with Taylor, and I really don't want her knowing any of this. Did you tell her?"

"Not a word. I promise."

As if on cue, Taylor got out of her pickup. "Everything all right now?"

"A misunderstanding," Kevin said. "Do you mind driving us to the airport so I can get my truck?"

"Climb in. There's not much room in the cab, but you two are family, so I don't suppose you'll be freaked out by the tight quarters."

Annie couldn't remember what Taylor might or might not know about the brief history of her connection to Kevin, but right then, it seemed like the last thing she wanted the woman to dissect.

Annie and Kevin didn't speak again until they were inside his truck, and Taylor had gone on her way. "I don't suppose they gave you food in your cell," he said matter-of-factly.

She laughed because he truly was one of the good guys. "I wasn't in a cell."

"I know. I was trying to break the ice. In case you were still pissed at me."

"I'm not pissed at you, Kevin. And, no, I did not have any food. No lunch. Or dinner, since it's probably time for that. I'm starving."

"Good. How do you feel about pizza?"

"Didn't you and Taylor have a burger?"

"We'd just placed our order when you called from the pokey."

Annie laughed again. "The pokey? You really are hilarious. But what about your girlfriend? Didn't we just blow her off?"

"Not really. I'm taking her out for dinner tomorrow night."

Annie waited for the punch line. When none came, she looked at him in disbelief. She'd referred to Taylor as his girlfriend as a joke. "Oh, my. You like her, don't you?"

"Well, she is sort of different. I like that."

"Sort of different" was an understatement when it came to Taylor. But Kevin was her brother. There was no guarantee that he would have chosen Brian—or, God help her, Mark—as a perfect match for her. But she bet he would have been supportive. So instead of telling him what she really felt, Annie said, "Good. Maybe you both deserve a little fun." She looked back out the window, at the sky that was turning pink with the sunset. "But please, don't mention anything to her about Fiona, okay? Until it's straightened out, the fewer people who know, the safer everyone will be."

He raised his right hand. "Scout's honor. Now let's get pizza. With all the restaurants on this island, it hadn't occurred to me that someone could starve to death."

"If your gun was loaded, you could always go hunting for our dinner. But not on Chappy. I've been told there aren't any squirrels there."

"Very funny."

"Thank you."

They laughed together, and he pretended to cuff her on

the arm—the way she had done to him—as if they were children.

"Besides," he added, "now that you've uncovered my firearm, there's something else about me it might be time for you to know."

Annie stopped laughing and looked at her brother, trying to determine whether he was serious or simply teasing her again.

"It's about my wife," Kevin said, once they'd been seated at Edgartown Pizza and placed their order.

Annie took a long drink of ice water and tried to will away a sense of impending dread. She wanted to ask, "Did you shoot her?" because she thought that might be funny, but Kevin's somber face warned her that the time for laughter had passed.

"What about your wife?" she asked. "Didn't she . . . leave?"

"In a manner of speaking, yes. But not how you think. She didn't pack up her things and walk away. It wasn't like that."

Then Annie had a terrible thought: Had his wife died, the way John had led Earl to believe? Deciding to let him tell his story without her interrupting, she waited, which wasn't easy due to her penchant for curiosity. So much curiosity, her dad had often said with his endearing chuckle.

"You know I owned a construction company," Kevin finally began.

She nodded.

"What you might not know is that Meghan—my wife—worked for me. Not in the office. She was one of my best workers in the field. In fact, she was a foreman."

"Really?" Annie said. "Good for her."

"She *was* good. And she loved it. Loved to get her hands dirty. Hell, I envied her. She had all the fun while I was mostly stuck in the office bidding on jobs, keeping the work coming

in, dickering with vendors. I always thought the most important part of my job was to make sure everybody got paid every
week. And that they stayed safe."

Suddenly, Annie's imagination usurped her curiosity. She
thought for sure that Kevin was going to tell her his wife had
run off with one of the construction guys. Someone younger,
maybe. A bad boy straight out of a romance novel. But he'd
said that Meghan hadn't packed her things and left.

Had . . . had he shot her with his gun? If she'd died, was
that how it happened? Annie wriggled on the chair. Her skin
felt prickly. Just because no one but her brother and the guy
who sold him the gun had seen it before she had, it didn't
mean Kevin didn't shoot Meghan . . . in the back. After all,
though he was Annie's half brother, she hardly knew him. For
that matter, she hardly knew her birth mother—their mother—
either.

"We did a lot of big jobs," he was saying. "Malls. Office build-
ings. That kind of thing. Three and a half years ago, just before
Christmas, we were trying to meet a deadline up in Swampscott.
We'd lost time because of bad weather. Anyway, Meghan was on
the job. Up on scaffolding. Four floors aboveground. I warned
her about the wind that day. I pleaded with her to take the day
off. When that didn't work, I told her to be extra careful. She
was a perfectionist; she wanted to get the last of the windows
in before the crew broke for the holiday. That's what she was
doing when the whole damn thing collapsed."

So Meghan hadn't left. She must be dead. Crushed in the
scaffolding. Which would mean that John hadn't been off base.
And that Annie felt terrible for mocking it.

The pizza arrived. Kevin stared down at it as if not knowing where it had come from or why it was there.

And Annie reached across the table, touched his hand, and
simply said, "Kevin. My God."

He raised his head again and looked at her, his eyes glisten-ing like the sun off the water. "After that, it was like I stepped onto the sidelines of my life. Out of action. On the bench. I'm only now starting to come around. Especially in these past few days."

"Kevin, I'm so sorry. I can't imagine what that was like. But I know what loss feels like. I lost my first husband, Brian, when we were still in our twenties. He was killed in a car accident. Did Donna tell you that?"

Kevin scowled. "Meghan isn't dead."

Now Annie was even more confused. "But . . ."

He stared down at the pizza again, his eyes moving from the peppers to the mushrooms to the pepperoni. "Mom insists on just telling people that I'm single again. Which makes it seem like I'm divorced. But I'm not. And Meghan's still alive. She has traumatic brain injury. I guess she's doing better physically, but she doesn't recognize me." He picked up his glass of water and set it down again without taking a sip.

"Kevin . . ."

"She's in a long-term rehab facility in Vermont. It's a nice place, but our insurance only covered two years. Now, it's self-pay. Which is the real reason I sold my business. I used a chunk of it to set up a trust for her ongoing care." His tears dripped onto the band of crust that circled the slices in front of him. "I should have stopped her from going up that day."

Annie guessed it wasn't the first time he'd said that. And many more times that he'd felt it. She knew that once guilt took hold of someone's heart, it often was a long time before it loosened its grip. She'd seen it in Brian's parents' eyes, the guilt over having convinced him to stay a few minutes longer before he'd headed home to Annie. But he never made it. Sure, he'd been hit by a drunk driver, but if he'd only left five or ten or fifteen minutes earlier . . . there would always be that "but."

"Do you still go to see her?" she asked.

"It's been over a year since I did. Mom is the strong one in the family. She convinced me that I wasn't helping Meghan, that I might even be making things harder for her. She said the time had come for me to let go and move on." He gave her a halfhearted smile. "It's taken a while, but here I am. Moving on."

Annie remembered John's remark that most people moved to the Vineyard either because they were in hiding or they were trying to start over. She wondered if Kevin might become part of the island, too. If he would find a new home there, the way that she had. Without further hesitation, she said, "I have an idea. Let's ask them to box up the pizza and we'll go to John's. If you want, we can stay up all night and talk. Or watch stupid old movies. If you want to sleep, I can go into his daughters' room. No matter what, you'll know you're not alone. Sometimes being alone really sucks."

He laughed. "No kidding. But if you don't mind, I'd be awful company and that would upset me more. Your offer means more than you'll ever know. In fact, it makes me feel a whole lot better. But I think I should go home and go to bed. Tomorrow is a Monday, and I have a high-pressure job these days." Not for the first time, Annie saw herself in his sensitive smile.

"Okay," she said. "But only if you're absolutely, positively sure."

"I am. Honest." He looked back at the pizza. On the half that faced him, he peeled off the pepperoni slices and stacked them on the other half. Then he signaled to the waitress. "May we have two boxes? She'll take the half with the extra pepperoni." The waitress left, and he turned back to Annie. "My stomach gets messed up when I'm upset."

Like brother, like sister, Annie thought with a sad smile.

It was only nine o'clock when Annie finally got back to the cottage. Her body, however, felt as if she'd been up all night. Plugging her phone into the charger, she crawled into bed. The gift of sleep washed over her—just as her cell phone rang.

She almost didn't answer it. She almost didn't even roll onto her side and pick it up to see who was calling. But a quick thought of Kevin flashed into her mind, followed by one of Claire. And Earl. She hadn't even thought of John, so she was befuddled when she lifted the phone and saw that it was him. Fear gripped her: Something bad must have happened.

"Jesus, Annie," he said when she answered, "what the hell's going on?"

Rubbing her eyes, she pulled herself to a sitting position. It was hot in the bedroom; she realized she'd forgotten to turn on the fan as she always did to bring in the cool night breeze. "Everything's fine." She paused. "Isn't it?"

"You tell me."

Now she was really confused. "Well, I think your mother goes to rehab in the morning. That's good, isn't it?"

"This isn't about my mother, Annie. It's about you. What the hell are you doing with a gun?"

"I don't have a gun." Then her brain fog cleared and the weight of her body sank into the mattress. "Oh. That was Kevin's gun. But don't worry—he has a license."

John fell silent. She wondered if he was sitting in his ex's house or if he'd sneaked outside to talk as if he still was married and Annie was the other woman.

"How's Lucy?" she asked.

"Don't change the subject. Do you have any idea what it's like to get a call from the state police telling me they'd brought you into custody? That you had a gun and said you were looking for Colin Littlefield?"

Oh, she thought again. That certainly verified that Officer Williams had known exactly who she was and about her relationship to John.

"Colin had nothing to do with the gun," she said. "In fact,

he's still missing. No one's seen him since the night of the Fourth. He probably went back to New York. It couldn't have been easy for him to be at his ex-girlfriend's wedding." Annie was still amazed at how much Vineyarders knew about one an-other's lives.

"Are you going to tell me the rest?"

Earlier that night, she'd wanted to share it all with him. But now she knew it would mean having to include everything that had happened since he'd left: how Fiona had been poisoned, for which the girl blamed her brother and now her sister, too; how the police—his coworkers—hadn't yet responded even though there was a toxicology report; how Annie had decided to try and help the girl. But with everything John was going through, it seemed ridiculous to bother him with it all. Espe-cially since she was so tired that she only wanted to sleep.

"Honestly, John, it was nothing. I was driving Kevin's truck. I stopped because I thought I recognized Colin Littlefield's Porsche." There was no need to say she'd actually been searching for it. "A police car came along and asked me what I was doing. When he asked for my license and registration, I went into Kevin's glove box for the registration and a gun was there. He has a permit. It wasn't loaded. So it was just a mix-up. But please, tell me about Lucy. Did she . . . ?"

"Have the abortion? No."

Annie wanted to ask what everyone was waiting for. She knew from experience that it was essential to have one earlier rather than later. She also thought it would be in Lucy's best interest to get it over with. Unless the girl had refused to have the procedure. Would a thirteen-year-old be allowed to have a say in such a huge decision?

"I don't understand," was all Annie could say.

John's sigh was long and heavy. "She wasn't pregnant after all. She says she thought she was because . . . oh, it's stupid. The fact is, she's still a virgin. Or she was until the doctor examined her. I don't know if that counts. Jesus, Annie, I'm in way over my head on all this."

"Did she . . . does she . . . have a boyfriend?"

"She thought she did. They did some groping . . . God, I can't even talk about this, okay?"

"Yes, but . . ."

"But I have to stay a while longer. No matter what has or hasn't happened, my kid is going through something painful. I need to be here to help."

Annie chewed her lower lip. "Of course. Of course you do. Which is all the more reason you don't need to worry about me. Or your mother, either."

"It was really a mistake? That business about the gun?"

"A total mistake." She hated to hang up. She hated that once she did, she wouldn't know when they'd talk again. Still . . . "Well," she finally said, "you'd better go."

"Yeah. I should get back inside."

So. He had been on the front steps or the back ones or sitting in his damn truck. As if Annie were the other woman, after all.

She said goodbye and rang off, then closed her eyes again. But this time sleep would not come, did not come until the dawn began to creep into the cottage and she simply was worn-out.

Chapter 21

"Did they say who owns the Porsche?" Fiona asked Annie the next day as they walked the side streets of the village toward the police station. "Colin lives in New York. Maybe he borrowed someone else's car."

"They didn't say. And I didn't ask. Frankly, I was more concerned that I was going to be arrested." Her words sounded harsh as if she were annoyed, which she was. Fiona hadn't asked if she was all right after the ordeal, nor had she apologized for dragging Annie into her mess. But Annie was older and supposedly wiser, so she tried to remember what Fiona had been going through and how she now felt alone. Until recently, Annie, too, had been alone—without a family—for years. Of all people, she should be empathetic.

They passed the sweet, small St. Andrew's church, where the front doors were open every day, then walked by the Black Sheep mercantile and café (no relation to the Black Dog) and the thrift shop.

They turned onto Main Street, then went past the cinema where Annie and John had spent many snowy nights. She wondered if next winter she'd still be on the island, and if she and John would still be together. Despite her inquiries and ads, she hadn't heard about another place to live. Maybe Taylor had spread the word that Annie Sutton was too fussy.

Passing the majestic Old Whaling Church, Annie and Fiona took a left onto Peases Point Way and finally made it to the station.

The man behind the glass window looked familiar, but Annie did not know his name; Fiona lagged behind, as if expecting her to take the lead.

"We need to speak with someone about a possible poisoning," Annie said.

"Human or animal?" the cop asked.

"Human."

"Me," Fiona interrupted. "Someone tried to poison me. You already have the toxicology report."

The officer stared at her for a few seconds, then said, "Wait there."

They stood in silence for several moments. Then a side door opened and the cop waved them in. Annie drew in a breath: being in two police stations in two days was a new and not terribly pleasant experience.

He led them to a desk in a corner where Annie saw John's friend Detective Lincoln Butterfield talking with a man who had his back to them. Lincoln was an older guy, married to a schoolteacher on the island, and they had three kids. Annie and John had been to their house for dinner a few times: It was a slightly cramped but inviting ranch out by Felix Neck, the Audubon wildlife sanctuary.

Lincoln stood and extended his hand. "Annie. Nice to see you again."

She was surprised that he'd ignored whoever sat by the desk until the man turned around: It was Roger Flanagan, her landlord, at least for the next few weeks.

"Roger," Annie said. She resisted the urge to say, "Fancy meeting you here." Why on earth did he keep popping up?

"Hello, Mr. Flanagan," Fiona said with a happy grin.

"Let's get a couple more chairs," Lincoln said. "I think we all should have a chat."

The officer who'd brought them in rallied two more chairs and set them facing the detective's desk. Roger adjusted his so they sat in a lopsided circle.

"So," Lincoln continued after everyone was seated. Annie, for one, was perplexed by the convocation and was eager to hear what he had to say. "It seems that everyone is here for the same reason."

Fiona blinked, then looked at Roger. "Mr. Flanagan, do you know who poisoned me?"

He ignored her and turned back to Lincoln. "As I previously said, I wish to speak to counsel."

"A lawyer?" Fiona asked. "You want a lawyer? Are you the one who did it?"

Roger rotated his eyes up to the ceiling. "Exactly as I suspected."

Lincoln rocked back in his chair. "Ms. Littlefield, apparently Mr. Flanagan is concerned that you might think he is somehow connected to the poison you ingested. He is worried you might bring a lawsuit against him by trying to suggest you'd been poisoned at his party."

"It was not a 'party,'" Roger said. "It was my daughter's wedding reception."

"But I was one of the bridesmaids!" Fiona cried, as if that was relevant. Annie put a hand on Fiona's shoulder to try and calm her, though the gesture did not seem to help. "Why would I think you tried to poison me? I've known you my whole life!"

Again, Annie didn't know what one thing might have to do with the other, but she did not want to interrupt. She couldn't imagine how she'd react if she were in Fiona's shoes. Flip-flops. Or whatever.

"He's not concerned that you think he did anything on purpose. More like you might want to sue him for negligence in providing poisoned food. In which case, he is prepared to sue you for defamation of character."

She swerved back to Roger. "But I told you I thought Colin did it!" Her eyes grew hazy; her thoughts must have felt even blurrier. "Now I think it might have been my sister, Sheila. Maybe they were in on it together. Why would I sue you? Why would you sue me?" She looked genuinely confused, though Annie wasn't. In her experience, the worst part of having lots of money was that people tended to look over their shoulders as if expecting that someone would take it from them.

Roger's thin lips seemed fixed in a closed position, as if he'd lined them with Gorilla Glue. Then he stood. "If you will excuse me, officer. I really don't believe I should engage in this conversation until I have consulted my attorney."

Lincoln remained sitting. "You won't leave the island?"

"Not until after Labor Day. Same as always." He glanced down at Annie as he began to leave. "Nice to see you, Annie," he said, as if they were at a garden party. Politeness seemed to abound on the island. But that thought reminded her that Roger was one of the garden tour patrons whose name she'd typed into the program from the list in Claire's pink file folder. He no doubt now knew she had filled in for Claire; she wondered if he expected Annie to say thanks.

Once he was gone, Annie spoke up. "This has become bizarre, Lincoln." She told him it appeared that Colin had left the island, though they did not know how or when. She started to tell him about the Porsche, but Lincoln said he already knew about her "encounter" with Officer Williams in the airport parking lot. A deep flush rose in her cheeks.

"Tell him the rest," Fiona said, nudging her. "Tell him about the honey cake and how Colin and Sheila were on the boat when that woman gave them the cake made out of the poisoned honey."

Annie sighed and related the entire story.

"Have you told John all of this?" he asked when she was finished.

She shook her head. "He's away," she said, as if Lincoln wouldn't have known that.

Lincoln cleared his throat and tapped a pen on his big metal desk. "Well, Ms. Littlefield, as I see it, whether or not you were actually a target remains to be seen," he said, looking squarely at her. "Anyone could have eaten the cake. No one force-fed you, is that correct?"

"Well . . . no, but . . ."

He raised his hand to shush her. "We've already checked, and there's no record of your brother having left the island by ferry or by air. So he must still be here, unless he was a walk-on on the ferry or took off in a private boat or plane, over which none of us has any control or way of knowing."

"He had a car," Fiona interrupted.

"Precisely. So our best guess is he's still here. Somewhere up island maybe. Your family has spent many summers here—I'm sure he has plenty of friends around. As for your sister, she has been seen at her house, though Seattle law enforcement hasn't yet caught up with her. It seems unlikely that she'd have come all the way across the country to poison you, then race back, doesn't it?"

"But . . . have you checked the airlines out of Boston and Providence? To see if Sheila was a passenger . . ."

Lincoln looked at her with a frozen stare. He didn't need to vocalize that they hadn't dropped the ball on this, but that it was summer and, yes, while they had better things to do, they were on top of things. He also did not remind her that no matter what had happened she was fine and had most likely not been in any real danger.

Annie squared her shoulders. "Will you at least talk with the people at Sweet Everything Farm? That's where the cake was made. The owners later learned the honey was poisonous, most likely from nectar extracted from mountain laurel. Myrna at the farm said they made two cakes; what I don't understand is how one wound up in the Littlefields' kitchen." If the police had already done so much groundwork, she was surprised that, busy or not, they did not seem to view the case as a priority.

Raising the shush signal again, Lincoln said, "You've obviously done some research, Annie. But, honestly, this appears to have been an accident. My bet is Colin saw the cake and brought it home to Fiona because he knew she likes them."

"He does!" Fiona cried. "He knows I do!"

He narrowed his eyes. "But that isn't everything, is it, Ms. Littlefield? What I mean is, this is not the first time you've reported that someone has tried to kill you."

Annie sat up straight.

Fiona went as white as the paint on the Old Whaling Church. "That was a long time ago."

"Three years is not so long." His eyes flicked over to Annie. "According to Mr. Flanagan, Ms. Littlefield accused a coworker in New York City of trying to kill her in order to get a part in a play."

"It wasn't a play," Fiona said. "It was *Swan Lake*. I was auditioning for Odette—the lead—for the first time. Mimi Hernandez cut the ribbon on my shoe. I know she did! I fell during the audition. . . ." Fiona started to cry.

Lincoln looked at Annie again. "Before Mr. Flanagan came in today, he'd already notified us about that incident. Apparently, he learned about it straight from you, Ms. Littlefield. He said he'd run into you at his daughter's apartment in New York, where you were crying because you hadn't gotten the part. Do you remember that? He also said you were upset because the police determined that ribbon had frayed, that it had not been cut. I spoke with the NYPD, who have corroborated that. As for the cake, while it might have contained tainted honey, as I said, no one force-fed it to you."

"But . . . but Colin and Sheila have always known it's my favorite. Even Dana knew. Like I already told you, every summer Colin and Dana made one just for me. . . ." She jerked her head toward Annie, then back to Lincoln. "Were she and Colin in on it together? But Dana is my friend! I was her bridesmaid!" Then she whined, "Oh, what on earth is going on?"

Lincoln shook his head. "I doubt that anything is 'going on,' Ms. Littlefield. Without further evidence, all signs point to it having been an unfortunate accident." He stood up, a clear sign of dismissal.

As they walked back to the Kelley House, Annie gently told Fiona that the detective might be right. "I know it seems to you that it was intentional, but maybe it was merely a strange coincidence."

Fiona didn't answer right away, then she said, "You don't believe me, either, do you?"

"I didn't say that. But maybe there's another side to the story."

"So what am I supposed to do? Stay here and wait for something else to happen?"

Annie thought about it while they walked. She wished she were convinced that Detective Butterfield was correct—her life would be much easier if she told Fiona that, then sent her on her way, and returned to her own to-do list. But something about Roger Flanagan's story seemed slightly out of sync—or, at the very least, the timing of it was suspicious. Then again, maybe Annie had been prejudiced by the fact that she now despised the man who had tossed her from her home. Maybe he was truly fearful that Fiona was out to get him for no logical reason. After all, no one else at the wedding had been poisoned, had they? But why would he think Fiona would want to sue him? Was his assumption based solely on an accusation she'd once made about another ballerina? And why would he threaten to sue her back? What was his real agenda? As they passed the ice cream shop and the bookstore, Annie said, "Fiona? Tell me about Dana."

"You think she was in cahoots with my brother and sister? I thought she was my friend. I know I'm younger than she is, but when we were growing up she was always nice to me. When she asked me to be in her wedding party, I was so excited. Sheila thought it was stupid, though. She said that Dana only asked because she felt sorry for me."

"Why?"

"I have no idea. Maybe because I'm almost thirty-four, and I've never been married? Dana was married and divorced twice before she married this new guy. The first wedding was an elaborate fête at St. Patrick's in the city. The second was smaller, of course. It was at the Old Whaling Church here. This time she got married in her backyard. It was the only time I was asked to be a bridesmaid. So, yes, maybe she felt sorry for me. Or maybe she'd used up all of her other friends with her more glamorous weddings. I didn't care. I was excited to be a bridesmaid."

That was all news to Annie, not that it really mattered. But married for the third time? She was tempted to ask Fiona how young Dana had been when Jonas had been born. It didn't seem that Jonas was Colin's son, but if Dana had gotten pregnant by another guy while still dating Colin, then dumped Colin and married Jonas's father, no wonder Colin would have bolted as soon as the ceremony ended. Then Annie wondered if the bride was as coldhearted about relationships as her father was about . . . well, about a lot of things in life. Except his precious grandson. Then Annie had another thought, one she suspected had come straight from Murphy. "Has Mr. Flanagan ever mentioned that he'd like to buy your property?"

Fiona thought for a moment, her flip-flops smacking staccato notes against the sidewalk. "No. Unless he talked to Colin or Sheila and they never told me. It would be like them not to tell me." Then she stopped. "But Mr. Flanagan knows I don't want to sell. I always thought he liked me, too. Do you think he'd try and buy the place out from under me?"

Annie refrained from saying that she would not put anything past her almost-ex-landlord.

Then Fiona gasped. "Oh my God. Did he want the property so badly that he tried to kill me?"

"Whoa," Annie said. "Don't let your imagination run away with you the way mine always does."

Fiona started to walk again, and Annie quickly caught up. "Tell me about your sister. Did the two of you get along when you were young?"

"Not really. I was born ten years after she was, seven after Colin. She used to say I was the 'afterthought,' the 'runt of the litter.' She hated it when Mom or Daddy made her look after me because she was the oldest and she was a girl. She went to college in San Francisco to get far away from home. Then she settled in Seattle. I always figured she stayed away because of me."

"But she must like it here if she wants the property to become a bird sanctuary."

"I have a feeling it would give her a tax write-off. She's always been good at knowing the ins and outs of money."

"When was the last time she came to the Vineyard?"

"I don't know. A few years ago. I don't think she's been here since our mother died, unless she came to see if Mom left any valuables. I'm not surprised that she's in Seattle and didn't show up for the wedding. Even if she wasn't in on this stunt with Colin, she's probably angry that Dana got married again. I think she'd always hoped Dana would have married my brother. Sheila had a crush on her from when they were little kids."

"Sheila had a crush on Dana?"

"Long before any of us knew she was a lesbian."

"What about your brother? He was in the marine corps, wasn't he?" She wanted to ask if there was any chance he was Jonas's father, but that felt more like gossip than something directly related to the problem.

Fiona stopped and stared at her. "Have you seen Colin's movies?"

"No," Annie replied, not wanting to admit to her Google search. "But I've heard about them."

They started walking again, then Fiona folded her arms around her waist as if she'd caught a sudden chill in spite of the heat. "Daddy encouraged him to do them. He said the work might help Colin be productive, find his place in life, you know? But Daddy died before Colin pulled everything together. I think that was why he thought Sheila would invest in the first one. Out of respect for Daddy." She shrugged. "Colin was wrong about that."

"Did your brother have problems after having been in Afghanistan? Like, did he have posttraumatic stress?"

If Fiona wondered how Annie knew Colin had been there, she didn't ask. "I doubt it. He worked in an office the whole time. Keeping track of what supplies were doled out where. No. Daddy worked some magic to keep Colin out of the fighting. As for my brother, the only thing he was ever very good at was not living up to Daddy's expectations."

"Does he work at all?"

"Not that I know of. We live in the same city, but we only see each other once or twice a year. Sometimes I text him to make sure he's okay, and he usually replies, so I guess that's good."

"Do you think he needs money? Is that why he wants to sell the house?"

"I don't know. Out trust funds aren't humongous. He might have blown through his, driving a Porsche and all."

Annie was overcome with sadness then. Sadness for a family that apparently had never quite gotten their act together, despite having had all the theoretical ingredients.

As they reached the intersection at Water Street, Fiona said, "I guess I need to go back to New York and pretend this never happened. I should let them sell the house and forget about it. But thanks for all your help. You're the only one who hasn't been against me." She sounded genuine, not like an immature ballerina who was merely seeking attention.

Every lick of sense left in Annie warned her that she should let Fiona go, that Annie had done enough, that there was nothing left to do. But as her pal Murphy had said many times, Annie had a bad habit of cheering for the underdog.

"Come on," she heard herself quietly say. "Let's go to Among the Flowers. I'll buy lunch. Or only tea, if that's what you want. Then I'll help you pack."

Fiona nodded. "Thanks. I'll try to get a flight off island tomorrow."

Chapter 22

When Annie finally got home, she planned to go online and check for possible postings of new rental listings. She knew she needed to step away from Fiona's problems and focus on her own. That's when Earl called.

"Claire's going to be released tomorrow. She's made so much progress, they said she is ready to go to rehab. I don't know what the hell to do."

Once she calmed him down, Annie learned there was no room for Claire at the island rehab facility. Which meant they'd need to find a place off island, to the Cape at best.

"What am I supposed to do?" Earl cried. "I sure as hell am not going to let her go anywhere sight unseen."

"We'll figure something out," Annie said. "Did you speak with someone from social services?"

"The doctor's office called. They gave me a name of somebody to call tomorrow. But I can't wait that long." His voice quivered, as if he was going to cry.

Annie bit her lip. She still didn't know much about the inner workings of the island, but she had an idea. "Are you home now?"

"Yes."

"Did you call John?" Maybe John could help. Maybe he could pull some strings. After all, he was a cop. And, for God's sake, this was an island family that had been there for nearly forever. They should be able to take care of one of their own.

"Will you call him for me? He'll hear how upset I am and, well, we'll end up arguing."

Arguing? "That's ridiculous."

"I know. But it's what we do. We get upset that the other one's upset, and we wind up raising our voices. Claire's always said it's probably a man thing."

Annie sighed and said she'd call. She and Earl rang off, then she quickly dialed John.

But his phone went right to voice mail.

She decided not to leave a message that his ex-wife might or might not delete before he saw it. So she called Earl back.

"I'll go with you to the hospital first thing in the morning," she said. "We don't need to bother John. Somehow, we'll find a way to keep Claire here." Though she had no idea how on earth to make that happen, Earl didn't contradict her. Perhaps he was too distressed.

Before going to bed, Annie finally checked the listings. There was only one new one: an overpriced, small cottage that looked moldy and neglected, the kind of place rodents would turn away from. She shuddered and quickly Googled the *Vineyard Gazette* site, and then wrote a brief editorial in which she thanked the anonymous tourists for calling the EMTs when they'd seen a woman collapse on North Water Street. Annie didn't use Claire's name, but reported that the woman was now doing well, thanks to those caring passers-by.

Shutting off her computer, she felt good about having remembered to do that. She would tell Earl in the morning, and he would be pleased.

Using that positive thought to avoid dwelling on John, she

cleaned up, changed into her nightgown, and slid between her sheets. But just as Annie closed her eyes, her text alert sounded. She softly groaned and checked her phone. The message was from Fiona.

Can't get a flight out until Thursday. I'll be at the Kelley House, if anything comes up.

Annie knew that aside from assorted flights, transportation from the Vineyard to New York was complicated; it usually involved a boat, a bus, sometimes a train, all of which had different schedules. She half-wondered why Fiona didn't call a car service—maybe it was too costly. But instead of asking, Annie simply typed **OK,** set the phone back on the nightstand, and went to sleep.

Tuesday morning, Annie woke up with an idea.

Brilliant! she thought.

Or, it could be a disaster.

She mulled it over while she showered, dressed, and poured a generous mug of coffee. After three sips, she decided it was worth a try. So she retrieved her phone.

"Taylor?" Annie asked. "You're an EMT. Do you have any connections at the hospital that might help us find a rehab bed for Claire?"

After a moment, Taylor said, "The best chance will be if I go with you. I know how to talk my way around those folks. But the sooner we go, the better. I haven't started working yet today. I've had a bit of a late start." She told Annie she'd meet her at Earl's and they could all go together.

It wasn't until they'd rung off that Annie remembered that Kevin had taken Taylor out for dinner the night before. Which might have been why Taylor had had "a bit of a late start."

Earl sat in the small office at the hospital; Annie and Taylor stood behind his chair. On the opposite side of the desk, a woman with gray hair and glasses peered at her computer screen.

"I'm sorry," the woman said. "No available beds show up in the system." She was not the person Earl had been told to call, but rather a woman Taylor knew.

"What about in real life?" Taylor asked. "Like, if we go over there, can't we make a room for her? An old storage closet, maybe? Come on, Martha, you know we did that for my mother after she fell and broke her hip."

The woman nodded and toyed with the short strand of wampum encircling her neck. She removed her glasses and addressed the three of them directly. "I remember, Taylor. I also know that was before the regulations were, well, well regulated. Monitored. It's different today. We have to watch every step we make."

"Who's over there now?" Taylor asked.

"In the rehab office?"

"No. In the beds. Who's there now?"

"I can't tell you that, Taylor. You should know that."

Earl hadn't spoken since they'd walked in and he'd said hello. But now he stood and said, "Sorry to be a bother, Martha. We'll see you at the potluck."

Until then, Annie hadn't realized that the woman must be a Chappy resident.

"No," Martha said, "I'm the one who's sorry, Earl. But hopefully Claire will have a quick recovery and be home before you know it."

He nodded and left the office. Annie and Taylor followed.

Once they were in the corridor, however, Taylor said, "I'm going over to rehab. Go and see that other person, if you want. But I'm not ready to rule anything out."

The person in the social services department was Mick McGuire. A nameplate on his desk included several professional initials that indicated he was a licensed social worker. "Sit, sit!" he instructed with a friendly smile.

Annie and Earl sat. After Annie related the dilemma, Mick McGuire got to work. For more than twenty minutes, he hummed and hawed between keyboard clicks.

"Got one!" he shouted at last, startling his audience.

"Where?" Annie asked.

"Weymouth. Not too far."

Earl snorted. "Over an hour from Woods Hole. Two hours counting the damn boat." He stood up. "Not to mention that it's summer, in case you haven't noticed. How the hell am I supposed to get reservations to bring my truck across to see her? Round trip? Every day?" He stomped out of the office.

Mick McGuire looked at Annie and shrugged. "Sorry. It's really the best that I can do."

Annie thanked him and said they'd let him know. Then she joined Earl in the hall.

"Screw them all," Earl said as he paced a few feet one way, a few feet back. "I'll bring her home. I'll get one of those— what do you call them?—visiting nurses or whatever. I'll have them twenty-four-seven. I'll do it my way."

"She'll still need to see a doctor, though. Maybe not every day, but . . ."

"I don't give a damn. Lived here all my life. Claire, too. I was born in this damn hospital. Well, not this one exactly, but the old one next door. So was John. Before that, the entire Lyons clan was born at home on Chappy. Generations of us, for Chrissake. And now they're telling me there isn't one lousy bed here to take care of my wife? After all we've done for this bloody island?" His face became a scary shade of red; his eyes had narrowed and turned dark.

Then Taylor came around the corner.

"All set," she said as she approached.

"No!" Earl shouted. "I am not letting Claire off this island. And definitely not to Weymouth. It's too goddamned far. And there are only strangers over there."

But Taylor shook her head, her auburn mane swinging from one shoulder to the other. "No. Here. We're all set here. I have a bed for Claire."

Earl stopped pacing. Annie swallowed, pressing her lips together, realizing that she'd been about to cry.

"Bessie Adams is going home today. She said she's sick to death of being here. I called her niece off-island; she's agreed to come and stay with Bessie for a couple of weeks. The doctor has agreed that she'll be fine."

"Bessie Adams?" Earl asked. "I didn't think she liked Claire. Not since Claire took first prize at the Ag Fair for her blackberry jam back in 1981. Up 'til then, Bessie always won. . . ."

"Earl," Annie said, taking him by the arm, "it doesn't matter now. Taylor has seen to it that Claire will stay right here." She turned to Taylor. "Thanks, Taylor. You have no idea how much this means. . . ."

But Taylor only replied, "Yes, I do," and let it go at that.

And Annie was left feeling that maybe Taylor wasn't such a bad sort after all.

Taylor left to take the bus back to the Chappy ferry; Annie and Earl stayed at the hospital until Bessie Adams was released and Claire was moved into the rehab unit—which didn't happen until after 3:00 p.m. Annie congratulated herself for having had the sense to grab them lunch from the hospital café before it closed.

When Claire finally was settled, she shooed them away.

"Since you're ornery as ever," Earl said, "I guess that means you're really getting well." He moved to the window and stared out. "At least you've got a nice view of Lagoon Pond," he added, then nodded as if everything was finally as it should be.

Promising to visit the next day, Annie decided she would wait until then to ask for last-minute advice about the tour. Maybe she'd even ask how well Claire knew Roger Flanagan, since he was a donor to the garden club. Maybe Claire knew if he'd ever expressed an interest in the Littlefield property, and if she thought he might resort to murder in order to get it. As long as Fiona was still on the Vineyard, what harm would there be in trying to find out more?

By the time Annie had dropped off Earl and was back home, she was too tired to open her laptop and work on her manuscript. Her brain didn't seem to want to re-engage in fiction; it somehow wandered back to Taylor.

Taylor knew almost everyone on the island—she'd proved that at the hospital. And chances were she knew way more than she'd admit.

Thinking back to the night Fiona had passed out on the lawn, Annie tried to remember if, when Taylor had first arrived, she'd said anything that might have hinted at something sinister about the family—its past or present. Anything that might provide a morsel that would steer Annie in a new investigative direction. But all Annie recalled was that Taylor had recognized the bridesmaid and that she'd said she'd seen Colin drive off the *On Time* when she was on her way back from seeing a movie. *Jaws.*

With a sigh of surrender, Annie realized that too much was going on for her to focus on her book. So instead of sitting idle—or, worse, making revisions that wound up being neither logical nor good—she decided to drive out to the Indian Burial Ground. Sitting on the hill, looking over Cape Poge Bay, might help clear her head. Though the view pointed east, if she waited long enough, she might get to see the sunset reflected in the sky and on the water. She might as well take advantage of the island's beauty before needing to pack up and leave the way Fiona was.

Grabbing her purse, Annie walked out the door just as her cell phone rang.

"Come for supper," Earl said. "We've got chicken for the grill. And while we were at the hospital, Francine made enough potato salad to feed a whole community supper in February."

"Ammie!"

It wasn't that Bella didn't know Annie's name, but it seemed easier for her to pronounce it with *m*'s instead of *n*'s. Annie laughed, scooped her up, and gave her a big hug. Lately, whenever Annie had a chance to see Bella, life was so frenetic she often forgot to pay close attention to the almost toddler with the big dark eyes. Nothing filled Annie's heart more than knowing that so many people had taken loving guardianship of the little one whose life could have turned out so differently.

"Wine?" Earl asked.

"Sure. It's long past five o'clock, right?"

"Ten past six by my watch."

She followed him into the kitchen, where Francine was busy gathering forks and knives and napkins. "Strawberry shortcake for dessert," she said. "Might be the last of the fresh ones."

One of the best parts of living on the Vineyard was that Annie had become spoiled by mostly consuming food that had been grown, milked, or churned locally. *Even honey,* she thought.

"You want to eat outside or in?" Francine asked.

"Outside is good," Earl replied. "The bugs won't be out 'til later."

Francine plunked the utensils on a platter that held a heap of chicken breasts. She disappeared out the back door as Earl handed Annie a glass of chardonnay.

"So . . . have you talked to my son lately?" he asked.

"Well, yes. Of course. The other night." It had been Sunday night when he'd called to quiz her about the so-called incident with Kevin's gun. *Wow,* she thought. Had that only been forty-eight hours ago? It seemed like a week, maybe two. So far, the summer was projecting a skewed concept of time. Maybe it was due to the heat. Or not.

Earl poured an inch of scotch into a glass. "Let's go into the living room and sit."

Annie sensed there was a reason why he hadn't suggested they join Francine outside. She hoped it wasn't because there was another serious matter.

She set Bella on the carpet and handed her a Baby Learning tablet that the little girl was too young to understand but loved watching the lights. She also seemed fascinated by the electronic voice that spoke whenever she touched a button: "B is for Baby," followed by the sound of a baby laughing; "F is for Frog," followed by a couple of ribbits.

Annie sat on the sofa, Earl in his recliner facing her.

"What's up?" she asked. "Claire's okay, isn't she?"

"Absolutely. She promised I'll kick the bucket before she does." He chuckled.

"Oh, God, please don't tell me you're sick."

"Me? Hell, no. I'll live to be a hundred. That'll teach my wife to be a smart-ass. No, I wanted to talk to you about John."

Oh.

Annie tried to ward off the gentle thump in her gut. Her efforts were futile. John must have told him what had happened at the airport; Earl would more than likely read her the riot act about interfering with police business, because John wasn't there to do it.

"I was wrong," Earl said bluntly. "He might not come back."

That time, Annie's stomach didn't thump. Instead, all the small muscles in her face went slack, as if she were suffering a stroke the way Claire had. She stared at Earl, as if she'd misheard him.

"C is for Cow," said the lady in the box, followed by an elongated *Mooooo*.

Taking a sip of wine, Annie tried to muster a reasonable response. Finally, she asked, "Do you mean, he might not be coming home? To the Vineyard?" She wanted to add the word, "Ever?" but could not get it out of her mouth.

Earl looked at her with a soft gaze. "I called him after you brought me home. I wanted to tell him Claire's in rehab. Anyway, he said that Lucy has some issues."

Of course Annie already knew that. "Yes, but . . ."

"His ex is not going to let her go, but I think it would be best if the girl came back here with him. It's pretty obvious that a big part of her problem is, plain and simple, she misses her dad. She misses the island. And her friends. I guess John figures the only way he can be there for her is to literally do that. Be there. Permanently. Or at least until she goes to college or outgrows this stage or something."

Running her finger around the rim of her glass, Annie fought back tears. "I don't know if I'm more stunned that he's going to stay there or angry that he didn't tell me himself."

"I think he knew you'd be upset."

"Well, he'd be right about that, wouldn't he?"

They sat in silence, then Earl said, "Can I get you anything? Cheese and crackers? A tissue? A morphine drip?"

She pretended to laugh a little, though her thoughts shifted to Kevin's gun for a brief second. She knew, however, that she wasn't capable of suicide. Just as she knew that remorse over lost love was a sad reason to do it.

"I'm fine," she said. "This is not my first rodeo, as my father would have said." The first time he'd said that had been when her mother had left him—had left them—the day after Annie had turned nine. She'd had no idea what he'd meant; she'd only known that life had continued almost as if nothing had happened. She had, however, learned to cook and do the laundry, and she knew that she'd been glad when her mother returned a few weeks later when the rodeo, apparently, had ended. Setting down her glass now, she stood and lifted Bella again. "Let's go outside and watch Francine cook. That will help me feel better than I do right now."

She walked through the living room, the dining room, and the kitchen, with Earl following dutifully behind. When she opened the back door and stepped onto the deck, she saw Kevin standing there. As terrific as she already knew that he was, Annie never would have thought she'd be so damned happy to see him.

Chapter 23

"Please stay!" Francine pleaded with Kevin. "I made too much potato salad and Earl will complain that he has to eat it for a week." She batted her dark lashes at him because Earl had told her she could get a man to do just about anything when she did that. At the time, Annie thought it was offensive that he'd said such a thing to a twenty-year-old, then Francine said she'd already figured that out.

"I love potato salad," Kevin said. "And I'm starving. I got busy rebuilding the Alvords' chicken coop and forgot to have lunch."

"Well then, your wish is my command," Francine said, waving a spatula at him.

"Sit, have a beer until it's ready," Earl said as he wove around Annie and clapped Kevin on the back. "And in the meantime, you can tell us all about your dinner last night with Taylor."

Kevin looked at him a minute, then broke into a smile. "How'd you know about that? Annie, did you tell him?"

"Your sister did not breathe a word. I saw it in the stars. Or maybe it was on page one in the *Gazette*." He retreated back into the house, no doubt to grab a beer for his guest.

Annie could not contain a smile.

"Geez," Kevin said. "I came to my boss's house to report on the awesome work I got done today, and I suddenly feel the way a skunk must feel when it's been entrapped. Or is that ensnared? Never mind. Please. No one make comparisons to what I just said with the way that I must stink. Like I said, it was a long, hardworking day."

The screen door slapped behind Earl and he handed Kevin a bottle. "Drink," he said. "Then talk."

"And don't leave anything out," Francine said.

"Annie?" Kevin pleaded. "Save me?"

"Too late. Around here, I'm afraid you must save yourself. If it's any consolation, though, Taylor is a hero around here today. It's because of her that Claire got into rehab on the island. But I'm afraid that doesn't let you off the hook. You still have to tell us everything about your date. Well, almost everything, I suppose."

Kevin scrunched up his face in a weak attempt to look exasperated, then he laughed and launched into a monologue about dinner at Alchemy, where he'd had the scallops and Taylor had halibut.

"Did she wear her flannel shirt?" Francine asked.

"No. She wore a dress. Black and short and very sexy with black stockings with seams. And did I mention her stilettos with the bright red soles?"

That comment shut up everyone, even Annie, for a few seconds. Then Kevin guffawed. "Ha! Got ya!"

Francine went after him with the spatula again. "You're such a dolt."

"Yes," Kevin replied. "I am at that."

The little group continued to jabber; Annie tuned most of it out. She went down onto the lawn and tried to help Bella attempt another walking step, but the baby kept falling onto her thickly diapered bottom and giggling. But with happy voices of people she loved in the background, and Bella's innocent tumblings, Annie felt the ache of John-might-not-come-back easing bit by bit.

By the time the chicken was grilled and potato salad and sliced tomatoes were heaped onto the plates, conversation about Taylor had dwindled, though Francine expressed sorrow that Kevin would not tell them more.

"There isn't any more," he said. "Scout's honor." He raised his fingers in a way that looked more like a peace sign than a Boy Scout pledge.

Dinner was delicious. By the time Francine served the shortcake and again announced that the berries might be the last of the local season, Kevin asked for a big serving because next year would be a long time to have to wait. He said it as if both he and Annie would still be on the island.

As the sun began to set, Earl asked to be excused so he could call Claire and say good night. Kevin and Annie cleaned up the dishes while Francine put Bella to bed. Then they said their goodbyes and got into their respective vehicles.

Annie headed to her cottage, and Kevin went toward the *On Time* to go back to John's town house. Annie wondered if John would sell it soon, if he'd break all of his island ties except those with his parents.

But, despite the way it had begun, the evening had been nice. Which was why, when Annie pulled into her driveway and Kevin pulled in behind her, the pain, the aching, the thump gripped her again.

He knows, she thought. *And he wants to talk about it.* How could she tell him she did not?

As it turned out, Kevin didn't know.

They climbed out of their vehicles and stood in Annie's driveway, leaning against the hood of Kevin's truck, when he asked what was bothering her. Rather than go into the sordid details that were bound to make her cry, Annie simply said

John didn't know when he'd be able to come back, that the situation with his daughter might need more tending to.

"It sounds upsetting," Kevin said.

"Well, yes. The bottom line is, Lucy is only thirteen. I think she really misses her dad. If anything, this helps to prove to me what a good man he is." She believed it. Sort of. But right then she was tired and didn't want to have to keep pretending that everything was fine. Nor did she want to continue talking about John. She only wanted to go to bed, pull the covers over her head no matter how warm the night, and will herself into sleep. She could not, however, give Kevin the brush-off. Not when it was apparent there was something else he wanted to say.

"So tell me how your date really went last night," she said with pretend enthusiasm. "Did you have a good time?" Despite how Taylor had saved the day for Claire (and Earl), it was still hard to picture Kevin with her. Still hard to picture Taylor with any man. The woman, after all, kept her feminine side well concealed from the general public.

"It was good. To be honest, it was nice to sit across the table from a woman who wasn't my mother or my sister. No offense."

She laughed. "None taken."

"So," he continued, "I've decided I'm going to talk to a lawyer."

Annie thought that by now she would have been accustomed to being startled by the kinds of comments that men sometimes made. But apparently she was not. Not even close. "What does that mean? A lawyer for what?" Dear God, he wasn't afraid that Fiona would accuse him, too, was he?

"I need to find out if I can get a divorce. I don't know what the rules are, but, for God's sake, Annie, I'm so trapped I'm choking. The woman I was married to for over a dozen years doesn't even know who the hell I am. There's a chance she'll stay like this forever. If I could have my wife back, I know I wouldn't feel this way, but to be honest, I've finally started to ask myself, 'What kind of life is this for me?' "

"There's no chance she'll get better?" Annie hated to challenge his motive, but for some reason Kevin seemed smitten with Taylor, and Annie didn't want him to do anything he might regret.

He shook his head. "I've done a lot of reading. The odds are no, especially since it's been such a long time. And every time I think of her I'm reminded that it was my fault."

"It wasn't your fault, Kevin. You tried to warn her, right?"

"I should have stopped her. In addition to being her husband, I was her boss. I should have told her I'd pull her union card if she tried to do something so stupid."

Annie figured that no matter what she said, he would continue to feel that the accident had been because of him. Until he could forgive himself. Though it was far from the same thing, Annie had often felt guilty about the accident that had killed Brian. If they hadn't been married, he would not have been heading home to her when it happened; he might have stayed at his parents' place or been en route to the apartment he'd had before they were married: It was on the other side of the city, so he would not have been anywhere near the drunk driver.

"I don't know what to say," she said now. "Except that I'm here for you, Kevin. And I will be, no matter what you decide. No judgment. Ever." She crossed her hands, held them to her chest. "Let me be your safe zone. Okay?"

With tears in his eyes, he gave her a bear hug. "I am so lucky you came into our lives." The "our," of course, referred to his life and Donna's, their traveling mother, who would be back—finally—in a few weeks.

Annie was about to tell him that he was her brother and she loved him when a rolling, rumbling sound powered through the moment. Kevin must have heard it, too; they stepped out of their hug and stood very still, listening to the trademark sound of a Porsche engine as it roared down the road and turned into the Littlefields' driveway next door.

That time, she wasn't dreaming. "Oh my God," Annie whispered, as if she couldn't let anyone but Kevin hear her. "He's back." She dropped into a squat and squinted toward the house, as if squatting and squinting would help her see through the thick evergreens.

"The bridesmaid's brother?"

"It must be."

"Should you call her? Is she even still here?"

"She couldn't get a flight until Thursday. But, no, I don't think I should call her. What if he's really a killer?"

Kevin laughed. "Death by honey cake? You've been writing too many mysteries, Annie."

"I'm serious. We don't really know what happened. The police are treating it like an accident. But Fiona disagrees. If I call her, she might want to come over and meet him face-to-face."

"Wouldn't that be smart? To get it over with?"

"Not if her being poisoned was intentional."

Kevin joined her now, brother and sister sitting on their heels as if they were children searching for four-leaf clovers in the grass. Or sea glass on the beach. "What if we go over?" he asked. "You and me? What if we confront him? Do you think he'll try to shove honey down our throats?"

"No," Annie said, and straightened up. "More than likely, he'll shoot us. If he has a gun."

Brushing off his jeans, Kevin stood up, too. "You mock me, dear sister. Well, I tell you what. I know this has been bothering you. So let's go over. Safety in numbers, right? If nothing else, maybe he'll tell you something you can take back to Fiona before she leaves."

She smiled. "You sound as if you care."

"You care. That's what matters to me. Besides, I'm starting to like it here. I figure it's not a bad idea to get to know the neighbors."

"They won't be my neighbors for very long."

"Maybe, maybe not. Shall I bring my pistol?"

Annie tossed him a loving glare.

"Okay, then," he said, "shut up and follow me."

Fueled by nervous energy for what they were about to do, Annie redirected him along the path that led between the two estates, praying they wouldn't run into Roger Flanagan. Now that Roger knew she was helping Fiona, he might have her arrested for trespassing. After all, she knew that, like animals, people could sometimes do strange things if they felt backed into a corner.

For the thousandth time, Annie wanted to turn to Murphy's ghost to be her loyal guide. But as she thought that, the familiar voice whispered in her ear: *This time, let your brother help.* Annie laughed and tramped across the lawn.

Through the tall glass windows of the sunroom, Annie saw Colin standing at the kitchen window. His hair was still blond, like in the image on Wiki; he wasn't tall—five nine, she guessed. Dressed in khaki cargo shorts and a white dress shirt, he looked every bit a preppy as she had envisioned. He was holding a cell phone, staring at the screen.

She motioned for Kevin to follow her to the door where she and Earl had once gained easy entrance.

They stepped undetected into what had been a laundry room, then into the kitchen.

"Colin?" Annie asked in a low, hopefully unthreatening voice.

He flinched. He spun around. "Who the hell are you?"

"Your neighbor. My name is Annie Sutton. I live in the Flanagans' guest cottage. This is my brother, Kevin MacNeish."

Colin's gaze darted from her to him. "I'd say it's nice to meet you, but I'm a little busy. I just learned my sister is in the hospital." He went back to the phone screen and began tapping a message.

"Wait," Annie said. "Fiona's all right. She's been released."

"Where is she?"

"Still on the island. But I'm not sure she wants to see you."

His eyes narrowed and moved back and forth again. "What the hell are you talking about? Who are you, anyway?"

"She told you," Kevin interrupted. "She lives next door. Your sister was in the hospital because she was poisoned the night of Dana Flanagan's wedding."

"And she thinks you did it," Annie interjected. "That you tried to kill her."

He gripped the phone, pursed his lips, and began to tap again. "I'm calling the police," he said.

"Good," Kevin replied. "They've been looking for you."

Colin paused. He studied them, the way Annie had studied him, with obvious caution.

While awaiting his next move, her eyes scanned the room and landed on a wastebasket. She stepped closer to it. It was empty. Perhaps confirmation that he had destroyed the evidence, as Fiona had claimed.

"Where is it, Colin? Where's the honey cake?"

He glowered. "The what?"

"The honey cake," Annie repeated, knowing she wouldn't have dared to say it if Kevin weren't there to protect her. "Where did you dispose of it?"

He folded his arms. "I have no idea what you're talking about. And even if I did, I can't imagine why you'd think it was any of your business."

"Your sister made it my business, Colin. So, please. Tell us what you did with it."

But he stood firm. "You're insane."

They had a standoff for a moment until Kevin cleared his throat. "I hate to tell you, Mr. Littlefield, but my sister is not going to budge. I'm pretty sure you know how stubborn sisters can be. So I suggest you tell her what she wants to know. Otherwise, she'll just stand here all night."

Annie bit her lip so she wouldn't break into laughter. She must remember to thank Donna for giving her an awesome brother, even though he apparently had quickly learned that she could be stubborn. And she must also remember to thank Murphy, who probably had seen to it that Kevin had come to the Vineyard in the first place.

Colin pushed a shock of hair off his tanned forehead, then put his hands in the pockets of his shorts. "Look," he said, his voice sounding almost reasonable. "I honestly don't know what you're talking about. I haven't eaten honey cake since I was probably seventeen. But if you insist there's one here, help yourselves. Check every drawer and cabinet that's left. I don't think you'll find any food, let alone a cake. We live rather minimally these days."

The appliances had strangely been removed since the winter. Annie decided not to mention that someone had put a mini refrigerator and a microwave on the floor. "Fiona said the cake was in a box," she said. "And that the box was next to the sink."

"Well," Colin replied, "then you're right about one thing. As you can see, there's nothing there now."

Annie sighed. "So you never saw a honey cake? And you're saying that a woman on the boat didn't give you one?"

He stared at her for several seconds. Then he said, "Now you say you think that a woman on the boat gave me honey cake? What did she do? Hand me a box and say, 'Here. This is poisonous. Give it to your sister'? Jesus, lady. With all due respect, you're nuts, you know?"

Annie started for the door. Then she turned around. "I don't suppose you want to tell us where you've been since the wedding?"

He glowered again.

Kevin stepped halfway between them as if to prevent a physical altercation, a fisticuff, Annie's dad would have called it. "Look, dude. We've been trying to find you since that night. We know you left Chappy then, but no one's seen you since. Your sister was poisoned just before you disappeared. The police checked the ferry and the commercial airline manifests, but there was no record of you having left the Vineyard."

"First of all," Colin replied, "don't call me 'dude.' I have a name. Second, perhaps I was not clear when I said my life is none of your damn business."

"Okay," Annie intervened. "Though I'm sure the police will think it's their business. The same way they'll want to know who the woman on the boat was. You were seen, Colin, coming from the Cape over to the Vineyard. There's an eyewitness."

He laughed. "I talk with lots of women, Ms. Sutton. Women usually like me. Present company apparently excepted."

"You were standing at the foot of the stairs between the top deck and the freight deck."

He frowned as if trying to remember the moment. The trouble was, if he was putting on an act, he looked believable.

"Was it Sheila?" she prompted.

"Sheila? My sister Sheila?" He laughed. "Hardly. The last place you'll find her is on the Vineyard. She's been very vocal about saying this place is for the birds. Which is why she wants our property to become an aviary. It's her way of thumbing her nose at the whole place—at my parents, actually. They never forgave her for coming out at the Pink and Green Weekend in front of all their friends."

Though Annie hadn't attended, she knew the annual spring weekend was the unofficial kickoff of the Edgartown social season. It seemed more than likely that Sheila had chosen the venue to make her announcement mostly to upset her parents. *Such a strange family,* Annie thought.

Kevin backed away. "If it wasn't Sheila on the boat, who was it?"

"Come to think of it, I did talk to Nicole." Colin nodded. "Yeah, maybe it was Nicole."

Annie wished she could shake the feeling that Colin was playing games with them. "Who's Nicole, Colin?" she asked. "Is she a friend of yours? Is she an islander?"

Colin laughed again. "Are you serious? You don't know her?"

Neither of them answered.

"Nicole Flanagan. Roger's wife. As in the mother of the bride."

In the short time Annie had conversed with Nicole Flanagan, the woman hadn't made a lasting impression. "I'm sorry, but this is a private party," the woman had said when she found Annie standing on their lawn in her long cotton robe. Annie remembered the overly sweet way in which she had spoken—*syrupy,* Earl called her—in contrast to the snobby way that she'd tilted her head.

"Why would Nicole Flanagan have been coming over on the boat the day before her daughter's wedding?" Annie asked. "Didn't she have enough other things to do?"

"If she did, they weren't as important as the fact she'd gone to Falmouth. I remember she had a big pocketbook. It was red. She said she'd picked up custom chocolates for the gift bags, that she didn't trust anyone to ship them. But if she had any cake, she sure as hell didn't give it to me."

Pulling his hands out of his pockets, he planted them on his hips. "Enough," he added. "I need to find Fiona. And I want both of you out of my house. Or I really will call the police and have you arrested for trespassing and for harassment."

Once outside, Annie motioned to Kevin to follow her up the driveway instead of sneaking back along the path. As she suspected, the Porsche was parked a few yards from the house. It had New York plates and it was black.

"It's the same one that was at the airport," she said. As she brushed past it, she glanced inside. On the passenger seat was the same wrapper from the protein bar and the small card that she'd mistaken for a ferry reservation ticket. "So he must have flown off island on a private plane."

"And then he flew back," Kevin said. "Which is even more bizarre if he had nothing to do with Fiona landing in the hospital." Their footsteps crunched over the clamshells. "So what next, Sherlock?"

"Well, just because Myrna gave Nicole—if it really was Nicole—the cakes to throw away, doesn't mean Nicole tucked one in her bag and decided to kill Fiona. First of all, why would she? Fiona Littlefield was her daughter's friend."

"True. And just because Nicole was on the boat doesn't mean Sheila wasn't there, too. Do you think Colin is trying to cover up for his sister?"

"I can't imagine why. He seemed pretty clear that he doesn't speak to either one unless it's to argue about whether to sell the property. But at least Myrna should be able to identify—or not identify—Nicole as the one she told to take the cakes."

"Have you considered that someone else might have wanted Fiona out of the picture?" Kevin asked. "Someone who found out about the cake, then jumped at the chance to poison her?"

"That's ridiculous. Who would it be? Whoever did it would have had to conveniently know that Fiona couldn't resist a honey cake. Sorry, but my editor would call that contrived. Something that would make the whole mystery neither credible nor believable." But as they walked down Annie's driveway, she had another thought. "Although . . ." she said slowly, "Dana would have known."

"Dana, the bride?"

"Sure. She and Colin made the cakes for Fiona every summer. I know that since she was getting married it seems preposterous. . . ."

"Yeah. Besides, why the heck would Dana want to kill Fiona?"

Annie shook her head. "You're right. Besides, it's not as if she would have been on the boat with her mother the day before her wedding. It's odd enough that Nicole was."

"Unless it took two people to bring the chocolates from the Cape. And unless someone else was with Nicole who Colin or Myrna didn't see."

"Maybe. But, honestly, of any of them, Colin is the only one who might have motivation. I'm not sure he was telling us the whole truth, but he did seem fairly surprised." She shook her head. "Maybe Nicole simply forgot to trash the cakes, brought them home, and somehow one made its way next door to Fiona. And it was an accident. And Fiona overreacted."

Kevin tossed her a look that said that was a stupid assumption.

They reached his truck that was parked behind Annie's car. "Come on. Let's go see her," Annie said. "I want to see how she reacts when we tell her what Colin claims."

"Now? You don't want to wait until tomorrow?"

"Tomorrow I'll be busy. The garden tour is Thursday, and I promised Claire I'd make the rounds to make sure everything is in place. Let's go in your truck. I'll walk back from the *On Time*."

"Have you noticed it's already dark out, as in nighttime? It will be even darker when we're done with Fiona. And as you've told me, there are no streetlights on Chappy. Not one."

"I'll grab a flashlight. I'm not afraid of skunks."

Chapter 24

It wasn't until Kevin rolled onto the *On Time* that Annie had another thought. "Kevin?" she asked. "Do you think Colin is right? Do you think Fiona is needy? The story the police told about what she did to the ballerina in New York . . . do you suppose there have been other times she's lied?"

Kevin shrugged. "Honestly, I have no idea."

Annie's head had started to hurt. It was so hard to know whom to believe.

The ferry captain started up the engine; there was no need to collect tickets from passengers or the drivers of the three vehicles on board: Tickets were only needed in one direction, from Edgartown to Chappaquiddick. The logic was that once you got there, sooner or later you'd have to make the trip back to the main island. The system worked.

Musing on that now, Annie looked over at Kevin. "One thing we know for sure is that Fiona ate the poisonous cake, right?"

"Well, yeah. Duh."

"What if it was her?"

"Her?"

"Fiona."

Staring straight ahead, Kevin frowned. "You lost me."

Annie twisted on the seat to face him squarely, the seat belt tightening across her chest. "What if Fiona was on the boat, too? And maybe it was Fiona, not Nicole, who took the boxes from Myrna. We don't know when Fiona arrived on the island for the wedding—or how. She doesn't have a car, but she could have flown into Boston, then taken the bus right to the ferry and walked on. Just because she and Colin are at odds doesn't mean she wasn't on the same boat. The *Island Home* has room for twelve hundred people. Fiona could have been one."

"But if she took the cakes from Myrna, she must have known they were poisonous. So are you saying you think Fiona poisoned herself?"

Annie raised an eyebrow. "Given all we know, is it so far-fetched?"

"But I thought you believed her."

"I did. I do. But . . ." Now that she'd started to reconsider, maybe it was even simpler. Maybe Nicole hadn't found a trash bin on the boat and brought the cakes home intending to dispose of them. Maybe Fiona saw them in Nicole's kitchen or in her wastebasket. Maybe she couldn't resist. Then, after her reaction, when she learned of the poison, she saw the chance to get some attention. And get back at her brother and sister for wanting to sell the property.

But that theory felt wrong in lots of ways, so Annie didn't tell Kevin.

Though it was a Tuesday night, he couldn't find a parking space near the Kelley House. "Grrr," he said, "summer."

Annie laughed and suggested they drive to John's, leave the truck, and walk back. It seemed like a good solution. But when Kevin pulled into the driveway, a band of emotion tightened inside her. She turned from the front windows. Though the sun had set, she was afraid the sky wasn't yet dark enough to mask a view of the silhouette of John's cozy sofas, his terminally wilting plants, or the braided rug in front of the fireplace where they'd often tossed pillows, made themselves comfortable, and drunk wine.

Then, as Kevin turned off the ignition, his text alert sounded. He glanced down at his phone. "Taylor."

"Read it," Annie said. "I'll wait on the porch." After all, she was an adult. Over fifty. Capable of handling the waves of life's emotions.

But the porch proved to be a challenge, too. As soon as she sat on one of the Adirondack chairs, she wished she hadn't. This was John's house, after all, the man she seemed to care more about now that he was gone; the man who appeared to care less and less about her as each hour, each day, passed; the man she might not see again for . . . who knew how long.

She stared at the garden, its blooms and colors lost to the night, fading in the dim glow of a streetlight.

When had they last been there? Two weeks ago? They'd sat in the evening, listening to the hum of the tourists who meandered through town on their way to or from dinner. Across the gap between the chairs, they had held hands. Closing her eyes now, Annie let herself be comforted by a fantasy that, any second, John would lean across the divide, wrap his arms around her, nuzzle his face into her neck. But the facts could not override her fantasy: John was gone, and would not be coming back. She tried to swallow, tried to wish away her tears. Instead, she sat. And ached.

"Annie? You okay?"

It wasn't John, of course. It was Kevin. "Sorry," she said, her eyes open now, her heart still again. "I was musing. Missing John."

He sat in the chair next to her before she could say, "Please don't." "I'm sorry you don't know when he's coming back."

Her shoulders rose and fell, hoping the response would ward off tears.

"I might have good news for you, though," Kevin added.

No matter how insignificant, good news would be welcome right then.

"Taylor heard about a year-round rental—a garage apartment—in West Tisbury. She wanted me to let you know."

How on earth Taylor knew that Annie and Kevin were together spoke to the ongoing question of how the woman learned everything that went on with Chappy people.

"She said you can see it tomorrow if you're interested. She left the owner's number."

"Well," Annie said, not wanting to admit that bothering to look for a place to live right then was not as high up on her agenda as it should be. "I suppose I could go after I'm sure everything is set for the tour." Over the last, emotionally charged hours, it felt as if she'd completely forgotten about the deadline for her manuscript. But she knew that with every minute she wasn't working, it would be tougher to pick up where she'd left off.

"Want me to come with you?" Kevin asked.

"Don't you have shingles to fix tomorrow? Fences to mend? Lawns to mow?"

"I do, but I also know how badly Earl wants you to stay here. He might grant me an exemption. Urgent family leave, or something like that."

"He wants me to stay on Chappy. Or, at the very least, in Edgartown. West Tisbury might as well be back in Boston."

Kevin snorted. "The dynamics of this island are certainly strange. But let's go see Fiona now before God knows what else happens."

"Sure," Annie said, her somber mood lightening. "In the morning, I'll call about the apartment."

★ ★ ★

Fiona was not in her room at the Kelley House, nor had she checked out. But when Annie tried to call, it went straight to voice mail.

"Let's walk around," she said to Kevin. "Maybe she's in one of the restaurants."

"She doesn't look like she eats very much."

"You wouldn't either if you thought one or more of your siblings was out to kill you."

"Or if you were busy trying to keep your story straight so others would think that."

"Good point."

"Does she have any friends on the island?"

"I don't know. Dana Flanagan must have been her friend if she was in her wedding. Though she was not in her first. Or her second."

"First or second wedding?"

"Right."

"Huh. That sounds like one of those 'contrivance' things your editor would hate. Unless you think the bride was involved."

"Highly doubtful. I think Dana would have had other things on her mind."

"True. But she's probably on her honeymoon now. And what with her father shouting about lawsuits, it's also doubtful that the bridesmaid has gone to the Flanagans'."

"Another good point."

They scanned the outdoor seating at the Newes and the long line at the door. Annie wormed her way inside as if she belonged there. Her eyes skimmed the crowd in both dining rooms, then checked out the bars. She even went into the ladies' room. No Fiona.

They crossed North Water Street to Chesca's, where it was also crowded and where a small ballerina might easily vanish within the high-spirited groups. They scrutinized l'Etoile, then crossed back to Rockfish and the Wharf, and circled down Dock Street to the Seafood Shanty. Fiona was nowhere in sight.

"We've missed several places," Annie said. "It would be easier if it were winter, when only a handful of restaurants are open."

"Maybe she just went for a walk. You're sure she doesn't have a car?"

"She does not. She's a New Yorker."

"So is her brother, but he drives a Porsche."

"That belongs to someone else."

"Hey! Maybe Colin is a car thief, too."

"If so, he might have picked a less conspicuous vehicle."

"Touché." He said it with a slight flourish that reminded Annie of Monsieur LeChance.

By then they'd reached the harbor and the *On Time* had chugged into its berth.

"Let's call it a night," Annie said. "I have a busy day tomorrow. I have to finalize things for the tour, pick up the programs, visit Claire for last-minute instructions, and call about that apartment in West Tisbury. In other words, I must start tending to my own business."

"Which," Kevin replied, "I assume includes finishing a manuscript?"

Annie groaned. "Right. I keep forgetting about that. Well, Fiona will be gone tomorrow, so maybe that will be a good thing. By Friday, the tour will be over, I might actually have somewhere to live, and I can get back to my life."

"Without giving the honey cake another thought."

Annie folded her arms. "You hardly know me, brother, and yet you know me so well."

"Well, I'm not comfortable with the lack of a resolution, either."

"Are you thinking that I should readjust my schedule? Like, check out the apartment first, and on my way back from West Tisbury, stop at the airport? See if I can find our ballerina wandering around with a rolling suitcase?"

Kevin smiled. "Not a bad idea."

She thought about it for a minute, then wondered if it might work. "I could go on the Internet tonight and find out what time flights leave tomorrow for the city."

"Or you could come back to the Kelley House early in the morning. Wait for her to leave. Then jump out of the bushes, scare the crap out of her, and demand to know if she poisoned herself. Catch her off guard, you know?"

"You, my brother, are definitely incorrigible."

"It's part of my charm."

"Which must be what Taylor sees in you."

"Ouch!" he cried.

She laughed and headed toward the boat.

"Wait!" Kevin called. "Don't forget to watch out for the skunks!"

Annie laughed. "Maybe I should try to find them before they find me. I read somewhere that they love honey, or at least honeybees. If I follow them, maybe they'll lead me to the left-over cake."

"Terrific," Kevin said with a wave, then turned and walked in the other direction.

Fishing her flashlight from her purse, Annie walked onto the *On Time* and settled on a bench. She wondered if, unlike Chappy, West Tisbury had streetlights so the night was not as dark.

No sooner had Annie snapped on the lights inside the cottage, kicked off her sandals, and tossed her purse onto a chair when there was a knock on her door. She turned and saw Roger Flanagan, his face close to the glass; she rued, not for the first time, that she'd never added a curtain that might have provided privacy.

Too late now, she thought.

"Roger," she said, opening the door. Based on their encounter at the police station, she saw no need to invite him in. For another thing, it was close to ten o'clock. At his age, shouldn't he be asleep? "How may I help you?"

"I'm checking to see if you've found another place to live. My grandson is getting antsy to move in."

She refrained from asking, "Seriously?" Instead, she forced one of her smiles and said, "I'm still looking. But as I'm sure you know, it's a tough time of year to find a place." She now doubted, however, that he would know, or that if he did, he would care.

"Maybe you'd have better luck off island. From what I understand, Cape Cod is nice."

Was he joking? "Yes, it is nice. But I live on the Vineyard. I plan to stay here."

He scratched at his chin as if deep in thought. "Still, you'd find the rental prices over there more affordable."

Annie knew that she had Donna MacNeish and her birth father (there were times Annie wished that Donna hadn't been so vague about him) to thank for the fact that she hadn't been born stupid. She also could thank Bob and Ellen Sutton for having made sure she had common sense, respectable values, and a good education. Between genetics, her adoptive parents, and perhaps a few street smarts she'd learned from her scam-artist ex-husband, Annie knew when she was being manipulated. Roger Flanagan would have loved it if she'd leave the island—which would result in one fewer person on Fiona's side if the girl went through with his cockamamie conjecture of a lawsuit.

Smiling a gratuitous smile that she hoped he would interpret as a smirk, Annie said, "I think it's premature for me to leave the island. As you reminded me, by the terms of my lease agreement, I still have a couple of weeks here in the cottage—which you graciously extended for another two. So I have about a month left altogether, if my math is correct. Until then, I won't be vacating the premises. Please pass that on to your grandson. Now, if you'll excuse me, I've had a long day. Good night." She began to close the door when he stuck his right Teva-ed foot inside. At least he wore a closed-toe style so she didn't have to look at an old man's unattractive toes—though a man like him probably had regular pedicures.

"I heard you're taking over the garden tour while Mrs. Lyons is rehabilitating."

"I am. As a favor to the family. They've done a lot for me."

"I'm a donor, you know. To the club. Including the tour."

"Yes, I know." She wondered if he was going to threaten to withdraw his funds. She leaned against the doorjamb. "I must admit, Roger, I found your donation curious. Other than your hydrangeas—which are lovely, by the way—I haven't noticed that you or your wife have a penchant for gardens. No hollyhocks, no foxglove, or other local blooms." She had no idea why she'd said that, other than his visit had put her in a combative mood, for which Murphy would have said she was justified. She only hoped Claire would agree if he stopped payment on his check.

He frowned. "Just because we support the garden club does not mean I'm a flower nut. I am a patron of the island arts community as well, but I can't draw a stick figure. Supporting community people and their activities is important, Annie. Especially since you never know when you might need them."

"You think you'll need the garden club?"

He laughed, which seemed rather bizarre. Then he said, "You're just a writer, so you wouldn't understand. But those of us in the real world know the importance of rubbing elbows with those who matter. Today I believe it's called networking.

Take one of our master gardeners, for instance. Monsieur LeChance. Are you aware that he's a full-time resident?"

It was odd that he mentioned Monsieur LeChance when a short time ago he had crossed her mind when Kevin uttered, "Touché." But, no, she did not know the man and his British wife were full-time island residents. She'd never considered that anyone who lived in one of the fabulous homes a block from North Water did not live in another house. Or two. But what did Roger care about him?

"Not only that," Roger continued, "LeChance has been on the planning board and is going to run for town selectman in the fall. As I said, you never know when you might need them."

Annie still didn't know what the connection was, if there was any, so she kept quiet and let him keep yakking.

He folded his arms. "And so you know, dear little Fiona will not be able to bring me down. I'm the one with the power and the influence here, and she best not forget that." Then he turned on one heel, stepped down off his invisible soapbox, crossed her porch, and shuffled off into the night.

Annie hadn't noticed whether or not he had a flashlight, but she supposed he knew every tree and root on his property, not to mention all the skunks. She wondered if those innocent creatures were aware that he, indeed, was the one with the power and the influence, so they'd better behave.

Message received, she thought, and once again took pity on Fiona.

Instead of going to bed, she poured a glass of wine and sat in the rocker by the window, wondering what kind of people the Flanagans really were beneath the obvious façade.

Roger clearly feared Fiona's lawsuit. But why? For starters, a man with his wealth and, as he'd claimed, "power and influence" surely had a bank of high-priced attorneys at his bidding who were capable of taking care of the "matter," though

Fiona had told him she had no intention of suing. "Why on earth would I think you tried to poison me?" the girl had cried. "I've known you my whole life!"

But Roger wasn't letting go, which didn't make sense.

Unless . . . unless Annie was missing something.

If he were one of her characters, Trish would tell her to explore his motivation.

Then Annie laughed. "Good grief. As if it's not bad enough that I talk to dead people, now I'm trying to channel my editor, too, who is very much alive and living in Manhattan."

She took a long sip of wine and decided to forget about this nonsense and go to bed. Then her cell rang.

It was John.

Chapter 25

Annie sucked in a breath as John's image appeared on her "Incoming" screen. It was a photo she'd snapped on a sunny spring day when he'd been leaning on the railing out at Dyke Bridge. He was smiling. Happy. Handsome.

"Were you asleep?" he asked.

"No. I'm having a glass of wine." Her mind raced as she tried to detect a hint of what he'd say. Would he tell her he'd decided to quit his job, give her up, and stay in Plymouth? Would he say he was getting back with his wife, that these past days had made him realize the divorce had been a mistake? Her palms grew damp, and her pulse started to patter at the base of her throat.

"I thought I'd check in," he said, "while I had a minute."

While he had a minute? Was he sitting outside on the front steps or the back ones again, out of earshot? Perhaps Jenn had gone shopping or was out doing other wifely things. Or maybe she was at her book group, sipping wine and boasting to friends that her ex-husband was back in the picture and back in her bed.

Annie cleared her throat. "Everything's fine." She hoped she sounded unaffected, as if, in that moment, she weren't hating herself more than she was hating him, hating that she'd said no when he'd offered to have her move in. But even if it weren't too late for that now, which it was, Annie knew she was not the kind of woman to manipulate a man in order to try and win him back. "Your mother should be out of rehab in a few days."

"Yeah, I talked to Dad. He's optimistic."

Because phone cords had gone the way of typewriters and cassette players, Annie toyed with the top button of the cardigan she'd put on because, for once, the evening had turned cool. "Yes. She's doing well."

"And Dad is holding up?"

"Yes. I had dinner with him tonight. With Francine and Kevin, too."

"Your brother has been a huge help."

"It looks that way."

The pauses between the lines were a beat too long, the way it happened when a television news anchor in New York tried to converse with a reporter who was halfway around the world. *How bad is the devastation?* Anderson Cooper or Chris Cuomo or Lester Holt would ask. Pause. Pause. Pause. *Well, Anderson* (or Chris, or Lester), *unfortunately, we won't learn the full impact for several days.*

Pause.

She wondered how long it would be before she learned the real reason John was calling.

"How's the Littlefield girl?"

Pause.

"She's all right. Your fellow officers believe it was an accident. Or that Fiona convinced herself someone had tried to poison her. They seem to think she likes the attention." That was enough to tell him. He did not deserve to know the rest, especially if he was thinking about quitting the force. Besides,

Annie didn't want to hear him say anything negative about a girl who clearly hadn't led the glorious, trust-fund-baby kind of life that some people might have imagined.

"Poor kid," he said. "From what I remember, she was always picked on. She was so young. And always tiny. The only one who was nice to her was Dana. But their parents weren't exactly friends. People like that sometimes like to try to outdo one another. The Littlefields seemed nice, but the Flanagans . . . well, you've seen Roger's nasty side the way he's kicking you out. By the way, have you found another place?"

Annie heard his last words, but was more interested in what he'd said about the Littlefields and the Flanagans. Not exactly friends. Trying to outdo one another. John was right: She'd certainly witnessed Roger's coldhearted side. And she'd had the brief run-in with Nicole, who, despite a smile, had seemed intentionally rude.

Suddenly, Annie had an epiphany, a glimpse of motivation that quickly gelled in her mind. Was it true? Had John triggered an important clue about the whole Fiona matter?

"Annie?" he asked. "Are you still there?"

"I'm sorry, John, I have to go. Call me later if you can." She quickly hung up. Sooner or later, she'd have to hear his clumsy admission that he was going to stay in Plymouth for an indeterminate amount of time. "Later" would be soon enough; right then, Annie had something more important to do.

That time, Fiona answered.

"We looked all over for you tonight," Annie said.

"I went for a walk."

"What time is your flight tomorrow?"

"Noon."

"Cancel it."

"What?"

"Cancel your reservation, Fiona. I'll explain tomorrow. I have a million things to do, and I need to check out one more thing, but please stay on the Vineyard for just one more day."

"Why?"

"I don't want to get your hopes up, but I think I know what happened."

There was a pause, not the tense kind of pause Annie had had with John, but more like one of disbelief. Then Fiona whispered, "Really?"

"Really. Now try and get some sleep. And don't open your door for anyone." She didn't know why she'd added that last directive; Annie only knew she wanted Fiona to be safe until she could prove her theory so the police would finally believe them.

In the morning, Annie called Kevin and asked for Taylor's cell number. "I have a hunch," she said. He said he had to work; she promised to keep him posted.

"For a minute," Taylor said when Annie reached her, "I thought you'd changed your mind about my apartment."

"It would have been perfect, except for the Internet issue," Annie reiterated. "But I'm going to try and see the one in West Tisbury today, so thanks. I have another question, though. One about the Littlefields and the Flanagans."

"I don't know much about them, but shoot."

Annie doubted that Taylor didn't "know much" about anyone on Chappy. "Have you heard anything about Roger Flanagan wanting to buy the Littlefield property?"

"Most anybody with big bucks would want the place. Beachfront acreage like that? On the harbor, not the open ocean that gets pummeled every year by storms or wasted by too much erosion? To top it off, there's damn little land left to go around—we've got less than four thousand acres on Chappy, and more than twenty-five percent is in conservation."

Annie didn't have time for a lesson in land management, but she clenched her jaw, determined to be patient.

"As for your landlord and the neighbor, sure. Roger wants the property. He tried to buy it right after the mother died and it fell to the kids."

That was all Annie needed to know.

Before heading out, she sent a quick e-mail to the garden club volunteers who would be stationed at the addresses to which they'd been assigned. She reminded them that each garden should only have six visitors at a time and that they must be moved along, but not too hastily. She added that the judges should be allowed to take their time, and that the refreshments must stay "fresh," especially since another uncommon heat wave was predicted. Wanting to close on a positive note, she reported that, according to a message she'd received the night before, ticket sales had now topped one hundred and sixty. At twenty dollars each, that meant over three thousand dollars had been earmarked for the schools, not counting last-minute sales or the generous checks from donors. *Like Roger Flanagan,* she thought, but did not add.

She clicked "Send," grabbed the pink folder and her purse, and headed out. The early start was easy; her first stops were the judges. She saved Monsieur LeChance for last.

He'd had a haircut and his eyebrows were neatly trimmed. He was awake, alert, and standing in his gazebo, practicing his violin. She didn't ask if he was planning to bring it with him as he judged each of the venues.

"Good morning, monsieur," Annie said with her brightest smile.

He welcomed her into the gazebo and asked if she'd like coffee. "And perhaps a croissant?"

"*Non, merci,*" Annie replied. "I'm afraid I'm in a bit of a hurry." She quickly reviewed the dos and don'ts of a judge, then said something more important. "I didn't know you are a year-round resident."

Nodding with his little grin, he said, "Seventeen years. But one is never considered a true islander unless one is born here. Every year Madame and I travel to France for a short holiday, but otherwise, yes, this is our home."

"And now you want to be a town selectman."

"I do. I am nearly eighty, but I still have much to offer. I have served on the planning board for a dozen years, which was only natural, as I was a city planner in Paris until my retirement." He brushed his upper lip as if he had a mustache.

"I need to come right to the point," Annie said. "I think there's a problem about a piece of land on Chappy. Can you tell me if there have been any inquiries about the Littlefield property? Specifically by Roger Flanagan?" She might be stepping out-of-bounds to seek information that could be confidential. Not to mention that Roger Flanagan might be one of the *monsieur*'s closest friends. But what did Annie have to lose?

"Everything is public record," Monsieur said, his voice and his head both lowering. "But off the record, I have never cared for Flanagan; he is a—how do you say it?—a bully?" A corner of his mouth twitched as he said it.

Annie had a feeling Monsieur LeChance knew exactly how to say *bully* and exactly what it meant. "So he wants the land."

"He has not declared it outright. But he has asked—behind the scenes, mind you, not officially—about the parameters of building codes, maximum square footage allowed for a residence, that sort of thing."

"It sounds as if he wants to tear down the Littlefields' and build a nicer place for his daughter and her husband. Or for himself and Nicole, and give the current Flanagan main house to Dana."

"I rather think he has a more grandiose vision."

"How so?"

"I think he wants to build one of those gauche monstrosities. What have they called them in Chilmark? 'One big home'?"

Annie had heard some of the controversy surrounding the up-island town where they had finally put a limit on the sizes of houses that could be built, after another fifteen-thousand-square-foot place had been erected. Though no one disputed the fact that building such places provided jobs for islanders and ultimately contributed to the economic health of the Vineyard, the basis of dissention was the drain on infrastructure and utilities and the cost to the environment and its ecosystem. She supposed the argument for limitations would be even stronger on Chappy, which, unlike on the "big island," needed to be more self-sufficient.

Right then, however, Annie only cared to know that Roger had big plans for the Littlefield property. And that Fiona might be the only one in his way.

"Thank you, monsieur," she said. "*Merci beaucoup.*"

He tweaked his invisible mustache again and picked up his violin. "Happy to help. As I said, the man is a bully." Then he began to play again, this time a piece from a sonata that Annie did not recognize.

She waved goodbye and got back to business, dashing to all twelve sites that would be on the tour, marveling at how their owners (or, in many cases, their owners' gardeners) had transformed their lovely gardens into storybook venues. Claire would have been pleased. Then Annie zipped across the north side of the island to the printer in what surely was record time.

Once she'd parked the carton of brochures—which looked terrific—squarely on the back seat of the Lexus, she retraced her path to Oak Bluffs. It wasn't quite eleven when she walked into Claire's room at the rehab center.

"Good morning!" Annie said.

Holding one end of an elastic strap in each hand, the midpoint wrapped under her right foot, Claire sat in a chair, bending and straightening her knee. "Physical therapy," she said. "Whoever thought this stuff really worked?"

Annie wouldn't quibble about that. After having fallen from her bicycle when she'd been ten, months of PT had helped her walk straight again. She sat on the end of the bed facing Claire. "I have a gift for you." She dug into her bag and produced one of the brochures. It had ended up to be four pages longer than Claire had anticipated because Annie had added several more pictures.

Claire's eyes widened and she let go of the strap. "Oh! Let me see!" Her speech was still a little slurred; her right arm still looked unsteady, but she managed to reach out and grab the treasure from Annie's hand. *Yes,* Annie thought. *Her progress is apparent.*

"Oh, Annie," Claire said while thumbing through the pages. "It's beautiful."

"I'm so glad you like it. I talked the printer into giving us a few extra pages at no added cost. The photos are all on-line, too."

"Thank Francine, please. Will these be at Sally Jones's house?" She stammered a little when she said, "Sally Jones's house," but Annie understood. Sally's was the designated "starting" point, where visitors would receive their official stickers to show that they had paid.

"Yes. Her table will be by her front gate, and she'll start greeting visitors at eight o'clock."

"I wish I could get out of here."

"You will be missed. But everyone sends their good wishes

for a fast recovery, and they say they fully expect you to be back in charge next year. Even Monsieur LeChance said you will not be able to shirk your duties so easily again." She didn't add that Claire might not be able to count on her help because Annie might not still live there.

Claire giggled. "I'm sorry I won't hear Monsieur play his violin. Earl says I have a crush on him."

"Do you?"

With a small wink, Claire said, "*Oui, oui.* A *petite* one."

Annie recognized the sweet reminder that romance, or even the dream of it, could bring a smile at any age. She promised not to tell Earl, then she reviewed the details for the preparations, and was pleased to answer yes to each of Claire's slow, but deliberate, questions.

When they were finished, Annie asked Claire how well she knew Roger Flanagan.

The woman sat back in her chair. "We're not friends. They've always schmoozed with people who are like them. Not people like us. Dana is just like them." She paused a moment, as if searching for the right words. Then she said, "For a few summers she was with that Littlefield boy. And she had that older brother. I always forget about him."

Older brother? Annie scowled. "I thought Dana was an only child."

"No, there was an older boy; I don't remember his name. He was nicer than the rest of them. He and Taylor were great pals for a while."

Annie winced. "Taylor? You mean . . . *our* Taylor?" One of these days she supposed she really ought to ask the woman's last name. Maybe Kevin knew.

A look of disbelief passed over Claire's face. "You don't know?"

"I didn't even know that the Flanagans had a son."

"Well, the boy is dead now. It was ruled an accidental drowning. But there wasn't a body. So no one could be sure."

"He died on the island?"

"In the water. He and Taylor had gone fishing. She came back. He didn't."

That was news to Annie. But did it have anything to do with Fiona being poisoned? "Were they caught in a storm or something?"

Claire shook her head. "The police said he accidentally fell overboard. Taylor was on the bow, and he'd been on the stern. She didn't realize he was gone until it was too late."

Her words had grown more slurred; Annie didn't want to wear her out. She stood and prepared to leave, just as Claire tipped her head back, drew in a long breath, then said, "Taylor couldn't very well dive in and hunt for him. Not in her condition."

Annie's hand froze on the strap of her bag. "Her *condition*?" As far as Annie knew, that word usually meant one thing.

"Well . . . it was only a rumor, but . . . people said it was the Flanagan boy's baby. Oh, what was his name . . . ?"

With her heart starting to race, Annie asked, "Wait. What happened to the baby? I thought Taylor went to Berklee, played in a symphony, then came back to Chappy years later when her father got sick."

"That's the 'unofficial version,' as we islanders call it. John didn't tell you?"

"Um . . . no."

Claire let out a tired sigh. "Men. They never share the gory details. Well, now that you live here, too, you might as well know the rest."

Annie wasn't sure that she wanted to.

"Taylor must have been around nineteen or twenty," Claire went on before Annie could stop her. "She went to Boston that fall, supposedly to college. The next summer the Flanagans came back to Chappy with their daughter, Dana, and a baby, a boy. Their dead son was apparently the father: They claimed the baby's mother was a teenager from the city who was grateful that Roger and Nicole wanted him. That part seemed sketchy, but they gave the boy a reasonably good home, at least money-wise. And the boy spent his summers here where his father had been happy." She pressed two fingers against her lips. "That's the boy who's moving into your cottage. The artist. What's his name?"

Annie was stunned. "Jonas," she said. Though no one had said that Dana was his mother, she'd assumed she was. She'd even thought that Colin might be his father. But now . . . ? "Are you saying that Taylor is Jonas's mother?" A headache began to nestle at Annie's temples. Even if it were true, she could not imagine what it might have to do with the fact that Fiona was poisoned.

Claire shrugged. "No one asked; no one told. But Taylor's father was a fisherman; they never had much money, so I always wondered who paid for her to wind up staying in Boston. Or how she and her mother managed to hold on to the property after her father died." Then she closed her eyes. "My goodness, I believe all this talk has exhausted me."

It had exhausted Annie, too. And had added another confusing element to Fiona's mystery. She wondered if Kevin knew that his new lady friend—potentially the secret mother of a not-so-secret child—had been the only witness to the accidental drowning of her boyfriend way back when. And that Taylor's son was the one uprooting Annie from the cottage.

She'd never fully trusted Taylor. And now . . .

Shaking off her bewilderment, Annie said, "Get some rest. I'll be back tomorrow night to tell you how the tour went. And don't worry about the weather; the gods have promised a nice warm day." She helped Claire from the chair and back into bed. Then, as she left the room, her eyes filled with unexpected tears. She knew that though Earl and Claire had been like a family to her, once John broke things off with Annie, everything would change.

But first, she had to focus on Fiona.

Chapter 26

Myrna wasn't home.

Annie had sped up island to Sweet Everything Farm in Chilmark and was grateful that she hadn't been stopped. Neither local law enforcement nor the state police had a sense of humor about speeders. Especially in season.

"She's not home?" Annie asked Rodney as if he might be mistaken about his wife's whereabouts. She'd power walked from her car up the hill when she'd spotted him strolling out of one of the barns. "Do you know when she'll be back? It's kind of an emergency." She wondered if she looked as ruffled as she felt.

"She's in Vineyard Haven at the dentist. Root canal." He grimaced.

"Oh, dear. That's unpleasant."

"Not as unpleasant as it was when she woke up during the night. The way she screamed I thought the damn house was burning down."

Annie smiled. "I needed one once. It's not high on my list of things I want to go through again."

His brows knitted together. "But you have a different emergency. Are you in critical need of poisoned honey? Sorry, but we destroyed that batch."

It took Annie a second to realize he was kidding. "Actually," she said, "I wanted to talk to her about what happened when she was on the boat. When she got sick and realized the honey cake was bad. Do you remember anything she told you?"

He shook his head. "Only that all she wanted was to get home."

"Did she tell you that she gave someone—a woman—the boxes to throw away?"

Scratching at what looked like more than a day-old beard, Rodney said, "Yeah, sure. I remember. She tried to call me from the ladies' room—that's always weird, isn't it?—but she remembered I wouldn't have my phone with me. She wanted to tell me she was sick and she knew it was because of the honey. She wanted to tell me it was bitter, and that a woman said she'd ditch both the cakes before anyone else could have a taste. As soon as Myrna was done with her story, I went into my processing room and tasted the raw honey. Bitter was an understatement. God, I still can't believe I missed that. I was sorry Myrna felt sick, but we're lucky it didn't go public. We've worked real hard to have a good reputation."

"It isn't your fault that Myrna gave the boxes to a woman and didn't toss them in the trash herself."

"I think she was otherwise occupied in a stall."

Annie tried to look sympathetic.

"But I feel terrible about what happened to that other lady."

"She's fine now, Rodney. Though I'm still trying to figure out how she wound up getting the cake." Then Annie had another idea. "How long have you been selling honey cakes, Rodney?"

"Good question. Five or six years."

Five or six years. Which meant that more than twenty years

ago, when Dana Flanagan and Colin Littlefield supposedly made honey cakes for Fiona because she "loved them," Sweet Everything Farm would not have supplied them. Annie didn't know why she'd thought there might be a link, or what it might mean. Suddenly she felt as if she was grasping at too many straws.

"We've been selling raw honey a lot longer than that, though," Rodney added. "Thirty—no, wait—almost forty years. Wow. Time goes by fast."

"Do you sell it to stores?"

"In the beginning, we thought we'd sell only to wholesalers. Then Myrna had a bright idea. Honey was real popular in the late seventies, so she said, 'Why not have a real honey wagon? I can travel around the island once every week or two.' We were newly married, God, we were so young! But she turned our beekeeping into a real business. Smart woman, my Myrna."

"Did she go over to Chappy?"

"Hard to remember, but probably. If you want, I can try to call her. Maybe she can help sort out your emergency. If she's not yet tied down in the chair."

"Tied down?"

He laughed. "I told her they'd better tie her down to stop her from running away when they came at her with the needle."

"Did she laugh?"

"No. She rolled her eyes and told me to shut up. She's used to me." He pulled a phone from a pocket in his overalls. "Let's see if she answers." He touched the screen, then held the phone to an ear.

After a couple of seconds, he puffed out his cheeks as if in exasperation.

And Annie waited, trying to sort out the myriad of facts.

Then Rodney shook his head. "Voice mail. Sorry."

"Okay. Thanks anyway. Maybe I can figure out something

else." She turned to walk back to her car, and then had another thought. "Rodney? Would you mind telling me where Myrna's dentist is? I hate to impose, but it's really important. I don't think I'm overreacting when I say someone's life might be at stake."

The dental office was on State Road, right past the Black Dog Café. Annie made a mental note in case she ever needed another root canal, though the thought made her grimace the way Rodney had.

Myrna was not in the waiting room. Neither was anyone else. Annie stepped to the reception desk, but no one was behind the sliding glass window. She stood, listening, not knowing what she expected to hear. Hopefully, it would not be Myrna screaming as if the building were on fire.

She jangled her keys; she coughed. She looked down a hall that had several doors on each side about ten feet apart. Still, no one showed.

The thought of Fiona sitting at the Kelley House, anxiously awaiting word from Annie, emboldened her.

"Hello?" she called out well above a whisper. "Is anyone here?"

The response came in the form of the high-pitched buzz of a drill. When the buzzing ceased, a young woman in scrub pants and a colorful smock stepped from one of the doorways into the hall. She removed a surgical mask. "Sorry," she said. "The doctor is with a patient. I'm her assistant, Grace. The receptionist must be out for lunch."

Good grief, Annie thought. She hadn't realized it was well past noon. "I'm here to see your patient," she said, employing her best smile. "Myrna . . ." Suddenly, she could not remember Myrna's last name.

"She'll be finished in a few minutes if you'd care to wait."

Annie didn't care to wait, but she felt she had no choice.

She sat in the waiting room and Grace disappeared back down the hall. Once again, Annie reviewed the facts.

Somehow, it now seemed obvious that Roger Flanagan was involved.

But why?

To get the land?

If he were hell-bent on that, it seemed he could have resorted to more appropriate means than poisoning Fiona. Besides, how could he have known that his wife would come back from the Cape toting not only custom chocolates for the wedding-guest gift bags but also poisoned honey cakes?

And what about his wife? It appeared that Nicole had been handed the cakes, and had been told that they were poisonous. Had she concocted the plan? Did she, too, want the Littlefield property so badly? Hadn't Earl once said he thought Nicole would rather be on Nantucket?

"Annie?"

She jumped at the sound and looked up to see Myrna. "Oh, hi! How's the tooth?"

"The pain is gone. I can't believe it. Are you here for the same reason?" Her words were a little slurred, as if, like Claire, she too had had a stroke. *Must be the novocaine,* Annie thought.

"No. I'm here to see you. I have a question about the woman you gave the honey cakes to on the boat. You said you thought she had light-colored hair. But do you remember if she was young or old?"

Myrna held one hand up to her cheek, then shook her head. "She wasn't young. But she didn't look too old. I remember thinking she must have had work done."

Bingo. Nicole Flanagan. So Colin hadn't lied about that.

"And then you saw her talking to the guy, who you then saw drive off the boat in a Porsche?"

"Right."

"And he was alone in the car."

"Yes. I'm pretty sure he was."

"When you saw them talking, did you notice if she was carrying the cake boxes? Please. This part is very important."

Myrna took her time. In the distance, the dentist drill whirred again. "No," she said. "She wasn't. She was carrying a large purse. It was red, as I recall."

"Would a man might have thought it was a tote bag?"

Myrna laughed. "Who knows what a man would say? It looked expensive, though."

"Was it big enough to hold the cakes?"

She shook her head. "No. Not even one. It was the wrong shape. Deep enough, but not wide enough for a box. Not even if she'd put it on its side, but why would anyone carry a cake on its side?"

"I doubt that they would."

Then Myrna suddenly said, "Wait. She had a box, too. A large one. It was tied with lavender ribbon and had a handle."

The chocolates for the wedding, Annie thought. "But you never saw the cakes again?"

"No. Wish I could help you more." She rubbed her cheek a little, dropped her hand into her pocket, and pulled out a set of keys.

"Oh, Myrna, you have no idea how much you've helped. And I'm glad your tooth is feeling better."

"Ha! Rodney will be, too!"

Annie grinned and went out the door.

On the drive back to Edgartown, Annie mulled over and over why Nicole Flanagan would have wanted to poison Fiona. Even if she'd known the tainted honey probably wouldn't have killed her, she would have known it would make the girl sick. Why would she have done that? To scare Fiona into agreeing with her siblings to sell the house so Nicole and Roger could buy it, tear down both houses, and no doubt the cottage, too, then build a mega-mansion like the ones in Chilmark that had caused so much controversy?

Had Colin and Nicole been in on this together?

Or had Sheila—the missing sibling who might or might not be at home in Seattle—been involved after all?

Or . . . could it have been Dana, the bride? Was her former relationship with Colin somehow significant?

"Where are you when I need you?" she admonished the sky, her words directed at Murphy. If her old friend hadn't died, by now they would have solved the puzzle. And Annie would be able to get back to her life.

But Murphy was unresponsive.

The desk clerk at the Kelley House rang Fiona, who said Annie was welcome to go to her room. She quickly found it again, but paused at the dark wood door, its brass numerals polished to a high shine. "A little help, please," she whispered, in case Murphy resurfaced. Then she knocked.

"It's open," Fiona's timid voice called from inside.

Turning the knob, Annie was about to caution Fiona about leaving the door unlocked, when she stopped short. Fiona sat on top of one of the beds; she was propped up by several pillows that looked as if they might swallow her tiny body any minute.

But what was more disturbing was that she was not alone. In the navy chair, one leg crossed over the other, sat Colin.

"Hello," Fiona said. "I guess you've met my brother." She wore a pink cotton robe and her hair was pulled back in a loose chignon that accentuated her jutting cheekbones and made her look like a teenager. *Like John's Lucy,* Annie thought.

Adjusting her purse on her shoulder, Annie replied, "Yes. I have."

"He didn't do it," Fiona said.

Colin stood; Annie braced herself for what might come

next. But all he did was walk to the window, look down onto the street, and shove his hands into the pockets of his khakis. "Did you ever hear of a guy named Edward Fenterly?" he asked.

"The filmmaker?" Annie knew the man had won several awards for his historical docudramas that took place during World War II and were centered around the men and women who had served.

"Fenterly is one of Roger Flanagan's old cronies. He flew in for the wedding. He supposedly wanted me to talk with his partner back in New York. We left before the fireworks because the guy was taking off for Paris the next day. I didn't think I needed to sign out."

"Are you saying the airline gave the police the wrong information and your name will be on the passenger list?"

"No. We traveled by private plane." Colin crossed back to the chair and sat down again.

So far, none of this had anything to do with Fiona being poisoned. "If nothing else," Annie said, "it might have been nice if you'd told your sister you were going."

"Look, I told you, I barely communicate with either of my sisters, except to argue about what to do with the mausoleum on Chappy." He folded his arms again.

"He knew about the cake," Fiona interrupted.

Annie's eyebrows shot up. Colin turned and faced her.

"I already told you I met Nicole on the boat," he said. "And, yes, we were talking about how crazy things get in summer. Then she told me about two honey cakes that a woman had in the ladies' room. The woman said they were poisonous and asked Nicole to throw them away. Nicole said she did. Then she reminded me Dana and I used to buy honey from the wagon that came from up island, then we made little cakes for Fiona. She loved them." He propped his elbows on his knees, and pressed his palms together as if he were praying—an act that seemed out of character. Annie wondered if, like Roger Flanagan, he was trying to manipulate her. And Fiona, too.

"She said one of them hadn't been touched, and that I might consider giving it to Fiona. She said maybe a good dose of illness might prompt my sister into finally leaving the island and agreeing to let me sell them the house."

"I don't understand," Annie said. "Why would Fiona decide to sell just because she got sick?"

"It didn't make sense to me, either," Colin said. "Until I figured out that Nicole wanted Roger to think that Fiona would sue him; she probably planted that in his head, as well as the threat that he'd sue Fiona back. Fiona has never liked confrontation; she's shy, just like our mother was. My bet is Nicole counted on scaring Fiona into agreeing to sell. She'd never allow Sheila to get her bird sanctuary, but if she turned over her voting rights to me, we'd be set. We only need two-thirds to sell to the Flanagans."

"Okay," Annie interrupted, "they want your property. I already know that." She could have sat on the ottoman, but she felt safer remaining by the door.

Colin continued. "Nicole wanted to tear it down and build what she called a 'show palace.' She's planned this since our parents died. Everyone thinks Roger controls that family. But it's really her. She's made Roger pump a ton of money into every island charity she knows of. She thinks that means the planning board and the selectmen bend the regulations when Roger applies for the permit."

Which supported Monsieur LeChance's theory as to why Roger supported the garden club, despite the fact that neither he nor Nicole had any visible penchant for flowers.

So far, Colin made sense. But Annie was careful not to let down her guard.

"Unlike Chilmark," he added, "Edgartown doesn't limit the size of residential homes yet. There aren't many house restrictions at all, except in the village where there are regulations about everything."

"How do you know all this about the Flanagans?"

He let out a low groan. "Not proud of myself, but Dana and I were friends with benefits, you know what I mean? She knew I'd never marry her; that family is too screwed up. But she told me about her mother's real estate plans. And that I should negotiate a wicked-high price."

"Fine," Annie said, "but talk to me about the honey cake. And tell me the truth this time."

"Right. Sorry I wasn't completely forthcoming, but, Jesus, I didn't know you. You could have been working for Nicole. Spying on me, you know?"

Annie could not disagree.

"Anyway, Nicole said I should retrieve the cake that hadn't been touched from the bin and give it to Fiona. She said it looked like it just came out of a bakery." He examined his fingernails. "I told her no thanks. Then she frowned—have you ever noticed how when someone's had too many face-lifts, when they try to frown you don't see any lines, but it makes them look like they're in pain?" He sighed. "Right after that, the steamship guy announced that drivers had to return to their vehicles, so I went down to the freight deck and got into my car. End of story."

"Not really," Fiona said.

"Right," he said quietly.

Annie waited. She'd developed a cramp in her right hip from standing motionless with her muscles tensed. Still, she didn't move.

"When Fenterly approached me at the reception, I ran home to grab my valise. When I raced through the kitchen, I saw a white box by the sink. It looked like a bakery box."

"Was it the honey cake?" Annie asked.

"I can't say for certain. I paid no more attention to it; I was in too much of a hurry. I do know it hadn't been there in the morning when I'd gone next door to help set up for the wedding. When I got home yesterday, it was gone. The hospital had left a bunch of messages on my cell saying Fiona was there. When you and your brother showed up, I was trying to find her. We might have our differences, but she's still my sister, you know?"

Annie had one more question. "Colin, who told you Fiona was at the Kelley House? How did you find her here?"

He shrugged. "Small island. I asked the captain of the *On Time*. He saw her walk up here."

Small island, indeed, Annie thought. Reminders were everywhere.

"I'm glad he found me," Fiona said quietly, and Annie realized she'd forgotten that the girl was there.

Then, as Annie turned to leave, Colin offered one last comment.

"If you want to know what else is going on with the Flanagans, I suggest you talk to Taylor."

Taylor? Her again?

Chapter 27

The only one Annie wanted to talk to was John. He would have been able to cut through the crap (as Earl would have said), solve the case, and move on. She didn't need Taylor's input, no matter what Colin had suggested. She didn't know whom to believe, and she was growing weary of trying.

"I'm done with it," she said to herself as she went back to the cottage. She texted Kevin to ask if he'd stop by after work. She wanted to tell him about the day's events, and that she'd tried her best, but frankly, if Fiona was poisoned again, it would not be Annie's fault.

Kevin texted back, saying he'd be there in an hour.

Deciding that she needed rest, Annie went into the bedroom. But as she climbed atop her comfy bed, someone knocked on her front door.

She wondered what would happen if she hid under the quilt and didn't respond.

The knock came again.

Still, Annie didn't move. If it was Taylor, she would have seen Annie's car in the driveway; she'd only have to glance inside and see Annie's purse, keys, and laptop on the desk to know that Annie was inside . . . at which point she might call the ambulance and police cruiser over from Edgartown in case Annie was dead or sick or, God forbid, had eaten poisoned honey cake. Countless people in the queue for the *On Time* would be forced to wait if Taylor cried "Emergency!" because, as Annie now knew, the ambulance and cruiser were first on the list of "cutters."

She got up.

But it wasn't Taylor at the door. It was a young man.

"Yes?" Annie asked, when she opened it.

"Are you Ms. Sutton?" He was tall, lanky, and looked to have escaped his teen years relatively unscathed. "I'm Jonas Flanagan."

Ah . . . Annie thought. *The new tenant.* She stepped aside. "Come in. You must be the artist." Her dad, after all, had taught her to always be polite. *Until you know it would be better not to,* he had added.

Jonas had the same blue eyes as his grandfather, though his hair tended toward ginger, a lighter shade than Taylor's, if the rumor about her was true. "I hope I'm not disturbing you," he said.

"Not at all. I just came home." She wasn't sure she should have called the cottage "home," but it hadn't seemed to faze him. "Would you like to sit down? Or would you like a tour of the cottage? I don't know if you've seen it. . . ."

He nodded. "I used to play in here when I was little. Gramps said he's updated a few things." He didn't make a move to sit. "I'm sorry you have to move on account of me. I wanted you to know it wasn't my idea."

Annie was baffled. She wondered how much more drama her brain could take that day. She stepped to one side. "Please, Jonas, sit down. Let's have a talk." If he was Taylor's son, his demeanor was much different. He seemed quieter, less breathless. Or brash.

He sat on the rocking chair and declined iced tea or water.

"Between you and me, I don't want to live here. But my grandfather says that if I do, I'll be able to jump-start my career. What I really want is to move to New York. That's where careers are made, not on an island where there's a captive audience only a few weeks a year."

Annie sat on the love seat across from him. "But you're out of college. . . ."

He laughed. "And I should be able to do what I want, right? The truth is, I need some financial support to get started, and Gramps will only help if I live here."

"Oh," Annie said. "Well, I'm sorry."

He nodded. "Yeah, me, too. So my plan is to stay here until I've made enough money to go to the city on my own. I'm hoping it won't take forever." Then he grew quiet, which led Annie to wonder if he'd really only stopped by to apologize for her being uprooted. Or if he knew something about the mystery going on.

"Jonas?" she asked. "Is there some specific reason you came over?"

His eyes flashed over to her. "Yeah. It's about Fiona Little-field. Is she in some kind of trouble?"

Annie tried not to act surprised that he had asked. "Why are you asking me?"

Averting his eyes from her to the woodstove, then to her bookcases, then back to her, he said, "I heard my grandparents talking about her, that she's gone nuts or something. I feel bad. Fiona's always been nice to me."

"Fiona is fine," Annie replied. "But we think someone might have tried to hurt her."

He lowered his eyes and rocked the chair a few times. "You probably don't know that my grandmother talked Dana into letting Fiona be a bridesmaid. She said it would be a nice thing to do, seeing as how they'd practically grown up together in the summers here."

Annie's thoughts raced. Had Nicole first hoped she could win Fiona over by having her be a bridesmaid . . . and then trying to convince her to change her mind about selling the house? But, when encountering the poisonous cake, had she come up with a different plan? Annie wondered how much more Jonas knew, or would be willing to tell. "Did you know that Fiona was poisoned?" she asked.

His gaze left hers and roamed the room. "I heard them say that. But she really is okay now?"

"She is. But we're still trying to figure out how it happened. To make sure no one did it on purpose."

He nodded. "Good idea."

Good idea? What an odd remark. Then a knot formed in Annie's stomach. "Jonas? Do you know what happened?"

It took a moment, then he replied, "Maybe."

Life is filled with the unexpected, her dad had said back when Annie had turned nine and her mother had run off with the elementary school vice principal. *The trick is to learn how to deal with it.*

She decided that the best way to deal with Jonas was to be patient.

"I heard my grandmother say the cake needed to go over to the Littlefields. She said there had been another one, but she'd dumped it out because someone had taken a bite. But she said that one was brand-new, and Fiona wouldn't be able to re-sist." He picked at the cuff of his cargo shorts that were similar to Colin's.

"When was that?" Annie asked.

"The day of Dana's wedding. After the ceremony. Before the party started."

"And who was she talking to?"

The boy fell silent again. Annie tried to stay seated, tried to stay calm.

"Taylor," he said. "She's my real mother, you know."

So there it was. A connection to Taylor, in more ways than one.

"Nobody knows I know that she's my mother," he continued. "But I sleep in the room that was my father's. I found love letters they wrote back and forth after she found out she was pregnant. They were going to run away and get married. He'd even bought airplane tickets for Hawaii. But he drowned before they could." His eyes moved to the woodstove. "Imagine that," he added somberly. "I could have grown up in Hawaii."

After Jonas left, Annie poured a glass of wine. She needed to think this through, starting with Taylor, who really was Jonas's mother. But was she involved with Fiona being poisoned? Had Nicole enlisted Taylor to deliver the honey cake? And if so, why? So Nicole would avoid suspicion?

Then Annie wondered if Taylor was under Nicole's thumb because of Jonas. The Flanagans had apparently supported Taylor and her family as recompense for giving them Jonas. Did they still? Was that why Taylor had commented that she and "Mother" did not need the income from renting their garage apartment?

If the Flanagans were their benefactors, Taylor could hardly have said no to whatever Nicole demanded.

By the time Kevin arrived, Annie had nearly finished her wine and her brain was still muddled.

"What's up?" he asked as he padded into the living room in his socks, having left his work boots on the porch.

"Help yourself to a beer," she said. "We need to do some serious thinking."

Once Kevin was settled on the rocker where Jonas had sat, Annie spewed out everything, including Monsieur LeChance's comments that Roger had been interested in the Littlefield property for years and had cozied up to the local politicians with that in mind, and that Myrna's further description of the mystery woman on the boat suggested it was Nicole. She then told him about meeting Colin in Fiona's room and hearing his confirmation that the Flanagans wanted the property. She added Colin's story about the filmmaker whisking him off to New York, then ended with Jonas's account of Nicole handing off the cake to Taylor with instructions to plant it at the Little-fields'. She didn't reveal the part about Taylor being Jonas's mother; later, there would be time for that.

By the time she was finished, Kevin had drained his beer. "Wow," he said. "Talk about too much information."

Annie nodded.

"But what do we do now?"

"I don't know. I was counting on you to come up with an idea. We know a lot, but the details get confusing."

Kevin got another beer. Annie declined a second glass of wine.

"Let's back up," he said, resuming his seat. "We know Nicole got her hands on the poison cake."

"Yes," Annie concurred. "That seems like a fact."

"We know that initially there were two cakes."

"Yes."

"But Nicole wasn't holding either cake when Colin was talking with her."

"Right again. According to Colin, Nicole suggested that he should retrieve the untouched one from the bin if he wanted to use it to coax Fiona into selling them the property."

"But he turned her down."

"Yes."

"So after Colin went downstairs to get into his car, Nicole must have realized she could do it herself. She must have gone back to the trash, retrieved the cake, and left behind the one Myrna had tasted."

Annie closed her eyes. "You are brilliant, my brother."

"I know. But both Colin and Fiona were staying at their

house. How could Nicole be sure that when Colin saw the cake, he wouldn't guess what Nicole was up to and get rid of it?"

"I guess the only foolproof thing was for Nicole to make sure Colin wasn't there."

"But he was there. He was at the wedding."

"And he was whisked off to New York by a big-time film-maker who just happened to offer him a meeting with a man who just happened to be leaving the next day for Europe. As far as I can tell, Colin has no work and probably needs money. And he was both flattered and excited to meet the guy. Nicole could have set him up through Roger's old crony who'd been at the wedding."

"To get Colin off the island."

"So Taylor could see to it that Fiona was poisoned."

"But Nicole made a mistake: It never occurred to her that Colin would run home to get his valise and spot the box."

"Or that her grandson had overheard her conversation with Taylor to deliver the cake."

Kevin moved the beer bottle in small circles, lightly swishing its contents. "Okay. But what doesn't make sense is why did Nicole call Taylor to do her dirty work? Earl is the Flanagans' caretaker, not Taylor."

Annie knew enough about her brother to tread lightly now. "Most people on Chappy know one another. Over the years, friendships probably grow in different ways."

He narrowed his eyes and smirked. "You sound like you're hiding something. You can tell me. I'm a big boy."

Inhaling a deep breath, Annie said, "First, Jonas told me that he doesn't want to live here, that his grandfather is rail-roading him into it by refusing to support Jonas if he goes to New York City."

"Roger has all the money."

"Yes. But apparently, Nicole doles it out. I bet she concocted the idea for Jonas to move in here in order to throw me out without tipping her hand. She plans to tear down everything—the main houses and the cottage—and build her 'show palace,' as she told Colin. With me gone, that would be one fewer obstacle for them. And who knows, maybe Roger was in on all of it, too."

"Okay. But that isn't what you've been hiding."

Eyeing her empty glass, she decided she should have reconsidered when Kevin offered her more. "Kevin, I know you like Taylor, but you don't know much about her." She paused. "Do you?"

"I know she went to Berklee and played the cello with the symphony, which is pretty funny because she doesn't seem the type, does she?"

Annie shook her head. "No. But is that all you know? I mean, about her major life things? Personal stuff?"

He frowned. "I know she came back to the Vineyard when her father got sick. But that's about it. Then again, I haven't shared with her the fact that my wife is still alive. Does she have a spouse stashed away, too?"

"Not that I know of. But, Kevin, she does have a child. A son. Jonas."

When they'd finished hashing out the story behind the story—the older brother of Dana Flanagan whose name Claire could not remember, the capsized boat, the rumored pregnancy, and Taylor's exit to Boston, Kevin put his hands on his head and cried, "People! They're all a little crazy, aren't they?"

"You need to include us in that proclamation," Annie replied. "Our family has had its share of secrets, too."

"Yeah," he said with a half laugh. "My father left when I was four, but I still don't know why. All Mom said was,

'Grown-ups sometimes do that; it isn't about you.'Well, I never saw the guy again or even got a birthday card, so I guessed early on that it had something to do with me."

"And I haven't pressed Donna about my birth father," Annie said. "But people are entitled to privacy. Especially if they think it will hurt the ones they love."

"Okay, but forget about us. What was Taylor's motivation to give up her baby to them? Of all people?"

"More than likely, it was money. Or blackmail. Maybe Roger threatened to have her arrested for killing his son, whose body, by the way, was never found. Maybe he felt they deserved to have Jonas because he was all they had left of their son. If they didn't press charges, they might have had enough influence so the accident wasn't investigated—or maybe they simply led Taylor to believe that. It was over twenty years ago. Who knows how things worked then? But it does seem plausible, doesn't it?"

Kevin nodded. "It also seems plausible that Taylor got a bucket of cash. And still does."

"Well, by not rocking the boat—no pun intended—at least she's been able to see her son every summer." The light inside the cottage turned a soft end-of-the-day shade of melon. "And if Roger and Nicole have threatened to tell Jonas the truth, they'd be wasting their time, because Jonas already knows."

Kevin stood up and looked out the window onto the front porch. "And Taylor doesn't know he knows."

"Right."

"We need to talk to her, don't we?"

"We do. I think it would be best for everyone if we can re-solve this before going back to the police."

Pulling his phone from his pocket, Kevin typed a text. A few seconds later his alert sounded. He glanced back at the screen. "Come on," he said to Annie. "Let's go to Taylor's and get this over with."

Chapter 28

"Mother has gone to bed," Taylor said when she greeted them outside. "We can stay out here or go in. It's up to you." Her hair was in a ponytail, held together by twine again; it made her face look severe.

"Here's fine," Kevin said and leaned against his truck.

Annie stepped around the vehicle and stood next to him. "We've been trying to help Fiona Littlefield," she said, "and your name came up."

Taylor shifted; her body stiffened. "What about me?"

"Nicole Flanagan had you deliver a honey cake to the Littlefields' house. She told you to leave it in the kitchen."

Leveling her gaze on Annie, Taylor said, "True."

"Can you tell us why you did that?"

Aside from the blinders she'd worn when she'd been married to Mark, Annie was usually good at deciphering body language. But whether it was due to the shadows cast by the sun as it began to dip toward the horizon, or concern for the growing feelings her brother had clearly developed for Taylor, she couldn't tell if the woman's rigid stance was caused by a guilty conscience that she'd participated in Fiona's mishap or by her need to protect her secret about Jonas.

"Fiona always liked honey cake," was the wooden reply. "It was no big deal."

"So Nicole just gave you a call in the midst of her daughter's wedding celebration and asked you to deliver a honey cake to her next-door neighbor?"

"Something like that."

Annie sighed and glanced over at Kevin, who seemed happy to leave the questioning to her. Maybe he didn't want to admit he felt duped by Taylor, or uneasy because he'd been duping her, too, by not being forthcoming about his wife. *People!* he had exclaimed. *They're all a little bit crazy, aren't they?*

"Taylor," she said, lowering her voice, "did you know the honey cake contained tainted honey? That it was why Fiona became ill and had the seizure?"

A mystified expression washed over the woman's face.

"What?"

"The honey was poisonous, most likely from the nectar of mountain laurel. It slipped past the beekeeper and wound up in the cake."

"Seriously?" Her shoulders dropped; she appeared more accessible, which Annie interpreted as a good sign.

"You didn't know?" Kevin asked.

"Christ, of course I didn't know! You think I'd knowingly give anyone something poisonous?"

Neither Annie nor Kevin replied.

"If I was going to poison anyone," she added, "it damn well would be Mother."

Annie flinched.

"Not because I hate her. But because she's only eighty-three but can't do a damn thing except take her pain meds and try to get from the bed to the bathroom without falling on her ass." She shook her head. "She'd never ask me to do it, but I know she wouldn't stop me. Put her out of her damn misery, you know? But I can't. I have a hard enough time shooting vermin. As for Fiona Littlefield, that girl never did anything to me. Why the hell would I want to kill her?"

Annie remained quiet, trying to temper the moment. Then she said, "It's rare that a human dies from poisoned honey. Animals, yes. Humans, not often. But they can get very sick, like Fiona did. And I suppose if the body is compromised by other issues, death might occur. Fiona might have been more susceptible because she's so tiny." Annie had made that part up, but wanted to placate Taylor. Annie felt the woman had been dealt enough blows in her life.

In the distance, the evening crickets had begun to chirp; a bat screeched from within the small forest of trees, a sign that it was starting its nocturnal rounds. Bats were one more species that had frightened Annie in the city, but which she'd come to terms with on Chappaquiddick. After all, it had been their home long before it became hers.

"Well," Taylor said, "I'm sorry about that. But I had no way of knowing the cake would make her sick. I was only doing Nicole a favor because she was under the gun, trying to keep the kitchen cleared for the caterer, who was already hustling hors d'oeuvres and champagne."

"So it was after the ceremony?"

"Yes."

"Were you a wedding guest?"

Taylor hesitated, then said, "No. It wasn't exactly my crowd, you know?"

Annie couldn't imagine what it had been like for her to have her son raised by people who weren't "exactly her crowd." "Taylor," she said, "would it surprise you to know that Nicole knew it was poisonous? That she intentionally wanted to make Fiona sick?"

"What?" Taylor asked, though Annie knew perfectly well she had heard her.

"Nicole wanted to make Fiona sick," Kevin chimed in. "It must have been before she talked to you that she arranged for Roger's friend to convince Colin to leave the island. We don't know how she did that, or why he agreed. But we do think she also might have hoped that, because Colin disappeared, Fiona would assume he'd been the one who'd tried to kill her. Which was exactly what ended up happening."

Then Annie chimed in. "We also don't know whether or not Roger was in on any of this or if Nicole acted alone. But that's up to the police to figure out."

"Sorry," Taylor interrupted, "but I don't believe this. It's true they're not the most warmhearted people on the planet, but I don't think either one of them would stoop this low."

Then Annie told her about Myrna on the boat, and that Nicole had been there. "It's not as if she planned it in advance, but she sure seized the opportunity. We figure that after Colin went down to the freight deck when the ferry was about to dock, she went back to the trash bin and retrieved the cake that Myrna hadn't touched. We have no idea if Nicole knew exactly how sick Fiona would get. But again, that's for the police to determine."

More crickets chirped as the sky began to morph from soft melon to deep purple.

"But she used me," Taylor said. "She set me up as the one who'd make sure Fiona saw the cake. What a sucker I've become."

Her comment did not require confirmation.

"Look," Taylor said. "I know I'm not always likable. Earl often reminds me of that. But we all have our reasons for being who we are, don't we?"

"Yup," Kevin replied.

She looked up at the darkening sky, not at them. "For almost twenty-three years, the Flanagans have pretty much owned me. Their grandson, Jonas, is my boy. His father was their son, Derek; he died one day when we were sailing. I don't think they ever believed it was an accident. But so help me God, it was. He slipped. He fell overboard. Unfortunately, I was pregnant. Nicole pulled some emotional blackmail shit on me: She said if I didn't follow her instructions she'd make sure I was arrested and convicted of Derek's death. Roger went along with her conniving bullshit.

"As for me, I couldn't imagine being accused of Derek's death. We really loved each other. In fact, that's why I go see *Jaws* every Fourth of July. I like to watch it on the big screen. Derek was an extra in the movie. He was only five, but, God, he was cute even back then." She paused; her face contorted, as if she were about to cry.

Annie reached out and touched her shoulder. "Oh, Taylor. I am so sorry."

Taylor shrugged off Annie's touch and continued talking. "They shuttled me off island to Boston, so the neighbors wouldn't find out I was pregnant. When Jonas was born, I agreed to let them adopt him. What else could I do?

"For starters, I was younger than Jonas is now. I had no way to support myself, let alone a baby. Nicole offered money. For my parents and for me. 'In perpetuity,' Nicole said. I remember I had to look that up to find out it meant 'forever.' I was, after all, the daughter of a fisherman, you know? Not one of their kind. A common story, the island girl with the rich summer kid. What would you call that in one of your books, Annie?"

"A cliché," Annie replied. She decided not to ask if the Flanagans still supported Taylor and her mother. That was a private matter between them, not suited for island gossip.

"Anyway," Taylor said, "my only consolation is that Jonas has had a decent enough life and a good education. Plus, I get to see him every summer. And he's never known that I'm his mother."

Silence wrapped around them.

Then Kevin said, "Taylor? Jonas knows."

Chapter 29

Annie and Kevin had a late supper, a salad she fabricated out of various greens, leftover rotisserie chicken, cranberries, and pecans. They had agreed to leave Taylor alone with her thoughts, alone with her decision about whether or not she'd go to Jonas and tell him he was right about her. *A child should know its mother,* Annie mused, her thoughts drifting toward Donna. *Just as a mother should know her child.*

Then again, she also knew that circumstances didn't mean those things were always in everyone's best interest.

As they nibbled on brownies that Annie had moved straight from the freezer to the microwave, Kevin said, "I guess if I plan to stick around, I should come clean to her about my wife."

"That's up to you," Annie said. "Secrets aren't always a bad thing. Though it does seem that, sooner or later, they manage to come out of hiding."

"You're right," he said. "I'll remember that. But I don't think it's up to us to tell the cops about Taylor and Jonas."

"Agreed. That should be her decision."

"We can just say she was helping the Flanagans out, which isn't a lie."

"True."

"When do you want to go to the police station?"

"Tomorrow is the tour. I think this can wait another day, don't you? It's not as if anyone will go anywhere, not even Nicole. For starters, anyone with a car knows they need advance ferry reservations to leave the Vineyard in July."

"So we'll wait till Friday. Are you going to tell John first?"

John. Was it possible that Annie had almost forgotten about him? That she'd gone through an entire day without having him cross her mind, not even once? She wasn't sure whether or not that was a good sign. "I don't know. Should I?"

Kevin laughed. "Depends on how you really feel about keeping secrets. But I'd bet that if you ever want a real relationship with him, or even if he never comes back, he'd want to know before you tell his buddies on the force. It's a male thing. Ego, you know?"

They finished eating, then Kevin said good night and headed off to the *On Time,* toward John's house, where Annie might have been living if she'd known more about the male ego.

After cleaning the kitchen and crawling into bed, she picked up her phone and stared at the screen. It was nearly ten thirty; did she dare call him that late? Did she dare call him at all? Kevin's words echoed: *If you ever want any kind of relationship with the guy . . .*

If she called and he didn't answer, she could leave a brief message so he'd know she had tried to tell him before she told Lincoln and whoever else would be on duty Friday morning.

If his ex-wife answered again, Annie would hang up.

Or if the woman screened his messages and deleted hers, Annie would see it as a sign.

Stop overthinking it, came Murphy's sudden voice. *You're tired. Go to bed.*

Annie laughed. She was, indeed, exhausted. And her news could wait until after the garden tour, couldn't it?

She quickly convinced herself that Murphy was right. Besides, there would be plenty of time to tell John before his ego could suffer. And plenty of time for Annie to get properly braced for his declaration that he would not be coming home. Ever.

The alarm went off at six o'clock on Thursday morning. As Annie leaned over and shut it off, she realized she'd been dreaming about Taylor.

It felt strange that she now empathized with the woman she'd once thought of as her adversary. Maybe she would actually come to like her if Kevin stuck around, and if the couple spent more time together. It was true that they both deserved happiness, which also sounded like a cliché, but life sometimes was one, wasn't it?

Thinking about that gave Annie a new mission, which propelled her up, out, and over to Edgartown by seven thirty.

Her first stop was halfway down South Water Street, where the garden tour was to begin.

Among the things Annie had learned about the island was that when it came to special events, people showed up in droves. And they showed up early. The line to the first stop already extended up South Water toward North, then spilled around Main Street at the bank on the corner. She couldn't see how far up Main it went. As magical as the exciting turnout, countless blossoms perfumed the air, infusing the village with energy and joy.

The hours passed quickly: Annie moved from venue to venue, talking with the home owners and visitors; savoring the joyful energy that exuded from the lemonade-sipping, photo-snapping, high-chattering throngs; making certain all things were in order, which they were. The participants had been involved for several years, so they knew what to do and what to expect. Even Mrs. Atwater, whose hollyhocks had been leveled when Claire had landed in them, was cheerful and welcoming, her garden incredibly appearing no worse for the mishap.

As directed, the judges had scattered to peruse the entries independently. Annie caught up with Monsieur LeChance on the north side of town, where he was performing his judging tasks near the Harbor View Hotel. Despite the warm day, he looked especially proper in a navy blazer, white pants, and straw bowler.

"Good day, Annie," he said as she approached. "A pleasant turnout, isn't it?"

"Absolutely. Much more than I expected."

"The gardens are spectacular. We've had just the right amounts of rain and sun this year for horticultural perfection. *Très magnifique.*"

Then a group of women sidled their way around Annie. Monsieur LeChance spoke to each of them, asking if they were enjoying the tour and which gardens they'd found most appealing. He scribbled the opinions in a palm-sized notebook, smiling and nodding the whole time.

As soon as the ladies wandered off, Annie said, "I have a question, monsieur. But it's not about the gardens."

His eyes and mouth widened, transforming his already elongated face into an Al Hirschfeld caricature.

"It's about your music."

"Ah. My violin has captured your attention."

"It has. And more than that, I have a friend who played the cello years ago. I don't think she's played for a long time, possibly because she doesn't know of an ensemble she could join. Do you have any suggestions?"

"As it happens, I am in a quartet. Two violins, a flute, a clarinet. My goodness, a cello would be a nice addition."

"Really?" Annie felt hopeful. "I thought you might know someone, but I never dreamed it would be this easy."

"Well," he said, tending to his invisible mustache, "we would need to have your friend audition."

"Of course. Do you give public performances?"

"*Oui.* In fact, we'll be at Union Chapel this Sunday morning. There's a special service honoring the men and women of the regatta."

Annie had forgotten that the annual regatta had been underway for a few days, though she'd noticed an exceptional crowd of sailboats bobbing in the harbor. "Thank you, monsieur. I'll be sure to tell my friend. Maybe you know her? She lives on Chappy and went to Berklee. Her name is Taylor."

"Taylor Winsted? We've never met, though I've heard of her. Her mother was a patron of our little group before she took sick." He clucked a bit and shook his head. "Poor old girl. She was a musician, too, you know. A flautist for the Metropolitan Opera."

Dumbstruck was the perfect word to describe Annie's reaction. "Mother" had been a flautist? A classical performer who'd been accomplished enough to work for the Metropolitan Opera? "I had no idea," she said.

"I didn't know her then. Apparently, she met Stan Winsted when she and her family vacationed here one summer. The gossipmongers told me she wound up in 'the family way.' She married him, gave up her career, and was relegated to life on Chappaquiddick. It was, of course, back when options for young women were still rather limited. Though, to be fair, that's not to say she'd have done things differently."

Annie suddenly felt as if she'd unintentionally peeked into someone's diary. Knowing Taylor's history, however, explained a lot: Aside from the obvious musical talent, which might also be the link to Jonas's artistic bent, Taylor's mother might have influenced her to give her baby to the Flanagans so both she and the baby would have a chance at a bigger, more exciting life. Annie wondered if anyone really escaped from having their past chart the course of their future. In a way, it was true even for her: If she hadn't met her first love on South Beach decades ago, would she have gravitated to the island so many years later?

Two elderly couples entered the garden gate then, and Annie stepped out of their way. She thanked Monsieur LeChance again and told him she'd relay the information.

It wasn't until she strolled toward the next stop that Annie realized that, after all this time, she at last knew Taylor's last name. Winsted. No doubt from old Yankee blood.

Final count: three hundred twenty-three visitors.

First Place Winner: Mrs. Atwater, who might have been the favorite due to the magnificent way she'd restored her assaulted blossoms.

Annie hurried down the corridor in the rehab facility, eager to give Claire the news. When she reached the room, she heard Earl's voice. *Great,* she thought, he can learn firsthand about the success. But as she whirled through the open door, she screeched to a stop; sitting at the foot of his mother's bed was John.

"Annie!" he said and jumped to his feet. As he did, Annie noticed a woman in the chair next to him. She had dark hair that was neatly cut and coiffed and wore a crisp linen shirt, stylish cropped pants, and high-heeled wedge sandals. Her bronze eyes turned toward Annie with obvious disinterest. She did not need an introduction.

A chill shot from Annie's brain down to her toes.

Neither Earl nor Claire spoke.

"Sorry," Annie said, her hand touching the base of her

throat, the little hollow where her pulse liked to race. "I didn't mean to interrupt. . . ."

"No," John said, "it's fine. You didn't know I'd be here. No one did. Not even my mother. Right, Mom?" He turned to Claire, who responded with a flat-lipped grin.

"He came in on the one fifteen," Earl announced, as if that explained anything.

"A quick visit," John said with a nervous chuckle. "I wanted to check in with Mom. To see how she's doing."

The fact that no one was addressing the woman in the wedge sandals confirmed who it was, as did the fact that Annie's stomach—which was astute at recognizing danger—was now doing somersaults.

"Um . . ." John continued, "this is . . . this is Jenn." At least he didn't add "my ex-wife" or worse, "my daughters' mother." Then he said, "Jenn, this is Annie Sutton. The writer."

The writer? Really? Annie was embarrassed that he had called her that, as if she were a mere acquaintance, just one more celebrity hiding out on the Vineyard.

"Hello," Jenn said without standing.

"Hello," Annie managed to reply.

Earl backed up his chair; the metal scraped the linoleum. "Maybe Jenn and I can wait out in the hall so you can visit Claire, Annie."

If Jenn wanted to disagree, she didn't say. Instead she got up, picked up her oversized canvas bag, strutted past Annie, and followed Earl out into the hall.

"So," John said once they'd disappeared, "surprise."

"Right. Surprise." There were a thousand things she could have said, starting with, "Isn't it nice that you and your ex came down to visit your mother," followed by, "You make such a lovely couple." Instead, she merely stood and stared into his pearl-gray eyes.

"If you two are going to argue," Claire said from her bed, "I'm going to call for a wheelchair to bring me to the day-room. I don't need to be in the middle of anything that's going to raise my blood pressure."

Annie turned to her, her stomach tumbles abating, her mind starting to clear. "There's no need for that, Claire. I only came to report that the garden tour was a great success. And that Mrs. Atwater won first place—mostly, I think, for the noble way she resuscitated her hollyhocks. Lots of money was raised, so you can be proud of that." Then she spun on one heel and said, "That's all I came to say. I'll talk with you another time." She walked from the room, amazed that her legs were still holding her upright and were able to power her forward. At least Earl and John's ex were nowhere in sight.

"Annie. Stop." John caught up to her in the corridor by the front door. "Let me explain."

She stopped and inhaled a deep breath. "No need to, John. Though I'm awfully glad I hadn't moved in with you. With three of us—to paraphrase what Princess Diana once said—it would have been a bit crowded."

He held up his hand. "No. It isn't like that."

She clutched the pink file folder that held the breakdown of the tour statistics; she felt foolish for having stepped into John's family and taken care of things for Claire while he'd been reuniting with his wife. She tried to remember that Claire was her friend. And that Earl had befriended Annie before she'd even known that John existed. But right then, that logic felt as thin as white wisps of clouds on a breezy summer day.

"She only came to talk with Mom and Dad," he continued. "It wasn't my idea."

"Well. She must miss your family, then."

"That's highly doubtful. No. She wanted to talk to them about Lucy."

That was as big a surprise as the fact that they were there at all. "What about her?" Annie no longer cared if John's daughter wasn't her business. After all, she had nothing left to lose.

He took her by the shoulders. Tenderly. As if he were going to tell her that he loved her. Or break up with her. "Annie," he said slowly, "I didn't know how to tell you. . . ."

She shook her head in quick, jerking motions. "Don't. Please. Don't say the words. I've been thinking that it's time for me to leave the island, anyway. I don't belong here. You have your family and I . . . well, I have Donna now. And Kevin. I've had a chance to get to know him pretty well, thanks to you. You don't owe me anything, John. You never did." She slipped from his grasp and headed toward the door.

"Wait," he called in his no-nonsense, police-officer voice.

She stopped again, her back to him.

"Please don't be angry," he continued. "If you're thinking I'm not coming back to you, you're wrong. In fact, if I don't get to sleep with you again—and soon—I'm damn well going to lose my mind."

A corner of Annie's mouth twitched once. Twice. Then turned up into a smile. An elderly couple walked past. "For God's sake, lady," the woman said, "do as he says. Otherwise, he might arrest you." Annie laughed. Island life. Small town. Yes, this was her home. She turned around.

John stepped forward and grasped her shoulders again. He rubbed her arms as he spoke. "But Lucy will be with me. That's why Jenn came today. To make sure my parents will help out with her. Deep down, I guess she's an okay mother. All of Lucy's acting-out shit has been because she's miserable on the mainland. She misses her home. And, damn, I guess she misses her dad, too."

Annie raised her hands and touched his chest. "So do I."

"But I won't have as much time if she's living with me."

"We'll make time, John. I'm busy, too." A ghost of guilt that resembled her editor emerged before her eyes. She laughed. "We're adults. We have lives . . . we had lives before we met each other. We can't drop them now just because we want to be together."

His gaze traveled her face. "So you'd be okay if I'm a full-time dad again?"

She shook her head. "I'd be disappointed in you if you weren't."

He tipped up her chin, then bent and kissed her mouth. And all Annie could think about was how much she'd missed that kiss. "Of course," she added when they pulled away, "I have nowhere to live." Then she remembered the place in West Tisbury. She had completely forgotten to call about it the day before. Taking a step back she dug through her purse. "Will you wait right here while I make a phone call?"

With his wonderful, cockeyed smile, John said, "I have a better idea. I'm going to get Jenn back to Plymouth tonight. Lucy and I will be back tomorrow. Will you join us for pizza? I want you to be a presence for her, too. But only if you want."

Annie searched for the note that had the number in West Tisbury. "Of course, I want," she said. "But for her sake, let's take it slowly, okay?" Without waiting for his reply, she said, "Now get out of here while I try to find a rental that with any luck will come with much less drama." She began to dial, then quickly added, "By the way, tomorrow I'll tell you about Fiona Littlefield, and how Kevin and I solved your case."

He opened his mouth to speak, but she waved him off. "Go," she said, then turned back to the door. "Hello?" she said into the phone. "My name is Annie Sutton, and I'm a friend of Taylor Winsted. Taylor told me you have a garage apartment. . . ."

Chapter 30

Before Annie left the rehab center, Kevin texted: **Want to do dinner? The Newes is packed. How about Edgartown Pizza? Ten minutes?**

It was nearly six; Annie figured he had finished work for the day and was back in Edgartown. Or maybe he was with Taylor, telling her the truth about his wife.

She texted back: **More like 15 with traffic.**

"So how was the grand tour?" he asked when she was done slaying the SUVs, mopeds, and people wobbling on bikes in the wrong lane, and slid onto a chair across from him.

"If you mean the garden tour, it was great. Better than expected. I never thought of myself as a joiner; I usually don't get involved with clubs or organizations. But there's something to be said for volunteering with people you don't know but who are your neighbors. . . ." She realized Kevin was looking into his lap as if he were texting. "Hello?" she said. "Are you with me?"

He looked up with what Murphy would have called a "shit-eating grin" and put his phone back into his pocket. "Sorry."

"Taylor?"

"Huh? Oh. No. But I'm going to see her tomorrow night. Going to tell her about Meghan then."

"So is this getting serious?"

He laughed. "Not really. I just think I should come clean the way she did."

A waitress arrived to take their order. They decided on what Annie supposed would become their "usual": medium pizza, pepperoni, lots of veggies. Then Kevin changed it to a large; he said that way he could have leftovers for a day or two.

"John's coming home," Annie said after the waitress left. "He's bringing his daughter Lucy. She's moving back to the island to be with him. And with her friends. And Claire and Earl, too, I'm sure."

Kevin bit his lip. "Well, that's good for you. Not so good for me. I'll get booted out of John's comfortable townhouse."

"Donna MacNeish's two adult children will be homeless," Annie said.

"Did you see that place in West Tisbury?"

She shook her head. "I forgot to call the owner yesterday. It's already been rented."

"Must have been a great place."

"Maybe. Maybe not. People get desperate here." She let out a sigh of exasperation. "It's my own fault. I should have known better."

"You still have time."

"A few weeks."

"Or . . ."

"Or I can try to find a cheap room for the rest of the season, then look for something in the fall. A winter rental if I have to."

"You want to stay here that badly? You want to keep moving around, hauling all your stuff with you?"

"No."

"Do you want to stay on the island because of John?"

"I suppose that's part of it now. But even when I didn't know whether or not he was coming back, I wanted to stay. I love it here. I loved it long before I met him. The truth is, I love everything about it except the summer traffic."

"So I guess you don't need me to offer one of my condos in Boston."

"Your what?"

He laughed. "I own seven condos around the city. Two in Jamaica Plain, two in Back Bay, one in the North End, two in Cambridge. Rental properties."

"You never told me."

"We only just met, remember?"

It was Annie's turn to laugh. "Sorry. I feel like I've known you my whole life."

He took a drink of water. "Shared DNA. At least part of it."

She shook her head and watched this nice, kind man, her half brother. Her brother, apparently, in heart and soul. "So I won't have to be homeless."

"Nah. Not as long as I'm around. Of course, you'd rather be on the Vineyard."

"I would. But, Kevin . . ." Her eyes grew misty; she did not know what to say. She looked up to the ceiling, wondering if Murphy was listening. Or her dad. Yes. That time, she wished it would be him.

"Well then, if you want to stay here, I guess we'll have to figure out a way to make it happen," he said. The waitress brought their drinks, and he took a swig. As he set down the bottle, Earl walked through the door.

"Fancy meeting you two here," Earl said and sat next to Kevin without waiting for an invitation. He looked at Annie, then Kevin, then back to Annie. "Is this a private party or can an old man join in?"

"Plenty of pizza," Kevin said. "We ordered a large."

"Good. I love pizza. Claire says I'm too old to be eating kids' food, but I do what I want when her back is turned." He chuckled and Kevin did, too.

Annie had an odd feeling that something was going on. "Well, the two of you seem to be having fun."

"It was a good day," Earl said. "You did real well with the garden thing, Annie. That meant a lot to Claire."

"I was glad to help."

"As for your brother," he added, nudging Kevin, "he's turned into a fine caretaker. I've been thinking about keeping him around."

"Then you'd better help find us both places to live," Annie said. "With John coming home with Lucy, Kevin will be in the same situation as I am. Only sooner. Like tomorrow."

"Well, Claire and I already decided he can camp out on the sofa in my man cave. Which, of course, used to be my study. But it's not as if . . ."

Annie raised a hand. "I know, it's not as if you study anymore." It was a phrase he'd coined God only knew how long ago and enjoyed repeating on occasion.

Earl chuckled again. "Right. Well, it will only be temporary. Until the outbuildings are finished."

The pizza arrived along with three plates, as if this entire get-together had been preordained. Annie put her napkin in her lap and stared at the two men across from her. "What outbuildings?" she asked. "What's going on?"

Helping himself to a hefty slice, Earl took a bite and chewed, all the while grinning the same kind of shit-eating grin Kevin had worn a few minutes earlier.

"Your brother updated me about the Littlefield situation," Earl said. "You kids did good."

Annie noticed he hadn't answered her questions, but decided not to press the issue. "I need to explain what happened to Fiona to the police tomorrow," she said. "I don't know if they'll arrest Nicole, but I want both Fiona and Colin to go with me."

"I want to go, too," Kevin said, diving into a slice. "I've already asked my boss for the day off."

Earl chuckled again and Kevin winked at him.

Annie folded her arms. "Okay, you two. What's going on? As you can tell by the strands of silver in my hair, I was not born yesterday."

Kevin nudged Earl. "You tell her. It was your idea."

With a slight shrug and a conspiratorial smile, Earl said, "We're going to buy it."

"Buy what?" she asked.

"The Littlefields'. Your brother and I are going to buy it and renovate it into the kind of property it started out to be— a beautiful waterfront property. The way we figure it, we can wind up with six big rooms with private baths to rent. We aren't made of money, but it will pay for itself in no time."

Annie blinked. "What?"

"Of course, we'll need you to run it, so we'll add on a separate wing for you—a nice little apartment with a separate space where you can do your writing. One that faces the water. Kevin and I think that might be a more inspiring view than an osprey pole."

"No kidding," Kevin chimed in between pizza bites. "Of course, your wing probably won't be finished by the time you have to vacate the cottage, but we can get you situated in one of the upstairs bedrooms in the main house. There's also a seventh bedroom upstairs; once we're done with the whole place, Francine and Bella can share it."

Earl picked up where Kevin left off. "Francine has already agreed to manage the household staff. She has some experience now, you know. And she says she can do the online marketing for the rentals, which your brother and I know diddly about, but she's young so she gets it. As much as Claire and I have loved having the girls with us, I think Claire will need some quiet time now that she's getting better. And God knows you need a place to live."

Annie sat, stupefied.

"We're also going to build two outbuildings," Kevin said. "One will be a garage. I'll live in an apartment above. The other building will be a workshop that you and I can share: I can do carpentry on one side, you can make your soaps in the other. And, of course, I'll be the caretaker. And I'll keep working with Earl. So the whole thing will be a family affair. So to speak. And for your information, you did not miss out on the place in West Tisbury. There never was one. That was Taylor's idea to help stall you another day so you wouldn't make any stupid decisions while we worked out our plans with Colin and Fiona."

"With both of them?" Annie finally found her voice.

"Thanks to you two," Earl said, "they might wind up being friends again."

"So," Kevin interrupted, "as you can tell, we've been busy while you've been dancing through the tulips."

"Hollyhocks," Earl corrected. "Tulips are in the spring. You'll have to learn these things if you're going to turn The Inn at Chappaquiddick into a 'destination,' as Francine calls it."

"So Francine has been in on this."

"Sure," Earl replied. "We've been working nonstop on this for the past few days. To be honest, I've been thinking about it for a few years. But then you two came along, and everything else happened, and . . . well, things fell into place. But we didn't want to disappoint you if we couldn't convince Fiona to sell. As it turned out, she said as long as we make it nice, she'll sign off on it. Maybe she'll even visit next summer. As a paying guest. We know it's happened fast, Annie, but hot damn, the timing has been perfect."

Annie felt as if she'd walked into a movie of someone else's life. "What about from October until June? Can we rent half of the six rental bedrooms to people who need decent places to live at rents they can afford?"

The two men looked at each other. Kevin deferred to Earl.

"Why not?" Earl said. "It might be a good way to keep the town folks happy about our enterprise. But are you thinking we'd leave the other three vacant all winter?"

Annie bit her lip. "No. Can we make them year-round rentals? And can we offer them at a reasonable cost?"

Kevin whistled. "Well, we can always turn the venture into a nonprofit. That way, we'd be helping people and helping the island."

Annie smiled. "You guys are amazing."

"Yes, we are," Earl said.

When Annie finally got home, she decided to call John. She no longer cared who might be in the room, or if he went outside to talk. This time, unlike with Mark, Annie knew she'd chosen a good man. Or he had chosen her. Or her dad and Murphy had conspired on her behalf, the same way Earl and Kevin had.

John answered. "Hi."

"Hi yourself," she said. "I called to tell you that I found a place to live."

He laughed. "So I heard."

She howled. "I can't believe your father told you!"

"He didn't. Kevin called a couple of days ago to ask if I'd be okay with it."

"My brother?"

"Yeah. About your height, same hazel eyes, a little stocky . . ."

Annie laughed. "This has been a huge conspiracy!"

"Did you agree to it?"

"Of course I did! How could I not? It's a perfect solution."

"For the long run, too. I mean, it opens new possibilities

for us, too, doesn't it? If down the road we decide to make some changes in our . . . um, living arrangements? Who knows how we could reconfigure your private 'wing' to suit more than you."

"I like hearing you say that."

"Me, too. But first you have a book to write."

"And you have a daughter to raise."

"And then you'll have an inn to run."

"And another book to write."

"And in between . . ."

"And in between we can share my bed. Sometimes."

"More often than sometimes, I hope. Like maybe in the mornings after Lucy's left for school and I'm not due yet at work?"

"Count on it."

"Good. Because I really like your bed."

"Me, too," Annie said. "And it's even nicer when you're in it."

Chapter 31

"Reckless assault and battery. The subject engaged in conduct that caused bodily harm to another person." Detective Lincoln Butterfield had escorted Fiona, Colin, Annie, and Kevin into the same room where, only days ago, Roger Flanagan had been planted in a chair, declaring that Fiona was a liar.

"So Nicole can be arrested for trying to make me sick?" Fiona asked.

"It's a felony. With a sentence of up to five years in a state house of correction. As a woman, she'll go to Framingham. If she gets two and a half years or less, she'll go to a house of correction. But not the one here on the island. Women have to go to Barnstable, over on the Cape."

Annie and the others listened in stunned silence. Like her, apparently none of the others had expected Nicole Flanagan would go to jail.

"Of course," he continued, "we have to prove it."

Annie cleared her throat. "We can. Nicole used Taylor Winsted to bring the cake into the house. When you talk with Taylor, I think you'll agree she didn't know the honey was bad." Unless the rest of those details were needed—about Taylor being Jonas's mother, or about the "deal" the Flanagans had made in trade for their grandson—little seemed to be gained by telling all to the detective.

"Nicole knew I wouldn't be able to resist the cake," Fiona added.

Then Colin jumped in. "The day before, I saw Nicole on the boat. She said I could use it to make my sister sick. Then the plan was to intimidate her by threatening the lawsuits, and that then she'd agree to sell the house."

"Which shows intent," Kevin added.

Annie edged forward on her chair. She knew that no matter how many mysteries she'd written, she'd never know every law. But bit by bit, she was learning.

"Tainted honey is rarely fatal in humans," Lincoln continued. "But . . ." Then he read the statute that said if someone knowingly gives another person food that contains a foreign substance, it doesn't need to be lethal; they only need to have known it could be harmful or cause discomfort. "I think it's safe to call poisoned honey a foreign substance."

"Wow," Kevin and Colin said simultaneously.

Fiona looked paler than when they'd walked in. "For all she knew, I could have died."

Lincoln shifted on his chair. "And you're sure Roger wasn't in on the plan?"

"No. We're not," Annie replied. "But I am sure you'll find out."

The detective winked at her. "I'm glad you saved some of the work for us."

"You're all so busy right now. . . ."

He nodded like a patient father. "Still, you should have come to us as soon as you'd spoken with Myrna."

She nodded. "Next time you can count on it."

Then the door opened. Roger Flanagan walked in first, followed by Nicole. Annie let out a small squeak when she saw who came in after them: John.

"I believe you all know Mr. and Mrs. Flanagan," John said. Everyone stared.

"Mrs. Flanagan has something to say."

Nicole raised her chin, a gesture that helped tighten her neck flesh so it nearly equaled the skin on her face. "I did it," she said, her voice sweet and syrupy, as Earl would have expected if he were there. She looked at Fiona. "I am so sorry, my dear. I didn't mean to cause such a stir. But you'd become terribly disagreeable."

That's when Annie noticed that Nicole's hands were behind her back; John must have put her in handcuffs.

"Apology to the victim duly noted," Lincoln commented.

"I do have one question," Annie interrupted. "Nicole, how did you get the filmmaker to agree to whisk Colin off the island?"

Nicole grinned. "That was easy. We knew Colin hadn't had a film made in a long time. Fenterly and Roger have been friends forever. He is Dana's godfather; he adores her. I told him Colin might try to disrupt the reception, that he still loved Dana and was angry she'd broken off with him."

"I don't still love her, Nicole," Colin said. "She's not even thirty-five and she's on her third marriage. We were kids when we dated, but she's never grown up, has she?"

Nicole aimed daggers at him with her eyes.

"I'll take her over to Booking," John said. "Roger, I suppose it's all right for you to join us." The trio left the room.

Annie thought for a moment, then asked Lincoln, "You already knew about Nicole?"

Lincoln laughed. "Word travels fast around here. And to ease all your minds, whether or not she winds up in jail, no one has to worry about the Flanagans anymore. Rumor has it their place is up for sale. They'll be moving to Nantucket."

No one in the room seemed sorry to hear that.

★ ★ ★

Once they were outside, they stood in the parking lot, next to the errant Porsche, which, Colin confessed, belonged to one of his friends in New York.

"I can't imagine who told John about Nicole," Annie said. Her list of suspects, however, was short.

Kevin's face reddened.

"You called him last night?" Annie asked.

"No. I told Earl. He must have called him."

"Or Claire did," Annie said, "if Earl had told her."

"Or Taylor," Colin added.

Yup, Annie mused for the millionth time, *definitely a small island.*

Fiona shook her head. "Enough! It doesn't matter. Nicole didn't get away with it. Though I'd like to think she thought the poison would scare me, not kill me."

"My sister believes that all people are inherently good," Colin said.

Kevin chuckled as if he understood. "I assume you're headed back to New York?"

"We both are," Fiona said. "But I'm not going to fly. I'm riding with Colin. We want to get to know each other again. Especially since we'll be working together."

"Really?" Annie asked.

Fiona nodded. "We're starting our own documentary production company. Our first film will be a history of ballet in New York, from the genius of Balanchine to today's schools for kids. I'm too old to dance now, and I was never prima material. But I know the industry, and I think others might like to see behind the scenes."

"No more war films, Colin?" Annie asked.

"Nope. Littlefield Productions will focus on the arts. Next we'll do art museums. Best of all, by selling the damn house, we won't have to hunt for investors."

Fiona rolled her eyes. "Or beg our sister, Sheila."

Annie could have offered to share the research on museums that she'd amassed for her novel, but she knew every artist needed to follow his or her own heart. Instead, she said, "If you're looking for a budding artist to feature, there's always Jonas."

Colin snorted. "You do know that whole thing was a scheme, don't you? That getting you out of the cottage was part of the plan so Nicole would be able to tear down their house, ours, and the cottage, too?"

"For her mega-mansion 'show palace' and its breathtaking grounds," Annie said.

"Yup. I wonder what kind of palace she'll build in prison."

"I don't care!" Fiona cried. "It's done! We'll be back for the trial, if there is one. Otherwise, I hope I never have to see the Flanagans again. Even Dana. Who might have been in on it, too, for all we know." She reached over and hugged Annie. "Thank you, my new friend. For everything." Then she hugged Kevin, too. "And you. I know you were a big help. Thanks for believing in me."

Colin hugged Annie, then shook hands with Kevin. "Nice to meet you both. Good luck with the inn. I have a feeling it will be a smashing success. Which will piss off the Flanagans even more."

Annie and Kevin watched the Littlefield siblings climb into the Porsche. Colin turned on the ignition and the engine rumbled to life—once again reminding Annie of Mark's car, the symbol of her ex-husband's material world. She wondered what he was driving now, wherever he was. Then she waved to Fiona and Colin, knowing that her life had grown too precious to waste any more of it thinking about Mark.

As she turned to walk toward her car, Kevin's text alert sounded. He looked at the screen and said, "Huh," then, "Wow."

"Something interesting?" Annie asked.

"You might say so. That was Taylor. She wants you to know

she's going to audition with Monsieur LeChance's ensemble, whatever that means. She also said that Jonas is moving into her garage apartment."

"Wow," Annie echoed his reaction. "That's incredible."

"Yup," Kevin said. Then his phone actually rang. He checked the screen again and smiled.

"Hey, Mom," he said, "you're on speakerphone. I'm on the Vineyard with Annie. How's the cruise?"

"You're on Martha's Vineyard?" she cried with what sounded like delight. "How wonderful! The cruise has been fabulous. I've made some nice friends. But Duncan's gone, no love lost there. He hooked up with one of the showgirls and disembarked in Sydney. So much for old men. But I'm so glad you two are together! How do you like the island, Kevin?"

He looked at Annie as if stifling a hearty guffaw. "It's an interesting place."

"Annie, did he tell you it was my idea for him to visit you?"

"No!" Annie cried, her mouth dropping open. "Seriously?"

"Guilty," her brother replied.

Donna's happy voice resonated through the phone. "I can't wait to hear about your adventures when I come home next month."

"Absolutely," Kevin said, because Annie was too flabbergasted to speak. "There's lots to tell."

They passed "love you's" around, then Kevin hung up. "Well, that woman is in for a surprise."

"I guess none of us is ever too old for surprises," Annie said. "I feel like there's been a giant conspiracy around me all this time!"

"If there has, it's only been with the best intentions for you to be happy," Kevin said.

"And John's back," she said, her head, her heart, warming.

"Right. And I'll start camping out on Earl and Claire's couch tonight. Lucy arrives tomorrow on the ten forty-five."

Annie's eyes quickly welled up. She gave her brother the biggest bear hug she could manage because, in that moment, she felt like the luckiest woman in the world.

Another cliché! Murphy whispered with disdain. *What would your editor say?*

And Annie laughed, safe in the knowledge she would meet the deadline for her manuscript, safe in the love of her twenty-first-century family, safe in the home that she'd found, at last, and intended to never leave.

Be sure to look for the first Vineyard novel
in this series, by Jean Stone

A VINEYARD CHRISTMAS

Available now
in bookstores and online

Read on for a special preview. . . .

Chapter 1

The turnout was better than Annie had expected. It was, after all, a bitter, see-your-breath kind of morning, with a brisk December wind whirling around Vineyard Sound. But sunshine was vibrant against a bright blue sky, painting a perfect backdrop for the evergreens and colorful lights that decked the lampposts along Main Street, the storefronts, the town hall. Around the village, the traditional Christmas in Edgartown celebration was underway: on her walk to the elementary school gymnasium, Annie had witnessed the beloved parade of quick-stepping marching bands; mismatched, decorative pickup trucks; and a Coast Guard lifeboat perched atop a flatbed trailer that carried Santa himself, who waved and shouted "Ho ho ho!" while tossing candy canes into the cheering curbside throngs.

The atmosphere inside the gym was equally festive as "Jingle Bells" and "Joy to the World" scratched through the ancient PA system. Browsers and shoppers yakked in high-pitched voices and jostled around one another—many were armed with reusable bags silk-screened with the names of island markets, banks, insurance agents. By day's end, the bags would no doubt bulge with knitted scarves, island jewelry, specialty chocolates, and, hopefully, one or two of Annie's handcrafted soaps.

From her station behind a table under a basketball hoop, Annie wore a hesitant smile. The Holiday Crafts Fair had been open less than an hour, but she'd already sold seven bath-sized bars and a three-pack of hand-shaped balls she called "scoops" because each was the size of a scoop of sweet ice cream. Her cash pouch now held fifty-two dollars—not bad for her first endeavor in making boutique soaps by using wildflowers and herbs that grew right there on Martha's Vineyard.

But as happy as the earnings made her, Annie mused that fifty-two dollars was hardly a sign she should quit her day job. Then a middle-aged woman in jeans, an old peacoat, and a felt hat with a yellow bird crocheted on the brim approached the table. *An islander*, Annie knew. A year-rounder, like Annie was now. She'd seen her somewhere in town—the post office, the movies, the library. With the days growing shorter and colder and the streets less cluttered with tourists, faces were becoming familiar. The woman in the peacoat examined Annie's wares, which were wrapped in pastel netting and tied with coordinating ribbon: pink for beach roses and cream; yellow for buttercup balm; lavender for violets and honey.

At the far end of the table, a young woman sniffed a scoop of fox grape and sunflower oil. Annie had gathered the buds, then added the oil for velvety smoothness, the way her teacher, Winnie Lathrop, had showed her.

"How much?" the young woman asked as she adjusted a basket on the crook of her arm. It was a big handwoven basket, the kind Annie's aunt had used to hold skeins of yarn. This one, however, held a sleeping infant, snugly wrapped in a thick fleece blanket.

Annie smiled again, the ambiance and the people almost warming her spirit and her mood. "Four dollars. Ten dollars for a three-pack of mixed scents."

The young woman, who looked barely out of her teens, had short, pixie-ish chestnut hair and sad, soulful eyes that were large and dark and looked veiled with sorrow. She set down the scoop, readjusted the basket. Then she picked up a piece of cranberry and aloe oil that was tied with red ribbon. She did not speak again.

Wincing at the snub, Annie wondered if she'd ever learn not to take the actions of strangers personally. "As hard as it is for us to believe, not everyone will love you or your work," her old college pal, her best-friend-forever, Murphy, had once told her after a tepid review of one of Annie's books. "Forget about them. They're pond scum anyway."

"Annie Sutton!"

Startled to hear her name, she quickly spun back to the present. Only a few people knew she now lived on the island; fewer knew who she was or that she had a backlist of best-selling mystery novels. She turned from the ill-mannered young woman and politely asked, "Yes?"

The caller's hair was as silver as the foil bells made by the first-graders that the custodian had hung from the gymnasium rafters. She wore a smart wool coat that fit her nicely—a Calvin Klein or Michael Kors. Her well-manicured fingernails were painted red and matched her lipstick; her purse might have been a Birkin bag—a real one, not a knockoff. She'd most likely arrived that morning on the *Grey Lady*, the special "holiday shopping" ferry that had come from Cape Cod straight into Edgartown for the festive weekend.

"You're Annie Sutton? The writer?"

Annie's cheeks turned the same shade as her beach roses and cream. "Guilty." An often-rehearsed, engaging grin sprang to her mouth. She hoped it was convincing.

The woman's eyes grazed the table. "And now you're a soap maker?"

"Just a hobby."

"Well, goodness, I hope so. When's your next book coming out?"

That, Annie wanted to reply, *is a good question.* But she could hardly say she was reassessing her life, that she had lost her inspiration to write, that she was now on a healing sabbatical. If the news ever went viral, Trish—her patient, yet perfectionist editor—would never forgive her. "Soon," she said, aware that several browsers at her table had shifted their focus from her products onto her, and that other shoppers were drifting her way. In her peripheral vision, she noticed that the young mother remained standing, silent, her head slightly cocked, as if she were listening. "Actually," Annie continued, shaking off silly discomfort, "I'm still working on it. It's the first book in a new mystery series."

"Well, hurry up. Your readers are dying to read it!" The woman put a hand to her mouth and giggled. "Yes, we're *dying* to read your next mystery. That's a pun. Get it?"

Annie nodded and said she did.

The woman picked up nine three-bar sets and plunked them down in front of Annie without checking the scents. "I'll take these. The ladies in my book group will adore them. Will you sign the labels?" She juggled her big purse and pulled out a credit card.

Annie had pierced a small hole for the ribbon on each oval-shaped paper label, which had an illustration of the island, the name of the flowers or herbs she had added, and a frilly typeface that read: *Soaps by Sutton.* There was no blank space for a signature. Embarrassed, she turned over each label and penned: *Happy Holidays! Annie Sutton.* It had not occurred to her that Annie-the-soap-maker would be "outed" at the fair, that she'd be asked to dish out her autograph.

"I love your books, too!" another voice called out. "Will you sign a bar of soap for me?"

"Me, too?"

"Me, three?"

The requests shot out from a line now swollen with reusable bag–toting patrons.

"Do you live on the Vineyard?" another voice hollered.

Annie sat up straighter on the metal folding chair. "I moved here at the end of the summer," she replied, summoning full celebrity persona now, the one she'd cultivated at Murphy's insistence.

"Did you buy a house?"

"No, I'm renting a guesthouse—a cottage—over on Chappaquiddick."

"I love Chappy!" someone else cried. "Whereabouts are you?"

"North Neck Road." She cleared her throat and spoke loudly and pleasantly, as if she were at a book reading.

"Does your new book take place here?"

"Is it an autobiography?"

"A murder mystery?" a different voice cried. "That would be a terrible autobiography!"

The crowd tittered, then another woman asked, "Will you be finished with it soon?"

The chattering rushed at her, the voices drowning out the PA system's "Jingle Bells." Annie remembered a time, not long ago, when she'd prayed to have a few fans of her books. *Be careful what you wish for*, she reminded herself, trying to keep her rising anxiety at bay. She forced a laugh, rang up another sale, signed another autograph, and sadly wished that this day were done. "My first book was the closest I've come to writing about my life. That was hard enough."

"Was that the one where your character was adopted?"

"Yes," she said, then collected more dollars, signed more labels. "It was before I started writing mysteries; I can assure you that no one in my life has been murdered!" Not that she would have minded learning that her ex-husband had met his demise.

The crowd laughed along with her, except for the girl with the sad, soulful eyes, who simply wandered away.

If this were an ordinary off-season Saturday night, Annie might have stopped at the Newes for a bowl of chowder and a glass of chardonnay on her way back to Chappy. But the 275-year-old, brick-walled, fireplaced pub would be packed with the weekend wave of merry, but tired, shoppers—mostly women with their friends, having lots of fun. She would hate being alone.

With the fair finally over, she stepped outside, took a long breath of the crisp night air, and willed herself to feel, if not completely happy, then at least content: there was no good reason not to. Yesterday, Earl Lyons—the white-haired, robust caretaker for the estate where she rented the cottage—had loaded four cartons of her soap into his pickup truck, driven onto the small ferry over from Chappy, and helped set up her table at the fair. He'd said he'd be glad to come back if she needed any leftovers hauled home. But now, carrying a single bag that held only a handful of unsold soaps and a fat envelope of cash and receipts, Annie decided to walk. Maybe the exercise would help her figure out if she'd found a new trade, after all—and help her shed what was beginning to feel like a dose of Christmas blues.

She put on her alpaca mittens ("The warmest you'll ever find," Earl had advised when he'd offered helpful hints about the island), then pulled the matching knit hat over her straight, silver-black hair that barely skimmed her shoulders. Though the night air was calm, the trek to the boat would be chilly, and the crossing downright cold: the miniature ferry that navigated the 527-foot channel from Edgartown to Chappy offered no shelter for passengers, only a three-sided glass cubicle where the captain stood. More like a motorized raft than an actual boat, the one running that winter was called the *On Time II* and only held three vehicles, or an SUV and a UPS truck, or some other meager configuration. Benches that hugged the sides could seat up to twelve walk-ons, though Annie hadn't seen that many people on the boat since tourism predictably had plummeted after Columbus Day weekend. A slightly larger *On Time III* crisscrossed the *II* in season, but was in dry dock now, taking its turn for maintenance, getting prepped for the next onslaught in the spring. There was no sign of an *On Time I*, though surely it once had existed.

Leaving the school grounds, she walked on past the new library to the fire station, where their original cast-iron bell, circa 1832, was displayed on the lawn. Like much of the village, the bell was decorated with hundreds of enchanting holiday lights.

She turned onto Peases Point Way, then crossed the street to avoid the graveyard, something Murphy would have found ridiculous.

Annie sighed. God, how she missed her best friend. She knew that the loss, the grief, were at the core of her glum spirits. Murphy once said: "Men can come and go in life, but best friends last forever." At the time, Murphy's hand had been clutching the stem of a glass of pinot noir, having come over after calling Annie at midnight with a rare need to escape from her "workaholic husband" and her "rambunctious boys." The two of them had smiled, clinked glasses, and taken another sip, neither of them having any idea how suddenly and sharply cancer would snap the "forever" of their bond.

Peases Point Way connected to Cooke Street, where Annie took a right and headed toward the harbor. But at South Summer Street, she changed her mind and turned left instead. She passed the eighteenth-century, gray-shingled building that had once been a poorhouse, but where the *Vineyard Gazette* had been located for over a century now. On the opposite side of the narrow street was the gracious, stately Charlotte Inn, known for its old-world charm. Annie jaywalked across the road, climbed the three front stairs, and stepped into the foyer.

A woman in a sleek black dress stood at the mahogany reception desk.

"I know the terrace isn't open in winter," Annie said, "but may I sit at a table if I only want wine?" She pulled off her hat and shook out her hair.

"Are you alone, or will someone join you?"

"It's just me," Annie replied, keeping her tone carefully neutral. The woman was just doing her job, she reminded herself. *She isn't mocking me for the fact that I'm alone.*

They moved into a candlelit room that was filled with diners who were conversing in intimate tones. Then, as if guided by the universe—or, more likely, Murphy—the hostess led Annie to a small table that had a view of the terrace. Annie thanked her, sat down, and gazed out at the redbrick courtyard. The wrought iron tables were gone, as were the navy umbrellas, which, early last summer, had shaded Annie and Murphy as they'd whiled away a sunny day. They'd been wearing flowered sundresses and open-toed sandals that showed off fresh pedicures. The sunlight had brought out the red in Murphy's shoulder-length hair. As usual, they'd shared plucky conversation about some things that mattered and many more that didn't. It had been a celebratory weekend, a girls' getaway to mark their fiftieth birthdays—Annie's had been in February; Murphy's, in April.

And now, on this December evening, Annie ordered a Chambord Cosmopolitan instead of her usual chardonnay. She and Murphy had sipped Cosmos that afternoon—Murphy claimed that vodka dressed up with Chambord and orange liqueur showed more enthusiasm than wine. "We made it to fifty; we deserve to live a little," she'd declared. A full-time behavioral therapist, the mother of twin boys (the rambunctious ones), and the wife of a well-respected Boston surgeon (the workaholic), Murphy prided herself in maintaining a positive attitude and mostly agreeable relationships with her family, friends, and an assortment of alcoholic beverages.

"If I drink this, I'll get drunk," Annie had said. "You know I can't drink the way you do."

Murphy asked the waitress to bring Annie more cranberry juice on the side. "Now," she said, turning back to her friend, "tell me about your next book."

Annie sighed. "I'm struggling with it. It's about two women who work in a museum where there's a huge art heist. And a dead body or two. I love the concept, but the plot isn't gelling."

"It will. You're not much of a drinker, but you've got the gift of blarney. Whether you're Irish or not."

Of course, Annie had no idea if she was Irish, French, or Tasmanian, though her dad often said she must be Scottish because of her black hair, hazel—not blue—eyes, and "outdoorsy" complexion, whatever that meant. Her mom and dad had adopted Annie when she was six weeks old; she'd never learned her heritage, not even later, when she'd had the chance.

"The truth is," Annie had explained, "my characters were best friends in college and are reunited when one gets a job at the museum where the other one volunteers. They're not us, though. Neither one of us knows squat about art history. And my characters are smarter, richer, and much more beautiful."

"No!" Murphy had screeched. "They can't possibly be smarter or more beautiful! But I do think the story sounds terrific. If you feel stuck, maybe you need a break. Even better, a vacation!" Then she'd grown uncharacteristically pensive. "Let's get serious. What's on your bucket list?"

"Stop! We're only fifty. It's too soon for one of those."

"No it isn't, Annie. Think about it. What would you want to do if you weren't such an infernally sober stick-in-the-mud? If you shake things up a little, you might reignite your creative genius."

Annie had a good laugh at that. Still, she wondered if her friend was right. Murphy, after all, knew her like no one ever had. Not like her parents. Not like her first husband—her first love—Brian. And certainly not like the next one, Mark, the man she'd wasted too much of herself trying to please. "Okay," she said. "If I had a list—which is not to say that I'll make one—the first thing I would do would be to move here. Live on the Vineyard. At least for a while."

"Where you met Brian."

"A thousand years ago. But even then, I knew this place was more than romantic: it's magical." Annie had chosen to set two of her mysteries there. While doing the research, she'd fallen in love with the island again, not only for the breathtaking land-scape, but also for its diversity of people, its immense support for art and culture, and its rich, unforgotten history—all of which combined to form an inspiring community.

"Do it," Murphy said in a serious whisper. "Make the move. It's time to open up your life." Annie knew that was Murphy's way of saying it was time to move on, time to shed the baggage of too many losses and disappointments. In hindsight, Annie wondered if her friend had had a premonition.

A month after that wonderful weekend, Murphy was diag-nosed with a rare, swift-moving cancer. Carving out time be-tween her family, work, and chemo treatments, she helped Annie find the cottage on Chappy, then, with her bald head cocooned in a gaily striped turban, she went with her the day that Annie moved. She said she needed to see Annie settled, to know that she was safe. That had been on Labor Day. Four weeks later, Murphy died. And Annie's heart had been irrevo-cably broken.

In some ways, Murphy's death had been Annie's greatest loss; no one was left now to help her navigate the day-to-day waters of life. But thanks to her advice, Annie was following her dream. She was here. On the Vineyard. Surrounded by unending beauty and the gentle rhythm of the place she now called home. And she knew that if she dared to leave, her old pal would come back to haunt her in her spunky, rap-on-the-knuckles kind of way.

Gazing out the window now, from the terrace up to the night sky, Annie saw the Milky Way, its wide, white ribbon shimmering like a twinkling sash. Just then, a comet streaked across, as if delivering a message of faith, hope, and love. With the curve of a soft smile, Annie felt her tears glisten like the stars. "I'm trying, my friend," she whispered to the heavens, up to Murphy, who surely was there.

Connect with U s

Visit us online at
KensingtonBooks.com
to read more from your favorite authors, see books
by series, view reading group guides, and more.

for sneak peeks, chances to win books and prize packs,
and to share your thoughts with other readers.

facebook.com/kensingtonpublishing
twitter.com/kensingtonbooks

Tell us what you think!

To share your thoughts, submit a review,
or sign up for our eNewsletters, please visit:
KensingtonBooks.com/TellUs.